# DANCE ON A
# SINKING SHIP

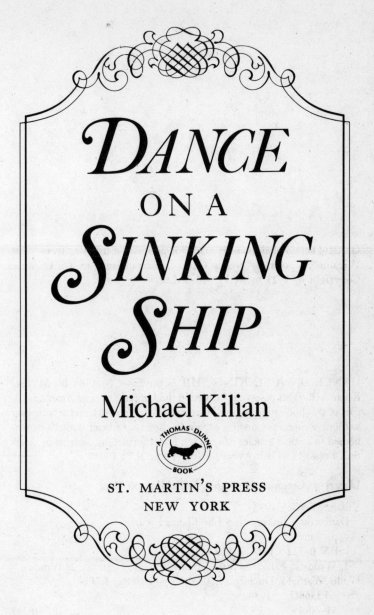

# DANCE
## ON A
# SINKING
# SHIP

### Michael Kilian

A·THOMAS·DUNNE
BOOK

ST. MARTIN'S PRESS
NEW YORK

Grateful acknowledgment is made for permission to quote from "The Wreathe", a poem by Nancy Cunard first published in *The Outlaws*. Copyright © 1921 by W.H. Allen, Ltd.

Library of Congress Cataloging-in-Publication Data

Kilian, Michael, 1939–
    Dance on a sinking ship / by Michael Kilian.
      p.    cm.
    ISBN 0–312–01413–9: $19.95
    1. Windsor, Edward, Duke of, 1894–1972—Fiction.   2. Windsor, Wallis Warfield, Duchess of, 1896–   —Fiction.   I. Title.
PS3561.I368D3    1988
813'.54—dc19                                                    87–26343

DESIGN BY DEBBY JAY

First Edition

10 9 8 7 6 5 4 3 2 1

# DANCE ON A
# SINKING SHIP

For Cleveland Amory,
a grand man and a grand friend,
for more than mere mankind;
and for Christiana Kochert MacDonald,
*de Paris, une bonne amie,*
*avec remerciements pour 1957,*
*et pour 1987.*

# ACKNOWLEDGMENTS

I am most grateful to my friend Cleveland Amory—by far my superior as a journalist and author—for the guidance, anecdotes, character assessments, and encouragement he provided me in the preparation of this book. As he demonstrated in his tour de force *Who Killed Society?* some years ago, he has preempted this field. The definitive book on the ill-fated Windsors can only be written by Cleveland. I hope someday he will write it.

Marian Probst, Cleveland's longtime associate and a wonderful friend, provided similar encouragement and help and I am truly thankful.

The research for this novel included a number of very useful and fortuitous conversations with people familiar with the Windsors or other individuals who appear as characters in the book.

I must count among them a short chat with His Royal Highness, Prince Charles of Great Britain, at a private reception in 1986. Though by long-held custom the contents of such conversations cannot be made public, I can say that His Highness proved helpful in clarifying the status of two of the principals in this story with the rest of the Royal Family.

Author Gore Vidal, who like Mr. Amory knew the late Duke and Duchess of Windsor, was also of assistance. Describing the Duke as "radiantly ignorant on almost every subject," he made it clear he was fonder of her than of him, but Vidal underscored a theme of this book in relating her complaint to him about "how empty and useless were their lives."

Aline, Countess of Romanones, was perhaps the Duchess's best friend, and, to this author's view, is far more the aristocrat, though born an American commoner as well. She would strongly disagree with the portrayal of Mrs. Simpson herein, but did during an afternoon's conversation give me some very useful guidance on the duke's conduct and demeanor and helped steer me clear of some inaccuracies derived from other sources.

Mrs. Brooke Astor of New York, who knew many of those in Prince Edward's entourage, made some keen character observations concerning them and advised on the superior qualities of Duff and Diana Cooper. Lady Diana appeared as a character in Mrs. Astor's recent novel, *The Last Blossom on the Plum Tree.* Lady Diana unfortunately died a few weeks after the novel's publication in 1986.

Andy McElhone, proprietor of the original and legendary Harry's New York Bar at "Sank Roo Da Noo," was the source of some wonderful information and anectdotes about Paris in the 1930s, as well as about some of the characters who appear in this novel.

I am also deeply indebted to an old friend, Mme. Christiana Kochert MacDonald of Paris, and a new one, Mlle. Marie-Gabrielle Schecher, for a much deeper and more knowledgeable appreciation of that magic city.

Nicholas Rayner and Diana Leavitt of Sotheby's were extremely helpful with data about the Duchess of Windsor's jewels and details about the couple's courtship and later life.

I am also grateful to Francis Cornish and John Hughes of the British Embassy in Washington for information concerning royal protocol and the ways of British royalty.

Friendship, advice, and support came from many sources: my colleagues Lisa Anderson and James Coates of the Chicago Tribune, Sugar Rautbord of Chicago and Dianne deWitt of New York, Tex and Jean Harris of Washington, and Heather Vickers-Smith of Berryville, Virginia.

I am enormously grateful to my friend and editor Thomas Dunne of St. Martin's and my friend and literary accomplice Dominick Abel of New York—and to Margaret Schwarzer and Sandy Wolf of St. Martin's as well. My thanks to Little, Brown and Company publishers for permission to reprint Lady Diana's remarks as an epigraph.

This book grew out of a conversation fifteen years ago with a wonderful English friend and legendary newsman, Reuter correspondent Ronald Batchelor, and from his subsequent loan of Chips Channon's diaries. I wish so much he were alive to read *Dance on a Sinking Ship* today.

As always, I am deeply grateful to my wife, Pamela, and sons, Eric and Colin, as only they can know.

She made him look good, that was her great talent. She made him appear brighter than he was. I got into it because of Wallis—he invited people to Fort Belvedere and on the *Nablin* to keep her company. I liked her, but we were never intimate, we never talked about any love affair. In the long run, it's been a blessing. He would not have been a good king. . . . We were lucky to get George VI and Elizabeth—they were by far the better loved in the end. Of course all the royal family were pro-German in the beginning. After all, they were German. Old Queen Mary could barely speak English, which most people don't realize—she was always working with tutors. But the duke was the worst. He'd make terrible anti-Semitic remarks. Sir Ernest Cassel was one of his grandfather's best friends, but whenever his name came up the duke would say, "What can you expect from the Jews?" And Sir Ernest's granddaughter was married to Dickie Mountbatten, the duke's own cousin! Whenever he talked like that, I'd shut my trap. Wallis never talked that way, to give her credit. Yes, in the end it was a blessing that Wallis came along and took him away.

—LADY DIANA COOPER, 1979


The defiant hilarity of a dance on a sinking ship.

—ALEXANDER WOOLLCOTT

# CHAPTER
## ONE

It was that lingering time between day and evening that Parisians called *l'heure bleue*. Eugene Fodor's new European guide for 1935, *On the Continent,* said of its unique effect on the city: "The contours of the buildings seem to soften and to merge into the dusk. You will see a few people standing on the quay and apparently angling, but in reality they are merely gazing into the air and reflecting what sort of aperitif they are going to drink."

Such a marvel of serenity, this tranquil Paris of the latest Fodor's. The guidebook said nothing of the rioting that had broken out like street fires in 1934 and had burst full force upon the heart of Paris in February—and was returning now in the warm autumn. Fodor's Europe was a place of pleasure, not the stinking political sewer still reeking of the old war as it fermented a new one. Discussing Germany, Fodor's complained of difficulties with the currency, noting only in passing that the traveler there can "hardly avoid the Jewish question."

C. Jamieson Spencer was avoiding the Jewish question—and all such questions. He had reflected on his aperitifs all day and was now consuming one rapidly—*un fine à l'eau*—at a sidewalk table of the Café aux Deux-Magots.

The café, as usual at this hour, was crowded, and the Boulevard de St. Germain close in front of it rattled and smelled from heavy traffic. But Spencer was not interested in serenity. He had earlier stopped at Harry's New York Bar in the Rue Daunou for a quick whiskey and to leave his afternoon's news story with the proprietor, Harry MacElhone, for the correspondent whose turn it was to run everyone's copy up to the boat-train at Gare St. Lazare. Normally he

*1*

would have had another whiskey at Harry's and perhaps stayed the night. Like many Americans, he preferred Harry's to all the other bars in Paris. But it was not a place to pick up women—and, for the first time in years, Spencer was in that mood.

He watched carefully each *jeune fille* passing along the boulevard as he drank his brandy, this night feeling as melancholy as he usually looked. A man four years from forty, with sandy hair, somber eyes, and a thin mouth with little smile to it, he was taller than most and narrow-limbed. He wore British clothes in an American manner. His gray flannel trousers were cuffed and his brown tweed jacket unbuttoned, a red-and-black striped tie that didn't quite match hanging loose over a rumpled white shirt. In his lapel was the green-and-yellow ribbon of the Médaille Militaire, which still gained him many courtesies in Paris. It was an honor he had won during his three months of flying with the French in 1917, before he had joined the Americans and Canadians of the 1st Pursuit Group. He had won only two victories in the air for the French, but he had survived those three months and there was also triumph in that. By 1917, three months alive in the air war was six lifetimes.

French, Americans, Canadians, even the Germans, they were now all brothers. *Les frères de la guerre, les mutilés de la guerre,* known to one another by the ribbons in their lapels or by missing limbs or other wounds still visible seventeen years after the armistice.

He signaled the waiter, a weary, hunched man with a huge mustache, ordering a cognac plain this time, with no water. Spencer was a man who drank little for months at a time and then drowning quantities of brandy or whiskey when sudden occasion demanded it. This was such an occasion. Whitney Ransom de Mornay had made it so. Again.

He rubbed his hands nervously. He no longer smoked. He had stopped during the war. A cigarette thoughtlessly lighted had set fire to the Spad VIII he had flown in more than three dozen patrols. He had nearly died in the flames and had almost been dismissed from the No. 27 Squadron for his carelessness. Four days later, the replacement ship they had given him, an old Nieuport 17 with a wheezing, underpowered Le Rhone engine, had come close to killing him in combat. He had not smoked since, except in China a few times, and that had been opium.

The brandy neat was better, warmer. He would eat late that night. Perhaps, if he found a woman, with her. Until then, he would drink.

The woman he really wanted was not some perfumed stranger. He craved the one he no longer had, the one who had a few days before abruptly removed herself from his life, leaving it to collapse behind her, not caring. Whitney Ransom was ten years and a generation and a war younger than he. She was as rich as he was no longer and blithefully happy as he had not been since he was a boy. And none of that mattered now. She was truly and irrevocably gone. She had loved him but had rejected all the grim realities he dealt with in his everyday life, that had come to define his life. In this way, she had confronted him with a terrible choice. Accept her and deny the truth, deny his work, deny himself.

He could explain his infatuation with Whitney. Every man who ever met her became infatuated with her. She was such a bewitching combination of American youth and French sophistication, cool reserve and madcap recklessness, loving generosity and impish selfishness, serene beauty and wanton passion, innocence and brilliant education, naivete and yet instinct for the essence of things. What he could not explain was why the infatuation had endured for what was now years. It had become an incurable addiction. She had intoxicated him the very first instant, and she still did.

Truth to him was love for her and a struggle to survive in a Paris, a Europe, and a world threatened by a human race gone vile and crazy. His life was sunsets that meant only that civilization had endured another day and sunrises that proclaimed it had endured another night.

Life to her was pleasant Paris gardens, no worry, and a husband who indulged her every notion and wish. Her truth was a bemused belief in the innate goodness and civility of every man. So then did she love Spencer, and love her husband—the one with passion, the other with fondness and gratitude, but both equally, in the perfect world she had invented for herself in this most wonderful and satisfying of cities. Life to her was always charming. As Bismarck had once said of the kaiser, she wanted every day to be Sunday—and it was.

He had chosen rightly in allowing her to leave him, though he was in agony over the price of his choice. He would not remain her pet man, a lapdog permitted by her ever-indulgent husband. He would not abandon his fascination with the violence-filled streets and famine-dead in China and the new monsters rising in Germany.

He had thought of taking a woman that night—any woman. But no woman would be Whitney.

Spencer drank, attempting to content himself with the moment, with the fabled *l'heure bleu.* He'd been Paris correspondent for the

*Chicago Press-Bulletin* since 1932, and in those three years had developed certain fondnesses. Those for the Deux-Magots and *un fine* during *l'heure bleue* were near the top of his list—up near Harry's New York bar.

At the very top, though, had been always and was still Whitney. Every happy thought always led to her. It did so now.

She was blonde and youthful in a fresh and free and yet very stylish way—very, very rich and married to a Frenchman even richer. She was from New York. Her family had a town house on East 75th Street and a large estate in Westchester. Yet she worked—for one of the Paris fashion houses. Whitney was a tall girl, large but well proportioned and blessed with wonderful legs, a dancer's legs.

She knew Paris even better than he. Spencer could not imagine a Paris without her. Yet there it was, all around him, Paris without Whitney. An empty chair at his table. At *all* his tables.

It was barely seven o'clock, and in the ebbing daylight, none of the women passing in the street looked particularly inviting. He finished the second brandy and ordered a third. He judged himself deserving of some indulgence. His day had been long and unpleasant, spent dodging the bricks of mobs, the clubs of police, and the craven hypocrisies of Premier Pierre Laval and Ministre Edouard Daladier. Spencer had written a long story on the new Paris disturbances, which his paper would likely cut in half and run on the obituary page. The *Press-Bulletin* was even more reactionary than its chief rival, the *Chicago Tribune,* and had been editorially fearful of a European-style uprising in the United States ever since Franklin Roosevelt's inaugural. Stories about rioting mobs in Paris might arouse the local socialists or, worse, the unemployed South Side steelworkers. It wouldn't matter, of course, that these particular Paris mobs were largely fascist. Or that the swarm of thugs who had tried to break into the Chamber of Deputies that morning had been right-wing Jeunesses Patriotes and Solidarité Française. To the *Press-Bulletin,* all mobs were socialist, or at least anarchist, which to them was much the same.

Spencer turned to observe a woman coming up the Boulevard de St. Germain from the direction of Place Mondor. She was blonde and, from a distance, might have been Whitney. Before she drew much nearer, a careening taxi distracted him, startling him when it suddenly swerved toward the curb and lurched to a stop. A flushed, familiar face, that of Bill Laingen of the *New York Herald,* poked out of a window.

"Jim!"

Spencer used "C. Jamieson" only as a byline. It probably accounted for at least twenty dollars of his weekly salary. A former publisher of the *Press-Bulletin* had had the name C. Jamieson Spencer—his late and bankrupt father.

Bill and Jean Laingen were also high on Spencer's list of Paris fondnesses. He pulled back a chair as a gesture of invitation. Laingen shook his head emphatically.

"There's big trouble up at the Place de la Concorde," Laingen said. "Come on!"

Spencer shook his head. "My paper isn't interested in any more trouble. I've already supplied my quota for the day."

"This is *très serieuse,* Jimmy! They're sending in Gardes Mobiles with rifles and sabers!"

Spencer stood, uttering the obligatory curse, and finished his drink with a stylish flourish. When he finally climbed into the taxi and pulled the door closed behind him, the blond woman passed by not three feet distant. She was not Whitney, but she was a splendor. Spencer was coming to dislike anarchists himself.

"*Allons!*" Laingen commanded. "*Vite, vite!*"

The driver responded with little enthusiasm but fair speed. As they swerved along, Laingen studied his friend unhappily.

"It's not like you to get blotto in the middle of a story. Not one like this."

"This story needs blotto," said Spencer. "The end of civilization. I'd meant to spend it with Whitney, but now I can't."

"You two quarreling again?"

"No row. No raised voices. She just walked out of my life. She divorced me."

"But she's married to someone else."

"*La même chose.* All the same to me."

They could hear the terrible shouting up ahead, even above the engine noise. Besides the riots in February, there had been a massive strike in Paris, one that had seen workers lock themselves in stores and shops for weeks, surviving on food brought to them at great hazard by their families. Now there was rioting again.

"End of civilization or not," Laingen said. "Here it is."

Entering upon the chaotic scene as cautiously as they might descend into hell, they urged the driver as close to the Chamber of Deputies as his nerve would take him. When he absolutely would go no farther and began to scream at them to emphasize that point, they leapt out and into the crowd, Laingen leading.

People were hurrying frantically toward as well as away from the furor across the Seine. A group of mounted Gardes Mobiles with drawn sabers came cantering by, and the two newspapermen trotted after the horsemen across the Pont de la Concorde. At the edge of the Place on the other side of the bridge, blue-coated infantry had massed themselves into a formidable wall. Laingen and Spencer moved along behind them, halting every so often to glance over troops' shoulders at the mass of human heads beyond. It seemed extraordinary to Spencer that such a vast openness could be filled so entirely with people all joined in the same dangerous and violent purpose. It was like the war.

Ahead, a large body of cavalry began moving out into the mob with slashing sabers, but they made surprisingly little progress. Shots were being fired in the distance, and flames of a burning vehicle were visible in the square. The din generated by the crowd increased till it no longer seemed a human sound. The sunlight was vanishing rapidly; nightfall would aggravate the tensions—and the passions.

"This is a bad spot!" Spencer said, shouting over the melée.

"Let's keep moving!"

They shoved, dodged, and scrambled their way to the Tuileries side of the Place, finding the battlementlike terraces jammed with more people. They were not onlookers but participants awaiting their turn, reminding Spencer of the reserves in the Great War, silently observing the carnage on another sector of the battlefield until it was their time to swarm out of the trenches and fight.

"I don't recognize these people!" Spencer said.

"They're communists! See those banners! We've got fascists and communists taking on the government side by side!"

Spencer nodded. All mobs were anarchists. In this at least, the *Press-Bulletin*'s judgment may have been correct.

There was a woman's scream, and some angry shrieks and bellows. Reinforcements for the mob were coming up the quay from the Louvre and were being met by firehoses. Stones and bricks began to fly overhead, some landing quite near. A piece of mortar struck Spencer in the cheek, causing him to bleed. Across the square, another crowd was moving toward them from the Champs-Elysées, their *tricouleurs* and banners identifying the group as right-wing war veterans of the militant Union Nationale des Combattants. Laingen stared transfixed. Spencer's adrenaline was failing—he was tiring rapidly and wanted another drink. He glanced quickly about, his eyes settling upon the façade of the luxurious Hotel Crillon, its windows crowded with onlookers observing the gathering clash as they might some sporting event or parade.

"Let's get up there!" Spencer shouted into Laingen's ear. "We can see better!"

They had to struggle through police to reach the lobby, but once there they could move about freely. Laingen headed for the main staircase and Spencer went for the bar. It was so thick with noise, tobacco smoke, and people he found it impossible to gain the bartender's attention, so, at an opportune moment, he stole a distracted customer's drink—from the looks and smell of it, a double brandy.

"*Victoire,*" he muttered, then hurried up the main stairs himself.

Laingen had gone out onto the third-floor balcony that ran across the front of the Crillon. Many others were braving the riot from there, a fair number holding drinks as well, lending the scene the aspect of a cocktail party, a cocktail party out of Poe's "Masque of the Red Death."

It was dark now but as hot as midday. Spencer wiped his brow with his handkerchief, pressing forward toward Laingen. There was swarming movement in every quarter of the square. The din was now so great that it could scarcely be perceived as sound, the sensation more of pain than hearing. Many gunflashes could be seen but not heard. Other fires were burning and more were being ignited. Smoke drifted thickly from the Ministry of Marine down the street.

The throngs in the Tuileries now swept forth as if on signal, dropping from the terraces and surging out the gates, lunging into the Place and pushing wheeling, rearing cavalrymen before them. Some sudden gunflashes drew a necklace of light along a section of the square, but Spencer could not see where the bullets struck.

He recognized other correspondents on the balcony. Dick O'Brien of the Irish *Times,* Ronald Batchelor of Reuters, Jim Jackson of *Time* magazine, Jim Coates of the *Chicago Tribune,* Bill Shirer of the Paris *Herald,* Melvin Whiteleather of the Associated Press. Janet Flanner of the *New Yorker* was also there, wearing an odd hat and a raincoat despite the warmth. Spencer nodded to Coates. O'Brien was scribbling furiously in a notebook and hadn't seen him. Standing just behind Whiteleather was a woman in a long, blue, backless evening dress. She was so exquisite she might have been the dancer Mistinguette, and Spencer had to blink and look again to make certain she was not. He emboldened himself with another sip of his cognac, then moved to stand next to her, very close. She was so utterly captivated by the violent tableau below that she noticed him not at all. Her perfect blue eyes were wide and staring, her thin lips held slightly parted. Though she stood absolutely motionless, she was breathing rapidly. If he were to put his hand against the bare skin of her back he knew he would feel a violent thudding of her heart.

He moved closer still, so near that he could put his arm completely around her waist if he dared. Despite the awful racket around them, he had an impulse to whisper in her ear. The heat and the mingled odors of smoke, gunpowder, and massed humanity had failed to sully the scent of her perfume. Even her hair, brushed to a golden sheen, smelled sweet. He leaned nearer, impudently and recklessly near, and studied the play of flickering light on the curve of her cheek and on the blue sapphire held by the merest glimpse of ear. He wished to kiss her neck, to inhale the fragrance of her skin.

He invented a name for her—Mathilde—and a husband—wealthy, attractive, and boring—like Whitney's. They would have a grand residence in Passy, or on the Île de la Cité, he imagined, and a country place on the coast between Honfleur and Deauville. She would be a patron of galleries and concerts, disliking Picasso but fond of his friend Erik Satie. She would smoke and drink only occasionally, but she would love to swim and ride, love dancing, love tea, love small pastries, love making love in the afternoon. She and Spencer would become lovers on an afternoon, and would lie sleeping quietly in each other's arms afterward, in a cool breeze from an open window. She would be impressed by his record as an aviator in the war but not want to hear about the combat. She would have a small blond daughter, whom she would favor with pink-and-white dresses. She would buy Spencer books as presents—modern French poets. She would make him forget Whitney.

Her eyes flickered. It was almost a glance, not quite in his direction. He was so close to her she would have to turn her head to see him. In an anxious passing of seconds, he alternately wished and feared she would, but a distraction led her gaze elsewhere. Another car had been set afire and its gasoline was burning brightly, a beacon of hatred in the gathering night.

Some people on the other side of the blond woman were speaking. He could not follow the words, but their accents were English. Many around them looked English. As he thought about it, so did she. This was a hotel much favored by the British rich. Had he led his imagination into error?

Another necklace of gunfire appeared. Ignoring it, he sought some measure of this moment with her, this extraordinary intimacy with a woman whose eyes had never looked upon him, into his, but in this infinite instant, their oneness needed only a touch to complete—or shatter.

The aimless bullet, soundless in the cacaphony, created a large, red, round hole in her forehead just above her left eye. Spencer felt the horror of wetness splattered against his cheek and neck as her head snapped back, life vanishing from her gaze before her eyes could focus upon him. He reached to catch her, as if keeping her from falling to the balcony floor could somehow undo what had happened. But he moved too late. She slipped through his grasp, her elbow knocking the glass from his hand, and landed twisted on her back. Her light hair was spread out all around her white perfect face, a madonna's halo. Slowly the hair began to darken.

He stood stupidly, staring down at her as might someone who had accidentally broken something in a store. It suddenly became very important to learn her name, her identity, this woman who had lived and died without him in her now-erased memory. But he didn't think to ask anyone. He simply stood as some men in hotel uniforms knelt over her and then took her away, leaving nothing but a shadowy stain on the tile floor.

It was only then that he heard the shouting and shrieking around him. Everyone on the balcony was fleeing for the Crillon's interior. Spencer could hear the gunfire now.

Laingen gripped his shoulder.

"Let's get inside!" he shouted. "I've got to file! You want to file?"

"File?"

"The story! This is a hell of a story! It's got to go out on cable!"

"That woman . . ."

In the square, firemen were trying to drag hoses through the melée to get at the blaze in the Ministry of Marine, but the arcs of water sputtered and fell. The mob was cutting the hoses. A machine gun stuttered, and then others. Masonry rained on them from a suddenly fractured cornice.

"Goddamn it, Jim! We've got to get inside!"

Spencer knelt and touched the stain, feeling grit and stickiness, then ran to catch up with his friend.

The crowded lobby contained a madhouse's disparity of moods and demeanors. There were the frightened, the drunk, the bored, the bold, the hysterical, the hilarious, the weary, the asleep, and the perfectly content. One extremely well-dressed woman sat holding a small lapdog while drinking decorously from a magnum bottle of wine. Next to her a barefoot girl in a nightgown huddled and whimpered. There were a great many police in the lobby, all looking dutifully concerned but without discernible purpose. The danger was outside. Unless some hapless cabinet minister had taken refuge in the hotel, the policemen's duty was elsewhere.

Laingen had somehow gained possession of a telephone at the hotel's main desk.

"Twelve dead? They said twelve dead?" Laingen saw Spencer and cupped the receiver's mouthpiece. "The police are saying there are only twelve dead!" He turned to speak into the receiver again. "There must be a hundred dead, damn it!" he said to the credulous person on the other end of the line. "I tell you they're using machine guns!"

Machine guns in Paris. Nazis in Berlin. Mass executions and government-mandated starvation in Russia. And in Africa, Mussolini was trying to butcher his way into mastery over the Abyssinians. There was no need of the great new war many said was now coming. The world was disintegrating quite handily without it.

Spencer gestured that he would probably return and went back to the bar. By the time he emerged, carrying two large whiskies, Laingen had finished filing his story but was holding the telephone for Spencer. He surrendered it quickly in return for one of the drinks, gulping from it quickly. "I've got to get back to the office," he said finally. "If you can stay alive, I'll see you in the morning. Breakfast? Here?"

Spencer nodded and took up the phone. The *Press-Bulletin*'s bureau was an office flat not far distant in the Boulevard Haussmann. Denise, his French assistant and secretary, was still there, as he had requested but not really expected. She was not alone.

"Jim," she said, pronouncing it "Jeem." "Monsieur Carlson is here."

Carlson was the *Press-Bulletin*'s chief of correspondents. Based in London, he had been traveling through Europe. Spencer had thought he was still in Berlin.

"Spencer? Where are you?"

There was an uncharacteristic excitement in Carlson's voice. He was a settled man, full of small and careful habits. He often complained to Chicago that Spencer was too impetuous.

"I'm dodging bullets at the Hotel Crillon. There's a hell of an insurrection at the Place de la Concorde. The army's here. They're shooting at everything. I was standing next to this woman—"

"I want you to come into the office, Jim. I have a really swell story for you."

"I already have a really swell story! Here, listen to it." He briefly held the receiver out toward the lobby entrance. "They're shooting up the town! There's a civil war in the city of light! The right wing are once again trying to overthrow the French government and the communists are helping them!"

"Don't be so overwrought. We'll let the wires cover it tonight and McGuire will be up from Rome tomorrow. You have too much to do. You have to get ready and make arrangements. You're going on a trip, a voyage."

"There may be hundreds dead, Carlson! It's going to go on all night! I was going to dictate a few paragraphs to Denise for a cable dispatch and then get back out there!"

Laingen was nowhere to be seen.

"Dictate to Denise and then get back here. This is important. Your story is Lindy."

"Lindy?"

"My dear boy." Carlson had spent too much time in London. "Lucky Lindy. The Lone Eagle. Charles Lindbergh. You're going to cross the Atlantic with Colonel Lindbergh."

"How can I do that? He's in the States."

"No, he's here. In Paris. Just a few blocks from you."

"Why would he leave America? They haven't juiced Hauptmann yet. In fact, I read in the *Herald* that Lindbergh's in New Mexico. Rocket experiments or something."

"A deliberate untruth. He's been in Europe for at least a week. He's just been in Germany. Did you know that? No one did. I was on the same plane coming back from Berlin. He's staying at the Ritz. The day after tomorrow he's sailing for New York on the *Wilhelmina* from Le Havre. I'm betting he comes back with his wife and son. Now that the Supreme Court has turned down Hauptmann's appeal, there's no reason for them to stay. They certainly don't want to be around for the execution."

"What's the *Wilhelmina?*"

"It's the newest liner of the Lage Lander Line, just out of the shipyards. It will be a maiden voyage."

"Why don't you go?"

"My dear boy. You know Lindy doesn't talk to mere reporters." Carlson paused. "Not even chiefs of correspondents. He hates us all. But I'm betting he'll talk to you, an aviator in the war. You could have the first interview since Hauptmann was convicted!"

"But he won't talk to me!"

"You *were* a combat pilot."

"Lindbergh wasn't in the war. He was just an army mail pilot."

"You flew airplanes. There's a chance he'll talk to you, and I think it's worth a try. Spencer, this is the best story you've ever had, that you'll *ever* have. This is Lindbergh! Among other things, I'm sure he's been with some very high-level Germans. And in secret! Now, dictate your paragraphs to Denise and then come in and we can talk some more."

Spencer hesitated. "I'll be in when I can. Traffic's rather bad tonight."

When he was done with Denise, he bid her an affectionate good night and hung up without speaking further to Carlson. A *Times of London* correspondent snatched up the telephone immediately. The noise outside had diminished, though he could still hear sputters and crackles. The hotel manager appeared before him, complaining to one of the desk clerks about some matter.

"*Pardon, monsieur,*" said Spencer. "*La femme morte* . . . the woman upstairs who was killed, *la femme en bleu:* can you tell me her name?"

"*Tragique. Si tragique. Ces communistes!*"

"*Sa nomme, s'il vous plaît.* Do you know her name, who she was?"

The manager shook his head. "The police took the body, monsieur. I do not know if she was a guest. So many injured, *morts.*" He shrugged. "Perhaps we may know more in the morning."

Spencer nodded. Back out on the street, he decided he would not return to his office that night. He would start work on Carlson's really swell story. He would go to the Ritz.

He never got farther than the Ritz bar, where, amazingly, the great hero never made an appearance, never sat down on a stool to slap hand on back, buy a round, and tell amusing stories about his new flying friends over in the German Reich. Spencer agreed with himself that he owed it to Carlson to spend much of the night on this really swell story, here in the bar, waiting for Lindbergh.

He ordered another brandy and returned to brooding on his memory of the woman's face. Europe had begun to devour its own. It had started with the most beautiful. He drank to her. Drinking was what he did when he wanted to cry instead.

On an upper floor of the Crillon, just above the balcony fronting the Place de la Concorde, in a suite absurdly registered to a Mr. and Mrs. Edward Prince, a smallish man with an unusually handsome if feminine face and beautifully brushed blond hair stood calmly in a dressing gown at windows overlooking the mayhem. Smoking a cigarette, he watched as a final charge by the Gardes Mobiles began to break up the mob.

"Please, sir," said a man overdressed in tweed hovering nearby. "It's not safe."

Because of the rioting, only one small lamp had been turned on in the large room, its pale glow contributing little more than a softening of the darkness.

The man in the dressing gown cocked his head slightly. He was deaf in the left ear. "Now, now, Inspector Runcie. This isn't the French Revolution, after all. I was considerably more exposed during the war."

"For God's sake, David," she said, calling him by the name that only his intimates used. "Please do as he says."

The words came from a woman, herself in a dressing gown and heavily jeweled, reclining on a deeply plush sofa set against the opposite wall. In the dim light she looked comely. Her dark hair was pulled back tight to accentuate her aristocratic forehead. In the darkness her outsized mole was not visible, nor could one fully see the largeness of her nose and hands. She held a glass of bourbon and water that was in need of ice. She drank from it by way of punctuation. David kept his back to her, biting his lip and frowning. Finally he turned to the man in tweed.

"Runcie, hand me your revolver."

"Sir?"

"Your revolver. Give it to me."

Startled at first, the man remembered his place and quickly did as commanded. The pistol was a heavy-caliber Wembley, an officer's sidearm from the war. The man in the dressing gown took it clumsily at first, then aimed it firmly at the window, at the crowds below.

"There you are," he said. "Now I'm ready for them." He looked back at the woman, giving her his what-a-bright-boy-am-I smile. She scowled in reply.

"They're moving them off the square," he said. "I wonder if our Horse Guards could manage that if called upon. I must ask Duff or Fruity. It's all in the sabers, I suppose."

There was a polite rapping at the door. The woman hurried to it, grateful for the interruption, especially when she saw who was there.

"Sorry for the intrusion," said one of the two men who entered, a dapper, amiable, and quite tall man named Major Edward Metcalfe, better known as "Fruity." After Lord Louis Mountbatten, he was probably Edward P.'s best friend, and now he was a good friend of the woman as well.

"It's quite important, sir," said the second man, Lord Perry Brownlow, one of Edward P.'s principal aides.

Edward greeted them both with happy enthusiasm and, cigarette in mouth, hurried to pour them whiskies. Each discreetly winced at the taste of bourbon—her habit, now his.

"No intrusion at all," he said. "We've been so bored, bored, bored up here. Get Kitty, why don't you, Perry, and we can have a little party."

"She's gone back to London, sir," Brownlow said. "I'm afraid all this rioting has completely unnerved her. And she's not been well. She sends her apologies."

"Oh. Well, thank you." He frowned.

"David," said Fruity. "Sir. We've been talking to the French authorities and a few of our own. They think you ought to leave Paris. They can't guarantee your safety, certainly not with the casual way you're traveling about. They've got the rioting under control for now, but the situation's deuced bad."

"Why did you talk to the French? I'm supposed to be incognito."

"I'm afraid the Crillon is not a good place for a masquerade, sir," said Brownlow. "It's now widely known you're here."

"We should have gone to the Hotel Meurice, just as we always have," said the woman, returning to the sofa.

Fruity Metcalfe smiled. The prince was extremely well known at the Hotel Meurice, and it was just down the street. They had come to the Crillon supposedly to escape public attention.

"There's trouble all over Paris," he said. "Bolshies. Black shirts. Anyone with a brick. It's worse than that bloody dust up they had last year over the Stavisky scandal. I'm sorry, David, but staying here simply won't do."

Edward P. sighed. "I just wanted a bit of fun, Fruity—for all of us. Wallis is so tired of the weekends at Fort Belvedere, though I don't know why."

"Oh, sir," she said. "I'd be so happy to be back there now."

"If anything were to happen to you here, sir," said Brownlow. "If you were to be injured in any way, the international complications could be quite serious. As it is, your father will be furious."

Edward Prince frowned. "My father is in a perpetual state of fury. He's not forgiven me yet for that trip to America years ago. Well, damn and blast. I'm not going to arrange my private life to suit my father. I perform my public duties. My private life is my own."

"He's ill, David. Seriously ill."

"I'm well aware of that!"

He turned his back to them, puffing on his cigarette. The woman arched her brow.

"Sir," Brownlow said, finally. "We simply cannot stay in Paris. We must leave at once, if only for the sake of the ladies."

"Oh, all right, blast you," said Edward. "But not tonight!"

"As you wish, sir, but no later than tomorrow. Please."

Edward wheeled about to face them. With his cigarette stuck at an angle in his mouth and his hands in his dressing-gown pockets, he began to walk about the room.

"I jolly well won't go back to London," he said. "Not yet. Baldwin has everyone caught up in that Abyssinian crisis. He'll use the situation against me. And no one in London's having the slightest bit of fun at all. I'm so tired of the damned Abyssinian crisis. It just goes on and on. Why don't those wretched niggers give it a rest?"

"You know what Chips says, sir," said Brownlow. " 'A crisis a day keeps the war away.' "

"I've already done my bit to keep the war away," said Edward. "I made that speech back in June to the British Legion. I was damned conciliatory to the Germans. I don't know what more Baldwin could ask. I really shouldn't be involved in foreign affairs. I really shouldn't."

Brownlow glanced at Fruity, who responded with the slightest of smiles. Edward's "Germany is our friend" speech to the Legion was viewed by many in the Commons as a signal encouragement for the Italians to have their way with Haile Selasse.

"Sir," the woman said quickly. "If you don't want to return to London, where would you like to go?"

"Why not the South of France?" Fruity said. "There's not much civil unrest at Cannes at the moment."

"No. We were just there. And there'd be reporters."

"Biarritz?" said Fruity. "Kitzbühel?"

"Sir," said the woman, "we haven't been there since February."

"Yes. Remember how angry Father was when he found out? He forbade me to go there again. And anyway, there's no snow. I've a dozen invitations to Germany just now, but that would not be appropriate, I suppose."

"Sir," said Brownlow, weighing his words with great care. "Your father is very unwell. I really do think it would be best if you returned to London."

"Perry, if you're trying to tell me my father hasn't much longer to live, why do you think I decided to take this holiday? I don't know when we'll have such an opportunity again. I know my duty. I expect to fulfill it, but not yet."

The woman's gaze upon him was unwavering, the small glittering in her eyes a reflection from the lamp.

"Coming to Paris was a mistake, David," Fruity said. "We should have advised you better. Too much French politics—and too damned many machine guns."

Edward stood in silence, the smoke from his cigarette hanging eerily about his head.

"I like Paris," he said. "I like it a damned sight better than London. Especially now." He sighed, turning and sticking his hand in his side pocket. "Very well, Fruity. I'll leave. But not for London. Don't even suggest that again. You must find us another place, someplace amusing. I'll give you an hour to do that. An hour only. Otherwise I shall jolly well do as I please. And that very well might mean staying here."

He grinned at them broadly. "Now go."

The two friends of the prince went to Brownlow's room down the hall, a large chamber that seemed lonely and empty without Lady Brownlow's presence. Brownlow poured Metcalfe a scotch whiskey and himself a brandy from large traveling flasks on his dresser.

Major Metcalfe went to the window. It looked south and had only a glimpse of a view of the Place de la Concorde, though he could see flickers of light from the fires reflected against nearby buildings.

"Should we have told him how serious it is?" he said, his back to his companion.

"It wouldn't have made any difference," Brownlow said. "He knows that once he goes back he'll never leave England again until the king dies. His only escape would be to Fort Belvedere, and I daresay that if he has to winter there it will come to seem a prison."

Fruity turned. "The reports from MI-5 were quite grave. Four suspected assassination plots."

"I've read them all, Fruity, old boy. Of course, this sort of thing is hardly new. They've had a standing report on a suspected Irish Republican Army conspiracy ever since the end of the Irish civil war."

"These are much more specific, Perry. Most particularly that one on the Russian agent."

"I'd hardly call that specific. 'Assassin: Stalin's best. Intended victim: A British royal.' "

"Specific enough," Metcalfe said. "And it frightens me awfully. We have no choice but to get the prince off the continent."

"You're the man of action. Have you any ideas?"

"You're the sage counselor, but I do have an idea. I've been thinking hard upon it the whole bloody day."

Brownlow paused with his glass halfway to his lips. "Well, then. Out with it."

"I think we should take the prince and Mrs. Simpson to America."

"America? Are you mad?"

"I didn't say anything about the two of them strolling up Fifth Avenue arm in arm, posing for photographers. I don't think we should let them debark at all. But if we could get them on a boat for a crossing back and forth, we could keep them out of danger for at least a fortnight. As soon as we returned, off we'd all go to Fort Belvedere, where we could keep him safe and tidy until . . ."

"Until the king dies."

"God save the king. But, yes. He'd have had his fling, and he'd have no choice but to conduct himself circumspectly for a while."

"He'd have to travel completely incognito. We couldn't afford the sort of attention he received on his 1924 crossing. We'd have to secure the utmost assurances of discretion from the shipping line."

"Of course."

"It couldn't be a British ship."

"And certainly not a German one. Nor a Frenchie. The press flock to those. We'd have to find the most obscure boat available."

Brownlow stood up and unbuttoned his jacket. It was oppressively warm in the room and he was perspiring.

"It's a sort of desperate notion, this," he said. "But we're in a desperate situation. On balance, I quite like your idea, Fruity."

"I see only one real problem."

"That a shipping line wouldn't cooperate?"

"No, Perry." He nodded toward the door that led to the corridor. "The entourage."

Brownlow seated himself, "Fruity, they're his friends."

"Nonsense. Most of them would abandon him in a trice if he weren't going to be king."

"I don't think that's entirely true. At any rate, they're the closest thing he has to friends, after you and me. And Lady Diana comes from one of the first families of the kingdom."

"She and Duff are the best of the lot. The others, I daresay, are ruddy trouble—especially the Mountbattens. And that Channon chap. He's the most outrageous social climber in the world."

Brownlow looked at him unhappily. The most outrageous social climber in the world was the woman they had just left in the prince's chambers.

"Lord Mountbatten is a cousin to the king," Brownlow said with great emphasis. "He is a prince of Hesse, a relative of virtually every royal family in Europe. Edwina, of course—"

"Is the granddaughter of a Jewish banker," Metcalfe finished. "But that's one of the best things about her."

The two stared at each other. Peregrine, Lord Brownlow, was from one of England's most aristocratic families. Major Metcalfe had been nothing more than a somewhat dashing Irish cavalry officer until he had met Prince Edward in India in 1922. His current high station was due solely to his friendship with the prince—and his marriage to one of the daughters of the legendary Lord Curzon.

"They'll have to stay with us, Fruity," Brownlow said finally. "He simply wouldn't have it any other way."

The major sighed. "Suppose you're right, old boy. Deuced right. We'll have to manage with them as best we can."

"It's still rather a wizard idea, Fruity. The best thing of all is that I think he'll leap at it. Two weeks at sea on a great secret adventure— he'll think it just the ticket."

"I daresay. That's what appealed to me most about it."

"For all that, it still terrifies me."

"Old boy, Paris terrifies me more."

The Mountbattens had taken a suite almost as outsized as the prince's and Lord Louis was alone in it, in bed in his carefully pressed pajamas. He was reading a new Royal Navy text on destroyer antisubmarine warfare with intense concentration, having drawn the heavy draperies across the windows to muffle the noise of the rioting. He and Edwina had left their servants behind at their villa near the Royal Navy base on Malta, and he was managing without them quite handily. His clothes, including a magnificently tailored navy commander's uniform, were hung in the closet with more care than they were usually accorded. The most methodically German member of the royal family and its branches, Mountbatten had arranged each garment himself so it did not touch another. In the morning, he would examine them all, certain he would not find a single wrinkle. He was absolutely certain about everything he did. He had never once, to his knowledge, been wrong.

The sudden ringing of the telephone alarmed and then irritated him. It could not be Edwina. She had already made her obligatory call explaining her absence, informing him she was in Montmartre in search of a new Miró painting for her collection. Yet it was so late the caller could be no one else. After pausing to mark his place neatly in the book, he snapped up the phone, saying "Hello!" in a cold, demanding tone, which vanished abruptly when he heard the voice of the speaker.

"Oh, David! Sorry, I thought it was hotel staff. . . . What? . . . America?" He sat up, stunned. "Oh! What a topping idea! Edwina will be thrilled. She could use a restful ocean voyage after that airplane trip from Australia. . . . Yes? . . . Oh, it should be no trouble getting time off. I have leave coming. I'll simply wire Malta in the morning. . . . Yes, David. I think it's a marvelous idea. Really do. Cheery bye."

He hung up, furious. There was a war on in Abyssinia. His destroyer squadron might soon be engaged. Edward's impulsive journey might consume two weeks. Mountbatten was well aware of the depth of resentment felt toward him by his fellow officers, junior and senior. He had dealt with that simply by being the most perfect officer in the history of the Royal Navy—at least since his father. This sort of flighty behavior would be considered self-indulgent and irresponsible. As if rules were not applicable to royals. Mountbatten's father's troubles in the Royal Navy during the last war had stemmed entirely from the fact that he had been born a German prince. Mountbatten's own derived from his trying to work his way up through the ranks to the highest levels of the navy as the cousin and best friend of the man who would shortly be king. "Rise above it, Dickie," Edwina always said of his fellow officers' animosity. "Rise above it." In his more generous moments, Mountbatten would admit to himself that Edwina was due part of the credit for his career advancement—Edwina, and his cousin Prince Edward. But his generous moments were indeed rare.

He had been quite content, indeed pleased, to be all by himself that night. But with Edward's call and the disagreeable prospect it offered, he found himself longing for Edwina's presence—as he hadn't in all the weeks and months she'd been away in the Far East. There had to be a way to extricate himself from the prince's voyage. He just needed Edwina to think of it.

It was far too early for her to have returned, but on the slight chance she might have crept in while he was engrossed with his reading, Mountbatten rose and crossed through the sitting room to her bedroom. The rioting had interfered with hotel maid service and the chamber was still in the awful mess it had been when she left, with shoes a jumble on the floor by the closet and clothes, including underwear, strewn everywhere. The bed itself, of course, was perfectly neat. She had not slept in it, or his, since they'd arrived in Paris.

He spoke her name to the emptiness, then, embarrassed by such folly, closed the door to her bedroom and returned to his own. He tried to resume reading but his mind had lost its fascination with destroyers. He picked up a book dealing with some of his ancestors, but not even his favorite subject appealed much to him. At length, he poured a brandy and took it to a hard-backed chair. Sipping uncomfortably, he stared at the drapes drawn across the window, wishing for Edwina and wondering how angry she'd be if he waited up for her. Life could be so terribly unhappy when it wasn't properly organized.

Albert Duff Cooper hung up the phone gently and lay back with his hands behind his head, saying nothing. He was content to watch his wife and Chips Channon continue the happy interlude of their game of bezique, which the affable Chips was losing, perhaps deliberately. No one who had been in the company of Lady Diana Cooper for one minute could ever take pleasure in depriving her of anything, even a trivial victory in an inconsequential game. At forty-two, she was no longer the blond goddess of London society the newspapers had devoted so much attention to a generation before, but the illegitimate daughter of the Duchess of Rutland was still extremely attractive. Her enormous blue eyes and warm, theatrical voice alone remained enough to enchant any man.

They enchanted Duff, though for him enchantment was not quite the same thing as fidelity. Diana tolerated this, sometimes with amusement, as she did his other passions for politics, drink, and gambling. Theirs was a happy marriage, if sometimes a crowded one.

He rubbed his short mustache, reflecting upon the telephone conversation just ended and the outrageous inconvenience that had been asked of them. Sailing off to New York at this juncture in world affairs would be a voyage Duff could undertake only with a sense of fatalistic abandon, but that was not far from his actual feelings in recent days. He was a man who had foresworn the offer of a title to devote himself to the Conservative Party and its pursuit of the national good. He had been in line for a major cabinet post. In fact, he'd been given reason to hope for the war ministry. But he'd just been turned down as too pro-French and too anti-Nazi.

"I've won!" exclaimed Diana. "Oh, Chips, you dear, you cheat so marvelously. And gallantly. I almost thought I'd done it myself."

Channon, a thoroughly English American expatriate with the manners and dress of a squire and the burning dark eyes of an Arab, patted her hand. "Nonsense, Diana. I haven't the skill to cheat. It's simply that my brain jellifies whenever I'm near a beautiful woman."

He was one of the more agreeable of the Coopers' friends, though others of their circle thought him odious, a snob, and an *arriviste*. Duff considered him a rather useless fellow, but pleasant company. He had come to their niche in British society oddly. The son of a nondescript Chicago millionaire, he had studied at Oxford and had traveled much about Europe in his youth and even lived for a time with Marcel Proust. Chips had also authored two awkward novels. But maturity had brought wiser ambitions. He'd married Lady Honor Guinness of the brewery fortune, who a few days before had borne him a son, and now he held the family Southend-on-Sea seat in Parliament. So passionately expatriate as to be a modern-day Lord Astor, he'd cleansed every trace of Chicago from his being, a folly the Coopers, who loved Americans, had indulgently forgiven. Chips was too amiable and amusing to be disliked for his affectations and incorrigible social climbing. His grandfather had in any event been English, having run away to sea as a boy from Somerset and become rich with a Great Lakes ship chandling business.

Diana came and sat down on the bed with Duff. "Who was the mysterious caller?" she asked in her husky stage whisper.

"That was our royal host," said Duff. "With awful news. He thinks a bit of sea air will do us all wonders."

"Not the South of France again?" said Chips.

"Nothing so balmy. He has in mind New York. Autumn in New York."

"You're serious, darling?"

"Yes. We leave as soon as Perry Brownlow and Fruity can arrange passage for everyone."

"Can you do this, Duffie, with the Abyssinian debate coming up and all that?" She took his hand.

"Of course I can't. But in thinking upon it, I have to say, why not? What bloody difference would it make? This government's not going to do anything about Abyssinia."

"I found meeting Mussolini gave me more of a thrill than meeting the Pope," Channon said. "Really quite an extraordinary man."

"I'll agree that he's certainly no Hitler. But his nasty little war is causing *beaucoup des frissons* and here we are about to go off on an idiotic romp to the United States. He'll doubtless make us pay our own passage."

Cooper was himself the son of the sister of a duke, but he and Diana were perpetually short of money.

"Don't be so bitter, Duffie," she said. "After all, we're supposed to be his friends."

"That's why I'm here, I suppose, but I don't think he's given a single thought to the consequences. Especially for Mrs. Simpson. That woman has simply no ken of the depth of the waters she's sailing in."

"But he loves her, Duffie wuffie. And if the king should pass on, they're both going to be in for a really dreadful time. We must help them as much as we can."

"Am I among the favored few to be booked passage?" Chips asked.

"Of course," Duff said. "He was most emphatic about that. He quite likes you, as you must know."

"Oh, God," said Chips, looking pleased despite his groaning. "America."

"You can stand it for a week or two, Chipsie," said Diana. She had toured the United States twice in a sort of play and enjoyed herself immensely—most of the time.

Cooper squeezed her hand, then slipped his from it and rose. "We'll go with him, but it won't be very bloody amusing. Now let's find some happy café, if there is one that hasn't been burned down. I'd rather not be here if he should ring up again. It might be he's decided instead to go to Moscow."

"No worry of that," said Channon. "I said to him this morning, 'No Englishman will realize the danger of the Soviet Union until we get communism at Calais.' His Highness nodded vigorously."

"Tonight there might very well be communism at Calais, and Dadaism at the Elysses Palace," Duff said. "Let's be off. It will be damned hard to find a taxi."

"We can go to Montmartre," Diana said. "Edwina's there. 'Looking for paintings.'"

"Painters," Duff corrected. "If she's in Montmartre, let's go to Montparnasse. The situation is scandalous enough."

"Tuppenny royalty, the Mountbatten," said Chips. "Tuppenny."

"Chipsie," said Diana. "Are all Chicagoans such snobs?"

Lady Emerald Cunard's response to Edward P.'s invitation was both genuine and immediate: "Oh, sir, it will be simply too, too amusing!"

As she considered after hanging up, holding the telephone cradled in her lap as if it were a small dog, the voyage could be much more than that. It was an opportunity to resolve the case of her friend and fellow American, Mrs. Simpson, far more than she'd ever been able to with the private little dinners she had arranged for the couple in her Grosvenor Square mansion. It was an opportunity that she as Mrs. Simpson's principal sponsor in British society, as well as the dominating figure in what was called "the Prince of Wales set," dared not decline.

She fretted with her hands. They were small and clawlike, and burdened with too many rings. She had much the absurd aspect of a bird, perhaps a parakeet, with yellow hair far too brightly colored for her sixty-three years. But she was a great hostess and commanding London figure. Many feared her, especially since the prospering of her friendship with the Prince of Wales.

America, though. Lady Emerald had been born there—with the actual name of Maud Burke. She was always uncomfortable about returning—for any reason.

She would certainly have to be careful. Ships were altogether different from hotels and all-night dinner parties. They would be much together. Emerald had what some called "a brilliant wit" and others described as "a vicious tongue." She had once introduced Michael Arlen as "the only Armenian who hasn't been murdered." When Somerset Maugham attempted to leave one of her all-night parties at an unseemly early hour in the evening, protesting, "Emerald, I have to keep my youth," she had replied, "Then why didn't you bring him with you?"

She would have to be much more circumspect at sea with the royal party. She was suffering enough from the scandal still attached to her estranged daughter, Nancy.

Lady Emerald rose and fretted more. She detested being alone like this, confined to a hotel suite without even the benefit of a servant. But with the rioting down in the streets there wasn't much choice. She'd tried the lobby for a few minutes, but had found it irritatingly crowded and oppressive. Since then, she had twice almost telephoned her daughter, losing the courage to complete the act both times. It was just as well. If Nancy were still in Paris, she'd likely be at the barricades with all the other Bolsheviks.

Lighting a cigarette, Emerald went to make herself something to drink. She loathed whiskey as something utterly common but compelled herself to drink it because Wallis did. It had been Emerald's resolve to make Wallis as comfortable and accepted as possible. And after all, His Royal Highness had taken up bourbon himself.

A happy thought intruded upon Lady Cunard's nervous loneliness, returning her to the telephone. Joe, as his English friends referred to German Ambassador Joachim von Ribbentrop, would be fascinated by her news. He delighted in learning everything there was to know about the Prince of Wales.

She started to give the hotel operator the number of the German embassy in London but realized that, at that hour, the chancery would be closed. Instead, she had the woman try von Ribbentrop's private number at his residence, though she was fearful Frau von Ribbentrop might come to the phone before he could. It would take a long time to get the call through, what with all the trouble, but it would be worth it. She would use the word *liebchen*.

It was the only German word Lady Cunard ever used, and she used it only with Ribbentrop. People complained she was part of the infamous "Cliveden Set" of anti-Semites led by Nancy Astor. That was rot. Joe von Ribbentrop was simply a very charming man with a very charming dimple. And Emerald loathed Nancy Astor— certainly as much as Nancy Astor loathed her.

"Joe," she said, cooing into the telephone when the connection was completed twenty minutes later. "*Liebchen*, you'd simply never guess. We're all off to America!"

Huddled in the backseat, the high collar of her dark-green coat pulled up close to her cheeks, the very beautiful woman in the speeding, lurching taxi was feeling very much alone and frightened as her ill-kempt driver sought to avoid the areas of rioting and yet get to her destination, the Place Vendôme and the Hotel Ritz. Finally, abandoning anything resembling a direct route, he drove along the left bank of the Seine, crossing over again at the Île de la Cité and passing the grim walls of what he pointed out as la Conciergerie.

"*Marie Antoinette est mort là,*" the driver said, with an evil laugh. "*Aussi Danton et Robespierre. Madame la Guillotine.*"

A light rain had begun to fall, glistening the streets. Nora shivered despite the warmth, cursing a small man named Ira Stein, her manager, agent, publicist, and—or so she had thought until the rioting began—her friend. He had begged her to leave with him, but when she would not, he had fled for the train station and London. "I don't need this kind of trouble," he had said. "If you were Jewish, you'd understand."

She hadn't understood. Though Nora Gwynne had starred in six films and had now been cast in a leading role in a play bound for Broadway, this was her first trip to Paris and she wasn't going to be cheated out of it by some mob, whatever its politics. She would remain for the entire holiday as arranged and take the new Dutch liner back as scheduled. She would do everything she intended, just as she had in achieving the transformation of Nora Reilly into Nora Gwynne, as she had in making Nora Gwynne such a brilliant success.

Still, Paris hadn't been much fun rattling around on her own. The mobs were scary, and being Jewish or not had nothing to do with it. She had seen cars and a building burning over by the Champs-Elysees. She'd heard gunshots. Nora shivered again. The taxi driver, who also scared her, was singing. Her French was meager, but she knew enough to realize the lyrics were quite filthy. He kept watching her in the rearview mirror and looked too pleased with what he saw. He was supposed to be pleased, of course. Nora had the face of a French Impressionist's model, with dark brows, softly burnished copper hair, and flashing eyes the dark-green color of her coat. Her studio managers thought her more striking than Constance Bennett, and had invested considerable money in that belief.

The studio managers made her nervous. This taxi driver gave her the feeling of having cold worms crawl over her naked flesh. She would fire Ira Stein at the first opportunity, assuming she somehow survived all this. It was her fault for having become so completely dependent on Ira, but that realization made her no less angry at him for chugging off in his train and leaving her in this violent city helpless and alone. She edged closer to the door, preparing to fling herself out of the cab should that become necessary, though she wasn't sure what that would gain her. She hadn't seen many other taxis, and was only vaguely aware of where she was in relation to her hotel. Through the rain-streaked window, she could see what looked to be a railroad station. Then it was gone.

In the sudden light of a street lamp, so near to the street Nora could see her face perfectly, was a girl, a tall, poorly dressed young woman with long dark hair, a wide pretty face, and piercing eyes. She had a large suitcase at her feet and had lifted her arm to hail the cab. Nora started to tell the driver to stop, then hesitated. There was something desperate, even dangerous, in the girl's look. Nora needed no more trouble. Clenching her fingers around the door handle, she let the driver proceed.

"*Plus vite,*" she said.

He took both hands off the wheel in a rude gesture. "*Plus vite,*" he said. "*Toujours plus vite.*"

But he increased their speed as she asked. She guessed that they were nearing her hotel. Ahead was a rosy glow—the fires set by the mob. But a moment later, the glow little nearer, they swerved into the Place Vendôme and rattled to a stop before the hotel. The doorman flung open the door before she had quite let go of the handle, half pulling her out of the cab. He launched into a stream of apologies. She handed him a franc note for the taxi driver without looking at the denomination and fled inside without waiting for the change.

A bellman standing by the lobby door all but jumped to attention, as did the head porter. A number of others turned to stare. Her celebrity meant something here at least.

She started for the lifts, then halted, the prospect of her empty suite suddenly uninviting. She was not much of a drinker, but she felt in need of people around her.

The tables in the cocktail lounge were all taken, so she went to the bar and seated herself as decorously as possible on a stool, as she had never been permitted to do in the neighborhood tavern her father had run in Toledo, Ohio, so many thousands of miles and years distant. She ordered a mineral water and glanced at those around her. On one side, a British couple were speaking softly to each other. On the other, a thoroughly drunken if handsome American man was talking to himself, reciting poetry and muttering something about a woman. His appearance was startling and appalling. He was well dressed, but the right side of his face and the shoulder of his jacket were covered with blood.

"Lucky Lindy," he said suddenly with a madman's grin. He raised his glass. "Here's to the Lone Eagle. Still flyin'."

There was no other place to sit. When her drink came, Nora gulped some of it down quickly and left. The drunken man paid her absolutely no attention.

Olga Maretzka trudged on numbly through the rain, abandoning all hope of a taxi and letting her large, heavy suitcase drag along the pavement. She had memorized her directions well and knew she could reach her destination via the Paris Métro. If well traveled, at least in terms of Eastern Europe, she was not a person much used to taxis. She could certainly bear the inconvenience of the subway. But she was so terribly tired. Her fatigue was a burden as heavy as her suitcase. She would have paid almost any sum for a restful ride in the dark backseat of a taxi, hidden from view and safe with her murderous thoughts.

Her Métro stop would be Porte d'Italie—the "Italian Gate" of the old city. A bus, if they were still running at that hour, would take her on into the suburb beyond, Villejuif, and to the address that would provide sanctuary and her next instructions.

"Villejuif." *Mein Gott,* what a name. It meant "Jew Town."

Perhaps there would be a taxi at Porte d'Italie. There couldn't be rioting everywhere.

She set down her suitcase and shifted her heavy shoulder bag from one side to the other. It contained books and, among some very personal items, another weighty object—a large, long-barreled revolver, a very accurate kind good for shooting from some distance. If the unfortunate Fanny Kaplan had used such a weapon in 1918, Lenin would have been killed instead of wounded.

Fanny Kaplan had been a fanatical member of the Social Revolutionaries. She and Olga's mother had been good friends. Olga had no use for the Social Revolutionaries, and had in fact informed on her mother to the OGPU for continuing to aid their hopeless cause. Olga was proudly a member of the All Union Communists. If no fanatic, she had always done what was necessary, what was asked of her.

She moved on, keeping close to the curbside, away from the shadows, though it meant getting splashed by the occasional automobile. There were no friends in the shadows. There never were.

# CHAPTER
## *TWO*

Count Martin Frederich George Fabian Hammond von Bourke und Kresse was already awake and half dressed when the telephone rang, though it was not yet dawn. He was planning to take the first flight from Berlin back to his home near Ortelsburg in East Prussia, and his morning preparations took time, even with the help of a servant. Fortunately, this flat he kept just off Kurfurstendamm was not far from Tempelhof airfield.

Awake or not, he did not appreciate telephone calls at this hour. Nowadays, they could mean anything—certainly nothing good. He turned, wincing, and limped to his bedside table. His leg muscles worked badly just after rising.

"Yes?" He spoke as curtly as possible.

"Count von Kresse?"

"Yes. What is it?"

"This is the Air Ministry."

"*Ist halb sechs!*" the count said, looking again to his clock. "*Morgenstund hat Gold im Mund. Wer Verschlaft sich geht zu Grund.*"

It was a proverb about oversleeping. Von Kresse was not amused. "What do you want?"

"The Reichscommissioner requests that you join him for breakfast this morning. *Hier. Um acht Uhr.*"

"*Unmöglich. Ich habe einen Direktflug nach Tannenburg um funf nach sieben.*"

"There are later flights, Colonel. The Reichscommissioner is requesting you attend him."

28

The use of the count's military rank rendered this a very direct order.

"*Sehr gut,*" he grumbled. "*Auf wiedersehen.*"

"*Heil Hitler.*"

"*Wiedersehen.*"

The count slammed down the telephone receiver and summoned his servant, Zimmermann, to continue with his dressing. The man hastened to hold his military tunic for him. Normally von Kresse wore civilian clothes, but when traveling he preferred to be in uniform. It made for fewer complications—in the new Germany.

The count wore the uniform and insignia of a colonel in the Wehrmacht, with a red stripe on the pants legs indicating he had served on the elite German general staff. He customarily wore regulation marching boots because the tight fit of the black leather helped ease the pain in his leg, though it was a special misery removing the left boot at night.

He had been a young captain at the beginning of the war, even accepting a reduction to *leutnant* when he had transferred to the air service so he would not outrank his commanding officer. Richthofen had been compelled to do the same thing, and had in fact first commanded his fighter *Jagdegeschwader* as a second lieutenant with lieutenants and captains serving under him. Richthofen had had rank enough simply by signing his orders "Baron von Richthofen." When it came time for von Kresse to command a flying unit, his signing "Markgraf von Kresse" sufficed as well.

In the last crushing months of 1918, when von Kresse had gone mad and abandoned the sanctified combat in the air to fight in the daily horror of the trenches, he had done so as a common private.

In the postwar years, he had taken absolutely no interest in military matters but had accepted the family colonelcy because he was his late father's only son. It was a responsibility that went with his title. He was not an ordinary count. A markgraf was a count of the marches. In addition to his proprietorship of the family estate near Ortelsburg, he was a master of the Polish marches, a hereditary defender of perhaps the most strategic and warworn land approach to Prussia and Berlin from the east. A regiment went with the position. It had been one of Uhlans—anachronistic lancers—before the war. Modernization had eliminated the need for cavalry so now he was simply a colonel of infantry. This was a trade much preferable to that of many colonels in Germany now.

Pushing his arm through the sleeve brought pain, as usual. He hated and rebelled against his infirmities, struggling daily to minimize them. He was not old, barely over forty. Though his hair was now nearly the same shade of gray as his cold, arctic eyes, he still resembled the handsome youth depicted in his wartime newspaper photographs.

Except for the scars. One ran in a jagged line just above his right brow. Another slashed across his left cheek. His back was an agony of scars, some inflicted by shell fragments and others by surgeons bent on removing them. The muscles of his left leg had been violently torn and wrenched apart by a shell explosion, imposing a limp for life and continuing pain. "Bones we can mend," a doctor had told him, "but with muscles we are helpless." Von Kresse carried a bullet in his right shoulder and burn scars on his right arm and hand that never tanned with the rest of him.

Still, women often professed to love him and to enjoy making love to him. The German passion for mythic heroes, he supposed, though few women would think him quite heroic if they knew his secret.

His sister Dagne was waiting for him in the sitting room, wearing a pale-blue nightdress and robe and smoking a cigarette. He had no idea whether she had risen early to see him off or had simply been awakened by the ring of the telephone and was curious about its meaning. In the old days, she might be coming in from all sorts of bedraggling revels at this hour, but since she had taken up politics a few years back, her sleeping habits had become very conventional.

She smiled. She was still pretty and girlish at thirty-six if not viewed too closely, and her smile enhanced the effect. She used it frequently. She was more German than he, and had hair and eyes as blond and blue as any of the archetypical Aryan maidens in the racial fantasies of Dr. Goebbel's propaganda ministry. The irony was that these characteristics derived from the Polish side of their father's family. The Prussian line was a dark one, visible in their late father's nearly black hair. He liked to tease Dagne that their strain of the Order of Teutonic Knights descended from the Huns and Mongols who had for centuries streamed across these lands from the distant east, that many an ancestral grandmother had been dragged from a burning hut and violated. Sometimes he invented a tale of related gypsies. She was never amused.

Dagne was his half sister. Their common father, like many Prussian aristocrats, had been half Polish. Martin's mother, the late count's first wife, had been an American of German and English stock. When she died, the old count had married Dagne's mother, a baroness from Silesia. Dagne was thus three-quarters German, to Martin's half. She never let him forget it.

"You look so nice in uniform, Martin. You should go on active duty."

"That may become inevitable with so many lunatics in charge of our foreign policy."

She grimaced but was bent on being pleasant. "Who was on the telephone?"

"No one for you."

"Who was it, Martin?"

"The Air Ministry."

"Your old flying comrade?"

"He was a comrade. Now he is Reichscommissioner. There is a difference."

"What did he want?" She had crossed her legs and was swinging her foot. As she was wearing high-heeled slippers with furry pompons on them, this was distracting.

"Me. For breakfast."

"You are honored."

"I'm not going. I'm taking the plane to Tannenburg, as scheduled, and driving to Ortelsburg. I have an engagement this evening."

"But he is Reichscommissioner! You'll be disobeying a direct order."

"I hold no command in the Luftwaffe."

"You're joking about this."

"Certainly not."

Zimmerman was in the hall with Martin's bags. Von Kresse started toward him.

"Martin," Dagne said. "It would be a serious affront. Goering will be angry."

"He'll be angry here in Berlin and I will be happy there in East Prussia, where I won't have to listen to him."

"If you don't care what trouble you get into, think of the difficulties you could cause for me."

"I told you, *liebchen,* when you joined the party, don't intrude your political affairs on my life."

She made a face at him, then rose and reached on tiptoe to kiss him on the cheek.

"When are you coming home?" he asked.

"I am home."

"I mean to the country."

"In a few weeks. We are very busy here."

"Unfortunately. *Wiedersehen.*"

"*Wiedersehen,* Martin. Don't be foolish about Goering. He will end up on top in all this."

"*Vielleicht.*" He bowed but did not click his heels. His bad leg made that difficult.

"*Heil Hitler,*" she said.

The car von Kresse kept in Berlin was American—a long, yellow, seven-year-old Duesenberg touring phaeton. Because of his sister's political position, they were permitted to fly two Nazi flags from the front fenders. The count agreed to this solely as an additional means of assuring fewer complications and more freedom of movement. He himself had refused repeated invitations to join the party, calling the Nazis "gangsters with votes."

Zimmermann helped him into the rear seat and then got the big engine going and sped off down the still-empty street.

"You are still going to the airfield, sir?"

"Indeed."

"Very good, sir."

"Indeed."

But the airfield proved to be as far as he could go. The Fokker trimotor stood unattended on the tarmac, still glistening with the moisture of the night's rains. There was no one at the counter in the airline office. Zimmermann went to one of several policemen standing nearby. They were all staring at von Kresse.

"The flight has been canceled, sir," he said, returning.

"Why?"

"Orders of the Air Ministry, sir. Perhaps the weather."

Von Kresse swore, quietly.

"The local weather, sir."

"Yes. Very well, Zimmermann. You know where we must go."

Zimmermann, who had served von Kresse as a sergeant mechanic during the war, quickly reached the turning that led to the huge *Ministerium* where Reichscommissioner Hermann Goering now made his home and principal office. In the war, Goering had been one of von Kresse's flying comrades, his temporary commander, and, very briefly, his friend. Now the count had come to loathe this most amiable of the Nazis and resist every contact with him.

The yellow Duesenburg was well known in official Berlin, and the *Ministerium*'s gates were swung open immediately. When Zimmermann pulled up at the grotesquely outsized main entrance, two guards in the uniform of the new Luftwaffe came smartly to attention and gave the Nazi salute. Von Kresse, after descending stiffly from the car, replied with a purely military one.

The *Ministerium* appeared as immense inside as Versailles, though without the furnishings. The enormous rooms were nearly empty except for the paintings. The strong suggestion of museum was intentional. Goering now possessed one of the best art collections in Europe, and was intent on making it grander.

The slewed cadence of von Kresse's limping gait made a strange echo as he followed his military escort through the maze of rooms and paneled corridors. At last they came to one of the largest chambers of all, the private office of "der Dicke"—"the fat one."

This room, at least, was abundantly furnished, with outsized chairs and a desk that might have doubled for a banquet table. Yet it seemed not disproportionate to the chamber's occupant. Goering suffered from a glandular condition little helped by the medication given him by physicians or the endless narcotic drugs he prescribed for himself. The heroic photo published of him in 1933, when he was commander of Hitler's Sturmabteilung, had been more than a little retouched. Goering's girth was becoming monumental. He rose from behind the great slab of a desk, a desk without papers, official or otherwise, but covered by a forest of telephones and outsized, framed photographs.

*"Gute morgen,* von Kresse," he said rudely, nodding his guest to a chair but failing to extend his hand. He sat down again quickly, almost as painfully as von Kresse did with all his old wounds. Goering had survived the war without any serious injury but, more fortunately for his career, had suffered a wound for Hitler. During the 1923 *putsch* in Munich, he had been shot in the groin. This had led to wicked and spurious remarks about his subsequent love life, but the injury had a more serious consequence. He had quickly become addicted to the morphine administered to him to ease the pain.

The fat man glanced at a golden clock suspended beneath a glass bell among the framed photographs.

"You are prompt, von Kresse." He grunted.

"I had assistance in that."

"Your charming sister. She telephoned to tell me you appeared to have misunderstood my invitation. She suggested I reach you at the airfield."

"And so you did."

"And so, shall we go now to breakfast?"

"I am completely without appetite. I could not eat a thing."

"Martin. Never defy my summons again. Never. On your life."

The two men looked at each other in silence for a moment. They had known each other for nearly twenty years. Friendships born of war endure much, but bonds overstretched can snap. For good.

As young pilots in the German Air Service, they had looked somewhat alike. Now they scarcely seemed to belong to the same species. In his Wehrmacht field gray, von Kresse was the perfect image of the utterly correct Prussian officer. Goering wore his bizarre uniforms as human plumage. With summer now gone, he had switched from white to powder blue with white facings and labyrinthian snarls and swirls of gold braid. These distracted from his chest paving of medals, some of them of nonsensical invention but among them two Iron Crosses won in the war. At his throat he wore the Pour le Mérite, the "Blue Max," a decoration the kaiser had bestowed on only seventy-two German airmen. Goering had been an inadequate and often irresponsible *Jagdgeschwader,* or group, commander, the last of those to succeed to the post of the great Richthofen, but he had downed twenty-two enemy aircraft. Markgraf von Kresse had been credited with forty-four victories, tying with Rudolph Berthold for seventh-ranking German ace. Von Kresse wore only two medals: his own Pour le Mérite and the plain Iron Cross he had won as a private in the trenches.

"And so, Herr Markgraf," Goering said, not pleasantly. "How goes it with you?"

Von Kresse replied with some civility, disliking himself for it. "It goes well, Herr Reichscommissioner. And you?"

Goering said nothing, setting his elbows onto the polished desktop and resting his heavy chin on folded hands. His eyes stared directly into the count's, full of shrewd assessment. Von Kresse looked for some manifestation in them of the paracodeine morphine derivative Goering used but saw no trace. There was only intelligence and human poisons.

"You are in trouble, Herr Markgraf," Goering said slowly and quietly.

"With you, Herr Reichscommissioner? Am I under arrest? If so, what have I done? Or doesn't it matter?"

"It's being said that you are the only German officer in the Reich who has failed to swear his sacred oath to the Führer," Goering said. "This has been reported."

When President von Hindenberg's death had allowed Hitler to

become both president and chancellor of Germany, all military officers were given a direct order to swear their undying fealty to him personally, as if to the old emperor. Such oaths were a matter of sacred honor to German officers, especially Prussian ones, and the order had not been universally popular.

The count repeated the charge, emphasizing the words "only German officer."

"This certainly is not true," he said.

Goering placed his hands palms down on the desktop and slowly pushed himself to his feet. "That is precisely what I said to the Führer," he said, and began to laugh, the basso quickly rising to heaving, squeaky sputters. With his great military waddle, he went to one of the tall windows overlooking an interior court, then turned.

"You are such a problem for us sometimes, von Kresse. Such a racial problem."

The count gazed at the large portraits that dominated the wall behind Goering's desk. Both were of beautiful women. That on the left was of Karin von Kantzow, a Swedish baroness who had hastily divorced her husband to marry Goering nearly fifteen years before. She had died in 1931, and this last April Goering had married the woman in the painting on the right, the actress Emmy Sonnemann, for whom he was said to have a great passion. Yet he continued to be devoted to his dead first wife, naming his country estate, Karinhall, after her. It seemed ludicrous that this sinister hulk could have once been a handsome and romantic youth, ludicrous that he could still be so romantic. Yet he was charming. There was no serious doubt of that. He remained now close friends of the Hohenzollerns and Prince Philip of Hesse, cousin to the British throne. Without the Goering charm, Hitler would never have gained power.

Karinhall had become host to the principal paintings in Goering's ever-expanding collection—most of them expropriated from rich Jews and other exiles fleeing the Fatherland, or looted from museums. Charm was not gentility, not honor, not pride.

"You are not interested in racial problems, Herr Markgraf?"

"Race has never concerned me. Not mine. Not anyone's."

"A dangerous attitude, von Kresse. Your race should concern you. You are a most un-Prussian Prussian."

"What are you talking about? My family held title to our estate in the rule of the Order of the Teutonic Knights. My ancestors fought Alexander Nevsky."

"Your father was half Polish."

"Poland and East Prussia are much the same country." Von Kresse moved his left leg to ease the pain. This line of conversation always irritated him. He endured it constantly from Dagne.

"But," said Goering, "as Baron von Richthofen would certainly agree, the Teutonic and the Slavic are hardly the same race. Your wife is Polish, isn't that so?"

"You know that very well, Herr Reichscommissioner. You attended our wedding."

"You haven't seen her since the war. Do you have any idea where she is?"

"Lalka is somewhere in Poland. I believe in Krakow. She occasionally writes to a mutual friend."

"In French, I believe. Would you like any help in reaching your wife? These days, anything is possible for us. We could have her in Ortelsburg for you tomorrow."

The Reichscommissioner's moods were as changeable as his uniforms. He seemed now to be offering this outrage as a genuine act of friendship.

"*Nein, danke.*"

"Your mother was not Prussian."

"She was American, as you know."

"Bernard Baruch, von Kresse," said Goering, distastefully, "is an American. What sort of American was your mother?"

"Her heritage was predominantly English. Some German, but mostly English. It doesn't matter though. She was a Virginian. Her people have been Virginians for three hundred years. It's the same as nationhood for them."

"Was she, are you, related to this Nancy Langhorne, this lady member of the English Parliament? She is from Virginia."

"My mother was not related to Lady Astor in any way. You must know this."

"A pity, von Kresse. You could use an anti-Semite in your family. It would be helpful."

"My sister Dagne should more than suffice. If not my stepmother."

"Your half sister, von Kresse. And much more Prussian."

"She is as much Polish as I am. And her mother came from Silesia, not Prussia."

"Yes, but Dagne is not English, not American. Unlike you."

"Did you have me ordered here only to discuss my genealogy? Is that all you people do these days?"

The Reichscommissioner's expression relaxed into the dumpling smile reserved for favorites and intimates. He gestured to the two high-backed chairs that sat facing each other by the high windows and lowered himself into one.

"If you will not take breakfast with me, Martin, would you like some schnapps?" he asked, all cheerful host.

"It's early."

"That makes it much nicer."

Von Kresse hesitated, then nodded assent. His nerves needed bolstering in this atmosphere, in this treacherous, evil companionship.

Goering touched a metal plate in the flooring with the heel of his boot. A military servant appeared almost instantly, and returned with a bottle and glasses nearly as quickly, as if they'd been waiting just outside. When he was gone, Goering leaned close.

"Martin," he said, his voice now wet with affection. He reached with effort and patted von Kresse's crippled knee. "I have asked you here for a very serious reason, for a matter of state."

"A matter of state that concerns me?"

"The war."

"What war? The last war?"

"The new war. The war that must not come. The war that you know and I know would destroy Germany, destroy Prussia, just as the last one almost did." Goering sat up very straight now, all seriousness. "They are saying that war ultimately is inevitable. Himmler. Goebbels. The Duke of Saxe-Coburg and Gotha. All of them. But they are wrong. The army does not want this war. *I* do not want it. And now a chance has come to hand, a small chance, a miraculous chance, but a real one, to prevent it. You would jump at such a chance, would you not, Martin? Because if we don't take advantage of this, war may indeed be inevitable."

Von Kresse said nothing, waiting. Art collections did not survive well in wartime. When Goering drank from his schnapps, he did the same.

"You are now very much the pacifist," said Goering, setting down his empty glass. "You wear this handsome uniform in Berlin, but home in East Prussia? Never. You are all tweeds and country clothes. Squire von Kresse. You are never with your regiment. Your adjutant virtually commands it. You have given up shooting. You read, play chess, dally with the ladies. You write letters abroad, very dangerous letters, to Poland, to England. To America."

"You have read them?"

"Of course. Welcome, please, to the Third Reich. My own letters

are read. Because you preach such a moderate, peace-loving philosophy to your correspondents, yours have been tolerated. Such senti-
ments are quite useful at this juncture. It is how we would like the
Reich to be perceived."

Germany was to be host to the world's nations the next year for
the Olympics. A docile England had just agreed to allow a German
U-boat tonnage equal to its own.

"You said 'matter of state,' Herr Reichscommissioner."

"A matter of the greatest concern. And it has always been my
principal concern. You know, Martin, my interests in helping to
bring the party to power were never the same as the others'. I of
course agree with everything the Führer believes and has said. But
the excesses that some—Himmler, Goebbels. Well, they go too far,
Martin. I am different from them. I joined the party because the
honor of Germany had been so abused. And our honor. The officers.
You remember how we were treated. *Mein Gott,* Martin, you had a
brick thrown at you in Leipzig! You, with forty-four victories! We
were spat upon, treated like swine. We heroes of the war!"

Goering had been born in Bavaria, the son of a minor diplomat. He
had grown up in a castle owned by a wealthy Jew. He had taken
much more joy in being a German officer—an *oberleutnant* by the
end of the war—than von Kresse had.

His talk was rot. As interior minister for Prussia, he had introduced
the secret police to Germany as a method of political control. He had
also introduced the concentration camp, a British invention of the
Boer War that Goering and Himmler put to much more ruthless and
sweeping use. Goering would always do whatever he felt was necessary to achieve a goal, no matter what it might mean.

"The matter of state, Hermann."

Goering seemed pleased rather than offended by the familiar address. "Germany will be restored, Martin. We shall regain what is
ours. All that the kaiser aspired to shall come to pass. But who is the
key to this?"

"The Führer?"

"Of course, but what I mean to say is, what country stands most
in our way?"

"The Soviet Union."

"They, as always, pose the greatest military threat, and are necessarily a preoccupation of yours, Martin. We cannot prevail if the
Soviets make common cause with the West. But I cannot imagine this
happening. We could march into Prague, Vienna, even Warsaw, and

I think Stalin would not raise a hand. They are so insular, the Russians, so xenophobic. The essence of Bolshevism is paranoia. No. The key to our future is England. Without the English, the French will do nothing. They have trouble now governing themselves. England is in many ways more our friend. If the English remain amiable, then we shall attain what we require peacefully. There shall be no war."

"As always, you are too optimistic."

"Mind your manners, Herr Markgraf, and listen. The old English king is unwell. Ribbentrop thinks he may not live a year. The heir to the throne, Edward, is friendly toward us. *Sehr freundlich.* He is very popular with the English people. When he is king, it should go very easy for us. There should be no war. There couldn't be war, since he would not oppose us. With his immense personal popularity, he could prevent the British Parliament from opposing us. And we have many friends there as it is."

"You seem quite certain about all this."

"The British royal family is German, as you know. It was an embarrassment to them in the Great War, but it is so. They are the most German monarchy in the world. Our Hanovers replaced the Stuarts. Marriages brought in more Germans—Brandenburg, Mecklenburg, Saxe-Meiningen, Saxe-Coburg and Gotha, Teck, Hesse. They change names. Saxe-Coburg becomes Windsor. Battenberg becomes Mountbatten. But they are German. The King of England is more German than you, Martin. You know all this."

"Queen Mary, the former Princess of Teck . . ."

"For all her Germanness—and she still can't speak proper English—the prince's mother is not so friendly to us. She is a major part of my concern. She believes in the English traditions. She was much against us in the Great War."

"Hermann, you are being most indirect. It is unlike you."

Goering shifted his weight, an elaborate effort.

"Queen Mary dislikes her son the heir, as does the king," he said. "And the heir dislikes them. When he becomes king, she will be irrelevant to the scheme of things. A cypher. As long as he stays king. With his brother, Albert George, the next in line, it is different. Mary adores him. He is in thrall to her. An obedient little boy. He has stayed clear of our friends, Prince Edward's friends. He is against us."

"He is not the heir."

"He is *der Nächste.* You know of Mrs. Simpson, Prince Edward's American mistress?"

Von Kresse nodded. "My sister is fond of gossip."

"We are all fond of such gossip. From Ribbentrop we get better than gossip. He has a well-placed woman friend, Lady Cunard. She is close to both the prince and this Mrs. Simpson. She provides a bed for them. Whatever else they want. Ribbentrop is certain he means to marry her."

"He should marry whom he wishes."

"Even a Polish music teacher, yes, Martin? Your own wife would be more suitable for Edward than this Mrs. Simpson. She's American, a commoner, a married woman, a divorcée, a social climber, a fortune hunter, a woman with a past in China, and so on and so forth. She may be a Jew. Her family name is said to have originally been War-feld, and her uncle's name was Solomon. Ribbentrop thinks Edward's marrying her will be marvelous, because of the influence he thinks he can wield over them through this Lady Cunard. Ribbentrop is an idiot. There is no political support in Britain for such a marriage. If Edward wishes to marry her, he cannot become king. If he waits until his father dies, he cannot remain king, if he marries this woman."

Again the Reichscommissioner leaned forward, and again he touched von Kresse's knee.

"If there is to be peace in Europe, Martin, Edward must be king, not his brother. If Edward is to become king, Mrs. Simpson must go. There must be no marriage, no romance. Someone must put an end to it."

"His family is trying to do just that."

"With arrogance, not cleverness. He is a fool, this Edward, but a stubborn one. Those who oppose Mrs. Simpson, he pushes away. Those who befriend her, he brings close."

The markgraf looked steadily at Goering. "I must again ask the obvious question."

" 'What has this to do with you?' I have a simple answer. Everything. I want you to end this romance."

Von Kresse laughed. "This is insane. You are crazy. All of you are crazy."

Goering thrust himself out of his chair with such speed and anger that it tottered. He raised his hand as if to strike von Kresse, as the count had seen him strike enlisted men in the war. "Silence! Silence, silence, silence!"

The count's face went blank, except for his gray eyes. They were ice. Goering's were burning with anger.

"Damn you, Martin! You will not talk to me this way! No! No, no, no!"

Von Kresse looked away. He sat in silence, waiting. His mind filled with images of his waiting home and the flat, forested East Prussian countryside, its long straight roads, leading east away from Germany through the pine woods.

Goering was breathing heavily. His skin was discolored, a motley pattern of crimson splotch and a bloodless, blanched paleness. Slowly the colors began to blend together again.

"I cannot permit you to speak to me this way," he said. "Do you understand that? Do you know why? Do you know what I must do if you persist?"

Von Kresse looked down at the sheen of his high black boots. His mother had talked repeatedly of moving back to America just before she died and had urged him to go there in her place. He had thought the notion silly. Now, once again, her wisdom was being dashed in his face. He could not escape this huge German country that his Prussia had become. He could no longer simply go home to his books and forests, his dogs and horses and occasional women, his private self, and ignore all politics. There was no longer refuge even in his nightmares and pain. Every day of his life now was like a day in Berlin, his nation a terrifying confusion of madness and genius, order and chaos. It had been fired with an unprecedented patriotic fervor marshaled to the most banal and despicable purposes. Its heritage was being sanctified yet drained of all its values. Germany was hurrying along to a destiny known only to the most cruel and capricious of the old pagan gods, and all Germans were being dragged along with it, including most especially Markgraf Martin von Bourke und Kresse.

"Very well, Hermann, but why me?"

"For all the best reasons, Martin. You are an aristocrat. Women are attracted to you. You speak English flawlessly. Your mother was an American, like this Warfeld woman. She is from Maryland, yes? A state next to your mother's Virginia. You are clever and resourceful. You are a patriot who will do anything to spare Germany another cataclysm. You are an old comrade. You realize how important this is to me. And I trust you, Martin. You and your sister, Dagne, I trust you both."

Cautiously Martin studied the jovial, malevolent face of the man who had once claimed his friendship. It had been in 1918 for the most part, in that brief time between the death of von Richthofen and von Kresse's own bout of madness. It had been a friendship of the extrinsic qualities of war in France, of the intrinsic qualities of war in the air, of shared survival, of tents pitched on muddy ground. It was a friendship of rainy days and long, soul-chilling nights, drinking schnapps on Goering's cot or cognac at von Kresse's writing table, talking of Goering's endless, nameless girls and of von Kresse's wife, Lalka, who had by then ceased writing to him. This was a friendship of a mutual waiting for death, which is perhaps what all friendships are, though seldom are they so intensely measured.

Goering had been a reckless and erratic flyer, compulsive and relentless in his efforts to kill. His comrades had attributed this to the intensity of his fear of dying. But now here he sat, a monument to ease, comfort, and self-satisfaction, having returned to killing as if to an old vice. Hundreds must have died at his personal direction, thousands under his bureaucratic authority, if the stories were true. And here with him now sat Martin von Kresse, drinking schnapps, as if it were one of those cold, rainy afternoons between the killings in the sky, as if it were all just as honorable.

Honorable. On a day of no rain, a day of heat and dust in 1918, von Kresse had led his *Staffel* with dozens of others in a desperate aerial assault against the British forces that had broken through the German lines along the Somme and were streaming east from Cambrai. They had caught a regiment off their trucks taking a rest break in Marecourt and torn them up with machine-gun fire and bombs. Flying low in a steady turn, the count had led his men in a murderous circuit of the village, firing as they rounded every tree and rooftop. Skidding about the spire of the church, he caught sight of the village square and a line of small figures running across it. A flare of sunlight had filled his eyes just as he pulled on the firing bar, the instant's perception of his target registering on his mind seconds and bullets too late. Among the soldiers, the dark, tiny, silhouetted figures were those of a woman and children. Many children.

He had then lunged his Fokker D VII into a wrenching turn around the church spire again, nearly colliding with some of his flight in the process, but on his second pass the reality had not changed, only worsened. They were on the ground, strewn and writhing, limbs flailing, flapping about like fish on a beach. He had flung the aircraft into another circuit of the church and, screaming rage at all deities to the limits of his voice and mind and strength and soul, had emptied his guns at his victims in the desperation of his remorse, the explosive clatter drowning his sense of their own screams, ending their agony, ending their war. But not his war. Or pain. Or guilt. And now, not his fear.

"We can have her in Ortelsburg for you tomorrow," Goering had said of his wife, Lalka. They could also have her in Berlin, in one of the now so numerous police stations.

"What is it you want me to do, Hermann?" Martins said softly, wearily, and very sadly.

Goering smiled. "The prince and his Mrs. Simpson are in Paris with a large traveling party. They will probably be leaving soon because of all the troubles. There have been riots. There is a possibility they may sail for America. In any case, you are to join them at once. You must get near them and deal with this wretched romance." He paused to pour more schnapps.

"No one else is to know of this, Martin. It would be very dangerous for us both. I will provide you with what help I can, but it will be your show. If things go bad, you'll have to deal with them. I can take no responsibility."

Von Kresse stared at him.

Goering leaned even closer, the sweetness of the alcohol on his breath. "For the sake of the Fatherland, Martin, for the sake of all you value above the Fatherland, you must succeed in this. Edward of England must not marry this Jewess."

When von Kresse had left, limping off into the labyrinth of echoing corridors and looking even more pained and troubled than usual, Goering summoned his secretary. The man, a longtime associate who had agreeably poisoned a colleague to demonstrate his loyalty and subservience to the Reichscommissioner, came hastily and stood at quivering attention.

"I want Himmler on the telephone," Goering growled. "I don't care where he is. Find him. I need to arrange a meeting."

# CHAPTER
## *THREE*

Nora lay still and quiet in her bed after waking, luxuriating in its silken comfort as she listened to the morning sounds of Paris outside her window in the Place Vendôme below. They were wonderfully normal sounds—the doorman's whistle, automobile traffic moving without urgency, two men shouting greetings to one another. It was all as innocent and cheerful as the clamor of the night before had been full of menace. It might at last be a happy day, as she had hoped all the days of her stay in France would be.

Closing her eyes, she remembered her small bedroom in the rear of the second-story apartment her family had occupied above her father's saloon in Toledo. Its view had been of a cramped little yard, an alley with grass growing up from cracks in the concrete, and, beyond, the scruffy rear of a similar building. A block and a half farther had been railroad tracks. In the winter, when the trees were bare of leaves, a narrow space between buildings allowed her a glimpse of passing trains. She would often lie abed there and, when a train passed, close her eyes and imagine herself on it, speeding away to some far off magical place—Chicago, New York, London, Paris.

But then the train and time would pass, and she would at length open her eyes, and there would be reality. She could remember it all now perfectly, could hear the noisesome drunks and the thunk and clink of her father setting out garbage cans filled with empty bottles. They had later moved to worse places, after Prohibition had put her father out of business. But she kept no image of the bedrooms that followed, only that one in Toledo with the view of passing trains.

She opened her eyes now, noting in careful examination of every detail how much this was not Toledo. She would remember this

Parisian chamber just as clearly as her childhood room—its spaciousness and elegance and extravagance. She had slept in bedrooms as pretty and pleasing in the days of her first real successes in California. The master bedroom of her house at Topanga Beach in California was twice this size. But this was Paris. There was no mistake. Nora Gwynne was at last where she belonged. And whatever might happen next, this morning in Paris would always be hers. She had been here. She had reached this far, and she could think of no farther to go.

The room was bright with the early sunlight. There were two huge windows, with doors that opened to a narrow balcony and the Place Vendôme below. She threw back her covers and ran to them, bare feet sinking in the soft carpet, her nightdress billowing behind her as she pulled open the doors and stepped forward to the railing.

It was indeed a wondrous, glorious, and special day. The sun was brilliant above the rooftops, the sky pure with blue bereft of cloud or haze, the breeze clean and cool against her skin. The street was full of people who seemed to have only agreeable concerns. She would be damned happy. She willed it so. On the following evening she would be sailing back to America, so she would make this day long and full of things to savor. She would go shopping in St. Germaine de Près and take a boat excursion along the Seine. She had been invited to a party that night at the home of a French newspaper publisher—Charles de Mornay. Ira Stein had not wanted to go, but now she would. She would dress fantastically and she would flirt. Possibly, she might even have a little to drink. She would have lots and lots of fun and it would all be very simply, wonderfully, and terrifically grand. Taking a deep breath of the Paris morning, Nora glanced along the horizon of rooftops, then whirled back inside, dancing over to the three-paneled full-length mirror. After slipping off the nightdress, she posed for herself, naked, tossing back her head. The haggard, fearful woman of last night had vanished, a splendid auburn-haired beauty taking her place. It would be a lovely day.

Spencer was late for his breakfast meeting with Laingen but, woozy, leaned a moment against a lamp post outside the entrance of the Crillon, gazing painfully over the remnants of the previous night's rioting while he waited for his equilibrium to return. He had to keep his eyes on something. If he closed them, he feared he'd drop dizzy to the pavement. He could not remember when he'd been so pulverized by drink. He could not imagine how the rummies he knew—

most notably the great writers Hemingway and Ford Madox Ford—
had survived as long as they had, let alone functioned so brilliantly.
Back in the bar at the Ritz, he'd told himself his own wretched
indulgence was because of the woman who had died beside him on
the balcony, that he needed to drown his memory of her. But the
truth was he had filled himself with brandy in a demented attempt
to keep that memory as intense as possible. In the distorted percep-
tions of his stupor, he'd been able to keep her alive, keep the curve
of her cheek, the sheen of her hair, the scent of her perfume, vivid
in his senses—until he'd passed out, killing her for good.

He'd awakened on a banquette in a corner alcove of the lobby of
the Ritz, tolerated there because of the rioting. He'd still not changed
clothes or washed. He rubbed his rough and scratchy chin. The vast,
deserted square seemed surprisingly clean considering the carnage
and mayhem that had rampaged over it for so many hours. There was
some litter—torn banners and placards, broken paving stones, a fallen
saber, a woman's shoe—but it was visible only here and there, like the
leavings in a public park following a Sunday's picnics. There were
no human bodies, only two mounds that were the carcasses of horses,
one near and one far, flies buzzing loudly about the one closest. There
was no sign of the cars that had been set afire. Spencer wondered at
the sensibilities of a society that would hasten to remove useless
burned metal while neglecting such heaps of dead flesh.

Squinting, he looked down at the sleeve of his jacket, the wool still
matted and stained with the dead beauty's blood. He recalled the
touch of the warm skin of her back as she had fallen, dead or dying,
through his grasp. He rubbed the palm of his hand gently, then
dropped his hands to his sides. It was time to go inside and join Bill
Laingen, to get on with his day, with the painful realities and terrifying mysteries of his life.

But first, an important gesture. He tottered out onto the paving
stones, clumsily snatching up first the discarded saber and then the
woman's shoe. The blade of the sword was remarkably bright and
shiny, without a hint of blood or violent use. The woman's shoe was
red only with dye, but scuffed and dirty. It had nothing to do with
the woman who'd been killed on the balcony, and yet it had everything to do with her. Clutching these souvenirs tightly, he entered
the Crillon's lobby, looking something of a lunatic. A man started to
leave the front desk as if to intercept him, but then thought better of
it, perhaps recognizing Spencer from the night before. A moment
later Bill Laingen was at his side.

"Jesus, Jimmy, you look a sight. Where'd you sleep, under a bridge?"

"Should have. Might have fallen in."

"What?"

"Couldn't find out her name, Bill. Nobody knew her name. There isn't any story unless I can get her name."

"Are you sober?"

"Not sure. Hungry, though. And I hurt."

"Let's get out of here. We'll go to Floride's. They'll take care of you."

Spencer would not surrender either the sword or the shoe to the dustbin, as Laingen asked, nor would he agree to a taxi, because of the noise. They walked away from the square past the Madeleine to the narrow side street off Boulevard Malesherbes that harbored Floride's café. It was not open, but Floride's husband, Pierre Hillion, saw who was at the green-tinted glass of the door and let them in. A handsome, balding man with a scar and a cigarette perpetually hanging from mouth, he'd been doing accounts at the bar. He abandoned that duty, bringing Laingen coffee and Spencer cognac, then picked up the saber.

"Fascist bastards!" he said, looking at the bloodied sleeve of Spencer's jacket. He poured Spencer another cognac, as the first was already gone.

"No, Pierre," said Laingen. "They didn't hurt us. *La tache de sang, c'est le sang d'une femme morte.*"

He told the story of the woman on the balcony. When he was done, Pierre poured himself a cognac.

"That is the saddest thing I have ever heard," he said. "To hold such a woman in the last moment of her life. And you'd not even been to bed with her. *Mon Dieu.*"

Spencer stared morosely at the cognac in his glass. The other two observed him silently for a long moment, then Pierre, leaving the bottle, returned somewhat reluctantly to the bar and his accounts. He appreciated Spencer and Laignen for their friendship but mostly for their conversations. He considered them almost Frenchmen.

"The official count is fifteen killed," Laingen said. "I don't know if that includes her."

Spencer said nothing. His reddened eyes were wet.

"I'm going over to the ministry," Laingen added. "I've got a source who will tell me everything they know. Maybe he can tell me who she was."

"Bill," said Spencer. "I'm scared."

Laignen had been with Spencer in North Africa and knew of his war record and what the man had survived in China. Laignen was surprised by this remark. "It was pretty bad last night," he said finally.

"That's not it, Bill. I'm afraid they're going to drag me back to Chicago. Paris is all I have and I think they're going to take it away from me, the way the woman last night was. The reach of the hand of God."

"What are you talking about? Why would they pull you away now? This is the biggest story we've had since we came to France. Hell, a few more days of this and La fucking République could go under. There's trouble in Spain now. All Europe's on the edge of the cliff."

"They're taking me off the story. They don't like it anyway. Carlson's in town from London. He's put me onto something else. It's . . ." Spencer lifted his glass, peering at it as a means of avoiding Laingen's eyes. "It's a good story, Bill. It's damn good, big. So big that if I told you about it with the promise you wouldn't go after it I'd hate myself. And if you did go after it, I'd hate you."

"Is it here, in Paris?"

Spencer drank, sipping this time. "No, not really. Starts here, but I have to go back to the States. That's what has me scared. It's a hard story to get, Bill. Easy to blow. If I do, they'll haul me back—throw me onto the police beat again, or send me down to the land of the hayheads to cover the state legislature. I know they will. I almost think they're arranging it that way, hoping I'll make a shambles of this thing so they can throw me away. The paper's been sold, you know. The new owners were enemies of my father. Carlson can't stand me. It's a matter of class, don't you know. 'The very rich are different from you and me.' He believes that. And he hates me for it, even though my father went bankrupt ten years ago."

Laingen searched for some gesture to show that such matters of class meant nothing to him, though Spencer had been a rich boy and his own father had owned nothing grander than a small hardware store in Minnesota. Finally he reassured himself that Spencer already knew that, that he himself already knew that. He poured a little cognac into his coffee. "Are you sure you're not just a little depressed and paranoid from your hangover, from last night?"

"I'm depressed and paranoid from my life, Bill. And I think they've really got me this time."

"If they try it, just come back. Get another job."

"Have you forgotten the Depression? The new people they're sending over are making half what we're paid, and there are thousands more after their jobs. I'm so flat, stony broke I'm not sure I could even raise passage money. As it is, I owe everybody in Paris except the prime minister and Whitney's husband. I owe Whitney three thousand francs. She's part of it, too, Bill. She gave me an ultimatum. Give up my job or give up her. She said she can't stand it any more that I'm always going off to riots or wars in Algeria or Nazi rallies in Germany. She wants to keep me, Bill, on the side, in some little nearby flat, paid for out of her boundless pocket money. I asked her to marry me, but she'd have none of that. Wants her husband *and* me. And now I'm going to be hauled back to Chicago. I'm going to lose her and my job here."

"Even if it turns out as you say, Jim, there are certainly worse places than Chicago."

"Paris in the spring; Chicago in the Depression. I can take all my old girlfriends from the Saddle and Cycle Club down to Halsted Street for a glimpse of Frank Nitti eating lasagne." He shook his head. "Damn. Listen to me. On top of everything else, I'm turning into a twit."

He pressed his face into his hands. Someone else came to the door and rattled its handle, but Pierre Hillion shook his head in a vigorous no.

Laignen studied his friend. "I'll tell you what I think it is, *mon vieux,*" he said. "I think you just can't handle what's happened to you and Whitney."

Spencer raised his head and sat back. Laignen had never seen him look so awful.

"What I can't handle, William, is Whitney, period. Too young, too rich, too married, too smart, too chic, too American, too classic and great, too . . . there are better French words for her." He glanced down at the glinting blade of the saber. "Christ," he said, picking up the weapon. "None of this matters to her, do you know? What happened in the Place de la Concorde yesterday. She thinks it's just noise in the night. Something that will pass."

"She cares, Jim. And she cares about you. She'll be waiting for you when you get back from the States. So will Jean and I."

Spencer rose and, with a clumsy flourish, drained his glass. He set it on the table.

"*L'audace,*" he said. "*Toujours l'audace.*" It had been the motto of a failed French general and the epitaph of the generation that had died in the mass murder that was the Great War.

"The trouble with you, Jimmy, is that you're so idealistic about your cynicism."

"What?"

Laignen regretted the remark, but there was no useful way of withdrawing it. "When you get back, we'll go down to Spain," he said. "There may be fighting by then."

"There'll be fighting, all right, but I'll be on Halsted Street. I've got that goddamn Whitney in my blood, Bill." He rested the sword blade on Laingen's shoulder, then lifted it in a sudden arc. "I love you, Bill. I love Floride. I love Pierre. Christ, today I am filled with love for those two dead horses." He took a step. "Okay. I go. *L'homme courageux.*"

Pierre Hillion watched sympathetically as Spencer wobbled out the door, then he lighted another cigarette. "Fascist bastards," he said. "*Nous les détruions.*"

Laignen sipped more coffee, then put money on the table, paying Spencer's bill. That was his gesture on the matter of class.

The horses thudded in a heavy trot along the muddy path paralleling the Allée de Longchamp in the Bois de Boulogne. Lord Brownlow, astride an overweight gray, took the lead, Fruity Metcalfe following close behind on an unhappy roan mare. Inspector Runcie, riding uncomfortably, brought up the rear on a smaller horse. Improbably dressed in gray flannels, an athletic pullover, and dark glasses, Edward P. trotted alongside Fruity's mount, clinging to the stirrup and breathing heavily.

He had developed this silly habit on a visit to Kenya in 1928, the same trip in which he and Lady Erskine had won lasting scorn for throwing all the gramophone records in the Muthaiga Club out the ballroom window because he thought them all wrong for dancing. He had gone down to the Nairobi racecourse at half-past six the next morning and asked Sir Derek Erskine if he might hang on to his stirrup and run while Sir Derek exercised his horse. He did this most of the mornings he was in Africa.

Nowadays he performed this ritual rarely—perhaps twice a year— and anything faster than a very slow trot was out of the question. Metcalfe was hard put to keep his mare to that. She'd keep slipping back into a jerking walk, compelling him to goad her into a trot again and then yank savagely back on the reins to slow her speed to that of the huffing, wheezing man beside him. Once a cavalry officer in

India, he hated to treat horses this way and despised himself for this morning.

Brownlow swerved his gray around a muddy spot in the trail. Metcalfe's mare shifted around it also, causing Edward P. to slip and stumble. Letting go of the stirrup, he skittered, sliding, across the muck, finding an anchorage finally at the side of a large tree. He stood with hands on hips, catching his breath.

"Damn you, Fruity. You can ride better than that, surely."

"Sorry, sir," Metcalfe said, unhappily. "Got taken quite by surprise."

"Yes, well, mind you don't next time. Give me a cigarette."

Metcalfe dismounted to hand the man one and light it for him, as the others came up. Runcie could not hold his horse still.

"Have I asked you how you're coming along with a boat?" Edward said.

"Yes, at breakfast, sir," said Brownlow. "But we were interrupted, by Mrs. Simpson."

"Oh, yes. Well, how are you coming along with getting a bloody boat?"

"We think we have one, sir," said Brownlow. "A Dutchman, sailing from Le Havre tomorrow. It's a maiden voyage and there won't be many passengers aboard. They've had to postpone sailing twice now because of some engineering problems, and most of the original passengers have booked passage elsewhere."

"Well played, Fruity. Well played."

"But we still think you should return home, sir," said Brownlow. "You're bound to be recognized."

"You're to see to it that I'm not."

"Yes, David, but—"

"On a first crossing like this," Brownlow said, "they'll hold the speed down. We'll be out of circulation for a very long time."

"That's precisely what I want," Edward snapped. "Now let's find a taxi and get back to the hotel. The path's much too muddy for running."

"But the horses," said Fruity. "We're more than a mile from the stables."

"Be a good chap, will you, Fruity? We'll wait for you at the Crillon. Or perhaps not. Wallis will want to do some shopping. I'm sure she hasn't clothes for a crossing."

Lord Mountbatten had risen early in hopes of finding Edwina at last returned, but once again he was disappointed. He went about bathing and shaving, poking his head out into the suite to listen for her in between times, but with the same result. Irritated now, he dressed quickly, choosing gray trousers and a natty navy-blue jacket, then sat down to wait for however long it took. To pass the time, he began rereading a genealogical work that dealt with his Spanish relations descended from his mother's cousin Princess Victoria Eugenia of Battenburg by means of her marriage to King Alfonso III. Despite his fascination with this subject, he fell asleep again.

When he awakened, it was to the sound of running water and, a moment later, a knock at the door to their suite. Edwina reached it before he did. She was wearing only a slip but she paid this indiscretion no mind, as usual, as she stepped back to admit a bellman carrying a tray. On it were a bottle of champagne, a bottle of vodka, a silver bowl of ice, and a single glass. Signing the bill, she smiled wickedly at the embarrassed attendant, then turned and started back toward the bath without waiting for him to leave.

"Be a dear and open the champagne, Dickie," she said through the open door as she removed the last of her clothing. "I'm in desperate need of something to drown a really crashing headache."

Mountbatten nodded curtly to the bellman, who hesitated a moment, then, with a quick glance in Edwina's direction, fled.

"Do you realize the time?" Mountbatten said, raising his voice over the sound of running water in the bath. "We will be late. Edwina, I am never late!"

"Please, Dickie. My headache."

"Edwina, you simply cannot go on conducting yourself like a girl from the Bal-Musette. We're traveling with the Prince of Wales! My cousin."

"Rot, Dickie."

"This is not La Boule Blanche! This is the Hotel Crillon! And we are due for lunch!"

"Oh, shut up, Dickie, and bring me my drink."

He stared at the doorway in helpless rage, as he had stared at the seaman who had brought him the signal from the admiral ordering his destroyer not to sail with the fleet for Abyssinia. Then, as if their quarrel had not occurred, he began whistling as he finally set about preparing his wife a cocktail half champagne and half vodka.

"Did you hear the news?" he said, bringing her drink into the bath.

"I've heard no news at all," she said, slipping into the tub. She pushed herself down until the steamy water reached to the top of her shoulders, then reached and took the glass. "I've been with surrealists all night. Had a very intense conversation with one of their leading lights, Louis Aragon. Fascinating man. Dreadfully common, of course. And very boring on communism. But otherwise rather extraordinary. A friend of Nancy Cunard's, don't you know."

"Not friend. Lover."

"Yes, well." She sipped from her cold drink, then closed her eyes. Mountbatten looked about for a place to sit, but her clothes were everywhere.

"The prince wants to go to America," Mountbatten said, leaning back against the wash basin. He suddenly realized his perfectly pressed jacket was getting wet from water on the basin's rim, but it was too late. He'd already struck his pose.

"Well, I think he should go to America, Dickie. That poor man deserves whatever he wants. And gets."

"Edwina. He wants to go now. With all of us."

"But we've already *been* to America with him. I don't like repeating things. And at all events I've spent a lot of time in America already this year and have only just returned from Australia. A spot of homelife in Malta now will do me just fine. They've asked me to do news broadcasts on the radio there, did you know? As long as this Abyssinian crisis is on. I really shouldn't have come with you to Paris in the first place. I'm needed."

The remark was a nasty little touch, implying he was not. The sea dog left at the dock.

She took another sip of her drink, then set the glass carelessly on the edge of the tub and began to scrub vigorously. A bath for Edwina did instead of sleep. His eye traveled along the soapy sheen of her leg. Edwina at thirty-four still had smashing legs and a very trim figure. She was paying the price for her manic indulgences in her face. Networks of little lines had formed about her eyes and mouth. They would shortly deepen, especially if she kept up these rough-country treks into the farthest corners of the world in between her bouts of debauchery.

"I'm sorry, Edwina, but he hasn't exactly given us much choice."

"It's impossible; Noel is coming over tomorrow from London," she said, revealing her real reason for not wanting to make the sailing, for not wanting to do much of anything with Mountbatten this season. Noel Coward had written a play about her, *Hands Across the Sea*, starring himself and Gertrude Lawrence. With this he had won her patronage and devotion forever. Edwina loved the theater. As she did not read, it was her only literature.

"He was very specific about not wanting Noel along. He's tired of being associated with fairies."

"Quite. He can go off to America without any fairies in tow and I will go back to Malta with Noel. Norma Shearer's coming as well."

"Edwina, please. He's the king."

She sat up, sloshing some water over the side of the tub and nearly toppling her glass. "Not bloody yet, he isn't. Come now, Dickie. You're the captain of a destroyer. There's a crisis. How can he ask you to desert your post?"

"Because my post has already deserted me." He put hand to chin, pouting. His ship, the H.M.S. *Wishart,* was part of the squadron that had been left behind at Malta when the rest of the fleet had steamed on to Port Said. He had taken it as an affront, sure that the admiral had deliberately sought to keep him out of the action, such as there might be. Under Mountbatten's command, the old *Wishart* had won the fleet gunnery trophy, scoring twice as many hits as any other ship, though at an extremely slow rate of fire. His destroyer had been named Cock of the Fleet, and teams from his crew had won the water polo and cricket competitions as well. Yet they had dared leave him behind. He ought to go off to America just to show his pique. And his royal association.

"It's not a real war," he said, "except to the Abyssinians. And Britain's not officially involved in it. The fleet doesn't seem to need my squadron no matter what."

"Of course it does, Dickie. You're there to guard Malta. That's the only reason you've been left behind. They couldn't very well leave Malta to the Italians."

"The Foreign Office told the prince there's a fifty-fifty chance the Italians will bomb Malta. I was going to send you away."

"Instead you sent us both." She splashed, reaching for her drink. After a large sip, she slid deep into the water again.

"Damn it, Edwina! I begged the admiral to let me take the *Wishart* to Port Said. But he wouldn't agree. I also have a duty to the king, er, prince. And if he needs me on this voyage, he shall have me. I'll miss some squadron maneuvers. But the Crown must come first."

"Too right, Dickie. What shit."

He wondered if it was time to retreat. He was tired of retreating.

"You could use a chance to return to the royal family's good grace," he said. It was a broadside, loaded with heavy shot, and intended as such. Edwina had been virtually barred from Court since 1932, when her affair with the black actor Paul Robeson had leaked in innuendo form into the press. She still seethed at the very mention of George V and had taken to allowing only the *Daily Worker* into her house, to Mountbatten's acute embarrassment, though he shared much of her socialist philosophy—or said he did.

"How low and common of you, Dickie. The prince himself is in bad graces with Buckingham Palace. Why do you think I tolerate his friendship, and all this endless fucking silliness? Because I know how painful it is for them. That's why I do everything I can to encourage this dreary affair of his with Mrs. Simpson. Because I know it's making them positively writhe, Dickie. Positively writhe."

Her skin was flushed a very ruddy pink from the hot bath water and her anger. Her brown eyes glistened as much as her wet, dark hair. Suddenly she stood up, water pouring from her beautiful body in dozens of small cataracts.

"I've changed my mind. I will go with you on this pointless voyage. The newspapers are sure to catch hold of it, and I can't think of a more splendid scandal!"

Chips Channon and the Coopers waited an extra half hour for the Mountbattens, then went off to the restaurant without them, beginning luncheon with a round of kiss-me-quicks, a strong but beguiling cocktail made with Pernod, Cointreau, bitters, and soda, poured over ice. All three were badly hung over. Chips looked pained, Duff was irritable, and Diana seemed queasy. She had assisted their search for happiness the night before with a discreet dose of cocaine.

"I wonder if Dickie and Edwina had a row," Channon said, lighting a cigarette. His dark eyes looked weak and bleary from his discomfort.

"Of course they had a row, Chipsie," said Diana. "They always have a row."

"At the least they could have sent someone to tell us."

"They never send someone to tell us," said Duff. He, too, lighted a cigarette, then peered into his wallet. He frowned, predictably. The Coopers belonged to one of the fifty First Families of the realm. Once again they were short of money.

"I say, Chips," Duff said, somewhat gruffly. "If His Royal Highness does persist in this American expedition, I may have to impose on your generosity until we return. I won't have time to draw on my account."

Diana lifted her head, pressing the back of her hand against her eyes in an almost theatrical gesture. She was wearing pink, which looked delightful against her blond hair, though her flesh this morning was utterly colorless.

"Of course, Duff. As I always say, any time." As the husband of Lady Honor Guinness, Chips could afford to be breezy about money. Guinness stock was down, according to the Paris *Herald Tribune,* but the Guinness family's brewery firm was far from succumbing to the world depression. Misery was its best business partner.

"Where's H.R.H. now?" Diana asked, lowering her hand and blinking.

"Shopping." Duff grunted. "With Madame." He signaled the waiter for a second round, then called the man back again as an afterthought to order a bottle of Guinness stout as well. It was as if this insignificant purchase was a payment on account for anything he might borrow from Channon, or perhaps a reminder that the riches Channon so freely dispensed were far from entirely his own.

Chips smiled. He knew he'd end up paying for the Guinness and all their drinks himself.

"Sea voyage or no," said Diana, "I shall be glad to get out of Paris. I've never seen it quite so beastly. You'd think it was the days of Robespierre and The Terror again."

" 'A thought from an Englishman is worth ten years' devotion from these squalid, misshapen, Jewish, vulgar, loud-tongued, insult-asking Frenchmen,' " Duff recited.

"What?" said Diana.

"Your words, darling," Duff said, "You wrote them to me in a letter once."

"How is it you've remembered it so perfectly?"

"I probably haven't. You probably wrote something much worse."

"Oh, dear. Well, I apologize. That was awful of me."

Chips could not tell whether she was sorry for insulting Jews or the French, and so remained silent.

"You were very young then," Duff said. "It was before the war. But I remember it still." Cooper hated the Nazis for their public persecutions of German Jewry and could not abide the reflexive anti-Semitism of his class, but he was not beyond an occasional slur himself. One rainy night when the enormously rich Philip Sassoon refused to lend him his Rolls-Royce, Duff had been heard to say "These bloody Jews are all the same." He had later apologized for it—to Sassoon, and to himself.

"Do you suppose H.R.H. and Mrs. Simpson might get married on the ship?" Diana said.

"You forget that she's already married," Duff said.

"So does she," said Chips, with a feeble laugh.

"If the ship's captain can perform marriages, then he ought to be able to grant divorces as well," Diana said.

"And to crown queens," said Duff.

They all laughed. The waiter returned with three kiss-me-quicks and a small Guinness, which Duff ignored entirely.

"Do you suppose it's true that she's Jewish? Mrs. Simpson?" said Chips. He'd been wanting to ask that question for days. His hangover made him feel reckless enough to attempt it now. "Someone said her name was originally Warfeld."

"Malicious gossip," said Duff.

"The problem is that she's common," said Diana. "Dreadfully common. But rather nice. I like her, don't you, Duffie?"

"She has great courage."

"I can't believe Emerald going off and leaving us for the day," Chips said, realizing it was time to change the subject.

"Someplace north of Paris," Diana said. "Château Reanville."

"Don't you remember who lives there?" said Duff. "That's where Nancy has a house."

"Oh, dear God," said Diana. "*Quel bruit.*"

Lady Cunard had the chauffeur of her hired car proceed all the way through Reanville and continue on along the road to the next village. He slowed and glanced back hesitantly after a few kilometers, but she urged him on with a whisk of her hand. She had postponed this reckoning for nearly five years, knowing that the passing of time only deepened the bitterness that divided her from her daughter and only child. Nearing old age herself and with Nancy herself now almost forty, these horrible feelings could well become a permanent condition, rendering any reconciliation impossible. In part, Emerald supposed she lacked the courage to confront her daughter now on any subject, but her reluctance stemmed also from a lingering conviction that she was absolutely right in her anger. Nancy had brought all this on with behavior so outrageously shameful it seemed intended to incur its obvious consequences.

The uproar had begun with a deliberately provocative remark tossed into London society like a well-aimed bomb by Lady Margot Asquith, wife of the former prime minister. She had swept into one of Emerald's luncheon parties to say, with memorable loudness, "Hello, Maud, what is it now?—drink, drugs, or niggers?"

The candid response to this calculatedly devastating public inquiry into Nancy's troubles would have been "All three." But Emerald— Maud, as she was still called then—had been too shattered to reply with any quickness. Though Nancy's indulgence in narcotics was occasional and largely social, her drinking was shocking even in a society as accustomed to alcoholism as it was to adultery. Nancy's affairs went far beyond simple promiscuity. Her love life was slovenly, casual, joyless, and constant. It was said she went to bed with men just to decide whether she wanted to get to know them better.

As a caring mother who could never understand her continual difficulties with her only child, Lady Cunard tried to accept this. What bewildered and confounded her most was Nancy's embrace of Negroes seven years before. She had immediately begun taking them to bed at every opportunity. At least Edwina Mountbatten's brief dalliance with Paul Robeson had been only that—a clumsy self-indulgence and churlish swipe at the monarchy she despised. Nancy had taken up Negroes with the fervor of a Christian seeking martyrdom—especially the American jazz musician Henry Crowder. When she was not living with him, she was supporting him with gifts, loans, and outright stipends.

With Margot Asquith using Nancy to bat down Emerald's pretensions as London's premiere hostess, Lady Cunard had had no choice. She was being made the object of laughter from friends and enemies alike. She had only one weapon against Nancy—money—and she began pulling the purse strings more and more tightly, till Nancy rebelled with horrendous social violence.

She had a pamphlet published in Paris lambasting Lady Cunard and all of British aristocracy for their racialist attitudes and conduct toward blacks and those who consorted with blacks. Then she helped produce and exhibit in London a notorious obscene film that could have caused her jailing. She traveled twice to the United States with Crowder, attracting scurrilous write-ups in the American press about her activities in Harlem. "Disinherited by her Mother for her Unconventional Conduct, the Heiress of the Famous British Steamship Fortune takes up Residence in the Harlem Black Belt," one long headline ran. A picture caption read: "Lady Nancy Cunard Enjoying Herself Among Her Colored Friends in Her Apartment in Upper New York." Her ultimate blow was the publication in 1934 of her enormous book *Negro,* which with poems, histories, and polemics said everything there was to say on the subject of colored people— none of which Lady Emerald Cunard wanted to hear.

At every turn, Emerald feared to do or say anything, lest she provoke Nancy to some new ghastly public act—for all Emerald knew, stripping naked on the steps of Trafalgar Square and taking on Zulu warriors. But the present impasse simply could not continue. Emerald's flirtation with von Ribbentrop, her close friendship with the Prince of Wales, her perpetual salon for Britain's titled and literary great—all these were extremely important to her, but they could not replace what she was losing from her daughter. Emerald had been brought up in California as the "niece" of the heir to the Comstock lode fortune. Nancy was her daughter, not her "niece." She would not let that go.

*"Monsieur,"* she said to the driver. *"S'il vous plait, retournez à Reanville."*

The house was long but modest, large enough only for one or two servants and a handful of guests. It occurred to her mother that, as Nancy would invariably take one of the guests to her own bed, the lack of space probably didn't matter much.

As they sat there, parked at the edge of the road outside Nancy's gate, Lady Cunard thought of sending the driver up to the door to fetch Nancy down. But her daughter might simply not come, and that would be the worst thing of all.

Emerald opened the door. *"Attendez ici,"* she commanded. He grumbled. The drive had been long. "All right," she added. "Go into the village and get something to eat and drink. Return in an hour. *Précis."*

*"Oui, madame."*

The house lacked heating, and on this sunny October day, all the doors and windows had been opened to the warmth. Emerald stood a long moment at the principal entrance. Nancy should have heard the car approach and stop, its door close; heard Emerald coming up the flagstone steps. But there was no sign of her. If Emerald knocked, it might only be ignored. That would justify escape. A few brisk raps, a long pause, and then Emerald would have done her duty. She could go.

Lady Cunard stepped inside. She found herself in a long, narrow room with a fireplace at one end and a doorway leading to the rest of the house just beside it. The chamber had not been cleaned since an apparent party the night before—or perhaps since months of parties. There was an empty wine bottle on the floor in front of the divan, and it looked quite dusty. Beside it was a woman's rumpled garment. On a nearby table sat a plate still heaped with uneaten food.

Emerald also saw a small crumpled square of metallic paper, as from a packet of cigarettes, though this it decidedly was not. Bringing it close before her eyes, Lady Cunard saw the residue of white crystalline granules.

"Mother?"

Nancy was standing in the doorway, her arms as usual covered from wrist to elbow in her signature: multicolor African bracelets. She wore a much-wrinkled green velvet dress—a cocktail frock, really—and looked much disheveled in it. The two women resembled each other greatly—small, thin-legged, rather birdlike. They were obviously mother and daughter, though Emerald seemed a bejeweled parakeet, caught in midchirp and chatter, while Nancy was deeply serious and almost beautiful, her large, pale, blue-green eyes a haunting presence in any room, on any occasion.

They were fully focused on her mother's face, but with the faintest movement Nancy glanced to what her mother held in her hand.

"Yes, Mummy," she said, her voice now as bitter as their years of separation. "Drugs, drink, *and* niggers!"

Beside her in the shadows was the dark, broad face of Henry Crowder, Nancy's Negro musician. He looked terrified.

Spencer spent much of the day recovering from his hangover in his flat, ignoring the Lindbergh story for the moment and staying out of touch with Chief of Correspondents Carlson, who had supplanted dictators, wars, mobs, and police bullets as the major menace in his life. It seemed altogether likely now that Carlson not only could send him back to Chicago but was bent on it, willing to seize upon anything at all untoward in his behavior as sufficient provocation to impose this most terrible of fates. Spencer avoided him as he might those leather-coated political police in Germany. Though he guessed, with good reason, that some of the calls might be from Whitney, he let the telephone ring on unanswered the several times its insistent summons interrupted his drowse and sleep, so fearful was he that it might be Carlson.

Spencer had his instructions. Denise had brought him his steamship ticket. It sat in a large, unopened envelope on the mantel, representing escape. Once he was aboard ship, Carlson could not reach him. Once he had the Lindbergh story in hand, it would not matter what awaited him on the New York docks—even a telegram recalling him to Chicago at once. As he thought upon it, the Lindbergh story would be more than just a protection against recall. It could secure his ultimate, indefinite, infinite freedom.

Spencer had resented Hero Lindbergh, the man that the bitter humorist James Thurber had devastated in his satire, "The Greatest Man in the World." Lindbergh was undeniably a superb navigator and a brilliant engineer, but no better a pilot than any Spencer had flown with in the war, perhaps much worse than most, for he had a reputation for abandoning aircraft and taking to parachute at the first sign of trouble. It was true that Lindbergh had demonstrated a lonely kind of courage in coursing through his thousands and thousands of miles of forbidding emptiness in that great solo trans-Atlantic crossing of 1927. But it was the courage of the gambler and the egoist, smaller stuff than the terrible ferocity and murderous skill called forth from those who had clawed at each other with such fear and passion above the trenches. Lindbergh had never danced the dance of death in the air. He had not known flame or the stinging bullet or the grotesquerie of the fall from flight of a smashed-up, burning airplane with its pilot still alive and flailing. Lindbergh had been a man who had stayed awake long enough to cross an ocean—nothing more.

But now Spencer cherished this strange, aloof, self-consumed man. He wished Lindbergh well with the most solicitous ardor. He forgave the man his every frailty and flaw and wept for all his sadnesses, including most especially the loss of his little child. Lindbergh meant Paris for Spencer; he meant the love and the touch of Whitney Ransom. He meant life—the only life that could sustain Spencer. Lindbergh had become a holy vessel.

Spencer had no doubt that he could get the Lindbergh story, or whatever was Carlson's vague idea of it. He did not question that he could achieve this prize, this goal so unattainable for so many of his colleagues. He would succeed as he had succeeded four years before in following a hard road of rock and dust more than a thousand miles to the village of Juichin in China's Kiangsi Province, from which he had returned with the story of the fanatical Mao Tse-tung's proclamation of a Chinese Soviet Republic. Lindbergh would be trapped aboard a ship for seven days or more. Spencer's newspaper and most of the world had ignored Mao Tse-tung's proclamation. No one would ignore what Spencer would have to say about the greatest hero in the history of mankind. They would learn of it even in Kiangsi Province. He would no longer be a journalist but the most successful journalist in the world, a twentieth-century counterpart to the *New York World*'s Henry Stanley, who had entered history by greeting a fabled eccentric in the African jungles with the words "Dr. Livingston, I presume." Spencer might become so successful that he could give up journalism, as Whitney so ardently wished.

His mind would not hold this dreamy vision. Instead, it went back to that long-ago road in China. To a hot, humid day with the air as thick with dust as it was with incipient rain, when he had come upon an old man sitting cross-legged at the roadside, his face a sculptor's expression of pain and years and fear, his eyes staring at the ages, not seeing. Spencer had continued on, but when the road began to climb again into the yellow hills, he had realized he'd taken a wrong turn and so retraced his steps. Coming upon the old man again, he found him in much the same cross-legged position but fallen over on his side. He was dead, but his expression was entirely unchanged. He'd been dead when Spencer had looked into his ancient face the first time. Spencer had seen the secret of life. The secret of life was death.

On the mantel next to the steamship tickets was a silver-framed photograph of Whitney. He rose and went to it, turning it slightly to avoid the glare of the light from the window. It was a rather formal picture, Whitney in white dress and gloves and picture hat seated on a carved stone bench in her garden, her hair and eyes as perfect as the cut roses she held cradled in her arm, the most beautiful woman Spencer had ever known, the most beautiful woman in the world. She was smiling slightly and her gaze at the camera lens was friendly. Her husband had taken the picture.

Spencer stepped back from the mantel, then went for his jacket. He would see Whitney that night. He would not leave for America without doing so, even if he had to break into her house.

Nora had had a truly fabulous day. She had spent hundreds and hundreds of francs, possibly thousands of francs, in a shopping binge that had taken her from the Galéries Lafayette to Lucien Lelong to the Samaritaine de Luxe on the Boulevard de la Madeline. She had taken lunch on the Champs-Elysées with a very handsome Paris film critic and tea with an American lady she met in her hotel elevator who proved to be one of the Vanderbilts. She'd dined aboard a floating restaurant in the Seine with several people from the Theater de la Michodiere. Now she was a starring guest at a party in the Passy district of Paris that was the most elegant she had ever attended, as glittering and aristocratic in her newly purchased Maggy Rouff evening gown as anyone there. Several attractive men had been attentive to her, the most persistent a French nobleman who wore medals on his jacket and possibly too much cologne.

He followed her out into the dusky shadows of the huge garden adjoining the house. She instinctively moved away, but found herself in deeper darkness. He caught up with her quickly, but, though he stood very close to her, he remained circumspect and deferential. Clearly he was chasing her, yet his conduct was so altogether different from the pawings and leerings she'd become accustomed to in Southern California that she was a little charmed. They walked. She kept her arms folded against her chest lest he take her hand, or reach for her breast.

"I cannot believe that you are leaving tomorrow," he said. "I have only just met you and now you are being taken away from me. This is most unfair. I am being made to suffer like King Tantalus."

Nora had never heard of King Tantalus and wondered if he were someone she should have met.

"Then, Monsieur le Comte," she said, "you must come to America."

"But I shall. Of course. Very soon. This winter perhaps. But that will be of little good to me in my sadness tomorrow."

She smiled. What was she dealing with here? Flirtation? Seduction? Love? Marriage? Perhaps all of these things. She was thrilled with the fact of this aristocratic attention, but felt awkward and somewhat helpless. She did not know what was expected of her or what she expected of herself. She wished for her father, or at least his advice, but he would only have told her to stick with her own kind. "The rich will never be any good to us," he always said.

She dropped her left hand, and the count decorously snatched it up, taking her arm in his. She had performed a scene like this in one of her movies, but in that she had known the ending—and the lines.

They halted. They were not alone in the garden. In a bower just off the path ahead was another couple. Nora recognized the tall blond woman as the young wife of their host, remembering the woman's long white backless gown. She could not see the man very well but he seemed familiar, and was remarkable in that he was not wearing evening clothes like the others. Nora had not seen him in the house and wondered if he had come in through a gate in the garden wall.

The two were arguing, with some anger, but this almost magically ceased and suddenly they were in each other's arms, their passion excessive for such a public place, even in France. Nora and the count, pretending not to notice, hurried past.

"I know that man," she said. "I mean, I've seen him before. Last night, in the bar of the Ritz."

"He is part of our little circle, though he has no money. *L'héros,* we call him. Madame dotes upon him. He was a flier in the Great War. Very brave, it is said. An American, like her."

" 'Dotes'? It's none of my business," Nora said, "but isn't it a little, well, flamboyant of them to be doing this here? I mean, her husband is just inside."

"*C'est bien entendu,*" the count said. "The relationship is very well understood—as you would say, old news. Monsieur, he has his mistress, the Marquise de Villefranche, whom you have met. Madame, she is very young, and she has her American *ami*. They recently had a *querelle*, a falling out, which upset her very much. *Une tristesse attardant*. This also made the marquise very unhappy because she feared Madame would turn her full attention to Monsieur. But now *l'héros* returns, and all now seems happy again. All is, shall we say, in balance. Did you know Madame in America?"

"No. I never met her until tonight. America is a very big country. There are one hundred thirty million people in America."

"France is a very big country, but we, in our circle, all know each other. *L'héros* and Madame did not know each other in America, but his cousin went to school with the older brother of Madame. You see, all very small, all very *ensemble*. Everyone knows everyone. It is the same in the theater, yes? In the films? You do not know everyone in California, but you know everyone in films."

In Toledo, she had known the grocer's daughter.

"Monsieur le Comte," she said. "I would like to dance."

He obliged her—for nearly an hour. She danced better than he because she was more familiar with the new steps, but he moved stylishly and they attracted considerable attention. Nora did not see the hostess and her American war hero again.

She allowed the count to take her back to her hotel and to fondle and kiss her breast in the taxicab. When this stirred him to great ardor and greater intimacy, she abruptly confronted him with the unassailable wall of her catholicism. There was hypocrisy in this, but not much. She had exacted a substantial price when she had first surrendered her virtue and had not reduced it much since.

The count was unhappy but made the best of it, kissing her hand in farewell and promising a spectacular pursuit of her in America. She allowed him to kiss her hand again, then left him with only a quick smile in reply. Entering the lobby, she almost regretted leaving him behind.

The night manager beckoned to her from behind the front desk. The hotel seemed to have returned almost to normal.

"Did my parcels arrive this afternoon?"

"*Oui, Madame. Mais,* there is a small problem about tomorrow. The car we had arranged for you, to take you to Le Havre?"

"Yes, you said I'd have to share it with a gentleman."

"Yes, but we have only that one automobile available at the moment, and, *malheureusement,* it is necessary that the gentleman have the car entirely to himself. I am very sorry."

"Why only for him?"

"The gentleman is traveling very discreetly. It is important that he do so. We will do our best to arrange another car for you, if at all possible, but perhaps you would prefer to take the train. It is much more reliable, and you don't want to miss your sailing."

"Who is this 'gentleman'?"

"I'm not at liberty to say. But if you knew, madame, I'm sure you would understand completely. Do not worry. We will see that you get to Le Havre on time. And in the greatest possible comfort."

She was more than irritated. She was offended. At the least, she felt that someone in her position should be.

"The 'gentleman' isn't very gentlemanly."

"He is not even aware of this difficulty. I regret, madame, that the mistake was entirely ours."

Olga Maretzka spent most of the day sleeping, shedding her fatigue with hour after hour of heavy slumber. Toward darkness, she rose and washed, dressed and ate, then set out on a long journey by foot and tramway to the other side of the city and her next destination.

The building was at the end of a short, dark alley. Olga passed by it first, continuing on to the next corner. She lingered a moment, waiting for the street to empty, then retraced her steps, slipping into the alley unseen.

The flat was a wheezing climb, all the way up dusty, narrow stairs to the sixth floor, and then to the rear of the building. The hallway was filthy and smelled slightly of urine. She did not look at the shadows or try to guess what might be crawling in them. She had seen much worse in Russia, but this was Paris. She expected better.

A cautious face appeared at the doorway, eyes blinking.

"*Znajoma,*" she said, speaking in the man's native Polish. "*Od Leningradski.*"

She was admitted immediately. His expression gentled as he stepped aside for her, but he did not otherwise make her feel welcome. The old Pole had been too long in his grim job. One day she would look that way.

He led her to a small, cramped sitting room with only one dim lamp, and served her hot tea from a samovar. The glass burned her fingers, but she held onto it. If he had intended this as a test, she would pass it.

"I am sorry, *dziewczyna,* that you were summoned on such short notice from so great a distance," he said. "You had no trouble?"

He was not being solicitous of her welfare. He was concerned that she might have brought trouble with her. This was in his eyes.

"In Germany." She had been compelled to kill a Nazi secret policeman in Trier before escaping into Luxembourg. "I cannot go home back through Germany again. I should not have traveled through it on the way here."

"Did anyone follow you?"

"In Germany. I took care of it. That is why I cannot go back there."

He pondered this, staring at her. "They could hunt you down here."

"No. I don't think so."

"Well, you won't be here long." He rose and went to his bookcase, taking a large brown envelope from the papers and volumes jammed into it.

"You will arrange a different way back for me?"

"Of course, *dziewczyna.*" He did not convince her. His eyes troubled her. He and his confederates might not be interested in letting her get back at all.

They were not alike. She had initially become an assassin to avenge her brother, who had been murdered by an agent of the émigré Whites. She remained one for a number of reasons, but they included the fact that she was well compensated—at least by Leningrad standards. He was an old revolutionary, hardened, mean, and now overly cautious. It was the old who cherished life the most. If she made him uneasy enough, she would soon be dead.

"We should have made better preparation for you, better arrangements," he said, handing her the envelope and reseating himself. He sat now more in front of the lamp, so that he appeared almost entirely in silhouette. "The opportunity has come up so suddenly. But it is one that must be seized."

"You're sure he is here?"

"At the Hotel Crillon. Yes. But not for long. The rioting in Paris has frightened them. They are all leaving tomorrow. They are taking ship for America. There are loyal communists on the hotel staff. We have learned this."

"America? What for?"

He shrugged. "With aristocracy, who knows? They amuse themselves maybe. I can tell you it's not to take a job cutting sleeves in a sweatshop in New York."

"A ship."

"Yes. A Dutchman, leaving Le Havre tomorrow evening. We had hoped you could make use of these street disorders to get at him. There has been much gunfire. But they leave tomorrow. There you are."

She held the envelope with both hands resting on the shoulder bag in her lap. A quick, easy movement and she could have the long pistol aimed at his wrinkled old face.

"You didn't try."

"There are only three of us left and between us we have eliminated eleven of them. That grand duke was my last. It is time to close down here. Waldi is now being followed."

"So I am to provide your *pièce de résistance.*"

"What?"

"You, the Parisian, do not know this term?"

"Don't mock me."

"I am being déclassé?"

"You are being insolent, *dziewczyna.* You have a holy mission. You are to bring justice to the most important surviving relative of the Romanovs. This is royal blood. It must be shed."

"Like that on the floor of the 'house of special purpose' in Ekaterinberg?"

"That was not enough. No one said it was enough. Not Lenin, not Bronstein, not Sverdlov."

"They never even admitted they killed the czar and his family, those cowards. It took Stalin to show such courage."

He leaned closer. "Your great Comrade Stalin wishes this royal death."

"That is why I am here."

"After all, they give us no choice. They are making common cause with the fascists in Germany."

"They?"

"That entire family. They are German. His cousin the duke is himself a Nazi. The Romanovs were German."

"Yet you say this last death will suffice?"

"I said it was necessary. I did not say it was the last. For now it will suffice. It will give the other Germans, the other relations of the Romanovs, deep pause."

"And this is to be done on this Dutch ship?"

He shrugged. "If it is possible. If not, perhaps in New York. Choose your moment. But he must not complete this journey. He must not come back."

She opened the large envelope, taking out a forged passport and a thick sheaf of French bank notes. "The photograph is not good," she said. "The forgery is imperfect and the name is ill chosen. 'Olga Marz.' It is too similar to my own."

"We thought that an advantage. Easier to remember for you, to keep in your mind."

"I don't require such little tricks."

"It was the best we could do in such short time. You are supposed to be very resourceful. Make the best of it."

"And the ship?"

"The *Wilhelmina*. She sails from Le Havre at six o'clock tomorrow night. Take the train from Gare St. Lazare. We made a booking for you but you will have to obtain your steamship ticket at the dock when you arrive. There's money enough for the journey. Nearly twenty-five hundred in American dollars there. *Vous serez très riche.*"

She counted it. "What accommodation?"

"Second class." He glanced over her clothing. "We did not think you could stand the scrutiny of first class. In third class, you would have to share a cabin."

She nodded. "That's all? You have nothing else to tell me?"

"No."

Olga snatched up the pistol and fired a shot into his chest, the sharp report rattling the tea glasses by the samovar. She was up and heading toward the door before his tottering body hit the floor.

She paused very briefly before stepping out into the hall, satisfying herself that he was dead. Though she disliked him, it was nothing personal. She had her orders.

Even late at night, with the ship tied up in port, the captain is always the busiest member of any crew. Hendrik van der Heyden, master of the S.S. *Wilhelmina*, had hoped for an hour or more of free time to write some letters and enjoy a glass or two of Bols gin. But, as on every night since he had come aboard, this was denied him. There were new troubles.

The *Wilhelmina* was to have been the crowning achievement of the

Lage Lander Line's aspirations, a flagship to put the company in a class at least challenging the position of the rival Holland-Amerika service. But the *Wilhelmina* had been plagued with trouble ever since she had come out of the shipyards at Saint Nazaire, which Lage Lander had gone to because of the superior quality of their work. First there had been difficulties with the boiler valves, which had almost produced an explosion. Then, in sea trials, the ship had shown such a tendency to excessive roll and list that a major and costly refitting was necessary, including the removal of the heavy marble in the first-class bathrooms and the addition of permanent lead ballast on the lower decks.

In the second sea trials, a fire had broken out in one of the oil-firing heating units that had spread through ducts to an adjoining compartment before the crew had been able to extinguish it. The repairs for that had been completed just three weeks before, and now there was a major problem with the electrical wiring in the main machinery supply switchboard in the after-turbo generator room. The engineers had been working on it all day.

As a final frustration, there were now late-night visitors, important men behaving unpleasantly. Because of the delays and rumors of her troubles, the *Wilhelmina*'s passenger list for this maiden voyage had been greatly reduced by cancellations. She would be carrying less than one-third of her full capacity of 1,420 passengers, and only a few dozen or so in first class. These gentlemen were adding a large traveling party—and new difficulties—to that number.

Van der Heyden took one small glass of the smoky gin neat and quick, then went forward to the expansive wheelhouse of the bridge. As they were in port, only the duty quartermaster and the young third officer, Kees Witte, were on duty.

"Where are they?" said the captain.

"Waiting in the first-class smoking room, sir. Waiting impatiently."

"*Wat ist er aan de hand?*"

"I don't know, sir. They insist on talking only to you. I think it may be about arrangements. *Het ist belangrijk.*"

"For this class of people, Kees, everything is important. '*Vlug, vlug, vlug.*'"

The captain turned away. Instead of descending to the deck where the two important men waited, he went out onto the starboard wing of the bridge. The *Wilhelmina* was tied up with her port side to the quay, prow facing toward the east end of the long harbor. She was still taking on fuel oil and provisions, and working lights made bright circles in the open areas of her decks. She was a long beauty, 854 feet from her high, proud bow to her tapered stern. Her beam was 90 feet, and she stood 165 feet high from keel to the top of her radio mast, drawing 28 feet of water. Her three smokestack funnels were smartly raked, adding the look of speed to her lines. In sea trials she'd been certified for twenty-six knots, not enough to win the *Bleu Ribband* for fastest liner afloat but adequate to make good on the bold promises of express service in Lage Lander's advertising.

Cunard had christened its grand *Queen Mary* the year before. Both the French Line and Holland-Amerika had also risen sufficiently from the world depression to have new ships in the works. With three of its oldest ships still laid up, crews dismissed and scattered and the remaining personnel working at three-quarters pay, Lage Lander had not yet risen from the Depression. The *Wilhelmina* was intended to accomplish the task. It was an expensive gamble, but it would be at least two years before Holland-Amerika's next *Nieuw Amsterdam* came down the ways. Lage Lander would have a fighting chance.

She was as complete a ship as any of the big British, French, or German—with swimming pools, Turkish baths, gymnasiums, racquet courts, a bank, smoking rooms, library, lounges, drawing rooms, cinema, shopping arcades, dog kennels, gambling rooms, and deluxe dining rooms and restaurants for both first and second class, and accommodations for third-class passengers not all that primitive.

If only the *Wilhelmina* would cease this endless succession of minor catastrophes. Van der Heyden was considered one of the most skillful navigators and ship handlers on the Atlantic, but he was also known to lose control of himself in a crisis, and he was rapidly approaching that point again. He had ripped into his chief engineer that afternoon for a mistake that had been made back at the shipyards. This was unfair not only to the officer but to the steamship line. They were risking everything on him, a confidence he did not deserve. He had lost not only his temper over the years. He had once lost a ship.

Now he must face a different sort of crisis—one in which he dare not even raise his voice. He closed his cabin door behind him, and descended from this elevated station into the world below that was his ship.

After a brief argument over the telephone, Reichscommissioner Goering relented and agreed to meet Reichsführer-S.S. Himmler at his headquarters in the Reich Main Security Office, a grandly glorified police station. "One principle must be absolute for the S.S. man," Himmler had proclaimed. "We must be honest, decent, loyal, and comradely to members of our own blood and to no one else." The activities on the ground floor and basement of this huge, gloomy building were a testament to his very literal adherence to this "principle." Hundreds disappeared within these walls almost daily.

Himmler had once been Goering's subordinate, head of the Prussian police and Gestapo during Goering's prime ministership of that state. He now considered himself der Dicke's equal, and gave every hint of a willingness to make himself his old comrade's superior.

Goering indulged him a little in this. He wanted no enemies in the S.S. He saw no great threat in the man's rivalry, for Himmler was not particularly sophisticated or competent—merely ruthless. Goering kept out of his way as much as possible, though, except when he needed to make some use of Himmler. Normally, he would not have agreed to bring his great personage to anyone's office other than Hitler's, but he wanted Himmler to feel placated. He had a very specific use for the Reichsführer-S.S. just now.

They exchanged "heil Hitlers," then Goering, still wearing his huge military overcoat, turned away, seeking and finding a large chair at some distance from Himmler's desk. The Reichsführer-S.S. was compelled to leave his bureaucratic throne and take a similar chair near Goering's.

"Get to the point, Heinrich," said Goering, massaging his pale, plump hands. "I have other engagements this evening."

With his pudgy face, thick round glasses, weak lips, and wispy mustache, Himmler looked more a bank clerk than a principal instrument of National Socialist terror.

"You are aware of von Ribbentrop's reports about the Prince of Wales?" Himmler asked.

"Long before you were, good comrade," said Goering, smiling not a little unpleasantly.

"You have sent an operative?" Himmler asked.

Goering stared.

"You have," pronounced Himmler. "That dreadful Polish Prussian, Markgraf von Kresse."

"How do you know this?"

"I know everything, Hermann. Just like you."

Goering looked about, frowning. "Refreshment, Herr Reichsführer?"

Himmler clapped his hands and a black-uniformed officer stepped forward from the shadows.

"I will have schnapps," said Goering.

"Schnapps, Fritz," Himmler said. "At once. A chilled bottle and one glass."

The S.S. man, doubtless a shop clerk or accountant before he joined the Schutzstaffel, clicked his heels. A large, cold bottle was produced instantly. After pouring, the officer withdrew into the shadows.

"I have indeed sent my old flying companion, Count von Kresse. He is to determine whether the Prince of Wales is actually in trouble over this Simpson woman and, if appropriate, to take some corrective action."

"What sort of corrective action?"

"I left that to his discretion. He is a subtle man, as well as charming and persuasive."

Himmler sat forward abruptly. "Hermann! He is a dangerous man. Totally unreliable."

"But eminently acceptable, socially acceptable. I can't think of anyone in Germany better suited to mix with the English aristocracy."

"This makes him no less dangerous, no less unpredictable. He should have been shot two years ago."

"*Vielleicht,*" said Goering, looking down at his thick, polished boots. "But now he is joining the Prince of Wales. I am confident he will attend to our interests as required. He understands the need for close friendship between the Reich and the British Empire, though I will concede that his domestic political attitudes are worrisome."

"Worrisome? They are treasonable!"

Goering smiled benignly. "I share some of your concerns. But this matter cannot be left in that fool Ribbentrop's hands alone. Von Kresse's intervention may not suffice. But it's the best I can do in such a hurry."

"He is a man who should be watched."

"And I am sure you are watching him. I would not be surprised if you manage to get one of your people aboard the ship with him."

Himmler grinned, which he almost never did. "State security is my responsibility."

Some passengers had already come aboard in preparation for the next day's sailing, but only a few were in the first-class smoking room. The two important Englishmen were unmistakable. They had taken a table in the corner, where one now sat and the other paced back and forth impatiently behind him. Both were wearing gray tweed suits and both had been served whiskey.

Van der Heyden approached with great dignity. Ships made for a social anomaly. At sea, captains were virtual monarchs, the most exalted personage aboard no matter who was traveling in first class. On shore, they were merely employees of their shipping lines—only sailors in port. Van der Heyden was not a man overly concerned about his status, but now conducted himself as the autocrat he would be once the *Wilhelmina* was underway. These two "gentlemen" irritated him. The simple fact of them did.

The one who was sitting rose and the other stopped his pacing. "Good evening, Captain," said the former. "I'm Major Metcalfe, and this is Lord Brownlow."

Though he had no mustache, the major looked a typical British officer, handsome enough but distinguished mostly by large, outset ears and far above average height. The other seemed an ordinary Englishman, distinguished only by the "lord" before his name. Van der Heyden reminded himself of how ordinary he and his officers must look out of uniform.

"Would you care to join us for a drink?" the major asked.

Van der Heyden seated himself. "A drink? No, thank you. But you wished to speak to me, so here I am. You have a problem, gentlemen?"

The other two took their chairs, Metcalfe leaning forward on the table, lowering his voice somewhat.

"We have booked passage," he said. "It's a most important booking, perhaps the most important of your career." The words, as he spoke them, sounded offensively pompous to his ear, but there was no way of withdrawing them.

The captain had recognized Brownlow's name, but wanted these English to be more forthcoming.

"You must know to whom we refer," Brownlow said.

"No, I don't. You are traveling with a large party, I believe. You are leading some sort of tour?"

"Certainly not!" said Brownlow.

"Actually," said Metcalfe, interceding, "it is rather like that. The difference is that our little group includes some rather high-ranking people, and one of them is perhaps the—well, one of the highest-ranking personages in the British Empire. I'll be perfectly candid. He's a member of the royal family."

The captain had suspected this but decided not to let it appear to affect him. "Yes? Well, I'm sure we can make him comfortable. This is a very well-appointed vessel."

"Quite. She seems splendid, sir. That's not what concerns us. What we wanted to talk to you about, is, well, whether we can count on your discretion."

"It's imperative that no one know he's aboard," said Brownlow.

"That's easy then," said van der Heyden, pushing back his chair as if to rise. "He should not come aboard."

"Captain," said Major Metcalfe. "Are you really aware of whom we are speaking?"

"*Ja. Ik weet.* But are you aware that this is not a British warship or a private yacht? This is a passenger liner. A *Dutch* passenger liner. This is not Cunard's *Berengaria.* This is the *Wilhelmina* of the Lage Lander Line. And this is not 1924, when your important personage last made this crossing. It is not my fault that he has since become notorious. Discretion for him is now very rare. And it's in no way my responsibility. You have made no special arrangements. You do not appear to have provided for security. You just march aboard without any prior notice and start making demands. You're being unreasonable."

"See here, van der Heyden," Brownlow began.

Metcalfe restrained him. "I appreciate that, Captain," he said. "We're in an awkward situation. It is inconvenient for this member of our party to return to England just now, and the unstable political circumstances make it unwise to remain on the continent. This voyage has become a necessity. In any event, it's what he wishes."

"He is not the King of Holland."

"Mind your place, van der Heyden," Brownlow said. "We're within our rights to book this passage. If you people make a muck of it, that's your responsibility."

"What Lord Brownlow means to say," said Metcalfe, "is that if this voyage succeeds, it will be well remembered by a man who in not too long a time is going to be King of England. I presume the Lage Lander Line would not be averse to royal favor, even from Great Britain."

Matters had definitely reached the point where van der Heyden should have been telephoning his superiors in Amsterdam for instructions. But that was not his way.

"Gentlemen," he said more warmly. "I appreciate the favor you bestow on Lage Lander in choosing us for this, what should I say, unique crossing. It is our interest to accommodate you the best we can in every way we can. But my concern must be for all our passengers. They cannot be inconvenienced in any way."

"Understood," said Metcalfe.

"If I seem troubled to you," van der Heyden said, "I have reason. We already have an 'important party' booked on this voyage. I don't know why fate has singled us out for this double honor, but it will not be easy to cope with. This other person is of far more consequence in the United States than your royal personage. He, too, has requested our discretion. It is extremely important that no one knows he is aboard."

"Who is it?" said Brownlow.

Van der Heyeden leaned farther back and folded his hands together before his face. He smiled, contempt and resignation in his eyes. "You see?" he said.

"We see," said Metcalfe.

"If you wish to succeed with this," the captain said more sternly, "you can make the same arrangements for your royal personage that we have made for our other guest. Bring him aboard tonight, during darkness."

"But he's still in Paris," Metcalfe said.

"It can be done," said van der Heyden, looking at his watch. "They will have to leave Paris within the hour, but they can make it. If they wait until morning, there will be all the other passengers arriving. And there will be some press. This is, after all, the maiden voyage of a major new liner. And we will have an American motion picture actress on board. Motion picture actresses have little interest in the kind of discretion you seek."

"Very well," Metcalfe siad. "We'll have him here before sunrise." He turned to Brownlow. "We'll put Lord Louis in charge of it. Sounds just his ticket."

"He'll make a muck of it."

"And once you get him aboard," van der Heyden said, "this royal highness. I suggest that you see to it he remains in his cabin for the entire voyage. That's what our other important passenger is going to do. He's having all his meals served in his cabin."

"Cabin?" said Brownlow. "We booked a suite for His—for our special passenger."

"I thought you were interested in 'discretion,' " the captain said.

Metcalfe laughed, and raised his glass of whiskey. "So we are, sir. So we are. But traveling in a mere stateroom. That is not discretion, Captain. That is degradation. I'm sure you understand."

Back in his cabin, his blue uniform coat removed because of the heat, van der Heyden went to the square little window by his desk that look out over the darkened harbor. The running lights of an off-duty tug moved slowly across the still scene.

If he called Amsterdam, the company would behave insanely. They had when they'd been informed of the other booking.

He decided he would not telephone them. As was his usual preference, he would deal with the trouble himself and tell no one of his conversation with the two Englishmen. If all went well, the company would be just as happy. If the voyage went badly, it wouldn't matter whether he told them or not. It would be his last command with them just the same. The time had come for his retirement. He recognized that, even if the company didn't.

He lay down upon his bunk. He would allow himself a few minutes' rest before making his rounds, a brief interlude in which there would be no special passengers. He closed his eyes. It seemed just an instant later that he heard the pounding on his door.

Opening it, he looked into the square dark face of his Javanese quartermaster.

"Captain! There's a fire in the engine room!"

# CHAPTER
## *FOUR*

The ever-thorough Reichscommissioner Goering had been more clever than usual. He had promised Count von Kresse an assistant in this intrigue, an accomplice who would feel as at home as he in the rarefied strata at the pinnacle of the British class system yet who would also be capable of helping him meet any danger or difficulty. And so Goering had provided him with his sister, Dagne.

She had courage and ruthlessness enough. She was quite a strong and still youthful woman who, like Martin, had been confronted with physical risk and challenge from early on in her life as a proper part of her upbringing. She had climbed almost as many mountains as he and won even more equestrian medals. He'd seen her kill a wounded stag with a knife, throwing herself on the thrashing, bellowing animal when her rifle had jammed, cutting its throat. Though she would not admit to it, he guessed she was now armed with a pistol. Dagne also possessed infinite loyalty—to von Kresse, of course, but also to Reichscommissioner Goering. She would doubtless inform der Dicke of every aspect of her brother's conduct throughout this adventure. She would insure that he carried out the Reichscommissioner's wishes, in every way, by her mere presence.

But Goering was more thorough even than this. Surely there must be another accomplice whose identity was not yet known to von Kresse, or possibly even to Dagne. There might be several. As one of the count's intellectual friends had said during a chess game in a coffeehouse near the Gedachtniskirche on a recent evening, the Third Reich was a universal concept. It was wise to assume its presence wherever one went.

Dagne was flaunting this truth. As the train rolled out of Gare St.

Lazare at the start of its swift journey to the Channel, she took from her traveling case a copy of The Leader's *Mein Kampf.*

"For God's sake, Dagne. Is that damned book a badge for you?"

They were alone in a first-class compartment, seated facing each other. Dagne was wearing a very fashionable beige suit, with matching hat and light veil. She lifted the book still higher before her face, a challenge.

"If the old count were alive he would have you thrashed," said von Kresse.

She began reading aloud: " 'And it is precisely for our intellectual demi-monde that the Jew writes his so-called intellectual press.' "

Von Kresse snatched the book from her hand and turned quickly to the front. "If you can't think of decency, Dagne, for God's sake at least think of your class. Listen to this, the men who fell in his pathetic Munich putsch, the men he dedicated this to, listen to who they are: 'businessman, hatter, bank clerk, bank clerk, bank clerk, locksmith, businessman, headwaiter, student of engineering, valet, businessman, court councillor, retired cavalry captain, engineer, engineer, businessman.' This is your 'New Order.' Clerks, valets, headwaiters, shopkeepers—'businessmen.' And let us not forget postcard artists. The lower-middle-class ascendant, the Countess von Bourke and Kresse in their train."

She resented his use of irony. Her voice was soft and cool, but she was defiant. "The Duke of Saxe-Coburg und Gotha has joined the party and he is Victoria's grandson."

"He's a silly fool, just like you."

She took the book back and hurriedly thumbed through the pages to a remembered passage. " 'The class arrogance of a large part of our people, and to an even greater extent, the underestimation of the manual worker, are phenomenae which do not exist only in the imagination of the moonstruck,' " she read smugly, as if this was a revealed truth from the scriptures. " 'It shows the small capacity for thought of our so-called intelligensia when, particularly in these circles, it is not understood that a state of affairs which could not prevent the growth of a plague, such as Marxism happens to be, will certainly not be able to recover what has been lost.' "

"The lunatic is not even grammatical!"

"You should be very thankful that at this moment we are not in Germany."

"You've no idea just how grateful I am for that."

"Martin! Do you forget what barbarism lies just three hundred kilometers from our home? In what sort of world do you think you live?"

"Pit barbarism against barbarism and the result is still barbarism."

She pushed herself away from him, into a corner of the compartment, lifting the book to completely obscure her face. "We have had this conversation, Martin. To no good end."

"Indeed."

He had a book of his own, Leopold von Ranke's *History of the Roman and German Peoples,* but it was hardly the stuff to suit his mood. He moved closer to the train window, folding his arms and extending his left leg to ease the pain. The passing tableau of gray Parisian suburbs was not an enticing diversion either.

Goering had given him a hastily prepared prècis of his mission, including a one-page biographical sketch of Wallis Warfield Simpson prepared by Reinhard Heydrich's Sicherheitdienst Security Service and some notes on her reported traveling companions. The count took this from the pocket of his gray double-breasted suit and read through it once again.

Though the author of the sketch seemed very excited about Mrs. Simpson's possible Jewishness, he was careful to note this was in no way documented. Rather, it was a belief held firmly in those quarters of Baltimore society resentful of her social progress in England.

There was evidence that the family had been in Maryland as Warfield since the English crown grants of the early seventeenth century. By Wallis Warfield's time, the family was in such reduced circumstances that they lived in a rundown house and took in boarders, or so Heydrich's German-American correspondents in Baltimore reported. Her widowed mother was able to rescue them from their shabby gentility only by marrying a well-off but alcoholic and disreputable local politician.

Mrs. Simpson's first husband was a U.S. Navy lieutenant. She had followed him to China in 1924. They had become estranged over his heavy drinking and patronage of Chinese brothels, but she had stayed on in China another two years, drifting from city to city and supporting herself in large part by living off friends and gambling. She was, according to the dossier, a skillful card player.

She was also, it said, highly claustrophobic and extremely self-conscious about her plainness, especially as concerned her oversized hands and nose and a large mole. She was given to salacious remarks and was reportedly very deft at the amusing conversational titillation so much in vogue in higher British social circles, which accounted for much of her initial social acceptance.

Mrs. Simpson apparently indulged the prince's flirtation as a means of advancing her social station in Britain, never realizing how deeply and dangerously it would involve her. She was obviously very uneasy with her situation and might be looking for a means of escaping it, according to the précis. Her rise to the position of king's "mistress," a term not necessarily to be taken literally, had sharply divided England's upper class into two hostile factions.

Von Kresse wondered how much Ribbentrop had to do with this report. Goering called him a fool yet was more than willing to act on his information. It was so like him to discredit his sources of intelligence this way. If things went wrong, there was a ready place to turn with the blame.

And there would certainly be no turning to the Reichscommissioner with blame. In the event von Kresse caused some disaster in this mission, Goering would be able to disclaim any responsibility. He would say he and the count simply had discussed the British royal romance over a companionable glass of schnapps that morning, and otherwise talked over old flying days. Goering would say he had once again tried to persuade von Kresse to join the National Socialist Party, but otherwise had not intruded politics on the conversation.

As for von Kresse's sudden journey with his sister, Goering would say he simply agreed that October was a marvelous time for a sea voyage, especially to America, where the count had so many relatives. And if the von Kresses chanced to provoke an international incident en route and damaged the New Germany's good standing with Britain, well, what could you expect from one of these arrogant East Prussians with unreconstructed class attitudes and intellectual pretensions, especially from one with so many dangerous friends and so much Polish blood?

So the reason for this bold intrusion upon the silly but awesomely consequential life of Edward, Prince of Wales, would remain their little secret, though it was perhaps the only matter on which von Kresse and his malevolent friend were in full agreement. Von Kresse had thought upon it for long hours after his morning with Goering. There was no other course to peace. England must be kept meek, friendly, and quiescent.

Hitler was bent on putting every living German under National Socialist rule, including the chancellor of Austria and the president of the Danzig Senate. The sort of confrontation this would entail carried every risk of war, and war meant ruin. Absolute ruin. The old Germany represented by von Kresse and the new Germany proclaimed by The Leader would both be lost. There were too few new airplanes in the production lines of the secret aircraft works and too many horse-drawn artillery caissons in the Wehrmacht. Hitler was talking about remilitarizing the Rhineland. *Mein Gott*, the French army in Alsace alone could stop him, and the French were still bent on disassembling Germany into the scattering of quarrelsome principalities and duchies it had been before it was forged into nationhood by Bismarck sixty-five years before. They would seize the first opportunity Hitler gave them—if the British were to back them up.

For all the evil and obnoxious things der Dicke had become in the course of his rise to power, he had not become stupid. He had foreseen the logical end of the first Great War even before von Kresse. The logical end of the next one was no less obvious. Hermann Goering, who stood shortly to become commander of all German military aviation, was steadfastly opposed to war. Swine and demon that he was, he would make every possible effort to deliver the Reich from doom.

But there was for von Kresse an unwanted question. If the destruction of Germany was the only means of destroying the Hitler regime, was it not a morally desirable goal? Von Kresse was not yet prepared to address this issue. He had not yet resolved his own moral dilemma. He had not yet decided whether it was moral that he himself had lived beyond the last war.

The count read on through the intelligence report, turning to the brief sketches of those reported to be the prince's traveling companions. Lady Emerald Cunard, object of Ribbentrop's clumsy flirtation and the diplomat's compulsive correspondent, was a principal member of the entourage—a rich, powerful, supercilious, and desperately ambitious woman passing from middle age to old.

Also of importance were the Mountbattens, he the very German British naval officer so closely related to all the royal families of Europe, she the wanton English heiress with, as Ribbentrop put it, the stain of Jewish blood in her veins. The ambassador suggested a German operative might want to perform the Aryan sacrifice of sleeping with her as a means of penetrating the royal circle. Von Kresse smiled. Just Ribbentrop's form of sacrifice.

The famous Coopers were in the party, the fading aristocratic beauty and the dissolute diplomat and politician. Their presence was reported with a strong warning. They were of the pro-French camp and critics of the Third Reich. Ribbentrop underscored the fact that Duff Cooper was a protégé of the feared and hated Churchill.

Last mentioned was a wealthy American named Henry Channon, a social climber from Chicago who had acquired the heiress to the Guinness fortune as a wife and had ingratiated himself into the prince's favor. Ribbentrop noted that he was an admirer of Hitler's and a friend of Germany's.

Von Kresse refolded the papers and put them back in his pocket. Goering had told him to destroy them before leaving Germany but he had failed to do so, probably in subconscious rebellion. If someone gave him trouble about them, well, Dagne could shoot that someone.

He laughed at his little joke. She glanced up, her pale eyes disapproving. She was so little like him and her ideas were anathema to him, but he still felt the bond between them strongly. His wife, Lalka, had left him. His parents were dead. The mother of his only child was dead and the child was dead. Dagne's was the only life still given unto his protection. For all her flaws and terrible ideas, he felt this responsibility deeply.

"Now you laugh. You are finding this journey amusing?" she asked.

"High comedy. A mirthful tonic to my fallen spirits."

"The purpose is very serious."

"All purpose is serious. That is why I avoid it."

"Yet here you are."

"As I must be someplace, better here than among all the gaudy flags of Berlin."

She closed her book and put it aside, then lifted her veil.

"You are so scornful, Martin. Of yourself, of everything. It's such a waste. You could contribute so much."

"To National Socialism?"

"To Germany. God allowed you to survive the war, yet you do nothing in return."

"I'm still puzzling over why He did it."

"You are a noble man. He has a noble reason. There is a great and noble task that you must perform. Perhaps this undertaking of ours, perhaps this shall be that task. You are an instrument of Germany's destiny."

"Following the orders of the creator of the Prussian concentration camps."

"I'm not talking politics."

"You are always talking politics."

She removed her hat and fluffed her hair. "We will talk about something else," she said with a quick look at his book. "Let us discuss literature."

He picked up von Ranke's volume. "This is history," he said. "And all history is political. But literature is appropriate. This conversation reminds me of a story by Henry James. You know him? The English author? He was once an American?"

"Decadent."

"You see, politics again. James's story was called *The Beast in a Jungle.* It was about a man who was convinced that something great, unique, and significant would happen to him. He lived a very long life, waiting and watching for it. But when he became old, he finally realized what that unique something was. It was that nothing at all important was ever going to happen to him. It will be the same with me. If I was made to survive the war for any reason, it was simply to demonstrate the pointlessness of war, of aristocrats, perhaps of life."

"In Germany now, no one's life can be pointless. Certainly not yours, Martin."

"I remain a useless man, living a pointless life."

"You have done significant things."

"Yes? I have killed a schoolteacher and her children and I have slept with my sister. For one of these I received a medal. But in the Third Reich, such things are now commonplace. Ordinary."

She turned her head and wiped her eyes. He had no idea what had compelled him to be so wounding. She would find some revenge. She always did.

"I'm sorry, Dagne."

"So am I, Martin. So am I."


Rouen. The train had stopped in the Rouen station. When it came to a halt, Spencer's window framed a sign on one of the depot pillars: ROUEN. A statement of fact.

Nearly all the Hundred Years' War was fought over this place. From here, fifteenth-century English generalissimos ruled the hapless north of France and even Paris. A last battle here had been all that saved France from being forever English. Now it was simply Rouen, a pausing on the road to the sea.

Spencer could easily take up his baggage and descend from the carriage now. He could find lodgings and become for the rest of his life a citizen of Rouen. All that he had in Paris, all that he had had wherever he lived and traveled, he could find in Rouen. A few fine cafés, a few worthwhile friends, a good woman. They would ask what had happened to C. Jamieson Spencer. Someone would remember and say, "He lives now in Rouen." Eventually they would no longer remember.

The train lurched, groaned, then slid forward, gaining speed. A procession of depot pillars hurried by, and then there was the sudden darkness of a tunnel. When they emerged into the hazy sunlight, Spencer saw houses on a hillside among drooping trees. Soon they were in the yellow-green countryside again, and all sign of Rouen was gone. His imagined café there was gone. The charming, fleshy, mothering woman he would have chosen for himself there was gone. His life there that never was had ended.

The door to his compartment slid open. Until they had pulled into Rouen, there had been a French family with him, father, mother, two daughters, and an aunt, shabbily dressed but highly mannered, traveling first class with much custom, though they looked not well able to afford it. They had left the train in Rouen, disappearing into that life that would never be Spencer's.

Now there was a beautiful face at the door, bright green eyes and copper hair. The young woman hesitated, then slid the door open farther and stepped inside, seating herself decorously opposite him. She was dressed all in green. He recalled that she had passed by once before, just after leaving Paris, and glanced in, when the French family had been there. She was looking at him now with both embarrassment and great curiosity.

"Excuse me," she said. She drew her hands together nervously in her lap. She was wearing dark-green gloves and matching shoes, very expensive. She dressed better than Whitney, which could be said of few women.

"Yes?" he said. He had been about to reply in French, but she was American. She was considerably more than that. He had seen her in a newspaper photograph—within the last few days.

"This is embarrassing," she said. "I wasn't sure where you'd be getting off the train. I wanted to talk to you before you did. I saw you before you got on. In the station. In the Gare St. Lazare." Her hands fluttered a moment, then came to rest, firmly. Her eyes now held his quite directly.

"Yes," he said. "I was in the Gare St. Lazare. That's how I came to be on this train."

"I've seen you in other places. You were in the bar of my hotel. The Ritz. And at a party last night in Paris. And now you're on this train. It's as if you were haunting me."

"Mademoiselle, I am often in the bar of the Ritz. I am often at the de Mornays', as I was last night, if that's the party you mean. The de Mornays are close friends of mine. I can't recall seeing you in either place. I had no idea you'd be on my train. I assure you, that's not why I'm on it."

"I'm sorry. This must sound very queer. I've had a difficult time these last few days, except for yesterday. I'm traveling alone. I guess I'm a little jumpy."

"These are jumpy times."

"You're a newspaperman, aren't you? That's what they told me, at the de Mornays'."

"I am a newspaperman. I believe you are Nora Gwynne, the actress."

"Yes. So you see . . . I mean, I thought you were somehow—I thought you might be hounding after me for a story."

"I am not hounding you, Miss Gwynne. People get thrown to- gether these days in a lot of strange ways. A woman died in my arms the other night, during the rioting in the Place de la Concorde. I had never seen her before."

"I'm sorry." Her look softened.

"You have nothing to worry about, Miss Gwynne."

"I'm sure. I'm sorry. I don't know what I thought I was doing, barging in on you like this." She rose and put a gloved hand to the brass handle of the compartment door. She paused. "You are taking this train all the way to Le Havre?"

"All the way."

"To board a ship?" She glanced at his luggage.

"Yes. I'm sailing tonight for New York."

"May I ask on what ship?"

"The *Wilhelmina.*"

She pulled open the door with a quick snap of the handle and darted hurriedly into the corridor. He thought of going after her but caught himself. If he took a step in pursuit, she might well scream.

He leaned back against his seat, turning his head back toward the window. In the distance, beyond the blur of trees along the track, was a large house with a red roof. The family within might be looking out the window, watching the passing train, perhaps thinking about the passengers—where they had come from, where they were bound. Spencer could not truly answer them.

He closed his eyes. This Gwynne woman was guilty of haunting him. She had descended upon him like a biblical visitation. She was trouble. It had begun with Carlson and now would follow him all the way across the Atlantic. As she'd made obvious, they would be fellow passengers on the *Wilhelmina*. She would be a herald going before him, denouncing him to anyone who was interested as a newspaperman, a prying reporter.

Charles Lindbergh would definitely be interested.

Le Havre embraced the sea and the estuary of the Seine, but it seemed hotter even than Paris. What breeze there was came from the south, scarcely stirring the air in the train sheds of the elegant new Gare Maritime. Out of long habit, Spencer carried his own bags. He had but two. Setting off down the platform, he moved out ahead of the other passengers, most of whom were still gathering their own luggage or calling for porters. He heard English voices, American accents, and a large number of French, though most did not look as if they were bound for a ship. As Spencer passed a tall, gray-haired man with a limp and a very stylish woman with blond hair, he heard them speaking in German. It seemed odd for citizens of the Third Reich these days to be taking ship from a French port instead of Bremerhaven or Hamburg. Certainly they must be Swiss or Austrian, though their accents reminded him of Berlin.

He pressed on, striding out ahead of everyone, arriving at the taxi stand first. The driver was greatly pleased to see him, or at least his minimal luggage. If he were quick, he might make three trips to the quay from this train.

"*Bonjour, monsieur,*" he said, putting the bags in front. "*Quel bateau?*"

"*La* Wilhelmina."

"Wilhelmina?"

"*Oui. Un nouveau bateau. Un paquebot du Lage Lander.*"

"*Ah, oui.*"

It was a very short distance from the railroad station to harborside, but the driver had to thread his way along the quays past two other liners, one of them the magnificent new *Normandie*. Spencer had been up to Le Havre for its departure on its maiden voyage that May, a grand occasion that had brought forth President Lebrun, Pierre Cartier, the writer Colette, Mrs. Morgan Belmont, and even the

Maharajah of Karpurthala. Spencer had spent most of that afternoon aboard the *Normandie*, touring the decks and mingling with the passengers and guests through all their amusements as if one of them. When the summons came for reporters and visitors to return to the dock, he had done so with great reluctance. Now he was being summoned again just as commandingly, back *onto* a ship. Ordered off the docks. Ordered out of France.

The Dutch ship was somewhat smaller than the great French liner, and its maiden voyage was going largely unrecognized. There were workmen standing or walking about at quayside, and a small group of men in black suits had gathered at a point just in front of the prow—obviously company officials conferring where they had the broadest view of the ship that had been the focus of all their energies and was now the focus of their worries.

Spencer had the taxi driver stop near them, though it meant a fair walk with his bags to the embarkation building. After tipping the man generously with some of the expense money Carlson had given him, he watched the taxi roll away. He stood a long moment in the heat, looking up at the ship. The haze deadened her color, dulling the Prussian blue of her hull and imbuing the white of her superstructure with a dingy grayness. Still, she was a beautiful creation, with a dramatic rise of bow and beautifully flowing flare and sweep of following line. Spencer had gone to sea in not a few rotting hulks in his time, rustbuckets that seemed scarcely able to steam out of harbor. Aboard the *Wilhelmina*, at least, it was not his life he would have to fear losing but simply all those things that made it worth living—if he failed.

He glanced about, as if one of the many human figures walking and standing about might somehow prove to be Charles Lindbergh, as if he might conclude his business with a quick, dockside interview and then be off back to Paris and Whitney.

There was no Lindbergh in view and no predatory crowd of reporters hanging about. If Lindbergh was aboard that ship, it was still Spencer's secret.

A couple was clearing the passport officer's station as Spencer entered. By the time he reached the counter and set down his bags, he was the only passenger present. The officer, a tall young man full of his uniform and authority, went through Spencer's passport with overzealous care, examining each visa stamp as if it contained clues to a criminal conspiracy. Spencer had been in and out of France at least a dozen times that year, and the youthful official apparently found this exceedingly suspicious.

Spencer cursed every country's passports and the war that had brought them into being. Before 1914 there had been no such bureaucratic requirement except for the internal passports of the Russian Empire, and a gentleman could cross frontiers wherever and whenever he wished.

He was no longer a gentleman, so it didn't matter that he must carry a passport.

"*Je suis un journaliste,*" he said.

The officer squinted at him. "*Pardon, monsieur?*"

"*Je suis un journaliste.* A newspaperman. That is why I have been traveling so much."

The man paused, then snapped shut the passport. "*Avancez,*" he said, handing it back to Spencer. He turned sharply, as if to attend to someone next in line, but there was no one.

A young ship's officer standing just beyond gave Spencer an idiotic servile grin, as if this submissive expression compensated for the passport official's rudeness and any and all other inconveniences this voyage might visit upon him. Beside the officer was a very Dutch-looking young woman, wearing a sort of naval uniform—a blue double-breasted jacket with a thin gold stripe and shoulder boards and a crisp white skirt. Spencer tried flirting with her, but she dealt with him very seriously, in the manner of the Dutch.

"Your ticket, sir."

He handed her the envelope, which he had not yet opened. She did it for him, with a quick tear, then pulled forth the folded document.

"All is in order, sir. Welcome aboard." She said this firmly but quietly, with only the faintest of smiles softening the line of her mouth. She seemed a little nervous.

Spencer nodded and moved on, joined instantly by two ship's porters in red jackets and red pillbox caps. They were Asian, Malays or Javanese, with merry eyes and happy faces. Each took one of Spencer's bags and hurried on ahead of him, up the gangway that led to gaping doors in the side of the ship at the level of main deck. As Spencer stepped aboard, he was greeted by two lines of similar Asian crewmen on either side of a red carpet rolled out over the lobby's purple carpeting. All smiles, they chanted "Welcome, sir, to the *Wilhelmina*" in something approximating unison. The porters, quickening step, hurried him over to the purser's desk, where he was asked for his ticket again by another young officer he presumed to be the assistant purser.

"Ah, yes, Mr. Spencer of Paris. Cabin 459," he said to a clerk scribbling into register beside him. "Welcome, sir, to the *Wilhelmina.*"

Spencer was handing tips to the two porters and his attention was distracted. As a steward came forward to carry his bags to the cabin, Spencer suddenly bade him stop. He had barely set foot aboard ship and already his enterprise was in trouble.

"What cabin did you say?"

"Cabin 459, sir."

"What deck?"

" 'A' deck, sir."

"That's second class."

"Yes, sir. You have a second-class ticket."

"There must be some mistake. I can't possibly have a second-class ticket."

The assistant purser examined another ledger, then turned it around to face Spencer, his finger aimed at an entry bearing Spencer's name.

"But, sir, there is no mistake. Your ticket was paid for by check, in the amount of second-class passage. You see? All very exact. Did you wish other accommodations, sir?" He glanced at Spencer's rumpled British jacket, as if he might not be worthy of anything better.

"No. No, thank you."

He could not believe Carlson's infinite stupidity. The man had taken him off the Paris bureau's biggest story of the year, perhaps of the decade, to pursue the extraordinarily elusive Charles Lindbergh. Everything depended on Spencer's cornering Lindbergh on this crossing—on his doing so undetected by any other newsman—yet Carlson had now rendered that accomplishment virtually impossible. There was no class mobility aboard ship—certainly not upward. The wits he would need to track down Lindbergh and somehow engage him in conversation would instead have to be devoted to the task of crossing the barrier that separated second class from the upper deck exclusivity of first. Just where did Carlson think Lindbergh would be traveling? After his epochal trans-Atlantic flight, the government had sent a U.S. navy cruiser to fetch him. The fury Spencer felt for Carlson was overpowering. He was on the brink of unleashing it upon this innocent functionary.

"Is there a problem, sir?" The purser had joined them.

"Yes," said Spencer. "I'm supposed to be in first class. My company purchased the wrong ticket."

The purser looked over the various entries. "Your company, sir?"

"The *Chicago Press-Bulletin*. I—" Spencer caught himself. He had been about to identify himself as a reporter. Discovery of this could prompt Lindbergh to flee the ship here in Le Havre, or lock himself in his cabin until the voyage's end.

"My father's newspaper," he said. "My father is C. Jamieson Spencer, the publisher. I always travel first class."

His mind fetched up the remembered image of a dreadful train he had ridden through the uplands of India, sitting on the roof of a third-class coach with all the untouchables.

The purser spread his arms, palms upward. "No problem, sir. We have many empty cabins on this voyage. We will simply change your accommodations." He scribbled on the ledger. "If you will just write us out a check in this amount."

Carlson would kill him if he spent one penny more than had been authorized. He would report it to Chicago as evidence of Spencer's profligacy.

"The policy is the same for all the shipping lines, sir. Passage payment in advance." He stood with arms folded, waiting. Perspiration was flowing down Spencer's cheeks and neck.

"I'll take second class," he said uncomfortably. "For now. If it isn't suitable, I'll come back to you."

"As you wish, sir." The purser returned to other business abruptly. His assistant eyed Spencer with some triumph, as the steward took Spencer's bags toward the staircase that led to A deck one humiliating level below. Lindbergh could be as many as three decks above and all the way forward, by the bridge, where the best staterooms and suites likely were. For Spencer's purposes, the Great Hero might just as well be making the crossing in the *Spirit of St. Louis*.

Edwina Mountbatten had opened a porthole by her bed, but with the ship still fast to the dock and not a breath of wind, it only seemed to increase the volume of heat-soaked air in her stateroom. She had removed her skirt, blouse, and jacket to change into clothes more appropriate for late-afternoon drinks, though she had not decided on which. Despite her very important guest, she wore only her slip. While she pondered what to wear, she would keep herself as comfortable as she could be in this infernal sweaty sog. Holding up one dress and then another, and then another, she finally tossed them all on her bed and sank wearily into a plushly upholstered chair, picking up her glass of vodka, lemon, and melted ice.

Her husband Dickie prided himself on being able to change clothes within three minutes, to the point of designing a damned foolish set of evening clothes with zippers he could get into in sixty seconds flat. Sometimes it took Edwina hours to change.

She crossed her still quite lovely legs circumspectly. She often sat about her bedchamber *dishabillé,* but the person with her now was not her husband or a lover or a servant but Mrs. Wallis Warfield Simpson.

Glancing up suddenly from her drink, Edwina caught Mrs. Simpson staring at her. The woman blushed and looked away, but not soon enough.

A chill ran over Edwina's shoulders. There were uncertainties about Mrs. Simpson that made her very nervous. The woman was the prince's mistress, but curious things were said about their love life and of that the prince had enjoyed with his previous mistress, Thelma Furness.

Memory increased Edwina's agitation. Thelma's sister, Gloria Morgan Vanderbilt, had lost custody of her daughter because of an outrageously public scandal over her liaison with Lady Nada Milford-Haven in a Cannes hotel in 1931. Gloria's sister, Consuelo "Tamar" Thaw, another notorious lesbian, was part of the traveling party. So was Wallis Warfield Simpson. She had ended her holiday abruptly, leaving the other three behind, but she nevertheless had been with them for several days, traveling with them all across France. And she did have such a masculine face.

She had often spoken to Edwina of her beauty. Lady Mountbatten assumed it was only envy. The woman herself was decidedly unbeautiful but, in her way, despite the manly countenance, deep voice, and brittle manner, she was still oddly attractive. Her nose, forehead, jaw, hands, and feet were all too large, but harmonious when observed ensemble. She was quick, smart, and carried herself well, and her body was lean and lithe enough to show her chic, understated clothes off to good advantage. The jewelry Edward showered upon her was excessive, but she wore it becomingly.

Another of Edward's earlier mistresses, Freda Dudley Ward, was vivacious and feminine and heterosexual enough, and he had stayed with her for nearly ten years.

Edwina flushed these soiled thoughts from her mind as she might pull the chain of a water closet. They were irrelevant to the needs of her relationship with Mrs. Simpson, which was strictly utilitarian. Besides, she had had her own run-in with Lady Milford-Haven, who was married to Dickie's brother.

"We should be underway soon," Edwina said, leaning back her head and closing her eyes a moment. She thought of sea breezes with great yearning.

"I'm not looking forward to it, actually," Mrs. Simpson said. *Une belle laide,* Cecil Beaton had called her. Beautifully ugly. "I'm not looking forward to it at all."

"It's only a fortnight, darling," Edwina said with a sleepy yawn. "Think of it as rather a long party."

Mrs. Simpson took a folded piece of blue letter paper from the pocket of her dress, glanced at it, then folded it more tightly.

"He wants to have a party this afternoon, when we cast off," Mrs. Simpson said. "When everyone is supposed to be out on deck. Lord Brownlow and Fruity Metcalfe insist that David stay inside, at least until the ship is under way. They think there may be reporters about. There's supposed to be an American movie actress aboard. They always attract photographers and press people. It's so loathsome."

If she spoke so contemptuously to impress Edwina, she erred. Edwina and Lord Louis doted on actors and actresses.

"Really?" said Edwina. "What fun. Who is it?"

"Norma? No, Nora. Nora Gwynne. She's quite common. Irish, I believe."

"She's supposed to be very charming. Norma Shearer says so, at any rate."

"Duff Cooper said she gave him a violent erection in one of her films. I told him he shouldn't exaggerate." She smiled, almost sweetly. Wallis Simpson had one of the most lascivious tongues in Mayfair. It was supposed to be one of her charms. She had made a few indiscreet comments about Edwina, all of which Edwina had heard about and let pass. For the duration of her liaison with Edward, Edwina would be her friend, no matter what.

"I didn't know Duff was so keen on the cinema," Edwina said.

"Perhaps not, but he's certainly keen on his erections."

Edwina said nothing. The woman wanted something but was holding back.

"I'd really rather not have a party just now," Mrs. Simpson said. "He's so out of sorts. Do you know that silly game he plays, when he tries to build a tower of matchsticks balanced on the top of a champagne bottle? He makes everyone who's around him stop what they're doing and watch. That's what he's been doing since lunch. But the ship keeps rocking. The silly towers keep falling over and he keeps flying into a rage. It's quite impossible."

Edwina felt up to a pretty good scream herself. Instead, she drank deeply of the warm lemony vodka. "Wallis. It's because he's out of sorts that he wants to have a party. After the terrible time we had in Paris, he deserves one. We all do."

"I just don't want him to start in with that heavy drinking again."

It was the most visible measure of Mrs. Simpson's domination over the prince, her having put an end to his practice of often getting hopelessly drunk at night. If he began to lapse, some might begin to think her hold over him was slipping. She obviously was not entirely happy with the relationship, but she seemed in no hurry to abandon it.

"Wallis. You're simply going to have to indulge him some of the time. He's been indulged all his life, and it won't be long before His Royal Highness becomes Rex Imperator. That we're his friends doesn't change who he is."

"I know, Edwina. I'm much more aware of that than you might imagine. I—"

She leaned forward now, the folded blue note clenched in her hand.

"Edwina," she said, "You are my friend, aren't you?"

"Of course, darling. How could you think otherwise?"

"And I can count on your discretion? Your complete discretion?"

"Absolutely. I shan't even tell Dickie. What is it?"

Wallis leaned forward farther. Her voice a little tremulous. "I'm very troubled, Edwina."

This was a confidence already shared by half of Mayfair. "I'm sorry to hear that, Wallis."

"In fact, I'm afraid."

"We're quite safe now, especially once we're out to sea."

"No. I don't mean that. I'm afraid of what's about to happen, to my friendship, my relationship with David."

"Don't be silly. He utterly adores you."

"That's what I mean, Edwina. That's why I'm afraid."

The two women looked into each other's eyes for a long moment, Mrs. Simpson searching, Edwina watching and waiting. The whistle of some boat sounded not far away. When it ceased, they could hear the loud scree of startled gulls. Suddenly Mrs. Simpson stood up.

"Here," she said, pressing the folded blue notepaper into Edwina's hand. "I really don't want you to read this. But someone must. I have no one to turn to. Edwina, I really, really need your help."

She turned and left the stateroom in clumsy haste, banging her leg against a side table but paying no mind. Edwina stared after her, not moving until she heard the door click shut.

The handwriting on the note was compellingly familiar. The prince and Lord Mountbatten corresponded frequently—at least as much as either of them did with anyone. "Tuesday, 1:30 o'clock A.M.," it began.

> Wallis—A boy is holding a girl so very tight in his arms tonight. A girl makes drowsel, but a boy cannot. He lies awake. He will miss a girl very much tomorrow, because he must travel separately to Le Hve. But he will see her again tomorrow night and will be such a happy boy.
>
> A girl must know that not anybody or anything can separate WE, and that WE belong to each other for ever. WE love each other more than life. WE must be joined for ever and ever as one, in every way. A boy thrills to think of holding a girl's hand, if she will not mind, far out on a beautiful sea, with eanum cares left far behind. God bless WE. Your David.

Edwina sat back, utterly astonished, as she rarely was at this cynical stage of her life.

"Make drowsel," she knew, simply meant to sleep. She had overheard them using this term with one another. The "WE" was easy enough to decipher—"W" stood for Wallis and "E" for Edward. The meaning of "eanum" was beyond her, except that it seemed to connote something weak, small, and pathetic.

The essential message of the note was absolutely unmistakable, however, for all its banality. The silly little man intended to marry her. The next King of England wanted to marry a divorced, married American woman from Baltimore.

Edwina picked up her drink and began to walk about the room. Freda Dudley Ward and Thelma Furness had been ideal companions for the prince because they were so irretrievably married to men important in London society, men who conveniently viewed their wives' royal attachments as something required of their high station. Wallis had seemed almost as logical and safe a choice. Though the Simpsons were hardly so prominent, Ernest Simpson, a Harvard-educated American who had joined the Coldstream Guards and become a British subject during the war, seemed to consider Wallis's connection with the prince as something good for the family ship brokerage business. That she had been married once before and divorced had made her doubly safe. Anything beyond "friendship" with Edward was unthinkable, was too, too ghastly to even imagine.

Yet the whimpering little fool must be bent on it. He was steaming on through all obstacles toward inevitable disaster and caring not at all. If nothing was done about it, the monarchy could find itself in its biggest trouble since the rise of Oliver Cromwell. The great British general strike and the rise of the Socialists were not that long ago. Times were very, very bad for many of the people in England. They were weary of all British governments. If the common masses still held the royals above all the political muck, they would not for long once Edward's scandalous self-indulgence became widely known. And there was nothing the stuffy, imperious Windsors could do about it, save hire someone to have Mrs. Simpson kidnapped. Once he became king, their royal house was a shambles.

Edwina felt a genuine pity for Wallis. Her sin wasn't social climbing, which was a way of life for most in her circumstances, but that she had been too good at it. Her scheming pursuit of the prince's attentions had taken her far beyond the pale, and she now had good reason to be terrified. Yet Edwina sensed something else in the ugly woman—a small, still-burning hope, a little flame of unquenched ambition. It was as if deep down she somehow yet believed that it was possible for her to become the wife of the man who would be king, that for all her fears it was worth hanging on, no matter what she might be dragged through. In asking Edwina for help, she was also seeking approving counsel, some sign that what she was doing was indeed the wisest course, that the slim chance that was the object of her small hopes actually existed.

If that were the case, then the ultimate catastrophe was inevitable. Edwina had no intention of intervening. Lord Mountbatten might if he could see it coming, but of course he wouldn't. Edward's stammering clod of a brother Bertie would be donning coronation robes as George VI before Dickie caught on that he'd been backing the wrong royal.

Edwina would be discreet. She would say nothing to her husband. She would be helpful and supportive of Wallis and her pathetic little dream. She would be her friend.

God save the queen.

Edwina laughed, swallowed down the remainder of her drink, then removed her slip and stood naked and sweaty. She would have another bath before she joined the others. However briefly, she would feel good again.

Captain van der Heyden had been three times down into the bowels of his ship that morning—once on a ritual inspection of his own to make certain that all was in readiness for sailing, then again to confer with the engineer, Jan Brinker, over a small problem with the steering hydraulics, and now with van Hoorn, the ranking company man from Amsterdam, who had wanted to see firsthand the segment of electrical wiring involved in the last night's brief fire.

It was in the long bank of immense electrical boxes that constituted the main machinery supply switchboard in the after-turbo generator room. This equipment extended approximately fifty feet across, and three of the units had been scorched black from the fire and surges in current. Two of these huge boxes would have to be replaced. The surges had also burned out several of the giant resistors in the nearly seven hundred miles of electrical cable that ran through the *Wilhelmina*'s innards.

Brinker held an electric torch high to illuminate the burned wiring as brightly as possible. Some new cabling had been installed, its black covering, not yet painted the institutional green that covered the original equipment, standing out starkly, proclaiming the accident, the mistake.

Van Hoorn peered more closely, examining some splices that had been added.

"You are certain as to the fire's cause?" he said, his eyes still on the cables.

"*Ja. Maakt kortsluiting.* The resistors at the junction box were the wrong size. We replaced them. *Maakt u zich geen zorgen.*"

"I do worry, Captain. Everything now depends on the *Wilhelmina*, and she is giving us cause to worry." He frowned and patted the metal, as if trying to placate a huge beast.

"The radiator and fan circuits on each of these switchboards," he said. "They're supplied through a single-pole circuit breaker, yes?"

"*Ja.*"

"And this is controlled from the bridge?"

"Yes, that is correct."

"And in the event of fire, the radiator and fans in the affected area can be shut off from the bridge?"

"Yes, this is so."

"Well, why weren't they? You could have contained the fire much more easily."

"I don't know, *mijnheer*. I was dealing with some passengers at the time."

"Well, you find out what went wrong, Captain, before we sail."

"We are going to replace two of these units and more than a dozen resistors. Our sailing will be delayed, but only an hour or so."

Van der Heyden took a deep breath, holding back any outward sign of his increasing anxiety. If van Hoorn was trying to make a case for canceling the sailing, the captain wished he would find the fortitude to resolve the matter quickly. It was not an easy decision. Another postponement of this maiden voyage and the Lage Lander Line could find itself facing bankruptcy again. But the time for departure was nearing, and van der Heyden still had many things to do— whether they sailed or stayed.

Van Hoorn still hesitated. "You have checked the voltages?"

"Several times. All is correct."

The company man frowned, as if any statement so confident could not possibly be correct. "I want to look at some more junction boxes."

"Brinker will show you whatever you want to see."

"Please accompany us, Captain. I don't want to come to any conclusion you do not share."

Before van Hoorn was finally satisfied, they passed through the entire length of the ship. After emerging at last by the forwardmost third-class cabins of C deck, they returned up the grand staircase to the navigation deck and van der Heyden's cabin. The captain poured the man a small congratulatory glass of Bols, following company custom, but none for himself. He would have nothing to drink until after the last watch that night.

Van Hoorn set the drink aside and asked to see the passenger manifest again. He sat down at van der Heyden's desk to look through it. At sea, no one would dare do that.

"Our special American passenger? He is aboard?"

"Since last night," van der Heyden said. "He is remaining in his cabin. He will take his exercise at night. This is how he wishes it."

"Very good. And the American actress?" She must be aboard by now. We improved her accommodations. Instead of a stateroom, we provided her with one of the suites on the sun deck. The best, actually."

"A worthwhile investment of company resources. Anyone else of consequence?" He flipped a page and drew his finger down the next list of names.

"Cardinal Bloch, the archbishop of Wurtzburg, as you know. Also, an English traveling party booked passage late yesterday."

"Yes? Prominent people?"

"Lord and Lady Mountbatten, Lady Diana Cooper and her husband." Van der Heyden smiled. "And Emerald Cunard."

"What? Lady Cunard? On our ship?"

"Yes. There's a vote of confidence."

"I wonder why."

"They seem to be on a lark. Aristocrats at play, discreetly. With us they might not be noticed."

"Anyone else?" Van Hoorn was now looking very nervous.

If van der Heyden revealed the Prince of Wales' presence, he was sure it would prompt van Hoorn to cancel the voyage. The captain wanted to give the ship a chance—to give them all a chance.

"In the English party?" van der Heyden said. "I'm not sure about the others. There's a man named Principus. Edvardus Principus, according to the registry."

"Yes, I see it. Sounds Greek."

"He's blond."

"Scandinavian, perhaps. That's all? No other special guests?"

"Just ordinary passengers, although I think there are a few big bank accounts and noble titles among them. No one else particularly famous."

Van Hoorn rose and went to the porthole. "Very few reporters," he said somberly, as if that were a bad sign. To the captain, it had been an unexpected blessing.

"Six," said van der Heyden. "Four Dutch, one French, one British. I have the first officer escorting them, in case any questions come up about the fire or any of the other problems. I think they're interviewing the American actress in the first-class lounge. I'm not sure they're even aware the Mountbattens are aboard. They'll be leaving directly."

"Don't advertise the Mountbattens. We want the publicity to come on the other side of the ocean, after you've gotten them across. Then we want the whole world to know about the Mountbattens. And Lady Cunard. If that doesn't reestablish our reputation, I can't imagine what could."

"Does that mean you want to proceed?"

"Of course. Did you have any doubt? Bring me my drink, Captain.

And pour a little one for yourself. Never mind the regulations. I know you bend them on occasion."

"As you say, Mr. van Hoorn."

"Just don't burst the boilers trying to make an express crossing. Safety first, no matter how long it takes."

"Safety first."

They stood facing each other with the porthole between them. The hazy sunlight was glinting on the water below.

Van Hoorn lifted his glass. "To your happy arrival in New York, Captain."

"To the *Wilhelmina*."

"Hear, hear."

They drank, emptying their glasses in a swallow. Van der Heyden relaxed. The biggest decision of this voyage had now been made for him.

Spencer lay on his bed, listening to the sounds on the dock outside as he leafed through the printed directory listing the names of the passengers. There weren't many. As he had been a late booking, his own name did not appear. He found a few others he thought he recognized, though none were friends or acquaintances. There was certainly no name on the first-class list that might be a variation of Lindbergh's.

He dropped the directory onto the night table, hoping an addendum would be published the next day to account for late bookings. He had to find someone to get him into first class. His current situation was akin to purgatory.

The garden photograph of Whitney was atop his dresser—in this narrow cabin, almost within arm's reach of his bed. Staring at it brought back such vivid memories. One came now of her beside him in an open car, her leg pressed against his as they sped through the Bois in the dark of a warm Paris night.

He had lied to her at their last, brief, passionate reconciliation during last night's party. He had told her he was going back to Chicago to see to his affairs and end his relationship with the *Press-Bulletin*. Then he would return to Paris and live as she wished— ménage à trois, Spencer a prisoner of her money—in an idyll of museums and recitals and picnics and bistros. And wild, fast drives through the Bois at night.

Why she had believed him he could not say. But she had, with childlike happiness. In this manner he had purchased time. Whitney was his until he returned to her. If this voyage was to change his circumstances, his life, he would have the time to accommodate it, to do what had to be done.

The dockside noise outside seemed to be increasing, the activity more purposeful, the rumbles and bangings within the ship more frequent. He had hoped for time to bathe and nap before they sailed, but he'd allowed the interlude to drift away from him.

He felt the ship begin to shudder and vibrate. The steam turbines were running. Through the open porthole came music from above—the ship's orchestra playing on deck. It was time to go to work. As he had dragged himself to his airplane in the war, as he had risen from the ditch and returned to the road in China, he rose from the bed and began to change clothes, pulling a creased blue blazer and gray flannels from the closet, getting bloody on with it.

He stopped at one of the two bars in second class for a gin and quinine, then carried it out onto the promenade deck. With so few passengers, there was plenty of spectator space at the rail. He took a place distant from the merry din produced by the band, watching with some amusement as the scatterings of people on the quay below did their best to create a celebratory noise in farewell.

The elaborate holdings of hawser and rope were undone and the ship was cast off. She came away from the dock smartly, two French tugs pushing and pulling her in a tight arc until she was pointed at the opening in the breakwater and gathering speed. The water began to hiss at her sides, audible despite the band music and horns and cheering. She was departing Le Havre as a bride might a church. Streamers were being flung gleefully and clumsily from the upper decks, and one fell over Spencer's head and shoulder. He let it remain, his mind still on Whitney, lifting his glass toward land in a final toast to her. He drank, slowly, the glass as smooth and cool against his lip as her kiss.

He felt the streamer move, not falling, but as if it were being slowly pulled away. He turned, almost as slowly, and found himself looking into a woman's staring face. It was a hard face, on the verge of age, with thin, unsmiling lips. But her eyes were extraordinary—huge, a haunting blue in color, and full of madness. She was thin and birdlike, her lower arms all but encased by a multitude of wooden African bracelets. She might have been very attractive once, before her lunacy. She was the kind of woman one encountered in bars rather than cafés—the kind of woman one avoided.

A large black man stood just behind her, looking elsewhere, as if embarrassed.

"Do I know you?" she asked Spencer, her voice very British.

"I do not believe that you do," he said.

"Are you a gentleman of Paris?"

"Very much so."

"Then I must know you."

"No. Sorry."

"A pity, then. Sorry."

Her eyes never moved as she spoke, remaining fixed on his. When she finally glanced away, it was as if Spencer was released from an imprisoning grip.

"Sorry," she repeated. "Quite, quite. Sorry."

She took the black man's arm and they moved off along the deck. Spencer shuddered slightly but stared after them. Hers would likely be a story of great pathos, sin, the bizarre, and—from the sound of her accent—a high birth squandered. Altogether, it would be a much more interesting story than Lindbergh's, though that was a truth no editor of the *Chicago Press-Bulletin* would ever dare admit.

The shoreline was receding on either side. As they passed through the breakwater, small boats came chasing up, then fell away. The offshore mist embraced them, illuminated ahead by the diffused light from the setting sun. Behind them, the land now faded into dark shadows.

The ship's horn thundered with a long, final farewell blast, then fell silent. Spencer lingered, transfixed, his nostrils full of the scent of the sea, his skin fresh with the sudden coolness of the landless air. The *Wilhelmina* was into the English Channel now, steering sharply west into the orange and pink haze. Other boats' whistles and ships' horns could be heard in the unseen distance, and an occasional ghostly shape would pass by. The water was churning and spewing now at the ship's side. He turned his head to appreciate the full extent of her line, to sense her heavy load of life—cut off from the land as if by an act of God and sent into the limitless void of ocean.

Spencer suddenly felt himself utterly free of all his ties and bonds, but it was not a feeling of elation—rather, one of loneliness and helplessness. The ship sailed strongly, steadily on, but he was adrift.

# CHAPTER
## *FIVE*

Olga Maretzka had turned on only one small lamp in the cramped second-class cabin she had taken a deck below Spencer's. It was an interior stateroom, more comfortably furnished than many accommodations Olga had called her own in Russia, but it lacked a porthole. In its way it reminded her of a cell, and she had been in too many of those in her short life. She feared she would suffer one of her recurring nightmares in trying to sleep, possibly the dream about the rat.

It varied each time. The rat never came from the same place. Sometimes it crawled in under the door. Once it came out of her navel. But the ending was always the same. The rat would go to her feet, sit staring at her, then hop on her leg and creep forward, slowly, inch by inch, until its staring, vicious little face was directly over hers, peering into her eyes, blocking out all else. The only way she was able to save herself was by waking, but it was a desperate process. Sometimes she cried out.

There were other lights she could turn on, enough to make the room quite bright, but she preferred the gloom. In the bright light, she feared she might actually see the rat.

She was sitting on her bed, her long legs drawn up protectively in front of her, resting her arms and chin on her knees. Her murder of the old Pole was lingering unhappily in her mind. He was a remorseless old rat himself, a weary, used-up, furtive killer who had begun to worry more about his own wrinkled skin than his duty, and of no further use to the special committee for whom he and Olga worked. Rather he had become a danger to it—and to her. She had killed him quickly and necessarily and efficiently, escaping without notice. It should not concern her any longer.

Olga had killed many, many times now. The first job had made her vomit, though afterward had come a strange elation. But all the rest had been more or less ordinary experiences—routine missions routinely carried out and forgotten. Her last assignment had been the murder of the wife and child of a party official in Moscow who had fled to the West upon being warned that Stalin was about to have him arrested. The woman had struggled and screamed and the little boy had tried to run away, yet she had shot them both, calmly, as instructed, leaving the gore for the neighbors to see so that the killings would be talked about and leave a lasting public impression, as intended. Afterward, Olga had gone on holiday at a borrowed *dacha* near a country beach on the Moscow River. She had drunk too much vodka, found a lover, and thoroughly, almost desperately enjoyed herself.

Now she sat totally withdrawn in the shadows, nervous and listless, silent and unhappy, guilty over ending the life of that wretched and worthless old man in Paris. Her hands twitched. The door to her cabin represented menace. Beyond it was everything she feared.

That was her problem—this cabin, this ship. It represented not escape but entrapment. She was locked in a floating box. If she had pursuers, they'd need not find her; they'd need find only the box. Once they opened it, she would be but a skittering insect with no place to go.

Always in the past she'd been able to escape into great masses of humanity. Now escape was denied her—at least until she had completed the all-important task that had brought her to the old Pole's flat and to this ship, until they were once again bound fast to the land.

With escape, the mind could be free of guilt. It was the threat of capture, the threat of judgment, the fear, that brought guilt.

She was becoming as craven as the old Pole, her thoughts fixed on her survival, not on how to attain the first-class decks and rid the world of this royal parasite. And receive her just and ample reward. They had promised her a Soviet equivalent of wealth and a degree of freedom for this one. When she thought realistically about it, she accepted the chance that her actual payment would be having her brains blown all over the wall of a cell in Lubyanka, just like Fanny Kaplan—or being made to "commit suicide," and so end like the hero and martyr Jacob Sverdlov, who had arranged the execution of the czar and his wretched family, and thus his own.

But this was merely a possibility, a speculation she could cope with afterward in better circumstances. The threat against her now was more immediate and certain. Just outside the cabin door.

Her victim was out there, up there. She hoped she would be able to have a few words with him in advance of the final event. Those who claimed the right to rule simply because of their birth should understand the need for their death. She was no ideologue, but she wanted him to understand. The traitor's wife in Moscow had understood.

Olga rose, suddenly and silently, like some wild night creature from its nest. After pausing at her door, she opened it a few inches, then, hearing nothing, slipped outside into the corridor. No one was there.

She calmed herself. She was rightfully in this place. A steward had led her to her cabin early that morning. But she dreaded being seen. She did not feel comfortable in second class. It was a mistake for her to be here. The old Pole had made a major mistake, maybe a deliberate mistake, in booking these accommodations, and it could cost her life.

Hurrying out to the forward staircase, she ascended it in a great rush and reached the door leading out onto the promenade deck. Pausing again, she waited to make sure the way was clear, then stepped out into the brisk air. The ship was nearly up to speed, furrowing the water and leaving a wide wake to glisten in the evening light.

The full night was nearly upon them, a few stars bright in the murky twilight. The sea was dark. Here and there, spray and wave caps were limned by the fading glow on the western horizon. She moved along forward toward a place where she could get a better view of the first-class decks ahead and above, leaning over the rail to see past the barrier that divided the classes. Not many were about at this hour, as it was nearing time for dinner. They would be dressing, according to class. She saw one couple just ahead, at the rail, still holding cocktail glasses, and laughing. Olga withdrew to a stanchion and pressed herself back against it.

A man was visible up on the boat deck. He looked to be a crewman rather than a passenger. There was a stairway leading up to that level on the second-class side, but anyone ascending it would be extremely visible. She would be much better off using interior stairs, picking a time of day when she could pass the barrier unnoticed.

She stepped away from the stanchion, rising on tiptoe to better see the cabin lights of first class forward of her position. Women would be putting on evening gowns, adorning themselves with jewels.

"Miss?"

Olga turned to find herself looking into a dark, Oriental face. A steward had come up behind her.

"Dinner time, miss. They are serving in main dining salon. Also in restaurant aft."

"Good. Thank you much." Olga's accent was heavy and her English not good.

The little man was staring at her clothes. "Excuse me, miss. Are you on right deck? Have you become lost maybe?"

"No." Olga started walking away. After a few steps, she glanced back, too furtively. The steward had been joined by a ship's officer. She walked faster.

"Miss," said a second voice. "Wait, please."

The officer was young but wore the emblems of some substantial rank. He had a friendly face, but seemed very suspicious.

"Yes?" said Olga. "What is wrong?"

She should not have responded in English. Her accent was thick and horrible, as bad as that with which she spoke French. She should have used German. They would understand German well on a Dutch ship, and she spoke German beautifully.

"I'm sorry, miss, but this is a second-class section."

"Yes? I am second class. I have cabin." She pulled forth her key from a pocket of her long wool sweater.

The officer studied the key. His suspicion became mostly nervousness. He seemed unsure how to proceed. All that was required was to apologize and go on his way, but he had some peculiar concern.

"I'm sorry, miss, but I'm afraid I must ask to see your ticket receipt. I'm sorry, but our captain . . . well, we have some special passengers aboard, and we . . . well, I have instructions to make sure all . . . well, miss, I'm sorry, but I really must . . ."

He seemed painfully embarrassed.

"Okay. Come with me then. I show you."

She led them back the way she had come, uncomfortable as she passed other passengers on their way to dinner. They wore suits and fancy dresses, and a few glanced at her curiously. Her hand was trembling as she unlocked her door and stepped into the faint light from that one small lamp. The officer followed her inside, leaving the steward to wait in the doorway.

Olga hesitated. Her ticket receipt was in her long shoulder bag. So was her pistol.

"One minute," she said, turning away so that he could not see as she dug through her belongings.

"Here," she said. "You will see is okay."

His glance at the ticket was almost cursory. But he looked at her very intensely, nervousness, suspicion, and friendliness all mixed together. She was relieved when he handed the receipt back to her. Now he would have to go.

"It all seems in order, miss. I'm sorry to have bothered you. It was just a routine check, really."

Olga shrugged. This was a nice, inoffensive boy. If he had stopped her, others would. At dinner she would be observed, perhaps stared at, because of her clothes, because she so obviously did not belong here. This was a bad idea, a very bad idea, her sailing second class.

"Wait," she said. "I am not happy with this cabin. Are there other second-class cabins free, without having to share? Cabins with porthole?"

"There aren't all that many passengers aboard, but I'm not sure about a porthole. Those may all be taken. In second class."

"What of third cabin? Would there be rooms with porthole?" She sat down on the edge of her bed, making him look away from her handbag.

"Probably, miss, but fairly close to the waterline."

"Are they all occupied? Would I have to share?"

"I don't think so. We haven't many third-class passengers on board at all—because of the delays in sailing."

Of course. People traveling that cheaply could not afford to wait all the extra, interminable days in a hotel. They would seek out other ships. Or go back to their old, unwanted homes.

"I want then to move down to third class, to cabin with porthole. If you have such cabin, could I move tonight?"

"Certainly, miss. I'll go to the purser and see what can be arranged. Will you be dining now? In the salon, or in the restaurant?"

She remembered the beauty of her eyes and used them suggestively in turning them away from him. "No. I am not hungry now. I may eat later. Now I wait for you to come back, so I know when I can move."

"Very good, miss. If there is a spare cabin like that, I'll be back after I make the arrangements."

"Good. I thank you much."

When he had gone, she lay back and closed her eyes. The old Pole's premise had been in error. Third class would not restrict her movements. Passengers in reduced circumstances were not the only ones quartered down there. Ship's crew and the servants of wealthy passengers slept on those decks. There would be a laundry, with fresh maids' uniforms. As a servant, Olga could go virtually anywhere a first-class passenger could. They were much together in this fashion, the very rich and the very poor who waited on them.

The party in the prince's suite got under way merrily enough, with Fruity Metcalfe attending to the gramaphone and the prince's traveling valet managing drinks. This was considered part of the egalitarian fun of the adventure. The prospective king's personal manservant was supposedly forbidden to perform service for anyone other than His Royal Highness. He went about this bartending as grimly as the Pope setting to the annual washing of the feet in the Sistine Chapel at Christmas Mass, mixing Manhattans, Bronxes, champagne cocktails, and the occasional gin and It as if logging each one as a transgression to later be avenged. He had forgotten whether Mrs. Simpson had wanted a small glass of American whiskey or her equally favored Vichy water, and so made her a mix of them both. He had learned to fear her wrath, but also relished the causing of it. He had little fear of the sack, at least until such time as she became Queen of England. In the interim, he had to be treated as a man who certainly knew too much. In service for more than twenty years to Buckingham Palace, he was not the sort to reveal anything to the public. But, as the prince was well aware, he could easily be provoked into a revelatory conversation with Her Majesty Queen Mary. Edward had wanted to dismiss him, but it was now far too late.

To spite his confinement to quarters for the duration of the voyage, the prince was costumed in flagrant violation of the ship's dress code for evening—barefoot, and wearing odd trousers and a Cap d'Antibes fisherman's shirt, with blue-and-white stripes and a widely cut neck. Mountbatten was similarly dressed, but wore shoes and socks. They stood together at the bar, singing a sea chanty badly and trying to get Chips Channon, who was already dressed in black tie for dinner, to join them. The American was usually rather good at this sort of amusement, but now he felt restrained and intimidated to be this intimately in the prince's presence, despite the long duration of their acquaintance. He had tried turning the conversation to Germany, which required no effort beyond voicing the prince's prejudices, but Edward was not in a mood for politics that evening. If his guests did not quickly prove livelier company, he gave every evidence of a willingness to seek the entertainment inevitably provided by drunkenness. He was already on his third cocktail. "Chin, chin. Happy days." It was his evening's refrain.

Unable to keep up with Mountbatten's nasal singing, he halted the number they were performing and went into his bedroom to find his ukelele. When he returned with it, Mrs. Simpson, observing from a settee across the room, winced and looked away.

She was seated next to Edwina Mountbatten, but her friend was much taken up by a conversation with Lady Emerald about her daughter Nancy—making Wallis a little jealous. The two women were supposed to be her best friends in the Prince of Wales' set—indeed, her protectors. They should be protecting her now from boredom and worry, and from inattention.

Mrs. Simpson's other companions were Duff and Diana Cooper, who were not living up to their reputation as one of London's brightest and most glamorous couples. Diana, in evening gown and tiara, looked tired and bored. Duff, in black tie, seemed merely irritable. Lord Brownlow could have joined them, but he kept to himself over by the door, sipping whiskey and peering from time to time through the porthole curtains. Inspector Runcie was stationed outside, but Brownlow was taking no chances. Until this voyage was done, he feared the monarchy was in dire jeopardy.

Diana took a sip of champagne, looking pained, as if from a headache.

"We were in Devon," Wallis said, "before coming over to France."

"Yes, dear dull little Devon," said Diana, steadying her glass. The ship was rolling slightly but making good speed through the water without much pitching of the bow.

"We didn't come upon it," said Mrs. Simpson, "but I hear there's an ancient fertility statue, a Celtic thing, somewhere in Devon. It shows a gentleman in a state of profound passion. The townspeople were so embarrassed that they planted a hedge around it."

"Privet?" said Duff, as if on cue.

Wallis paused, and then gave her naughty-little-girl smile. "No, I think it's honeysuckle."

Diana smiled back vaguely. Duff stared grimly at his soft, pudgy hands, a drink in one and a cigarette in another. He wanted to get down to dinner, to meet the American actress Nora Gwynne; he wanted, too, to partake in the usual first-night-out shipboard drunk and also get a card game going, if Chips would advance him an adequate sum. Instead, he was being assaulted by all this prattle. The trouble with this party, with this entire crossing, was that they had already been in each other's company for far too long. Mrs. Simpson had attempted this feeble honeysuckle joke just two or three days before. Duff should have tried to talk the prince out of this lunatic voyage at the outset. That they were now at sea in a strange, new ship was testament to Duff's irresponsibility and fecklessness. It shamed him. To think he still flattered himself with hopes of being named minister for war.

Edwina was far more distressed than her empty chatter indicated. She'd been overjoyed to learn that her old friend Nancy Cunard had joined their traveling party, and subsequently devasted to hear from Emerald that her reconciliation with her daughter was far from complete and that Nancy was keeping herself to the second-class decks, playing the exile. Edwina and Nancy were odd as well as old friends, sharing an ardent socialism and a few mutual lovers but seldom together socially—not really since Nancy had disappeared into Paris back in the 1920s. As much taken with leftist causes as Nancy, Edwina had always come upon her trail too late—whether in Juan Miró's Montmartre or Henry Crowder's Harlem—held back by her husband Dickie and his leechlike adherence to the royal family and the Mayfair set.

"It's utterly impossible," said Emerald, jeweled fingers nervously rattling against her champagne glass. "She promised me she wouldn't bring him along. She promised me we could devote this time together to working out the problems that have come between us. Instead, she plays Desdemona to his beastly Othello. I daresay he's the blackest man I've ever seen."

Edwina glanced at the prince, who was strumming and singing an approximation of "Moon Over Miami." "This is not the most congenial atmosphere for what I'm sure is going to be a painful process for you," she said.

"Then she shouldn't have come along at all," Emerald said.

"Then you shouldn't have invited her, darling."

"Stop it, Edwina. You're being *insurgé*. This is really quite intolerable. It's almost as if she plotted to humiliate me. I'm merely trying to be a mother. It's not easy, especially for a woman in my circumstances."

When Emerald had been mistress to the endearing old George Moore and later to the fiery Sir Thomas Beecham, there was some reason to understand her "circumstances" and her neglect of her only offspring. Spending her days now wilting before the flattery of that pompous dolt von Ribbentrop, playing hostess to mountebanks and arrivistes, and suckling this childlike prince and his surrogate mother in London society were not "circumstances" that excused anything.

"If she won't come up here," said Edwina, "why don't you go down there?"

"To second class? My dear, that's just what I mean, just what she's about. My humiliation—before my dearest friends."

"She's just looking for common ground. She could have traveled third cabin, you know. She usually does."

" 'Common' ground indeed."

The prince, cigarette in mouth, had come over to serenade them. As he leaned near, Mrs. Simpson closed her eyes. Duff Cooper looked at his watch. Diana Cooper smiled, and yawned.

"I'll go down and talk to her," Edwina said to Emerald.

But Lady Cunard had returned to her public self. "Do be careful of whom you talk to if you go there, my dear. You don't want to 'darken' your reputation any further."

The prince returned to Mountbatten's side. The two linked arms and commenced a clumsy dance.

"Topping!" Mountbatten shouted above the music.

Despite the tension between them, Markgraf von Bourke and Kresse and his sister entered the elegant, dimly lit, and largely deserted first-class dining room looking the picture of graciousness and amiability, he in somewhat old-fashioned black tie and she in a sleek black satin gown that handsomely set off her smooth white skin and blond hair. They were late, almost at the end of the serving. They had waited for an invitation to the captain's table, as befitted their aristocratic rank. They waited for it much longer than the count's pride normally would have permitted, but he was strongly mindful of their need to make contact with the British group as soon as possible. And that gang, he knew, would be guaranteed the best seats in the house.

A preposterous honor, such seats, signifying nothing. But von Kresse would seek it. He would do whatever was necessary.

He inhaled sharply. Though there was no sign of it in his calm expression, his leg was hurting fearfully from the exertions of the day's long travel and he had to lean on Dagne for support. She kept her arm around his waist to hold him tightly.

The maître d' assigned them a large table near one of the large square windows looking out over the sea, now invisible in the darkness. Dagne was even more indignant than he that they had not been invited to the captain's table. Judging from the passenger list, there were very few aristocrats aboard, and—except for the incognito royal traveling party—none higher ranking than she and Martin.

Von Kresse decided to be grateful for the captain's slight. He was greatly tired, and hardly up to the conversational rigors of a formal dining party and the rituals of the ship captain's company. Glancing discreetly at the British group, he saw that the captain had absented himself from his table, leaving the ranking place there to be taken by a subordinate who looked to be either the first officer or the ship's doctor. Some of those there appeared to be Dutch—doubtless officials of the shipping line and their wives, but the rest were unmistakably English. One imposing blond woman looked familiar to him.

He turned away, gazing for a moment at the blackness of the window. "Dagne. Are those the Coopers, over to the right?"

She lifted her wineglass, peering over it carefully.

*"Ich glaube das ist richtig, liebchen,"* she said. "The aviator's unerring eye. I don't recognize the dark-haired man with them, but the old woman next to him must be Lady Cunard. *Sicher."*

"Her laughter is very shrill."

"She leads a shrill life."

"I was wrong to wait so long in the stateroom, then."

"Perhaps not. I don't see any of the others—the principals." She turned back to her brother and lighted a cigarette. "His Highness and Mrs. Simpson must be dining in secret."

"I'm sure they are staying in their cabins."

"But where are the Mountbattens?"

He smiled. "I'm sure he thinks he's as well known as His Royal Highness, and so must hide. If her dossier is correct, Lady Mountbatten will likely be belowdecks, entertaining herself with one of the crew."

Dagne studied the group again. "I wonder which of them was invited in our place. Who ranks as high as we? Lady Cunard and the dark-haired man? Perhaps one of the Dutch couples? The archbishop there? In the New Germany, this would not be."

"God outranks everyone, Dagne. Even National Socialists."

At the other end of the captain's table were what sounded like two young Americans—an attractive dark-haired and dark-eyed girl with a wide, wonderful smile and a foolish, eager boy. "There are the ones taking our place," Martin said. *"Die Jungen."*

*"Vielleicht.* They look rich, and she is very pretty. An obvious choice."

The soup arrived, and Dagne put out her cigarette. The count was staring at her, but not warmly.

"You still haven't answered my question of this afternoon, *liebe schwester*. Why is it we are in one stateroom, the two of us? Who made our booking, Reichscommissioner Goering?"

"Someone in his ministry. I was consulted."

"Yes? This is a very large ship. There aren't many passengers aboard. Don't you think we could have managed two cabins?"

She patted his hand. "It's all right, Martin. I'll be your nurse."

"I am not an invalid, Dagne. I am a serving Prussian officer."

"A serving *German* officer. But you still need help dressing and undressing."

"There are servants available."

"None that knows your every little need as do I." Her look was far too intense, far too affectionate.

"I do not think this is a very good idea, Dagne."

"All will be well, Martin. Or were you planning on entertaining lady guests?"

"Certainly not. I mean to accomplish what has been asked of us. I will not jeopardize that."

"Brave words, Martin," she said, looking past his shoulder. "But now they are going to be put to the test."

A woman had entered, hesitating nervously at the maître d's stand. She was easily the most attractive woman in the room, perhaps on the entire ship, with hair the color of late sunset and a gown the black of midnight. Von Kresse recognized her from the train, remembering Dagne's sharp comments concerning his overlong gaze at her in the station. The conversation in the long room had fallen. Everyone was watching her, causing her some distress.

The maître d' hurried toward her, but Dagne abruptly halted him as he came by their table.

"*Ober, neemt u me niet kwalijk,*" she said to him, in perfect Dutch. "*De junge vrouw,* the lady alone. If she does not wish to sit by herself, my brother and I would be most pleased if she would join us. We've only just started. The others seem to be finishing."

"Certainly, Countess. I will tell her."

He rushed away. Whatever difficulties it might face, this maiden voyage was at least assured to be a glamorous one. The maître d' had been expecting Nora Gwynne all evening, and had prepared a special table for her. She properly belonged at the captain's table, but van der Heyden had been reluctant to invite her. He had three company officials from New Amsterdam there, one of them a noted imbiber and philanderer, who was traveling with his wife. As he sought to avoid any mechanical calamities on this all-important crossing, he did not want to cause any social ones, either, especially involving anyone as famous as this American actress.

Now these German aristocrats had intruded. The maître d' had no choice but to attend to their whim, but he would find another opportunity to perform some grand service for Nora Gwynne. She was an American motion picture star and this was a North Atlantic liner in the American trade. She was more special than they.

She looked quite pale. Her hand rested on his wooden stand as if she were in need of it for support.

"Good evening, Miss Gwynne. Welcome to the *Wilhelmina.*"

It seemed to her that she had been welcomed to this ship about five hundred times since stepping aboard. She wondered if they would bid farewell to her as many times upon reaching New York.

"I'm sorry I'm late," she said. "Is there still time for dinner?"

"Of course, of course. For you the kitchens will always open."

She smiled weakly. She had worked in restaurant kitchens, briefly—in Ohio and in California. The thought of food and steamy, greasy pots and pans was far from pleasing. She'd been feeling quite queasy since the ship had left the dock. A long rest had helped, encouraging her to the prospect of dinner, but now she wasn't sure. Just standing made her feel dizzy.

The maître d' offered his arm. "You may sit wherever you wish, of course. I have a very nice table set aside for you at a window. But if you would like company, the gentleman and lady opposite have extended an invitation to join them."

She blinked. "I don't know them."

"To be sure, but on board ship, acquaintances are always made, *n'est ce pas?* They are German, from Prussia. They speak English very well, for Germans."

Lying on her bed on the gloom of her bedroom, she had found the loneliness and fear of her first days in Paris returning. She needed friends, acquaintances, someone, anyone. She did not want to dine alone. Nora had always hated that, and in California often dined with her maid.

"I—I'll eat with them. Yes. Thank you."

The maître d' took her arm, gliding her across the carpeted floor to the von Kresses. Painfully, but with no clumsiness, the count got to his feet.

"The Count and Countess von Bourke and Kresse," the maître d' said, sonorously. Then, beaming, he presented Nora with a sweep of his arm. "Mademoiselle Nora Gwynne."

She blushed. Still slightly dizzy, she almost tipped over her chair lowering herself into it, blushing all the more. In Hollywood, she was allowed to behave more or less as she wished without fear of censure. Here it seemed that her every movement was being watched and judged.

"Another count," she blurted out, as von Kresse seated himself.

"*Bitte?*" said Dagne.

"I'm sorry," said Nora. "I met a count yesterday, in Paris. A French count. We became friends. And now, here are you."

"Yes," said Dagne, with a glance to her brother. "I'm sure we will get along famously."

"You are very kind to join us," said von Kresse, his smile very charming. "It was looking to be a very dreary voyage. Your company brings us good cheer."

"Thank you." She looked from one to the other. They were a handsome couple—especially the count. He spoke English very well, and with an accent more American than British. He seemed ill, or injured in some way. A long scar cut across all of his left cheek, but it was not disfiguring. He had haunted—and haunting—eyes, and long, beautiful hands. Her image of Prussian aristocrats was the bald, monocled stereotype given Americans by Hollywood's Erich von Stroheim. Von Kresse was something entirely new to her.

The countess's English was precise, but heavily accented. She looked very much the aristocrat. Nora wondered if they had any idea where she had come from, if they even knew of Toledo, Ohio.

Her soup was served, a bisque. She eyed it squeamishly—little bits of shellfish floating in a thick pink sauce.

"I'm sorry," Nora said. "I think I've lost my appetite. I'm not used to ships. This is only my first trip abroad. I hardly ever got out of my cabin on the way over. All the rocking up and down."

"But the sea is calm," said the countess.

"Not calm enough, I guess."

"A little secret," said the count, more friendly now. "Potatoes and bread. Eat like a peasant your first day out and you can handle the rest of the voyage with ease."

"Thank you. I'll remember that. 'Eat like a peasant.' Normally I don't eat much at all." She looked back at the countess, not sure which of them she should be addressing. "Do you and your husband travel much? You sound like veteran sailors."

He seemed amused, but she did not.

"We are not married," he said. "The countess is my sister. We had the same father but different mothers, which is why I am not so beautiful as she. Yes? My mother was American, like you. She was from Virginia."

"I'm from Ohio. It was part of Virginia once, long ago."

"Ohio," repeated the countess, as if she had just heard the name of some new colony in Africa.

"To answer your question," said the count. "We travel very little now. It is very difficult for Germans to travel outside of their country these days. It is also very difficult for them to travel inside their country."

"My brother exaggerates," said the countess. "You must understand that the New Germany is undergoing tremendous change, recovering from all it was made to suffer because of the war. Some loss of personal freedom is necessary."

"Especially if one is Jewish," said the count.

Nora began to wonder if she should have stayed in her suite. "I've never been to Germany," she said.

"You must come," said Dagne. "It is the most impressive place now in all Europe. And next year the Olympic games will be played in Berlin."

"If the athletes are not all arrested."

"Please, Martin. Stop this."

"I'm sure it will be very exciting," said Nora. "But I'll be making a film next year."

"Film?"

"Yes. I'm an actress." Hadn't they heard of her? If the manager of the Ritz Hotel in Paris had known instantly who she was, shouldn't two sophisticated European aristocrats, especially one who was half American? What kind of country was Germany?

Perhaps she was being egotistical. What would it matter to these two aristocrats what she was, even if they knew?

"An actress!" said the countess, leaning forward. "Do you know Leni Riefenstahl?"

"Yes. I mean, I never met her. But I know of her work."

Nora had in fact seen only one film by the German actress-director. It had not been one released for the public cinema but a print of some footage of Riefenstahl and some other Nordic-looking women—most of them blond, like her—exercising in a clearing in the woods, in the nude. A producer at her studio, a small, bald, ugly man, had shown it at one of his parties, had shown it several times, over and over. The film had fascinated him.

"I have met her twice," said Dagne. "She is wonderful. She is Germany's greatest artist."

"Though not so great as the postcard sketcher who runs the country," the count said.

Nora wanted no part of this sibling quarrel, which seemed on the verge of becoming much worse. At a loss for what else to do, she decided to eat some of her soup, hesitating only when she realized she had picked up a teaspoon and not the soup spoon sitting now so obviously before her. Blushing again, she studied the teaspoon, as if appreciating its beauty, then set it down and picked up the proper utensil. Someone had told her a simple way to remember: with each course, take the fork or spoon farthest from the plate. But the waiter had not put the soup spoon farthest from the plate. It was unfair. She meant no harm. She tried hard.

Spencer was in no mood for dinner, or even to move from his bed. He lay on his back, his eyes still mostly on his photograph of Whitney, or the ceiling. Ostensibly he was planning his next move, but his thoughts drifted. There was a painful irony. Whitney, who loved most security and serenity, was there in a Paris torn by riots and political hatreds, while he who had made such a career of accompanying death and violence was now steaming peacefully to the isolated haven that was the United States.

He thought of Whitney's wondrous belly, the softest imaginable flesh rising in a graceful curve from fine blond pubic hair to the first hard line of rib. He had kissed every square inch of that marvelous work of God.

The isolation of his cabin was becoming oppressive. He decided he would visit the second-class bar. Someone there might at least be talking of Lindbergh. As things stood, Spencer had no more tangible evidence of the man's having booked passage than Carlson's word. Spencer had once traveled all the way from Hong Kong to Siam to report on a supposed coup and massacre that proved to have taken place largely in an editor's hyperactive imagination.

Leaving his cabin without consulting his ship's directory, Spencer had to ask directions to the bar, which was a deck below. As he descended the stairs, the door leading to the next passageway opened almost in his face. He stepped back against the wall as a ship's officer, a young woman, and a porter entered and started down the stairs to the next deck. The woman had a wild look about her, her hair too long and unkempt, her clothes old, too heavy for the season, and probably cheap. She followed the officer as if being led away, the little porter trudging behind with her old-fashioned luggage. As she made a turn in the stairs, she caught sight of Spencer in the shadows. Her startled look made him feel like a lurking footpad or cutpurse.

He found the lounge following the sound of piano music, a thin, effeminate man playing the new Cole Porter song, "Easy to Love." A few couples were seated near him, listening raptly or talking softly among themselves. Spencer went to the bar at the other end of the room, taking the end stool. The only others there were a man and a woman, seated a stool apart, but together, talking. Hearing her cool, strange British voice, he realized they were the two who had stopped by him out on the deck at sailing time—the quiet black man and the insane woman whose arms were covered with African bracelets.

She noticed him and stopped talking. Spencer wished she hadn't. He wanted only passive involvement with others this night, to observe and listen and be ignored. But this was seldom possible aboard a ship. Those with the best chance of being ignored were those who strove hard not to be.

"The gentleman of Paris," she said.

The low light made her more attractive, but no less mad. He decided she had been a beauty once, with hard, hard years coming after. She must have disliked what she had been very much—and what she was now. There was a lot of gin in her voice, but also aristocracy. Yet she was drinking with a black man, although her glass was empty, and he had none.

"May I buy you both a drink?" Spencer asked, after ordering a stinger for himself.

"The man of Paris is a gentleman, but incautious. We are a dangerous couple, Henry and I. Quite, quite. We are being made to play Alice and the White Rabbit to the bartender's tyrannical Queen of Hearts. He won't serve us together, so we are sitting separately, but he won't serve us separately, for fear we will then sit together."

The bartender coughed and looked away. One forgot the way the real world was, living so long in Paris.

"Give them what they want," Spencer said in vaguely remembered military manner. "Do it or I'll complain to the captain. I'm an American newspaperman. He'll be angry with you."

"Would we be served down in third cabin?" said the woman, pushing her bracelets up from her wrists. "Yes, yes. Quite, quite. Third cabin is for the proletariat, and the proletariat can mix and swarm and miscegenate with whomever it wishes, as long as it stays in its class. Would we be served up in first class? But of course. The upper classes are to be indulged. But here in second class, the suffocating middle class, the bloody bourgeoisie, here we are to be restricted. Denied."

"Sir, I—" the bartender began.

"Just give them what they want," said Spencer. "Don't make unnecessary trouble. They've paid their passage. Don't harass them."

"Straight gin," said the woman. "Henry would like a whiskey. Any kind of whiskey."

"A double straight gin and a double scotch whiskey for the gentleman," said Spencer.

The black man said nothing. After they were served and Spencer had signed the bill, he turned to look over at the pianist, who was playing "Night and Day." Two of the couples from the tables were dancing.

"What can I do to thank you?" said the British woman, sounding perfectly sane.

"Have you seen Charles Lindbergh?"

"Have I seen Charles Lindbergh?" she repeated. "No, but I've seen God."

"That won't do. I need Charles Lindbergh."

"Do you prefer Lindbergh to God?"

"Do you think that if God were to descend to the Earth He'd be treated any more magnificently than Lindbergh has been?"

"Probably not so magnificently. He might not get served in this bar. I think God must be black. Part of Him must be black, for the Negro people to love him so."

Ignoring her companion, she took her glass and moved down to the stool next to Spencer's.

"Do you have any cocaine?" she asked.

"Is that how you meet God?"

"Sometimes. How do you meet Charles Lindbergh?"

"Perhaps God will introduce us. But I'm sorry. I have no cocaine."

"Then let's dance. A jolly little razzle tazzle."

"The music is slow and quiet."

"All right. A quiet little razzle tazzle."

She was amazingly light, almost frail. It seemed to him he could lift her effortlessly by the wrists, toss her high into the air, break her arms with a snap of his fingers. She pulled very close to him, her face turned against his shoulder. Her dark-blond hair, to his surprise, smelled quite clean. She was wearing a very pleasant perfume. Residual manifestations of her past life, he supposed. She was an older woman, his age, a few years, perhaps, from hag. Yet he was attracted to her. It was like drinking the last of a fine but fading wine.

Whitney was so far away. He found himself directing his anger over the distance at her.

"Are you really a newspaperman?" she asked. Her Negro friend was watching them, as he sipped from his drink.

Spencer had done it again. He ought to simply wear a press card, perhaps taped to his forehead.

"Not really. My father was the publisher of a newspaper. That's my newspaper connection."

"I thought so. You seem much too well bred to be a reporter."

"Not so well bred as you."

"My father was a baronet. My mother is an heiress, from America, don't you know. As the wife of a baronet, perforce an English lady. Her Ladyship. I am simply a lady, also English. I would like to be a reporter."

She staggered somewhat. Regaining her balance, she clung to him more tightly. The pianist faded the tune and, without stopping, slid into "You're the Top."

"Why do you want to be a reporter?"

"Because I hate the rich and powerful, the privileged classes, and the rich and powerful hate reporters. Strange, isn't it? The two have such a symbiotic relationship. Reporters are history's paid spectators. I want to be a spectator when the rich are destroyed—front row, orchestra. I want to write it down and show it to them so they'll be able to see it and know bloody well that they've been destroyed."

"Aren't you rich?"

"No, no. Certainly not. I have a little from my father, but my mother cut off all the rest." She nodded toward the black man still watching them from the bar. "Because of Henry. Because of all my Negroes."

"I'd like to meet him. You didn't introduce us."

"Henry can wait. I'm telling you why I want to be a reporter. I want to go to Abyssinia. I want to go to Spain, to the Spanish

Republic. Do you know the Spanish well? They are such a marvelous people. They will be the one nation of Europe able to keep out the fascists."

"You hold out no hope for the French?"

"*Non. Rien. Pas de tout.* The French live well and think well and eat and drink well and fuck very, very well, but they're rather no good at dying, and it will take a frightful lot of dying to beat the fascists. The Spanish are good at it. They have the inner power. The inner resolve. They are born to die."

"The Spanish are simply Arabs who've taken up catholicism and wine."

"That's bitter and cruel. They are more than Arabs. They have more than temper; they have passion."

"Even for anarchy."

"Anarchy is the quintessence of passion. Listen to my poem. I wrote this poem:

> '*Love has destroyed my life, and all too long*
> *Have I been enemy with life, too late*
> *Unlocked the secrets of existence! there*
> *Found but the ashes of a fallen city*
> *Stamped underfoot, the temple of desires*
> *Run through with fire and perished with defeat . . .*
> *My loves have been voracious, many coloured,*
> *Fantastic, sober, all-encompassing,*
> *Have flown like summer swallows at the sun*
> *And dipped into a wintry world of water.*' "

They had stopped dancing. She urged him back to the rhythm of the music. He could feel her pelvis close against him.

"Your poem," he said.

"It's called 'The Wreathe.' It was in a book of poems I published. Nearly fifteen years ago. *Outlaws,* it was called. Let's fuck."

"What?"

"I want to fuck you."

"What is your name?"

"Nancy."

"What about your friend?"

"He'll be fine. He's just Henry."

Spencer was alone, adrift, on a ship, on the road in Chinese mountains, in the air in his fighter plane, floating across the yellow dead hills of wartime eastern France, the wind thrumming in the wires of the wings. Whitney was somewhere else, not in this world, in this life.

"First let's have another drink."

"No. No drink. Just a lovely little fuck precisely now, as a footnote to my poem."

Captain van der Heyden let the door slip closed behind him, then stepped through the entranceway curtain into the dim red light that illuminated the bridge of every ship at night. Only three men were present, uniforms and faces the same color in the glow from the lamps—two junior officers and the quartermaster. The latter stood almost motionless at the helm, which was on a raised platform at the rear wall, one of the shipbuilders' more pointless concessions to the past. Any wave that could swamp the bridge would be so high on the ship it would sink it.

"Good evening, Captain," said the senior of the two officers. "Did you enjoy dinner?"

"Too much talk about business." He went over to side of the bridge where his chair was mounted, but instead of sitting, just stood staring out one of the forward windows, both hands on the wooden railing.

Even so many decks above the engine room, he could feel the throbbing pulse of the shafts and turbines—a womblike sound, the constant beat of a mother's heart, constant, and comforting. Mingled with the cyclic rise and fall of the ship's pitching bow, it always brought peace to the captain.

But contentment was not what he was about this night. He turned reluctantly and went to the chart table, where the other officer was marking their course. They were well into deep water. Soon the French and English coasts would be falling far behind, leaving them to the open sea.

Van der Heyden went to the wire basket where the weather dispatches from the wireless room were deposited. The latest was less than an hour old. It noted warm and humid air lying over the Bay of Biscay and the channel approaches. That could mean fog. A static warm front was established to the north of them, but a cold front was approaching from the west. They would encounter dirty weather sometime the next day. The false October summer would at last be snatched away from them, replaced with the North Atlantic's more customary blustery thrashing.

The ship was sailing well, as gracefully as her sweeping lines had promised.

"All ahead full," said the captain.

With a clang of brass, one of the officer's sent the message for increased speed over the Siemens ship's telegraph to the engine room far below. He glanced at the captain somewhat apprehensively.

"Let us make time when it is pleasant to do so," said van der Heyden.

"Yes, sir."

The entrance curtain fluttered and young Kees Witte, the third officer, joined them.

"I looked for you in the dining room, Captain," he said.

"Captains spend too much time in dining rooms."

Arthur Rostron, a Cunard captain, had once said that a passenger liner had three sides: the port side, the starboard side, and the social side. For van der Heyden, that side was always the one to weather. In addition to commanding a new and difficult vessel on its maiden voyage across the world's most troublesome ocean, he had to play jovial host to his company's most demanding officialdom, plus perform the rituals expected by the passengers. He had tried to make Lady Cunard feel a very special and honored guest, but she had proved a snappish and unpleasant woman, assaulting the conversation with barbs and witticisms his Dutch guests could scarcely comprehend and devoting almost all her attention to her British companions. She showed no interest whatsoever in his talk of ships and the sea. She wanted only gossip, preferably British.

He had made a point of not inviting the famous American movie actress to his table, not knowing how she and the British would interact. He had kept away the proud Prussian nobleman and his sister because he thought they might be Nazis. He had enough troubles without Nazis.

"All is well then, Kees?"

The young man would be officer of the deck the next watch, until late into the night. Van der Heyden was working him now, having him deal with passengers' special problems, not out of meanness but because he trusted greatly in Kees's abilities.

"Yes, Captain. There was a fight between two of the Malays. I had them locked up. There was a lost little girl, whom we reunited with her parents, and a woman in second class who really belonged in third. It's all taken care of."

"And our very important passengers?"

"All in their quarters, behaving themselves and staying out of sight."

"For tonight," said the captain. "We have five more nights to go, at the least."

Civilization was a commodity that did not travel well. With each successive day of boredom, inactivity, and isolation from the rest of humanity and its laws and customs, passengers always began to lapse into their primitive state. Every voyage seemed to end just in time. Van der Heyden had sailed on a few ships when the voyages had ended a day or two too late.

"Don't let them get out of hand," he said quietly to Kees. He looked up to the officer in charge. "I'll be in my cabin."

"Aye aye, sir."

"Good night. Good sailing."

His cabin was just down the passageway. He locked the door behind him, slipped off his uniform coat, and sat down on the edge of his bunk. He poured himself a small glass of Bols. It would not hurt. All was well.

Spencer lay still in the woman's slender arms, still feeling the hard marks of the wooden bracelets in the flesh of his back. She was talking, and through the fog of his drunkeness and fatigue, he tried to listen. The air was heavy with the scent of their bodies and their lovemaking. He felt sweaty and physically beaten. It was she who had made love to him, not with tenderness and affection but with brutal gymnastic ardor. She knew many more things to do with hands and lips and genitals than did he, and had demonstrated them to him, but as practiced performer, not lover. He felt exhaustion, release, curiosity and gratitude, but not love. It was his impression that she felt nothing at all. She seemed as detached as a long-suffering martyr, or a prostitute. Perhaps both.

He was no innocent. He reminded himself of that. He had just committed adultery against Whitney. But she committed adultery against him, every night she slept with Monsieur Charles Antoine de Mornay.

Nancy sat up, still talking, pausing only to light a cigarette.

"But you are pleased, are you not?" she said, exhaling. "You are satisfied, fulfilled?"

"Yes. Enough."

" 'Enough.' When I was young and pretty, this dainty scrap of flesh was considered more enchanting than 'enough.' I'll thank you to know, O man of Paris, that an affair with me was often worth an entire book. You seem a literary chap. Are you familiar with Michael Arlen?"

"Not to speak ill of your friends," he said, "but I found him slick and superficial."

"And Armenian. But marvelous with words. His novel *The Green Hat?* Iris March? *C'est moi.* Lucy Tantamount in Aldous Huxley's *Point Counter Point? C'est moi aussi.* Yes, I slept with the horrid little man. Quite, quite. I've forgotten why. It was like having slugs crawling all over you."

Spencer looked groggily at his wristwatch. After a moment of squinting and blinking, he sat up.

"It's nearly three in the morning."

"Yes, well. It often is, if one stays up long enough."

"What about your friend, Henry?"

"He's fine. He always is, unless he needs money."

"Is he in his cabin?"

"This is his cabin."

"He's out there somewhere? A Negro man alone on this ship at night, with no place to go?"

"He's quite all right. He always is."

"Nancy. I must go."

"I think I rather like you, or could. I should like to get to know you."

"Yes, but not now, Nancy. Another time perhaps."

"Would you like to hear about Mother's traveling companions? Some of them might interest you, newspaperman."

"Later, Nancy."

"One of them is the Prince of Wales." She stared at him intently, but her expression was friendly.

"Michael Arlen I can believe, but I must draw the line at the Prince of Wales."

"Suit yourself. There's obviously something not quite right with your nose for news."

She gave him a chummy smile. He dressed clumsily. She didn't bother. His last glimpse of her was of her bare bony back and buttocks as she leaned over her night table, pouring a drink.

The bar would be closed. Bumping into the wall with the roll of the ship, he made his way down the deserted passageway to the doors leading out on deck.

They were in misty waters. He could see a wavecap or two beyond the rail, but nothing more. No one was in view forward from where he stood. He turned and started aft, in search of a cold and tired black man, alone in the fog. Passing under a companionway, he came across a tall figure hunched against a stanchion, a tall man in a raincoat. Was Henry tall? He had not been wearing a raincoat. Just a black sports jacket and turtleneck sweater.

His footstep quiet on the moist wood of the deck, Spencer approached, trying to think of a friendly, useful thing to say.

"Henry?" he said, touching the tall man's back.

Without a moment's hesitation, the man moved away. He didn't look back at Spencer until he was at some distance. In the mist, his face was ghostly—youthful, but forbidding; familiar, but utterly strange. It was a cold face, like the weather. It was gone in an instant. The man was there, and then he wasn't.

Spencer blinked. He could barely hold up his head. He could scarcely remember his cabin number. He needed sleep. Half a day and night he'd been on this ship, and he'd accomplished nothing except to fill his belly with too much alcohol and warm the loins of a sad and crazy woman.

In his dreams, he saw the man at the rail again. Awakening fitfully near dawn, he couldn't remember the details of the dreams, except that they had something to do with flying. He and the man he'd encountered at the rail were trying to kill each other. In airplanes. The dream left him sweating. He'd had such nights before, but in recent years there'd been Whitney to comfort him, cradling his head against her bare white breast.

# CHAPTER
## *SIX*

Kees Witte took over the watch at midnight, stepping into the eerie red half light by which the bridge was illuminated in the hours of darkness and coming to attention before the first officer, Van Groot, who only grunted. Studying Kees a moment, as he might inspecting some deck seaman on parade, the senior officer then gave Witte their current position and noted that the course changes for the watch were on the chart table. Grunting again, he disappeared through the curtains and out into the passageway. Kees presumed he was heading for one of the lounges, not for drink but to peruse the women. The first officer always made at least one conquest every voyage, though seldom was the woman his first or even second target.

Karl Poeder, another junior officer, was already on the bridge. He was three years older than Kees but had several months' less time in rank. They were friendly but not friends. The other officer seemed resentful of Kees's seniority and the trust that van der Heyden had placed in him. Kees was not going to concern himself with that this night. He kept Poeder busy at the chart table, remaining himself near the dark front windows by the quartermaster and the helm. What view there was was mostly of the open working deck at the bow. It was faintly lit with just two light bulbs and full of shadows among the coiled hawsers, housings, and other gear. The sea before them had merged completely with the murky night. Kees peered forward into the black, his forehead pressed against the moist cold of the canted glass.

The throbbing turbines vibrated the deck beneath his feet, giving him the sense of standing inside some living creature. The roll of the ship was still gentle, shifting his weight almost imperceptibly as he

126

leaned against the wooden railing that ran along the interior of the bridge beneath the forward and side windows.

The two of them spoke only infrequently, the Malay quartermaster not at all. Kees was able to tune his hearing to the ship, to every buzz and stutter of the electrical equipment, the lift and crushing fall of the bow upon the sea, the tuneful humming of machinery running in concert. He itched from nervousness, and felt the still-lingering heat of this autumn's absurd tropical summer weather. Every one of his senses was laboring hard, crowding his brain with messages. Though nothing even mildly alarming had happened, and the ship seemed as fit and sure as any vessel he had sailed on, slicing through the water like some great, eager fish, this first watch of his was an ordeal, the worst of his career at sea.

Kees had never before commanded the bridge. What he had thought would be a proud and glorious experience, one he had long daydreamed about, was proving to be unrelenting misery. No wonder van der Heyden sometimes drank.

Kees gulped coffee, cup after cup. From time to time he left the darkened windows and paced the bridge. It didn't help, and made the others nervous as well. He was already exhausted. His body ached for sleep but his mind burned with an almost electric wakefulness, a painful awareness of his responsibility and all the lives that the captain and first officer had placed in his trust.

For a moment he thought he saw a glimmer of light ahead, but it quickly vanished. It should not be another ship. None was reported in the area their course was traversing. But it could be. It always could be.

A light in the dark ahead. He remembered a translation from the Old Spanish of the ship's log of Columbus's *Santa Maria* on its first voyage: "The Admiral, being in the sterncastle, saw light, even though it was such a dim thing that he did not wish to assert that it might be land."

What might a light at sea be? Anything. On the sea, one's fears were limitless, one's expectations without constraint.

For Columbus that next morning, the mysterious light proved to be the island of San Salvador—and the New World. Kees needed no such miracle. Only the familiar port of New York. To tie up at the familiar old pier at 52nd Street. That would be New World enough. That would be heaven on earth. It was nearly a week away.

"Kees," said Karl Poeder, who had come over from the chart table. "What do you make of the English we have in first class? One of the stewards said he heard that the Prince of Wales was among them.”

Kees laughed, with something of a nervous squeak. *“De Prinz?* If he were aboard everybody would know. I think these are mostly lords and dukes—friends of the prince, maybe.”

“Lord Mountbatten, the one who’s a naval officer. He is the prince’s cousin, isn’t he?”

*“Ja,* but he’s not so much. A lieutenant commander, I think.”

“Maybe we should invite him to come up to the bridge sometime.”

“We have enough problems.”

The harsh, chilling clamor of the fire alarm took Kees by terrible surprise. He spun around, his coffee cup flying from his hand and striking the bulkhead with a loud bang.

The other officer all but ran to the panel of lights that presented an almost schematic representation of the alarm system—and the ship—an electronic picture of all twelve decks.

The twinking red light was on E deck, deep in the bowels of the engine compartments.

For a moment Kees could not move. The ringing bell seemed accusatory, informing everyone on the ship that something was horribly wrong and his inescapable fault.

He shook his head violently, clearing his mind. This alarm was ringing only on the bridge. If a general alarm was to be sounded throughout the ship, it would be up to him to activate it. He snatched up the intercom receiver and rang the engine room.

Brinker, the chief engineer, was not present. A subordinate, Berthold Ohms, answered sleepily.

“Where is the fire?” Kees asked.

“What? What is that you say?”

“This is Kees, on the bridge. There’s an alarm! The panel shows E deck. One of the circulating pumps, I think.”

“All is normal here, Kees. You may have a short circuit or something in the alarm panel.”

“Check the pumps, all the circuitry.”

“I can’t. I have strict orders to stay here and monitor the gauges constantly. I’ll send someone. But I see no sign of fire. There is no fire. No smoke. All is well.”

“I’ll check the pumps myself. Get a crew ready with fire extinguishers.”

“As you say, Kees.” He paused. They were friends for some time. “Sir.”

Kees ordered a reduction in speed to half ahead and instructed Karl Poeder to maintain course exactly. Then he tore through the curtain at the door and hurried down the passageway, abruptly stopping with a slight skid.

He was by the door to the captain's cabin. It was imperative—a company rule and a requirement of the emergency—that van der Heyden be wakened and told of everything. Yet Kees hesitated. Finally, with a grimace, he turned and slowly opened the cabin door.

He could see little in the darkness, but could hear the captain snoring, and smell the faint, smoky aroma of Bols gin.

Kees pulled the door closed and hurried down the stairs. He dared not call the first officer. That would mean the end of the captain. Kees would have to deal with this all alone.

Edwina had drunk so much that the alcohol worked on her nerves through the night, causing her to wake after only a few hours' sleep, her brain pulsing from the accumulated chemical. She was in her bed in the smaller bedroom of the Mountbattens' suite and had forgotten she was aboard ship. For an instant its rolling movement terrified her. She sat up, sweating with fear, then remembered and calmed herself. In habit, she smoothed her hair.

She rose from the bedclothes, naked as she always was in slumber, the tingling feel of the cool air against her bare skin arousing, as always. She was alone. It was a rare night that this was so.

Edwina went into their sitting room, which had one dim lamp left on above the bar. She turned it off and tottered barefoot to one of its two portholes, looking out into the gloom. There was nothing to see but a few white flecks of whitecap, but it gave her a better sense of the ship's passage. A royal passage, the vessel ennobled by the presence of the heir to the throne of the very greatest and grandest nation that there ever was. With Edward as passenger, no matter where it went, this ship had high purpose.

Edwina giggled at herself for the absurdly overblown thought. She ran her hands down her sides and over her buttocks. The coolness had vanished and she was feeling warm. Taking a deep breath, she felt woozy, though still incapable of sleep. She didn't want another drink, but she needed something to do. An odd sentimentality had come over her.

She crossed to the door of her husband's sleeping room, hesitating, feeling unusually affectionate—in part from loneliness and sexual need, but also from a genuine if half-forgotten fondness. She and Dickie Mountbatten had indeed once been a "golden couple," theirs the "wedding of the century," as some of the papers had put it.

Edwina remembered a letter he had written her, before their engagement, on the eve of his sailing for India with Prince Edward on a royal tour in 1922. "You will be my 'guiding spirit,' " he had said. He had closed with: "Bless you, Edwina, my own darling, I just love you with all my heart."

Provoked by whim, ardor, and rebellious impulse, she had taken ship to India herself, intercepted him there, and secured their engagement. At the time, his income was a little more than £600 a year, a not inconsiderable sum for a naval lieutenant. But her grandfather, Sir Ernest Cassel—the richest man in England and the best friend of the late King Edward VII—had left her a fortune of £2.3 million, which she had shared with Dickie gladly. There was more than enough for the two of them, more than enough for a dozen fashionable people to live comfortably. He was the only naval lieutenant on Malta with a cream-color Rolls-Royce, with Noel Coward a frequent guest in his destroyer's wardroom.

She had a duty to tell him of the letter from Edward that Wallis had shown her—to warn him of its unpleasant if not dangerous implications, of the folly of pursuing this royal friendship any further. Dickie's true friend was Prince Edward's awkward, stuttering younger brother Albert. Quite possibly now Albert would soon become king and his doughty Scottish wife Elizabeth queen, his decorous little daughters heirs to the throne. Edward might well disgrace himself in this fatal fashion even before he could even assume the throne upon the expected passing of his father.

If hardly faithful, Edwina was instinctively dutiful. She'd never let Dickie muck his career. Never, no matter how furious or bored she might at times be with him. She turned the knob. The bloody damn door was locked! She kicked it hard, hurting her toe. No sound came from the other side. She swore, then she laughed again, somewhat drunkenly. Edwina didn't feel drunk, but she was thinking bloody drunk indeed. She sat down in one of the upholstered chairs and turned to look at the portholes, which were limned with a faint gray light now that seemed to have no source.

He was probably sleeping in his naval uniform, lying perfectly still so as not to crease or wrinkle his clothing. The ass.

Edwina swore again, rose, and went to the bar. After turning on the small light just above it, she poured herself some vodka into a crystal glass. A mildly exciting thought struck her. The odd autumn heat was still with them, aggravated by an increasing humidity. It was a little past four A.M., and there would be no one about. Their suite was just one door from the exit to the sun deck. She had never before been naked at sea.

Her bare skin atingle, she peered out into the passageway and then, hearing no sound but that of the ship's engines and its heaving thrust against the sea, tiptoed a bit farther. Still hearing no human stirring, she stepped out into the corridor and hurried to the exit and out onto the deck. It was colder than she had expected and there was a visible mist, but she found being there wonderfully thrilling. She went to the rail and raised her glass, then took a happy swallow, coughing.

A movement to the left caught her eye. A seaman who had been standing idle on the deck stared at her a few seconds, then hurried away. She almost wished he hadn't. She pressed her belly and breasts against the metal of the railing, and drank. When her glass was empty, she found herself nervous about her nudity and suddenly very, very tired. Weaving and bumping into the walls, she returned to their suite. As she opened the door, she glimpsed another figure—a woman this time, dressed in a maid's uniform—coming toward her along the passageway. She was struck by the woman's long unkempt hair and large, haunting eyes. The maid hesitated for an instant, but otherwise paid little attention to Edwina's nakedness. Edwina hurried inside the suite, quickly closing and locking the door behind her.

"This voyage," she said to herself and Dickie's bedroom door, "is going to be far from quite divine."

Nora Gwynne bolted from her bed and rushed to her bathroom, choosing to throw up in the wash basin rather than the toilet, the thought of which only made her feel more ill. She had ignored the German count's advice and now was paying the price. She should have trusted him more.

He had intrigued her. Though stiff, formal, and possessed of the aristocratic bearing and extreme self-confidence she had encountered only in museum portraits and motion picture directors, he had a certain gentleness, a sad, lonely, and vulnerable man vaguely discernible beneath the Prussian correctness. He was in some pain because of his old injuries. Perhaps it was that.

Perhaps it was her own newfound infatuation with nobility. The French and English aristocrats she had met on this tour were none so proud as the Count von Kresse. He had given every sign of genuinely liking her, and she had been thrilled. And for all his ailments and scars, he was very handsome.

But she could not imagine herself sleeping with him. Bringing pleasure to such a damaged and tortured man required more skill and knowing methods than this Catholic schoolgirl from Toledo could ever hope or want to possess. And she found the count's sister positively spooky. By dinner's end, she had the clear impression that the sister would want to join in whatever activity she and the count might conceivably have agreed to.

Happily, there was not even the suggestion of any. Before dinner was quite done, the count had risen and kissed her hand in farewell, then limped away, the nervous sister hastening to follow after, taking his arm.

Still, Nora was not averse to a romance on this return voyage, if only as compensation for the horrible time she had had in Europe—as compensation for the wretched, exploitive love life that awaited her on her return to California, that was the unfortunate lot of every actress.

She noticed the daylight when she returned from the bathroom. She had a full day before her—almost a week of them. Time enough, she supposed, for all sorts of romantic possibilities. She had seen a number of handsome men aboard this ship.

Nora lay down upon the bedcovers, closing her eyes again, and thought of the Count von Kresse in the sky in his roaring airplane, high in the blue, a thousand miles high.

Von Kresse was in the sky in his own dreams. He was killing Englishmen, his sleep jarred by intermittent images of British pilots dying from his guns, machine-gun bullets exploding heads and shattering limbs, producing sprays of blood and engine oil, and flaming engines.

The dream produced a dozen or more airplane crashes, one after the other in quick succession—thud, thud, thud. Then a plane was falling that never crashed, spinning down through the air toward a whirling patch of earth that came ever closer but never near. The plunge was terrifying, and endless. The pilot was condemned to a limbo devised in hell, to a permanent horror, the worst a pilot could imagine for himself.

The pilot was himself. The plane was his Fokker D VII. He had had many such moments in the war, but they had always passed quickly. This was the last moment of life, the first moment of death, prolonged interminably.

He awoke, calling out. His back and leg were hurting very badly.

A sharp pain ran up his thigh to the base of his spine when he sat up.

Dagne sat up also, then quickly ran from her bed and to the edge of his. She was wearing her favorite blue silk nightgown.

"*Das verdammt Schmerz,*" he said, with a slight groan. "It started at dinner. Sometimes I wish they would just cut those nerves and let me live the rest of my life numb in a wheelchair."

She lowered him back to the pillow.

"Turn over, *bitte, liebchen bruder.* I will help you."

It disturbed him when she did this, but he hurt so much now that he welcomed her ministrations. Rolling over onto his stomach, he lifted himself on his elbows as she pulled back the sheet. With one hand, she worked the muscles alongside his spine. With the other, she kneaded his calf and thigh.

"*Nicht mehr dann das, schwester. Nur das, bitte.*"

"*Sehr gut, liebchen bruder.* I felt so sorry for you tonight."

"Last night. It's almost sunrise."

"Yes. I think we shall accomplish something today. Perhaps we may even enter the royal circle. That Duff Cooper kept looking at our table."

"He was looking," von Kresse said, halting to groan again as she touched a particularly painful spot, "at our tablemate, the beautiful lady from Hollywood."

"He looked at both of us *damen.* In any event, I think we shall be invited to join them today. It would do well for us to stay with Fräulein Gwynne as much as possible. If she will permit us."

"She seemed friendly enough. But I should remind you that our interest here is the Prince of Wales, not this Duff Cooper."

"He is a trifle plump and has a silly mustache, but he has a lovely face and such marvelous eyes."

"He is irrelevant, Dagne."

"Not at all. He is a protégé of Winston Churchill, and a confidant."

"Of course you would know that, Dagne."

"Of course. I know many things that you will never learn sitting off in Ortelsburg, reading your decadent books."

"As a matter of fact, I learned that interesting fact from a dossier supplied me by your dear friends in the S.D. But I do not feel comfortable about what we are doing. I don't feel at all sanguine. I almost think we should leave these people be and just sail on to America, and never come back."

"You are a Prussian officer. You would not permit yourself to do that." She struck the most painful spot with great determination, causing him to cry out. "And that is something I would not permit you to do in any case."

Lady Cunard slept little but remained abed late. She felt terribly isolated and lonely, though she had stayed up late with her companions and would be joining them again very soon. Nancy had done nothing to contact her—not a word since they had left Le Havre. Several times Emerald had had the impulse to call her daughter's cabin, but could not find the courage. She feared that the Negro would answer. She had never spoken to him, not even in that dreadful encounter at her daughter's house in France, and could not imagine what she would ever be able to say. "Good morning, Mr. Crowder. Is my daughter in your bed?" Preposterous.

She succumbed instead to another impulse, dialing the stateroom of the Coopers, just down the passageway.

A very sleepy Lady Diana answered. "The king is not here," she said.

"Don't you mean the prince?" said Emerald.

"The prince is not here either."

"I didn't ask for the king," Emerald said. "Or the prince."

"That was clever of you, because neither of them is here."

"Diana, come down to my stateroom. I'll order some pick-me-ups. I simply can't face the day without one. And certainly not the sea."

"Oh, Maudie sweet, I'm afraid it's simply impossible for us to face the day under any circumstance. And we're quite beyond being picked up. Poor old Duffie can't even lift his chin. He's snoring over there looking like a lovely beached walrus." She made a kissing sound. "I adore walruses, especially beached."

"Diana, I've no doubt His Royal Highness is going to require a full day of us. We should prepare ourselves. And I must confess I'm bored. I've been by myself for hours and hours and I never realized I was so utterly boring."

"You're not boring, Maudie darling. But we certainly are at the moment. I think we may even be dead. We'll do whatever His Royal Highness requires of us, but I'm afraid we'll have to do it without waking up. Bye-bye, darling. I'm asleep."

Silence followed. Emerald called the Mountbattens. No one answered after seven rings, though she knew that did not necessarily mean no one was there. She'd seen Edwina talk on through almost continuous ringing of her telephone while paying it absolutely no attention at all.

Her Ladyship then rang Fruity Metcalfe, and then Lord Brownlow, but neither responded. That would definitely mean they weren't in their cabins. Likely they were outside the prince's suite, with the Scotland Yard detective.

Emerald did not dare call up the prince or Mrs. Simpson. One simply did not risk irritating him, for sometimes he became quite angry about the telephone.

She took a long, deep breath and then reached for the phone once more. Nancy didn't answer, but the wretched black man did, almost incoherent with sleep, or something else. "What is it, Mr. Crowder?" she might have asked. "Drugs, drink, or my daughter?"

Instead she quietly asked for Nancy. Crowder mumbled something, and then Nancy came on, very sharp and crisp, almost brittle.

"Mother dear," she said. "How sweet of you to call."

"Nancy. I want you to come up here at once."

"No, no. Quite, quite. Much too terribly busy. Henry and I are thinking up ways to get our picture into the New York papers when we arrive. I thought perhaps I might have him carry me down the gangplank."

"Nancy!"

" 'The English Lady,' they'll write, 'borne by her black brute.' "

"Nancy! I want you up here. Not just for the moment but for the rest of the voyage."

"I'm more than content here, mother. These are far better accommodations than I'm used to in my travels. Quite, quite."

"I'm paying for those quarters."

"Is that a problem, mother? I heard your investments were in trouble. Perhaps Henry and I had best move down to third cabin. There aren't many there, I daresay. There's hardly anyone at all aboard this ghastly ghostly ship."

"Please don't be so difficult."

"Can't be helped. As Michael Arlen said, I'm just a more beautiful version of you."

"Nancy. I had hoped—I'd intended—that this be a reconciliation, and you won't even come up and talk to me."

"Not while your surrounded by all those toffs."

"Don't use that vulgar, lower-class word."

"Come down here, Mother. We can meet in the second-class lounge. I bet you've never seen one."

"Don't be ridiculous, Nancy."

"There are some very nice sorts down here, Mummy. I was with an extremely nice gentleman last night, in fact, and he gave me an extremely nice and very gentlemanly fuck."

"Nancy!"

"Yes, yes. Quite, quite. An actual gentleman, and a newspaper reporter at that."

"A reporter?"

"Some sort of newspaperman, at any rate. An American."

Emerald felt like screaming. "There's a newspaperman aboard and you talked to him? Do you realize the trouble you could cause?"

"Worry not, Mother dear. Your wretched little secret is perfectly safe. I actually did tell him the Prince of Wales was aboard at one point and he didn't believe me for a moment. He didn't say anything more about it. He thinks Charles Lindbergh is aboard. Can you imagine that?"

"Nancy, are you sober?"

"Why, so I am. How thoughtless of me, Mother dear. You must be scads of vodkas ahead of me by now. I'll call you back when I'm squiffy."

Lady Cunard hung up. As she knew she would end up doing, she phoned Chips Channon. He agreed at once to come over, and appeared a few minutes later at her door, wearing furry slippers, pajamas, and a dressing gown.

"I ordered gin and orange juice," Emerald said.

"Insufficient," said Chips, moaning as he dropped into one of Lady Cunard's armchairs. "Order a pitcher of stingers."

"You seem already stung, Sir Henry."

Channon had not been knighted, nor done anything to warrant it, but there was talk his name would appear on the king's next honors list if the list would be that of a King Edward VIII rather than a King George V. He had told a few close friends like Emerald that his ultimate goal was an earldom.

"Never stung enough. Not until stung to death."

"You came close last night, darling, but then so did everyone. How ever are we to survive this voyage? Not only are we being taken away from all that we hold dear, we're being taken back to America."

"Stick with the prince," said Chips, "and we shall never be far from all that we hold dear.

"Including your little son, perhaps," said Emerald.

Channon's wife, Honor, had given birth to their son, Paul, just three weeks before, yet here was Chips at sea with the Prince of Wales.

He looked sad, and angry. She'd been very unfair. He adored that little baby. But he also adored the idea of becoming Sir Henry. It was the American in him, just like her.

"I'd point out, Emerald, that I've seen much more of little Paul in the last three weeks than you have of your daughter Nancy in the last decade."

She glared at him, remaining silent.

"Sorry, darling," he said. "I forget your *travail du jour.* I say, do you know who that couple was sitting with the American actress? The Count and Countess von Bourke und Kresse. With the kaiser gone, you can't get much higher than that."

"What do you mean? Dickie's brother is the Prince of Hesse. And there's their cousin the Duke of Saxe-Coburg und Gotha."

"Hesse is not Prussia, dear one. Anyway, she's quite high in the Nazi party. An intimate of Goering's, I'm told. I don't think he's very political. A hero in the war and still quite a military fellow, guarding the Polish marches with his brave regiment. I should like to meet him. Men like him are all that keep the Bolshies at bay."

"Let us arrange a little dinner here in my stateroom," she said, wanting to make up to Chips for her thoughtless remark about his baby son. "I can't stand much more of the captain's table. When God invented the Dutch, he invented boredom."

"Topping idea, Emerald. I wonder if we could invite His Highness? He'd love to meet some new Germans. If only we could be sure of their discretion."

"I'm sure we can, Chips. The nobility, at least, are true to each other. And anyway, I've already told Joe von Ribbentrop about this crossing."

Chasey Chatham Parker, following the custom of young women at her high level of Philadelphia society, had been very circumspect about her drinking and had arisen feeling rested and refreshed. Her eager and unfortunate husband, a year younger than she, had instead been foolish enough to swill along with the English aristocrats at the captain's table glass for superfluous glass, eventually falling unconscious beneath the table. He had thoroughly disgusted her, especially when he vomited over one of the stewards who tried to help him to his feet, but now she felt forgiving.

She peered down at him closely. His face, so flushed the night before, was now ghostly pale. She stroked his cheek, though somewhat tentatively, fearing he might wake.

His mother would be displeased were she to find out about this episode, and she would hold Chasey responsible. She disapproved of Chasey, though the Philadelphia Chathams were far the social superiors of the Baltimore Parkers, the Parker's money notwithstanding. Chasey was pretty, well bred, popular, and accomplished—and thus posed a threat. Chris Parker was an only child. Since their marriage, he had been in thrall not to his divorced and lonely rich mother but to his strong and independent wife.

Chasey left their bed and went to the bathroom of their stateroom, immediately turning on the shower. As the little chamber filled with steam, she took a quick look at herself in the mirror. Dark haired, with brown eyes and flawless rosy skin, she was an exceedingly attractive girl and exceedingly well aware of it. She had a slender and athletic body, the product of ancestry and a passion for tennis, and a quick mind well trained by four very successful years at Smith College.

When not puking, her husband Chris was very attractive himself, but more in a feminine than masculine way. She sometimes thought he had longer eyelashes than she did. But he had shown himself man enough on this their honeymoon. He was an ardent and caring lover. This had somewhat surprised her.

As the steam erased her face from the mirror, she thought of the reasons she had married him. The match had pleased her mother, bringing a badly needed fortune into the family, if not a particularly distinguished bloodline. Chasey's mother's family had been in America since the seventeenth century. They made a very attractive couple. And Chris could be fun at times, at least when he wasn't drinking. He was very witty, in a boyish Harvard way. She quite liked him.

Chasey understood, of course, that she would ultimately be unhappy. He was much too young and would never catch up. He would still be a boy by the time she was beginning to worry about getting older. But for now she was pleased with her marriage. If nothing else, it was a comfortable place to rest before moving onto the next major part of her life.

With hot water striking hard against her back, she wondered what lay before them on this voyage. They had intended to spend it entirely by themselves, but, thanks to the nice Dutch captain's invitation, had been caught up in a traveling party of English nobility and thus had been rendered members of the ship's elite. Chris had been thrilled. Chasey had been flattered and amused, but also a little frightened. Chris, like his mother, was almost absurdly an anglophile. Chasey felt much more an American, at least her parents' kind of American.

One of the Englishmen, a very bright, middle-aged, and slightly plump member of Parliament, had intimated an interest in going to bed with her. She had been startled. She had little idea of how to deal with so worldly and sophisticated a man. But she had not retreated. It was an unthinkable idea, but not necessarily an unpleasant one.

Or was it? There was something about these people she found very threatening, especially to her so-very-vulnerable husband.

Chasey tilted back her head and let the hot water stream over her well-boned face. They had a secret, these people, and she was not sure she wanted to know what it was.

Fruity Metcalfe and Lord Brownlow had descended to the promenade deck and were making a perambulation of it, in need of both exercise and privacy. They had each passed a largely sleepless night, but the sight of the open ocean in daylight and the stimulating breaths of fresh sea air revived Metcalfe. Brownlow looked bored, or at least unhappy. Fruity supposed he might be worrying about his ailing wife.

"Well then," said Fruity. "We've done it. We have him aboard and we've passed a peaceful night."

"Such boastful talk makes me quite nervous. We've five nights remaining, perhaps more with the poor headway they're making."

Fruity glanced over the rail at the small, sidling waves. " 'Tis a bit slow, isn't it? No matter. The longer he's on this ship the more we stay out of trouble."

"As you keep saying. I do wish I'd had a chance for a longer call to Kitty at Le Havre. She doesn't understand this at all. She was quite upset."

"She understands the rigors of being in the service of His Royal Highness."

Brownlow frowned. His wife's illness was possibly more serious than Metcalfe had thought.

They had reached the bulkhead aft that separated the smaller second-class portion of the promenade deck from that belonging to first. The doors that led through it were locked. Turning into a sheltered walkway, they crossed to the starboard side of the ship and started forward toward the bow.

"I think I should send a wireless message to MI-5," Brownlow said.

"To inquire after Kitty?"

"No. To ask if they have any more information about all these murky assassination plots."

"I shouldn't do that, Perry. Those fellows are rather selective about their discretion. Word might get back to the king. It's well enough known that, wherever you are, the prince is likely nearby."

"Oh, very well. But I'd like to visit the signals office sometime. I'd be most interested in seeing what sort of wireless messages have been sent and received thus far."

"Not just yet, Perry. Let's poke about belowdecks. See what some of the other passengers are like."

"Did Inspector Runcie have anything to report from his sentry duty last night?"

"Only Edwina Mountbatten, going for a late-night stroll on deck—in the nude."

"My word."

"Nothing to be concerned about. She didn't notice him. No attempt to lure him from his post."

"Come now, Fruity."

"I've just now sent Runcie back to his cabin. He has to sleep sometime."

Wallis heard the prince's valet enter their suite and proceed to Edward's bedroom door. His knock was followed by some loud cursing from His Royal Highness, but she heard nothing after that. The valet had entered his bedchamber and was doubtless busily engaged in whatever ministrations the prince required. Sometimes she was jealous of these private attentions; sometimes she was just as relieved to be spared having to perform them. But they made her curious.

As she expected, there was a small blue envelope protruding from beneath her own bedchamber door. He had awakened her once during the night to borrow a headache powder, but had somehow found occasion after that to write her one of his "sweet" thoughts.

She pulled on her dressing gown and, walking barefoot to the door, retrieved the note, taking it to a chair by one of the portholes. She looked at the royal crest on the back, for a moment thinking of what her own initials would look like there. Then she tore open the envelope, with some impatience.

My darling girl,

A boy could not make drowsel, despite the powders and the lull of the sea. I feel so eanum to be these few steps from you while you sleep, but a girl must have her slumber, to be all the more perfect for a boy.

A boy loves a girl so much—every hour of every day. WE shall triumph.

E.

Wallis crumpled the note, the stiff, elegant stationery hurting her hand as she did so. They were half a day or more closer to America. She had sent a wire to her Aunt Bessie in Baltimore saying she would telephone from New York—but she did not disclose the name of the ship or invite her aunt to join her. Though that dear, generous woman was the only human being Wallis had much love for in the world, there was simply too much risk in their meeting. There were too, too many reporters in New York, and Wallis remained terrified about what might happen if the story of her romance ever became public. Especially in the British press. She had been popular enough in London society before Edward, and her status as his ostensible favorite had propelled her to the very center of the *haut monde*—the geographical locus of which was probably Emerald Cunard's drawing room.

But to step even an inch farther was the most dangerous thing she could imagine herself doing. Already she could sense a hostility and wariness growing even among the prince's friends. As for Margot Asquith and King George's court, they likely viewed her as they might some Hindu untouchable.

No matter. She would have her day.

Wallis stood, clenching and reclenching her fists in nervous habit. There was nothing she could do for the moment. Her fate was entirely in Edward's hands, which was to say, in Fruity Metcalfe's. She had great faith in the fellow, but no idea how he planned to get them off the ship in secret once they got to New York. She feared Fruity had no idea either. Her dread was that he meant to keep them aboard until they returned to Europe, all closed up in their quarters.

She and Edward had been given the largest suite aboard, but even its huge sitting room seemed small and oppressive and her bedchamber a virtual cell. Wallis had tried to look upon this strange voyage as escape and release and this new ship as a long needed sanctuary. But it had become a prison.

Her breathing was becoming rapid—a recurring and feared symptom. She hurried to the porthole, fumbled with the catches, and finally flung the glass cover open, inhaling deeply of the sea air and finding relief in the sense and view of the limitless blue-gray water that stretched to a hazy horizon.

If only she could fly out over those lapping waves, break free of this ship and all its frightful people. But she was trapped. She must go and stay where he bade her, forever and ever and ever.

Spencer sat yawning, looking blearily through the papers that had been pushed beneath his cabin door. One was a printed sheet headlined "Today's Forecast" and containing nine squares. Eight were line drawings of clouds, the sun, and whatnot, with captions reading "Stormy, Hazy, Windy, Rainy, Sun Breaking through, Cloudy, Showers, and Sunny." The ninth was a blank square captioned "Expected temperature." The square marked "Hazy" was circled. The blank square bore the figure "70 F." He was amazed. It was October on the North Atlantic, and the weather was that of the Cote d'Azur in spring. They might just as well have been sailing toward Suez.

Another paper was entitled "Ocean News" and listed a dozen items that had been picked up by the ship's wireless during the night. The beautiful black entertainer Josephine Baker had performed before the President of France at a charity gala at the Paris Opera. The Italians had bombed Adowa in Abyssinia, destroying among other things a Red Cross hospital and killing an estimated one-thousand seven-hundred people, including nurses, women patients, and children. Mussolini had turned down another offer from the League of Nations for a peaceful settlement. Berlin authorities again threatened to deport American newsmen for stories unfavorable to the Reich. Roosevelt had signed the Farm Mortgage Moratorium Act, allowing farmers to live on and work foreclosed property if they paid a rent stipulated by the courts. The acreage lost to the "Dust Bowl" had decreased slightly from the year before. The American Federation of Labor had announced plans to set up a Committee for Industrial Organization to exploit provisions of the Wagner Act that allowed them to organize by industry instead of by company. A musical by George Gershwin titled *Porgy and Bess* had opened on Broadway to ecstatic reviews.

Spencer reread the item about the bombing of Adowa, imagining the smoke and flame, the clouds of dust and flying masonry, the screams and the crying. He had once bombed marshalling yards in eastern France near Nancy. His ordnance had for once exploded, among boxcars carrying munitions, and the resultant pyrotechnics had been startling and deadly. He had tried never to think of it, but surely he had killed civilians—railroad workers, people living near the yards. Doubtless they had died just as awfully as those at Adowa.

He should be in Abyssinia, telling the good, complacent people of Chicago about these things, making them scc them and hear them, making them understand what was coming. Instead, he was on a luxury ship, chasing a phantom.

He unfolded the next paper, a schedule of the dining-room and restaurant serving times and of the day's events. There were exercise classes in the gymnasium, trap shooting and golf practice (for the first class) on the sports deck, squash and deck tennis for first class only, and games of backgammon, mah-jongg, bezique, and bridge in the lounges. The afternoon movie was *The Secret Six*, starring Wallace Beery, Jean Harlow, and Clark Gable. It was the voyage's captain's dinner that night, black tie for both first class and second, though the captain would confine himself to first class and First Officer van Groot would be host in second.

That evening and night, as every evening and night, there would be dancing in both first- and second-class lounges. The orchestra in first class was American and that in second class was Dutch.

On the bottom of the sheaf was what Spencer had been waiting for—a small beige booklet containing the passenger list as amended to include those who had booked late. With defiant absurdity, he turned first to "L," but could find no "LINDBERGH, Mr. C."—only a "LINDBLOOM, Mrs. T."

He began leafing through the pages, scanning each quickly. Some familiar surnames flashed by: ABBOT, Miss S. He had known a Stephanie Abbot, but she had moved to San Francisco and was married. CHANNON, the Hon. Mr. H., M.P. He recalled an odd fellow of that name from his preparatory school in Chicago, but this was obviously an Englishman. KUNGSHOLM, Mr. D, but his friend Dag Kungsholm, a reporter for *Morgenbladdid*, had been killed by a Bedouin raiding party in Morocco. Mecklen, Quint, Rothenberg, Tuttle, Winterling. Familiar names, but not of anyone he thought he knew.

His lamentable amour of the night before had not lied. There was a Lady E. Cunard aboard, but no reference to a Nancy. Then he found her after all. She was listed as Fairbairn, Mrs. N. She had used the name of the ex-husband she had told him about. He wondered why—to disguise Henry Crowder as a spouse? To disguise herself as a respectable person again? To make some peculiar gesture against whatever demons were plaguing her?

She had told him something about Fairburn. Theirs had been a romance, and a marriage, of the Great War—a relationship made of drugs and drink, danger and distance, horror and awful sadness held at arm's length. Unlike the lovers of all of Nancy's women friends, Sydney Fairbairn had survived the war. She said she had never forgiven him for that.

Spencer closed the booklet and slapped it against his leg. He looked up at his photograph of Whitney. Her eyes seemed to be studying him intently.

He would return to her, to Paris. He would succeed, somehow.

Third Officer Kees Witte heard voices behind him, calling his name. On hands and knees, he backed slowly and painfully out of the compartment in the bulkhead, sharp steel hard against his back. It occurred to him he had irrevocably soiled his uniform.

The face he looked up into was that of van Groot, fresh from a night's sleep. His expression was more curious than angry, but his voice was very gruff.

"Kees, are you still on duty?"

Kees looked at his wristwatch. It had been more than three hours since he had left the bridge.

"I forgot the time."

"We have been steaming at half speed. On your instructions. Not the captain's. Or mine."

"Sorry, sir. It was a precaution."

"What in hell have you been doing?"

"Checking out electrical circuitry, sir. We had a fire alarm. It appeared to be false, but I wanted to make sure, after all the—"

"Kees, how many electricians do we have in this crew?"

"Six, sir. Well, five, with one in sick bay."

"You left Poeder in command of this vessel."

"He's competent."

Van Groot's thick, dark eyebrows clenched together as he scowled. "Kees. Poeder had us six degrees off course to the north. Off course, in calm seas and clear skies."

"Yes, sir."

"I am going to put you on Schuur's watch, as assistant."

"Yes, sir."

"And I am going to inform the captain."

"Yes, sir. Is the captain on the bridge, sir?"

"No. He is still asleep. It is just as well. He has been working hard, and this will be a long voyage."

# CHAPTER
## *SEVEN*

A shaky and roughly shaven Captain van der Heyden entered the first-class dining room late that morning, finding only van Hoorn, the company director, and the young American woman, Mrs. Parker, still eating breakfast at his table.

The young woman smiled amiably as van der Heyden took his seat. He nodded politely but otherwise ignored her, despite her prettiness, which had much held his attention the night before. Her drunken young husband had displeased the captain, so undisciplined had been his behavior. For all his own problems with alcohol, van der Heyden had never himself been that drunk, on duty or off. Drunkenness was a commonplace of trans-Atlantic crossings; but boorishness was not.

"Sorry to be so late," he said, looking at his watch as a means of avoiding van Hoorn's eyes. "There was an electrical problem last night. I wanted to talk to the duty officer about it."

"So I understand," van Hoorn said. "It was nothing serious, I presume."

"*Niets belangrijk,*" the captain said, shaking his head. "A minor short circuit that set off an alarm. The third officer in charge over-reacted."

"Your young protégé, Kees Witte. You told me you had great confidence in him."

"Oh, I do. I do. He was just a little overly cautious. Better that than someone slipshod and casual."

Mrs. Parker's gray eyes were intent upon them. When they fell silent, she said, "Good morning, gentlemen," and left the table briskly, before they could quite rise.

"Why did you sit this Parker couple at your table?" van Hoorn asked.

"Rich young Americans. Lively company. I thought they would go well with our British party."

"Yet you kept the German count and countess away, along with the American motion picture actress."

"We were not certain she would be dining in the salon. Count von Kresse had her brought to his table before we could do anything about it. Why all this happy welcome to these Germans?"

"They are very important Germans, van der Heyden. We are fortunate to have them with us. And it is unforgivable for the actress to be neglected this way." He paused to dab at his mouth with his napkin. "We have a great opportunity here to make a good impression, Captain. We must not waste it."

"As you wish, *mijnheer.*"

"I wish only what is helpful to the Lage Lander Line."

"I will have the German count and his sister to my table. And of course the actress."

"I will make it up to the young Mrs. Parker and her husband," van Hoorn said. "Margrethe and I will sit at another table tonight and have them join us. I'll make it a special invitation."

Henry Crowder was in the second-class dining room, seated alone at a distant corner table, but happily there was no sign of Nancy Cunard. Spencer nodded to the colored man, for whom he felt very sorry, but went on to the other end of the room, near a window overlooking the sea. He had to admit that the preceding night was not without its pleasant moments, for all its strangeness, but he was in no mood to have Miss Cunard with breakfast. He had not eaten dinner and was now very hungry.

He ordered amply from the menu, stirring two teaspoons of sugar into the steaming cup of coffee brought by the steward. His first sip was dreadful. The coffee was horribly bitter. The steward, a Javanese who spoke poor English, had stepped away, but he hastened back.

"Something wrong, *mijnheer?*"

"Something very wrong," said Spencer. "This coffee tastes like boiled sea water."

"Sea water, *mijnheer?*" said the steward, a very young fellow with a fat, round face. He pointed to the view out the window.

"No," said Spencer, pointing to his cup. "Sea water here. In the coffee. Worse than sea water. It tastes like piss. Bloody awful."

"Bloody awful, *mijnheer?*" He peered down at the cup.

"Drink it."

"Drink your coffee, *mijnheer?*"

Spencer sighed. Whitney would be delighted with such a scene. "No. Don't drink it. Just take it away."

The steward smiled eagerly. "I take it away."

He returned with Spencer's meal—fried eggs, Canadian bacon, Dutch biscuits, French jam, Belgian potatoes. Spencer sprinkled them liberally with salt, and was not really surprised when his first mouthful of egg proved to be sickly sweet. He signaled the head-waiter.

"Oh, no, sir, oh, dear. You, too."

"Me, too, what?"

The headwaiter picked up Spencer's salt shaker, sprinkled a few grains into his hand and tasted them. "Yes, sir. You, too. Someone has exchanged the sugar for the salt at several tables. A very poor joke, sir. I am so sorry. It happened during the night. I am very sorry, sir. We shall not let it happen again. Are you all right, sir? Would you like more eggs? We are concerned about you. We shall not . . ."

"It's all right," said Spencer, waving the man away. "I'll make do with this."

Scraping the sugar from his egg, he reminded himself of what he had made do with in China. He must have eaten a dozen snakes.

"You will, sir? Are you sure? This is fine? You are not sick?"

"Fine, fine. Leave me be."

"Yes, sir." He backed away, then paused. "Sir. Please do not forget ten A.M. lifeboat drill."

"Lifeboat drill." On the tramp steamers Spencer had used for many of his travels, lifeboat drills were usually dispensed with, as in some cases were the requisite lifeboats.

"Yes, sir. Please, sir. Do not forget the lifeboat drill. Your lifeboat station number is on your cabin closet wall behind your life jacket. Everyone must take part in the lifeboat drill. We are concerned about you."

The bells ringing through the ship came as a muffled tinkling to Wallis in her bedchamber high above the lesser decks, but she was startled and alarmed nevertheless. Having breakfasted with the prince in her dressing gown, she had returned to her bedroom to change for the morning. He had gone back to sleep, complaining of his hangover, refusing to see anyone again until a curative could be produced.

All his valet and Fruity Metcalfe could suggest was a stiff drink, and Wallis feared that would only lead to another and another, all of them dragged along again on one of his binges. He was getting out of her control, he really was. For all his ardor and hand holding and pathetic, impassioned notes, he was still quite capable of brusquely disregarding her. If people called him her little boy, as she had heard, he was too often a quarrelsome, disagreeable, and most disobedient little boy.

She hurried into the sitting room, opening the door to the outside deck. Inspector Runcie's head appeared almost instantly.

"It's lifeboat drill, mum," he said. "Nothing to be worried about."

"Shouldn't we take part?" She had never missed lifeboat drill on her voyages. It was something of a superstition with her.

"I should think that would be difficult, mum."

"Go find Major Metcalfe. Tell him I want to take part in the lifeboat drill. Some way must be arranged."

"Yes, mum. I'll be back double quick."

Wallis closed the door, wishing circumstances permitted her to leave it open. Returning to her bedroom, she left that door ajar, and then hurried to the closet, pulling forth her life jacket and setting it on her bed.

She still had to dress, and quickly. Something sporty would be the most appropriate, a pair of white slacks and a light-blue blouse—shoes with low heels. She would wear little jewelry. Just the sapphire necklace and the gold and indigo bracelet.

Someone, something, struck the small of her back—hard—propelling her forward into the closet. Wallis tried to turn to face her attacker but stumbled and fell, clutching a dress that slid off its hanger and tumbled over her face. She heard the closet door closing and the sound of its lock turning. She screamed. After tearing the dress from her face, she found herself still in darkness, locked in darkness, imprisoned on a ship far out at sea with bells ringing in the passageways. She screamed again, fighting for breath, gathering oxygen to scream yet one more time. In the midst of it all, she heard the prince shouting, as if from a distance.

Spencer, secure in his bulky life jacket, stepped out on the deck. The card mounted above his cabin door said his lifeboat station was No. 11, a point aft. But the drill presented him with a wonderful opportunity. As safety precautions required, the door in the deck partition separating the first- and second-class promenades had been opened.

His invasion of the forbidden territory attracted no attention. The first-class promenade had few passengers on it. The group at the first lifeboat station he came to consisted of an officer, two crewmen, and just three passengers. But no Lindbergh. Sea law required that all passengers attend these drills. Everyone had to be accounted for—on a first-class ocean liner. He kept moving.

At the forward end of the promenade, just below the starboard bridge wing, was one of the ship's two steel motorboats. A group of passengers quite larger than the others was gathered before it, in white clothes for the most part, heads held high and stiff by their life jackets as they listened to an officer speaking to them with his back to the rail. He was telling them of the wine, beer, tinned cheeses, and other provisions stored beneath the motorboat's seats.

Spencer lingered, standing behind a tall blond Englishwoman who was chatting with a man in a mustache who looked to be her husband or lover, completely oblivious to what the ship's officer was saying. Spencer glanced over the others, recognizing the actress Nora Gwynne in profile, struck again by her beauty and also by the seriousness with which she was listening.

There was another face beyond hers far more arresting, a line of nose and jaw and dark, glittery eyes eerily familiar, a face remembered from the painful long ago of early adolescence, someone he had seen nearly every day for three terms of school, someone amazingly unchanged. Henry Channon was indeed on this ship. There he stood.

There was little reason for him to have changed, to bear the weary facial lines and vaguely haunted look of so many of Spencer's contemporaries. The man had sat out the war serving with the Red Cross in Paris.

He turned toward Spencer. He was a little fleshier now, but essentially still the same. The dark Moorish eyes were the same. "CHANNON, Mr. H., M.P." the passenger list had said. Spencer had no idea what peculiar twists of fortune could make this strange and consumingly selfish American from Chicago a British member of Parliament. Since school days, Spencer had encountered the man once in Paris during the war—they were joined at dinner by Channon's apparent friend, Marcel Proust—and again in London in the 1920s. Spencer supposed a parliamentary seat was not entirely unreasonable, given Channon's intense Anglophilia—and consuming social ambition. In any event, there he was, Henry Channon, once the bait of school bullies, now traveling in very fast company indeed.

"Henry," said Spencer. "Henry Channon. Is that you?"

The ship's officer stopped talking. The others turned, Nora Gwynne staring at Spencer with a mixture of anger and disgust. Channon blinked, then signaled recognition with a nervous smile. He nodded, rather curtly, as if that would suffice as his contribution to the encounter. Spencer recalled that reminders of Chicago had embarrassed Channon in their earlier meetings. He had abruptly changed the subject whenever Spencer had brought up their school days on that strange evening with Proust.

But the situation could not be left at that so awkwardly. Spencer did not move on. Channon finally stepped around the others and came to Spencer's side, his smile increasing a little as he limply shook Spencer's hand.

"C. Jamieson Spencer. Of all people. What interesting luck running into you."

"It's been years, Henry. I'd wondered if you'd gone back to Chicago."

Channon looked at him coldly. "Ha ha ha. Your wit is still as mordant as ever, old boy. I was back last year, very briefly, to see Mother. I'm married now, don't you know?"

"To Mary Landon Baker? I'd heard you were engaged."

The coldness in Channon's eyes turned to angry flame.

"No," he said, his teeth on edge. "To Lady Honor Guinness, daughter of the Earl of Iveagh. She's just given me a son. He's named Paul, after my friend King Paul of Yugoslavia."

The others seemed to be uncomfortable witnesses to this dialogue. Channon was refusing to introduce Spencer to them, and they were compelled to observe this strange reunion silently and awkwardly.

"Well, then," said Channon. "Here you are aboard our ship. I suppose we'll see you at dinner. You weren't about last night."

"Sir," the ship's officer said to Spencer, irritated at the interuption. "Is this your lifeboat station?"

Spencer ignored him. "Actually, probably not," he said to Channon. "My secretary made a mistake and booked me second class."

"Then what are you doing here?"

"Sir," said the officer, "if this is not your lifeboat station, you must leave. You must go to your proper place. It's required."

"Right, then," said Spencer, shaking Channon's hand once more. "Some other time."

"Indeed," Channon said. "Some other time." He emphasized the word "other."

Spencer walked away with as much dignity as he could muster, which was not much. Nora Gwynne seemed truly appalled by him.

There had been an afternoon, in a basement corridor of Chicago's so-very-prestigious Francis Parker School, when he'd found Channon on the floor with two other boys on top of him. For a fleeting instant he had wondered if it were a homosexual incident, but then he realized that one of the boys was choking Channon while the other held him. Spencer, the tallest in his class, had pulled both of them off Channon, smacking one in the side of the head.

They'd fled, and Channon became his friend, though never explaining what he had done to make his attackers so angry.

Now he was the son-in-law of an earl, and Spencer was merely a second-class passenger on a one-way voyage back to Chicago.

When Spencer finally returned to his cabin, he found the carpeting of the passageway outside soaked with water and several crewmen tussling with a hose.

"Sorry, sir, but someone turned on a fire hose during the lifeboat drill," one of them explained. "We have a joker on board."

Fruity Metcalfe entered the prince's suite with Inspector Runcie just behind him. Screams from Mrs. Simpson's room and angry shouts from Edward's halted them, Fruity uncertain where to go first. There was no man in all the kingdom more loyal to the Prince of Wales than Major Metcalfe, but the woman's screams were more compelling. He threw open her door, looked frantically about. When she cried out again, he hurried to the closet. It was locked, and there was no key. After pulling on the doorknob to no avail, he crashed against the paneling. Noting the effect, he tried again, with more vigor. A third attempt rent the wood and the door easily came open. A hysterical Mrs. Simpson, large eyes made huge by fear, was on her knees. Recognizing Metcalfe, she ceased her screams and then began swearing.

Edward was sitting up in his bed, with Runcie hovering over him. The royal eyes were red with anger and last night's drink.

"Fruity. Where the devil were you? Someone came into our suite."

"Did you see who it was? Wallis was pushed into her closet."

The prince sat up, shocked and gray-faced. "My God, no."

"She's all right. Did you see the person? What happened?"

"I saw only the door opening, and someone's hand. I shouted, and then the door closed again quickly. Always looking out for my safety, you say. Subjecting us to constant annoyance and inconvenience and harassment. For our protection, you say. And so, Fruity, some phantom enters my bedchamber unmolested, hundreds of miles out to sea. Not well played, Major."

"I'll talk to the captain at once. It might have been one of our people, or a servant, but why would they lock Wallis in the closet?" Fruity patted his royal friend's shoulder. "Well, they're gone now. It's all right. We shouldn't have left you alone." He looked up at Inspector Runcie. "We won't leave you alone again. Let me get you something for your nerves; at the very least, that stiff drink you wanted."

Metcalfe started toward the door to summon the visit, but stepped back quickly as Wallis came storming through, charging at the prince's bed. "How dare you let this happen to me?" she said, her voice low, threatening and thoroughly intimidating. Metcalfe left quickly, wishing suddenly he were home with his wife.

The captain nodded to Kees, who ushered Major Metcalfe into van der Heyden's cabin. No one spoke until the young officer left.

"Things are not going well? For our important guest?" the captain said finally.

"No. Decidedly not," said Fruity. He related what had happened to Edward and Wallis during the lifeboat drill, omitting only Wallis's obscene language.

The captain sighed, the sound concluding with a slight whispering wheeze. "I have already so many problems. Now this."

"You have to do something. It could have been someone trying to kill him. Think of that."

Van der Heyden sighed once more. "Major, forgive me. I can't tell you how sorry I am about this."

"You'll have to do more than be sorry, Captain."

The Dutchman rubbed his badly shaven chin, then shook his head. "Let me think what to do. I'll have all the ship's personnel interrogated."

"Our Inspector Runcie found a maid just down the passageway. She said she'd seen nothing."

"We'll talk to all of them. We have weapons aboard. Even two or three machine guns, I think. We can post armed sailors in the passageway. Seal off the area around the prince's suite. But you had stressed that discretion was paramount."

It was now as imperative for van der Heyden as it was for the British party. Any word of this could ruin him and the shipping line.

The *Wilhelmina* was as surrounded by potential ruin as it was by the sea.

"I would suggest that the ship be thoroughly searched. Just to see who or what we might turn up."

"Again, discretion."

"Find some pretext. A repair crew. Something wrong with the ship."

Van der Heyden nodded, sadly. "Well. That could be done."

The captain rose. He needed to think. He needed to be alone again. Van Hoorn should now be told of the prince's presence. He would be furious. Perhaps that could still be avoided, if Metcalfe and his people cooperated.

"Discretion, Major. At all costs. I have an officer—the young man who showed you in. He is very trustworthy. I will put him in charge of this."

"Have him see me. As soon as possible."

"This afternoon. After lunch, when everyone is resting. I will assign him to be the shepherd of your traveling party—your lifeboat officer, everything. I rely on him very much."

"Thank you. We'd also like to look through the wireless messages."

"That would be an intrusion, Major. May I remind you once again that this is a Dutch ship."

"I understand our lack of jurisdiction, but I must ask you to be reasonable about this. We need to know as much as possible about everyone who's aboard—and why."

"All right, Major. But please be careful. Guarding the secret of the prince's presence here is nearly as important as guarding his life."

"Thank you, Captain. I think you and I understand the situation. We're quite likely the only ones on board who do."

Chips Channon was the center of rapt attention. Edward had taken a sedative—and a drink—and was now asleep in his bedchamber. But the others had gathered in the sitting room of the prince's suite— ostensibly to comfort Wallis, but mostly to have something to do. The news of the intrusion had alarmed them, but the incident was not so fascinating as what Chips was now relating to them.

Edwina had asked the identity of the tall American who had come up to them during lifeboat drill. Channon, uneasy, had said something about an old friend from Chicago, uttering the words "Francis Parker School" with an emphasis that implied they should be impressed. This was of course absurd in such superior company and he had been embarrassed by his words as soon as he had spoken them. But he needed to give Spencer some stature—for anyone Chips knew perforce should have stature, especially someone from his Chicago past. So he had stated a fact that he guessed correctly would produce some respectful interest.

"Jamieson Spencer is actually rather famous in his way," Chips said. He paused to smile. He intended it to be a worldly expression, but it appeared as something of a smirk. "Jamieson is the one who first, well, relieved the Countess Alice de Janzé of her virginity."

He could not have produced keener interest if he'd said Spencer planned to kill Hitler. Alice de Janzé was one of the most notorious women in the British Empire.

Edwina's eyes widened. Lady Diana Cooper gave a start and then giggled. "Not sufficiently, it would appear," said Lady Emerald. Mountbatten and Brownlow looked on intently, waiting for Channon to continue. Wallis Warfield Simpson, supposed sophisticate noted for her titillating conversation, stared blankly at him, her large fingers toying nervously with her jewels.

"Who is Alice de Janzé?" she asked, regretting her ignorance. Once again she was the outsider.

"Alice de Janzé is the most famous beauty in British East Africa," said Diana, "if no longer the most beautiful beauty, though who of us is anymore?"

"She's certainly the most infamous beauty," said Emerald. "*The* vamp of Nairobi. And vamps are all there are in Nairobi."

"I've never heard of her," said Wallis. "How can that be?"

She had quite recovered from her earlier fright. A bourbon and Vichy water had helped.

"His Royal Highness met her, I think," Diana said provocatively. "They danced together at the Muthaiga Club. Poor lamb. It's said he trembled with apprehension. All those brave things he did in the war, but dancing with Alice de Janzé was the bravest thing he's ever done. That any man could do."

"He's never mentioned her," Wallis said. She inhaled deeply, as if inflating her composure. She set her large hands flatly down on the arms of her chair. "Tell me," she said. "Tell me all about it. About this de Janzé woman." It was spoken as a royal command.

"She's really quite beautiful," said Diana. "She keeps a lion. She's got wonderful dark hair and violet eyes, and wears corduroy trousers."

"Hypnotic eyes," said Chips. "The most beautiful eyes I've ever seen."

"She's had more lovers than most women have had dance invitations," Emerald said. "Josslyn Hay, the Earl of Erroll? The handsomest man in Kenya? He's been the longest. But I hear she lost him this year to a very common blonde, Diana Caldwell."

"Nouveau," said Channon. "But I'm told far from riche."

"I don't understand why Alice didn't commit suicide," said Emerald. "She usually does when a man leaves her. Her doctor must have the busiest stomach pump in East Africa."

"The poor dear," said Diana. "I've heard she thinks thirty is the end of life, and now she's thirty-five."

"And this friend of yours, Chips, was her first?" Wallis asked.

Channon settled himself more comfortably in his chair, delighted to see how eagerly all the others waited for his words.

"Alice is American also, from Chicago, don't you know," he said, "like many who've found a happier circumstance in the Old World. Bertha Palmer, for example, Potter Palmer's widow and a friend of my mother—she became a favorite of Edward VII, His Highness's grandfather."

"Get back to Alice de Janzé," said Duff, "and this historic rogering of her."

"She was descended from Scots' felt textiles, through her industrialist father, William Silverthorne," said Channon. "Her mother's family was Armour meat. They were quite one of the wealthiest families in Chicago. But far from happy. Her father drank. Her mother was slightly crazy. Alice is altogether crazy. At her coming-out party, she pulled off her dress and danced on a tabletop in her undergarments and stockings. That was in 1918."

"Is that when your friend . . . ?" Wallis began.

"Oh, no. Jamieson's denoument was much earlier. When she was just fourteen, and he but a year older."

"Fourteen?" said Emerald. "Isn't that against the law, even in America?"

"Of course. But it was her doing, not his. I was there. We had a dancing class at the Saddle and Cycle Club. She'd brought a bottle of liquor she'd taken from her father and shared it with us. Her chauffeur took them home. Jamieson lived on Astor Street, too. Apparently she had the driver stop near some bower in Lincoln Park on the way home, and, well, there you are. For all I know the chauffeur held her clothes."

"Scandalous," said Wallis. "I never heard of such a thing. Good grief. In Chicago?"

Channon said nothing but certainly could have. On his royal visit to Chicago in 1924, the prince had gotten drunk at the Saddle and Cycle Club himself, and rutted with a local society belle outside in the bushes. She'd become pregnant, the only woman known to have been made so by His Royal Highness. The husband moved the family to New York but there was no escape from the scandal, and they ultimately were divorced. Wallis doubtless knew nothing of that either.

"Alice and Jamieson weren't the scandal," Chips said, pausing to treat them to an impish grin. "It was her father, a terrible drunkard and a lecher. His reaction to learning of her amorous proclivities was to take advantage of them. Her mother had died of consumption when she was five years old, you see. After one rather dreadful incident with Papa, Alice was made the ward of her uncle, but her father still took her to Europe on occasion. Dressed her up in lacy frocks and took her on rounds of Paris nightclubs when she was barely sixteen. She became keen on cocktails and animals. Used to walk along the Promenade des Anglais in Nice with her baby black panther."

"She met her husband in Paris, le Comte de Janzé," Diana said. "He was a writer. Very, very rich."

"Wait," said Wallis. "I think I know something about this. Didn't she shoot him?"

"No, no, no," said Edwina. "She shot her lover, Raymond de Trafford, a man she met in Kenya while on safari. She had gone back to Paris to ask de Janzé for a divorce. Raymond followed after, trying to dissuade her. He refused to marry her, begging off because of Catholicism."

"Blew his bloody brains out, poor dear," said Diana.

"No, no," Edwina said. "He lived. She caught up with him in a railroad car at the Gare du Nord as he was leaving Paris. I remember reading about it. She knelt down in front of him and then pulled out a pistol and shot him in the chest. Then she shot herself in the stomach. I don't know how either of them survived, but they did. It was her fifth attempt at killing herself, and she was only twenty-seven."

"She abandoned her children," Channon continued, trying to re-gain the center of attention. "Left them with Count de Janzé's sister, saying she'd be a hopeless mother. Then she returned to Kenya for good. Took up with lions instead."

"Probably slept with them, too," said Emerald. "She was quite the one for getting sex and death all mixed up."

"Not only lions," Edwina said. "After her divorce from de Janzé— she abandoned him, as well—she actually got de Trafford to marry her. It was three years ago. They separated after three weeks."

Wallis looked down at her hands, sitting primly, knowing not what to say but fascinated with Channon's story—though not so fascinated as Edwina, who seemed electrified. Lord Mountbatten appeared uneasy.

"And she, this Alice from Chicago, loved your friend Spencer first," Wallis said. The man's name was jarring to her—not only the same as her first husband, Navy Lieutenant Earl Spencer, but in some vague way remindful of him—of something in her past.

"Yes," said Chips. "Nothing much came of him later, I shouldn't think. He was a flier in the war and then traveled. His father was in publishing. Fairly rich, when I knew him, but that may have changed, what with this awful Depression."

"And now here he is with us on the *Wilhelmina*," Edwina said.

"Hardly, darling," said Emerald. "He's in second class."

Olga Maretzka sat in her new cabin with the lights off, concentrating her thoughts, angry with herself and bitter at her luck. She had proceeded without adequate knowledge of her hunting ground and had acted rashly, without certainty, without preparation, plunging into the luxurious upper-deck suite and finding herself in the wrong place.

She put her face in her hands, saying *"Glupi, glupi, glupi,"* over and over. "Stupid, stupid, stupid." What had motivated her rashness? Her own contemptible fear. Her urgent desire to be done with this. She had allowed herself to become intimidated by the social stature of these sickening people and the strangeness of her circumstances. She'd become impatient, a deadly thing to do to herself.

Rising, slipping her pistol beneath her pillow, she began to remove the maid's costume she had stolen from the ship's laundry. In the future she would make more prudent use of it.

Spencer had taken a deck chair near the end of the second-class promenade, by the entrance to the aft lounge. Just above he could hear first-class passengers playing deck games, taking advantage of the still-warm weather and their high station. In Paris, Whitney and her husband might well be amusing themselves with games—tennis or croquet. Monsieur de Mornay was a great Anglophile.

Slouched deep in the chair, Spencer was trying with some effort to read a book, wearing gray flannels and a tieless white shirt with the sleeves rolled up. He had brought a sweater, but the weather was too warm for it.

His book was Evelyn Waugh's just-published *A Handful of Dust.* On the deck beside his chair was a copy of Guy Chapman's *A Passionate Prodigality,* which the Sunday *Times of London* had pronounced the finest book to have come out of the Great War, though Spencer preferred *All Quiet on the Western Front.* Both works had much intrigued him but he found he had no mind for them now, no more than he had for the notebook in his pocket.

He had planned to begin scribbling his thoughts and observations, distilling from them some conclusion, some idea for action. Though his encounter with Chips Channon had ended embarrassingly, it offered a chance now for some access to first-class passengers, at the least for a more specific goal to pursue.

But he could think of none. His notebook contained only two words: "Charles Lindbergh." He'd become stupefied staring at them.

He lifted his eyes to the horizon visible beyond the white-painted rail, watching it rise and fall with the gentle pitch and roll of the ship. Only the ship's wake, a broad avenue of flattened pale-blue water stretching to the end of all thought and ken, gave evidence that they were not adrift. Their course was one away from all things yet seemingly toward nothing.

He closed his eyes, trying to think of Whitney, but his mind refused her. Finally he slept.

When dreams came they were of Nancy Cunard. Fighting them, he awakened to her presence. She was sitting sideways on an adjacent deck chair, hunched over, chin in hands, staring at him with her huge, mad eyes. Her arms were still encased in those African bracelets, but she had changed her dress. The new one was very fancy, and bright red. As Spencer sat up, he saw Henry Crowder at the railing a few feet away, looking on unhappily.

"Good morning, gentleman of Paris. Did I tire you last night?"

"Worse than that, your ladyship. You seem to have broken my mind."

She sat straighter, sharing a secret smile with herself. "Yes, yes.

Quite, quite. You'll find no need for it. Not on this ship. Shall we take luncheon together?"

"Oh, no. I'm not at all hungry. I had an enormous breakfast. Full of sweets."

"Would you like some more screws? Have you had your screws today?"

"Nancy, please. I'm not much good today, really, I'm afraid. I'm exhausted. Too much rioting back in Paris. Not enough sleep. Sorry."

She shifted, moving her legs up onto her chair and reclining, her face stark in profile, an outline of beauty, filled out with haunting signs of age.

"Don't sleep," she said. "Tell me whether you think France is going to go fascist."

"Please, Nancy. I can't talk politics. I can barely remember my own name."

"You don't know if France is going to go fascist."

"France is already fascist. The whole world will shortly be fascist. It can't be helped."

He recalled the face and hair of the woman in the blue dress who had died in his arms on the balcony of the Crillon.

"Your mind is muck, O man of Paris. Go to sleep, then. We shall watch over you."

Despite her presence, he did sleep again. In time—a few minutes, perhaps hours—Nancy awakened him once more, with the rustling sound of her movement as she sat up and with the anger of her tone.

"Damn her to hell," she said. "Look who's coming. My famous friend, the predatory bitch."

Henry Crowder had vanished. Spencer saw a smartly dressed and very stylishly attractive woman coming toward them along the deck, smiling in a very restrained British way. She wore a tennis skirt, white blouse, and pink cardigan sweater, with a large strand of pearls at her throat. Her hair was dark and perfectly groomed. Her tanned legs were magnificent, her stride quick and purposeful. She had been among the lifeboat party with Channon.

"So there you are, Nancy, darling," she said crisply. "Why have you been keeping yourself from us?"

"You all knew where I was, goddamn you to hell," said Nancy. "You've always known where I was."

"Yes, quite. But whenever you were there, I was somewhere else. I was in Australia this summer. America, too."

"It's been three years, Edwina."

"Has it really? But here we are." She turned to look down at Spencer. "I don't know your friend, though he paid us a visit this morning. I was expecting you would be with Henry Crowder, Nancy. Or so your mother said."

"He's gone off somewhere. This is C. Jamieson Spencer. Lieutenant C. Jamieson Spencer, a flier in the war and now a man of Paris. Lieutenant Spencer, this is Lady Edwina Mountbatten. She's rich, and her husband's a commander in the navy, so I suppose you're outranked."

Spencer started to rise, but Edwina waved her hand in disapproval and then sat down on his deck chair beside him. He could see small lines about her face, but she was quite pretty. She seemed even more British in her speech and manner than Nancy. He found himself enormously attracted to her, and guilty again. Nancy was charity. This woman was lust.

"Why are you here, Edwina?" Nancy demanded.

"Because I'm your friend, Nancy. Because your mother has failed to persuade you to join us, which you simply must. I know she's been beastly to you, and most especially to Henry. But she does love you, and you can't continue on your separate ways. On board ship, it's quite absurd. If Henry doesn't want to deal with your mother, that's certainly understandable. But you should come. Come along with me now. Perhaps Lieutenant Spencer would like to join us. He's a friend of Chips's you know. Did you know Chips Channon is with us?"

She leaned back slightly, pressing the curve of her left buttock against Spencer's hip. He was reminded of Whitney, but he chased her from his mind.

"Chips is an odious little snob," Nancy said.

"Quite," said Edwina. "But also your mother's closest friend, and indispensable to our party."

"The hell with your party, Edwina. If you were true to yourself, you'd have nothing to do with any of them."

"I'm true to Dickie," Edwina said, "and so I must have to do with them. They're everything to him."

"True to Dickie?" Nancy's voice was shrill.

"In a sense, an important sense."

"True to Dickie?" Nancy stood, clasping her arms and her bracelets. She laughed, the sound like ice shattering, then turned and walked away, her arms still folded, her head tilted back, as if she were talking to God. "True to Dickie?"

God did not answer her. When she was gone, Edwina turned around, her hip and thigh now pressed fully against Spencer.

"Poor dear," she said. "I'm really quite fond of her, but I'm afraid there's nothing to be done." She smiled, this time with warmth and friendliness and interest. "I do think you should join us, though. We can't have a friend of Chips's locked away back here in second class with all the bourgeoisie, now can we?"

"*Tout le monde sont bourgeoisie.* It's the human condition."

"Don't be vulgar. Now come along, Lieutenant Spencer. I'm going to stand you to a drink."

"I've not been a lieutenant since 1919."

"Well, we have to call you something, don't we? Now come along."

She led him, with some haste, to a bar just off the second-class lounge where they each had a quick pink gin, a Royal Navy drink for which she seemed to have developed a marked fondness. Edwina said very little, while talking constantly, conducting a monologue about the rigors of air travel from Australia. She was nervous now, impatient.

"Can't stand traveling, really," she said. "But then I can't stand not traveling either. Mine's a very frustrating life." She gave him a neat but mischievous smile. "What is your cabin number, Lieutenant Spencer?"

He hesitated, then told her. She took a small gold notebook and gold pen from her handbag and made a notation in it, with much satisfaction.

"Now," she said, rising. "Let us have a tour of it."

"Of my cabin?"

"Yes. I want to see if it's suitable. To see if I can't make you agree that you'll be much happier in first class. Come."

Holding his hand tightly, Edwina took him down the passageway as a jailer might a prisoner, demanding his key as they approached his door. Inside, she noticed the photograph of Whitney and went up to it, studying it as if it were an interesting painting.

"French?" she asked.

"American. Her husband's French."

"Rather too young for you, don't you think?"

"Sometimes." He frowned.

"No substitute for experience," she said, setting the photograph face down. She came up to him and kissed him, urgently and hungrily, both arms around his neck. Then she pushed him gently down into a chair and stepped back, slipping off her sweater.

"You will find me quite beautiful," she said. Her skirt followed, falling almost silently to the floor. Gracefully she removed her blouse and then the satin slip beneath. She was wearing no brassiere. Her breasts were small and lovely. She lifted them gently with her hands.

"Not bad, Lieutenant?"

"Exquisite, your ladyship." He was not merely abandoning Whitney; he was plunging recklessly away from her, out of their relationship into a maddening unknown.

All that remained were Edwina's stockings and lace underdrawers. She turned her back to him. Bending forward, she gracefully pulled the stockings down and off, draping them on a chair. Then with a slight wiggle, she lowered the last garment to the floor, stepping out of it and then standing motionless. Her body was very firm and trim, her buttocks white and smooth, her arms, legs, and back very tan, her skin lustrous in the hazy sunlight from the porthole.

"Now you, darling," she said, still with her back to him. "I hate to watch men undress. You look so silly taking off your socks."

He rose, competing urges compelling him to choose between doing as she commanded and fleeing out the door.

"I'm ready," he said, when he was.

"Come to me, then," she said, still facing away. "Come close."

He went up to her and reached around her arms to cup her breasts and kiss the back of her neck. He felt her shiver, happily.

"Come closer, darling. Very close. I want to feel you."

He did as bidden, pressing against her, blood racing.

"Oh, lovely lovely lovely, my dearest darling Lieutenant Spencer."

He slid his hands slowly down her belly, but suddenly she pulled away. She turned to face him, taking his hands but stepping back.

"Why, you're beautiful, as well," she said, and glanced down. "Perfect. Perfect, my darling." She touched a rough, disfigured patch of flesh on his thigh. "From the war?"

"Yes. A burn."

"Does it still hurt?"

"No." He was breathing rapidly. "Just the memory of it."

"I won't make you hurt, darling." She pulled him gently toward the bed. "Now show me all the things that you know. And I'll show you all I know. We must know many, many things, you and I, my darling perfect aviator from the war."

Afterward, eyes closed, he savored the memory of the scent of her neck and cheek and hair and the driving, muscular grasp of her loins and the silkiness of the small of her back. He rolled over, breathing slowly now, and deeply. Never in the war, never in the singsong houses of Shanghai, had he experienced anything like this. He still loved Whitney—he told himself this almost angrily—but Whitney had never given him what this woman had just done.

Lady Mountbatten moved on top of him, leaning on her elbows, looking dreamily into his eyes.

"Not bad, Lieutenant?" she said.

"No, ma'am."

"Bloody marvelous?"

"Bloody marvelous."

"Better than crazy Alice?"

"Than who?"

"La Comtesse Alice de Janzé."

"How in hell do you know about Alice de Janzé?"

"Anyone who's been to British East Africa knows about Alice de Janzé."

"How do you know about Alice and me?"

"Your chatty friend, Chips Channon, darling. He told a most amusing tale. Of sweet, young love, in some place called Lincoln Park."

"My chatty friend, Chips, is a rotten son of a bitch."

"Quite, and common as dirt. But don't be offended. He spoke of it rather proudly. After all, Alice is rather a legend."

"Is that why you sought me out?"

"That begs the question. Was I better than Alice de Janzé?"

He remembered a dusk and distant traffic moving along the lake shore in a migration of pale yellow headlights. He remembered a face little more than a child's and wide, wild, excited eyes, underclothing pulled down and the midwestern air cold against their partial nakedness. He remembered clumsiness, and pain. Afterward she had laughed, but also cried. He had felt like doing the same. He had felt so sorry for her, and for himself. It had been worse than shame.

"It is a silly question, your ladyship. Of course you are."

She stroked his cheek with the backs of her fingers.

"You dear, dear thing." She smiled. "We shall have dinner together tonight, you and I. Here in second class. And afterward I'll have a surprise for you. A marvelous surprise."

As Captain van der Heyden permitted, Major Metcalfe and Lord Brownlow went through the wireless messages in Signal Officer

Brevoort's cabin, under his stern supervision. Those in Dutch they automatically disregarded. Their last-minute, almost random choice of this ship virtually precluded any involvement by ship's crew or the *Wilhelmina*'s initial passenger complement in any action against the prince.

The others included one from Lord Mountbatten, who, ignoring their agreement, had sent a signal to his fleet headquarters on Malta advising them he could be reached on this ship. There were some American and English messages apparently relating to commercial business. Emerald Cunard had sent one to her butler regarding the cancellation of a social event. A French woman had informed her husband in Lyon that all was well, and there were a number of signals in German. Two, sent on separate days, repeated the same message: *"Ein gut Reise. Ich bin gar nicht seekrank."* "A good trip. I'm not at all seasick."

It was sent by a Herr Braun.

"Who is Herr Braun?" Metcalfe asked.

Signal Officer Brevoort shook his head. "A male passenger. First class. That's all I know."

"Was he on the original passenger list, or one of the later ones, like us?"

"I will inquire," said Brevoort.

"Discreetly," said Metcalfe.

Brevoort's cabin telephone rang. To his surprise, and apparent displeasure, it was for the major.

It was Runcie, rather upset. "More trouble, Major. You'd best hop it back here."

"The intruder again?"

"No, no. Nothing like that. It's Commander Mountbatten, sir. He's trying to organize a game of tug o' war with the crew for His Royal Highness."

"Tug of war?"

"Something they did on the *Berengaria*, on His Highness's first crossing to America. You'd best hop it, sir."

The distance was not far. Metcalfe ran, with Brownlow puffing after. They found a small group on the boat deck. It included five Indonesian crewmen, Mountbatten, Duff Cooper, and Edward—His Highness wearing dark glasses and stripped to the waist. He was very fond of going about half naked. His father had insisted on absolute power of decision over his heir's dress from the time Edward was an infant until he went to the front in the war. Edward now flouted him whenever possible.

"Thank heavens you've come, Metcalfe," said Mountbatten. "We've only the three of us for the British team. Chips won't play. Afraid he'll hurt himself, no doubt."

Metcalfe shook his head. "Lord Mountbatten. Can it really, possibly, actually be true that the Royal Navy has seen fit to give you command of a destroyer? Do you really think this sort of spectacle on the first-class deck is what His Royal Highness needs at this juncture?"

"Now, Fruity," said the prince. "We're just trying to have our bit of fun."

Olga heard them coming down the passageway, knocking on doors, a terrifying thing to hear—in her country. She heard them at the cabin next to her, surprised to learn it was occupied. The voices were amazingly clear. They included that of a ship's officer, who sounded both young and familiar.

She was surprised by this search. Another mistake, a dangerous one. The pistol was under her pillow. The maid's uniform was in her laundry bag. She should have long ago found a secure hiding place for both outside her cabin.

Olga had to act, at once. There was no place to put the revolver. She had to keep them away from her bed.

Hearing the young officer's voice again, recognizing it, she knew at once what to do.

Kees and his search party, consisting of a steward and two seamen, moved on to the next cabin. Kees was weary, yet there were many more to go. None could be passed up. He had two other search parties working other decks of the ship but this would take the entire day. They had yet to finish interviewing all the servants on the ship.

He rapped on the door with some insistence. He desperately wanted to get this ordeal over with.

There was no answer. He knocked again and then again. He knew for certain this was an occupied cabin. As they had been ordered to do, he then opened the door with his pass key, hearing someone murmur just as he flicked on the light.

A young woman was on the bed. As she opened her eyes, he recognized her and remembered what cabin this was. She was the girl he had moved down from second class. She was completely naked, lying atop the sheets of her bed, legs sprawled.

Kees stammered an apology and backed quickly away, closing the door tightly behind him.

"It's all right," he said to the steward. "I know her."

The Parkers had been dressing for dinner when the knock came from the messenger bearing the invitation from van Hoorn. Young Parker, still inserting his shirt studs, took the envelope from the crewman with anticipatory pleasure. Not only would they be at the captain's table for the captain's dinner, but were probably being invited to a private party, as well—likely hosted by the British aristocrats they had met the night before. Somehow, he and his lovely, dark-haired wife had impressed them. He'd gotten sick, to be sure, but they'd had a swell, happy time beforehand.

He tore the envelope open, read it twice, then angrily crumpled it and threw it against the wall.

"Is something wrong, Chris?" Chasey asked. She was standing in her slip in stocking feet, brushing her hair.

"Everything is wrong. Damn it all!"

"Did you get a message from home?"

"No, damn it. It's an invitation to dinner. The wrong invitation."

There were tears in his eyes. She studied him a moment, then retrieved the note from the floor.

"It's from that Mr. van Hoorn," she said. "He's asked us to dine with him and his wife. What's wrong with that?"

"It means we won't be sitting at the captain's table."

"I suppose it does, but so what? Van Hoorn is a director of the Lage Lander Line. He's one of the captain's bosses."

"You don't understand." The tears were flowing now. "We were at the captain's table. Now we're not. We've been rejected."

"Oh, Chris. Stop it." She put her arms around him. "We're having a wonderful time. It was wonderful on the boat going over, it was wonderful in France and Spain. It's been wonderful coming back. It doesn't matter where we sit. We'll dance. We'll meet some new people. It'll be lovely."

"No, it won't." He held her tightly. "Damn it, Chasey. What's wrong with us?"

With the customary assistance of his sister Dagne, Count von Kresse had completed his dress for dinner, looking as impressive a figure in civilian black tie as he did in his dress uniform. He had spent much of the afternoon lying down and afterward had done some exercises. He felt better.

Dagne was wearing a long, white satin dress with a plunging back. A stunning woman, his half sister. If they could purge her brain of its vile chemistry, she would be one of nature's more beautiful creations.

The count tapped the invitation card against his cheek.

"*Solch Grobheit,*" he said. "I've never seen such English rudeness. It is captain's night and instead of taking part in the generous hospitality, Lady Cunard dines in her cabin and invites other passengers to join her."

"Invites us, *liebchen.*" Dagne smiled, handing him his glass. She seemed almost merry. "It means our success. This is better than the Coopers."

"*Vielleicht. Vielleicht nicht.* We don't know who else might be coming. It might be only her, pining for that ass Ribbentrop and wanting to talk with us about him. I can't think of anything more nauseating."

She hovered close. If it weren't for his old injuries, she would have sat upon his lap.

"Despite your grousing, we might very well be dining with the prince himself tonight. At all events, it is a handsome start. We shall be insinuating ourselves into the royal traveling party. And so early in the voyage."

"It will require that you be your most charming. National Socialist diatribes are not in order."

She gave a quick laugh, tossing back her head. "If the Reichscommissioner is correct, it will require only that we be German."

## CHAPTER
# EIGHT

Edwina stopped, looking up abruptly. The second-class dining room had been rapidly filling with passengers, all of them in evening clothes.

"My God," she said. "We've forgotten to dress."

"Should that matter to an aristocrat?" said Spencer.

"I am not an aristocrat. I am a socialist."

"You are a socialist." He repeated the phrase as if she had just said she was a hippopotamus.

"*Bien sûr.* I despise our government. And your government. And the French government. I positively loathe the German government. I think Nancy Cunard is the sanest person on this ship—about politics. The monarchy is vile. The aristocracy, essentially, is vile. The bourgeoisie is very, very vile. In a way, you know, you quite seem dreadfully middle class yourself. But I know better, my dear sweet cynical aviator. I think you, too, are a socialist."

"Nancy thinks I'm an anarchist."

"Anarchists are of consequence only in Spain. If you were an anarchist, you'd be in Spain."

He took her hand. Many in the room were watching them.

"Why aren't you in Spain, brave Lieutenant? Why aren't you in Abyssinia? Why are you on this ship?"

"If you're a socialist, your ladyship, why are you so rich?"

"That's an impertinent question."

"Yes, but an obvious one."

"I'm rich, if you wish to be so vulgar as to discuss that matter, because I was born that way. It has nothing to do with how I think."

"What does have to do with how you think, your ladyship?"

"The things I've seen. The suffering. I've traveled every bit as much as you have. Probably more. I was in New Guinea this spring, in New York all this summer. By New York I mean Harlem, where I have friends. I've seen the kind of suffering you've told me about in China and Africa. I've seen it not only in primitive backlands but at the center of civilization. And it appalls me. The only good thing I can say about that otherwise worthless Prince of Wales up there is that it appalls him, too, and he's the only member of the royal family who's gotten off his noble ass to do something about it!"

"What has the Prince of Wales to do with this?"

"Nothing. Absolutely nothing."

She pulled her hand away. She disliked intensely the mood he had put her in, and debated whether or not to swiftly end this liaison. She could not decide.

Edwina adopted a neutral tone. "Would you prefer that I conduct myself like Nancy? Screaming at the newspapers all the time? Getting her picture taken with black men? Sponsoring obscene films to get attention? She's injured every cause she's sought to bless. I have my innings, don't you worry. I'll bring this pack of cards atumble, in my fashion."

"Your husband sits atop this house of cards."

"Don't discuss my husband, Lieutenant Spencer." It was a decree. Edwina Mountbatten, *imperiatrix mundi.* Empress of the world. He assented to it by looking away.

She took back his hand. "Let's not have a row. Let's go somewhere and dance. I'm suddenly mad to dance. Please."

"We'll go to the second-class lounge. There's a band there. And tonight we should have it to ourselves."

He was wrong. They danced a fox trot to "It Had To Be You"—performed it, really; she was a marvelous dancer and obviously fond of being admired for it. When they returned to their table, they saw Nancy and Henry Crowder at the bar. Worse, Nancy saw them. She rose regally and, head high, approached them with exaggerated slowness, swinging her arms and bracelets in great arcs.

"Oh, dear God," said Edwina.

Nancy put both hands down on their table, hunching over them, imprisoning them with her wild eyes.

"So, duckies," she said, shrilly and loudly. "What have we been about this long, long day? Fucking? Have we been fucking, Edwina dear? Have we had our screws? Why not? What is there to life but fucking? We fuck and die, fuck and die, but before we kick, we give birth to little wretches, so that they may grow up to fuck and die."

She needed to stand as she did, leaning on the table for balance. Without it she might have toppled.

Edwina rose, commanding Spencer with a gesture to do the same. She looked hard at Nancy, who was grinning with some unexplained triumph.

"Nancy. You are drunk." Edwina might have said just as usefully, "Quasimodo. Your clothes do not fit you properly." Nancy Cunard replied with her ice-shattering laugh.

Edwina took Spencer's arm and they left the lounge, hurrying down the passageway. But Edwina took a wrong turning and, ultimately, through forbidden doors.

"Lady Mountbatten, this is first class. I can't go here."

"You can now. It's the surprise I've arranged for you." Slowing, she searched through her purse and handed him a cabin key. "It's number fifteen. Just down the corridor from mine."

He took the key but did not pocket it. "I don't understand."

"Don't be so bloody obtuse, Lieutenant Spencer. I've had your things moved to first class, where you belong. They said they'd have it ready by eight-thirty, and it's almost that now. They're having some mass inspection of the ship, and everything's been delayed, but your stateroom should be ready."

"When did you arrange this?"

A ship's officer passed, smiling deferentially.

"While you were asleep. It's all settled. Don't worry about it." She gave him a quick glance. "You shouldn't let your secretary inconvenience you that way again."

"I shall repay you."

She laughed. "No. Don't bother. It's nothing to me."

He held the key up before his eyes, as if the number on it bore some message. "Just down the corridor from you—and Lord Mountbatten."

"Don't give it a thought. Have you never spent an English country weekend? This is how it's done."

This is how it would be done if he remained with Whitney. Just down the corridor. Just down the street. Send the bills on to the lady.

Edwina took the key from him at the cabin door, fumbled with it in the lock, then entered quickly and snapped on the light. She had tipped them all heavily and they'd more than done their work. It was an enormous stateroom with an anteroom and a huge bed. There were flowers, and a bucket containing a bottle of champagne.

Without further hesitation, she began taking off her clothes. "Get undressed, Lieutenant, and pour us drinks."

When both were naked, she came to him and took his arms, but held him away. Her dark eyes were very intent.

"Are you poor, Lieutenant Spencer?"

"What do you mean?"

"There are the rich and the poor. Are you poor?"

"I was my father's sole heir."

"And was he poor, when he died?"

"He was in reduced circumstances."

"How do you support yourself in Paris?"

"With debts." He paused. "And writing."

"Do you still have a connection with your father's newspapers?"

"There was just one newspaper, and the answer is yes." He realized where she was heading with her remarks. "Nancy said the Prince of Wales was aboard. I thought it was just more of her madness, but I wonder now if it isn't true. Your husband is his cousin, isn't he, and one of his best friends?"

"You're a reporter."

"The more dignified term is foreign correspondent."

Her eyes questioned him even more deeply. "You're not going to get us in trouble, are you? Not me, not Dickie, not any of us?"

"I would do nothing to make you unhappy. Nothing."

She came into his arms then. "Then we'll each keep our secrets."

He kissed her, but with some distraction. It might, after all, not matter whether Charles Lindbergh was aboard this ship—or whether Lindbergh ever existed. The Prince of Wales was likely just down the passageway.

The dinner for four in Emerald Cunard's stateroom was intimate, elegant, and, in terms of the task before the von Kresses, a success— mostly because of Dagne, who was indeed as charming as Martin could remember her ever being. The count himself sat stiffly, in social as well as physical discomfort, as he found himself disliking these British people, but his inherent courtesy passed for graciousness and the evening proceeded without awkward pause.

"I can't think of a better place to dine on captain's night," said Chips Channon, as one of the two hovering stewards poured after-dinner brandies.

"It's so nice to be away from all those boors," Emerald said.

Chips did not know whether she meant "boors" or "Boers," a

reference to the Dutch at the captain's table. Then, realizing she meant both and had made a joke, he looked amused.

"Certainly this is the most exclusive table aboard ship," he said to the Germans. "Emerald and I are about all there really is to London society, after the Prince of Wales."

"We must hope then that the ship doesn't sink," said Dagne. "I should hate to think of London without any society."

"Oh, it would be a horrible blow," said Channon. "But Berlin I daresay would suffer an equal loss. You two are quite the most civilized Germans I've yet met—except of course for Emerald's dear friend von Ribbentrop." The latter reference was a lie, but one he knew Emerald insisted on believing.

"It's plain, simple Ribbentrop," von Kresse corrected gently. "There is no 'von,' though he now claims one. It was gratuitously bestowed upon him by an adoptive aunt." The count could not resist adding for Dagne's sake: "He was a champagne salesman, you know, before the recent success of his political party."

Lady Cunard seemed unhappy with these remarks, as did Dagne.

"I rather like what your Reich is doing, you know," Channon said. "But there are so many brutes about. I appreciate what Mr. Hitler has to say, of course, and he's the most amazing man, but the way he says it! Such beer hall polemics, and such awful German. Still, I don't know where we'd be without him. Communism at Calais, as I say. At all events, it's reassuring to know there are people like you in the National Socialist Party. On our side of course we have Tom Mosley and the Mitfords, eminent lineage all round. They've made English fascism quite respectable."

"If terribly unamusing," said Emerald, "Tom's deadly serious about everything and the Mitfords are all quite mad."

"Tom's unscrupulous," Chips said, "but not an unattractive fellow. Too much of a lust for power, though. His first wife, Lady Cynthia Mosley, was one of Lord Curzon's daughters, don't you know? The sister of Major Metcalfe's wife, Alexandra. You've heard of Major Metcalfe, one of the prince's intimates? Cynthia was one of God's gentlest and loveliest creatures. Pity she's gone. The Curzon name would give British fascism quite a boost, I should think. Major Metcalfe, by the by, is on the ship, part of our party. He's not much for fascism, though. Cynthia's mother Mary was an American from Chicago. Died of the Indian climate. Her husband was viceroy in Delhi, you know. He—"

Von Kresse spoke very slowly and evenly. "I am not a member of the National Socialist party. I am simply an officer in the German army."

Dagne's hand quickly fluttered to his arm. "With his military duties and running our estate in East Prussia, my brother hasn't much time for political activities."

"Or inclination," he added.

"More's the pity," said Chips. "You're certainly needed. In Britain, people like Tom Mosley would be put in jail if all the Jews and communists had their way, and sometimes I fear they might. We've Jews serving in the British Cabinet, don't you know? Leslie Hore-Belisha is minister of transport. He is an oily man, half a Jew, an opportunist, with the Semitic flare for publicity. Sir Philip Sassoon, however, the undersecretary for air, is quite something else. Married into the Rothschilds. Wonderfully grand house in Park Lane. Philip and I mistrust each other; we know too much about each other, and I can peer into his Oriental mind with all its vanities. But I admit he is one of the most exciting, tantalizing personalities of the age. Though Jewish himself, he hates Jews. I'm really quite fond of him. A bit pushy, though. Lately he's been after Emerald to secure him Hore-Belisha's job."

"After Edward becomes king," said Lady Cunard, "which is taking entirely too long. The old king is really being a boor about lingering on so."

Von Kresse rose with some difficulty. "I'm sorry, but I must return to my cabin. My sister will explain."

"Martin was badly injured in the war," Dagne said quickly. "There is still pain, and sometimes it gets the better of him."

"Please excuse me," the count said, reaching the door. "You needn't come with me, Dagne. You should stay. Her ladyship and Mr. Channon are such wonderful company for you."

He actually felt quite well, once out on deck, refreshed by the still-warm sea breeze and the immense relief he felt at having removed himself from the dinner party. If Chips Channon was typical of British Conservatives, there was no danger at all of Britain going to war with the Reich. An alliance was more likely.

Limping on to his stateroom, the count was surprised to see an envelope sticking out from the door. He thought it must be for his sister, assuming she was sending messages to Germany, but it was addressed to him. Written in English, the note it contained was brief and profoundly puzzling:

If you are the aviator Martin von Bourke und Kresse who flew with the Richthofen Jagdgeschwader No. 1 in the war, please arrange to be on the Sports Deck at midnight. We are of equal rank and like mind.

It was unsigned.

Company director van Hoorn had a plump, pleasant Dutch wife who spoke approximately six words of English. It was left to the director and Chasey Parker to maintain what remained an uninteresting conversation about shipping as van Hoorn's wife nodded amiably and Chasey's already tipsy husband Christopher stared longingly at the captain's table across the room. Half the chairs there were empty. Only Lord Mountbatten and the Coopers were present from the British party. They'd been joined by Cardinal Bloch and the actress Nora Gwynne, whom Chris had yet to meet. A play of hers was coming to Philadelphia for a tryout in the next few weeks, and his friends would be impressed if he could claim her friendship. He'd been trying to waylay her on the deck, without success.

For her part, Nora had not even noticed the young Parkers. She was much too preoccupied trying to hold her own in table conversation that included Mountbatten's and Captain van der Heyden's recollections of naval battles in the Great War as well as the Coopers' confectionary chatter. There was also the matter of Duff Cooper's leg. Seated on her right, he kept pressing his knee against hers. With Captain van der Heyden on her left, she had no room for retreat. Perplexed, she endured, wondering what would come next.

Mountbatten's interminable account of action he saw aboard the H.M.S. *Lion* with Admiral Beatty toward the end of the war proved too much for Diana. For all his tediously detailed description of the functions of a flagship, it was clear that as a seventeen-year-old naval cadet, he hadn't much to do with the action at all.

"Do be a dear, Dickie," Diana said finally, "and let Duff have a turn telling us about what it was like in the trenches. I think it was probably rather less exciting in the trenches than it was afloat, but I fear Duffie's becoming bored, and it's bad for his digestion."

Her casualness about the war was deceptive. Duff was the only one of her many youthful suitors who had survived the fighting. Most of them had died horribly.

Mountbatten gazed at Duff coldly. Cooper had recently served as First Lord of the Admiralty, but it was as a young infantry officer in the Great War that he had won the D.S.O.

"Tell us, Duff, about the trenches," he said.

Cooper took a sip of champagne. "Bloody awful."

"That's all? Bloody awful?"

"All right. It was truly bloody awful."

Diana had accomplished her purpose. "It certainly was. Now let us hear about something more pleasant. Miss Gwynne, tell us about your next film."

"My next project, actually, is a play."

"A play," said Diana. "Oh, how marvelous. I was in a play once."

"You weren't in a play once," said Duff, his leg still tight against Nora's. "You were in it forever."

Nora had remembered who Diana was. As Lady Diana Manners, her maiden name, she had toured the United States in the 1920s in *The Miracle,* a production that was more tableau than play. Her role was that of a silent madonna, who stood stock still in profile for most of the performance. The acting required was minimal, but it must have made her a lot of money. It had played the United States off and on for years.

"I saw you," Nora said. "*The Miracle.* At the Civic Hall in Cleveland. It was in 1924. I was a very young girl." She blushed at that last blurting. She had been told Diana Manners had been given the part because she had once been reputed to be the most beautiful woman in the world, though to some she looked like a blond, blue-eyed sheep. Age had made her a lot more sheeplike, though she certainly seemed attractive to men.

"Cleveland," Diana said with some surprise. "I wasn't so happy in Cleveland. There were these dreadful Siamese twins in the audience one night. I'm sure they were dear boys, the twins, but there they were, weren't they, sitting back to back, watching me sideways. I did rather like Cincinnati, and I adored Toledo, though I can't recall whether we played there or were passing through."

"I'm from Toledo."

"From Toledo? How marvelous. I hated Chicago. I had Noel with me in Chicago. Noel Coward. I'm sure you've met. But even with him about, it was rather awful. Dreadfully cold and brutish. Noel scrawled something like 'Noel Coward died here' on my dressing room wall and the theater's manager left it there as some sort of icon. I received a note about it from Clifton Webb—surely you know Clifton?—two years later, when he was using the dressing room in a play. Noel and I went to some awful déclassé house while we were in Chicago, an architect's mansion, actually. Terribly famous, though

I've forgotten his name. It was one endless boudoir. Noel and I decided he'd invited us there in hopes of a romp with the both of us. But that was still better than Boston. In Boston I had this dreary lesbian lady following me about wherever I went. But I love America. Truly I do. Now, Miss Gwynne, tell us about this lovely little play of yours."

"It's called *Lemonade*," Nora said. "It's a comedy, by Archibald McCutcheon."

Duff put his hand on her knee.

Confined to his suite, the prince had remained shirtless and in shorts and sandals the entire day, and had dressed for evening simply by adding a shirt. Wallis was dressed in an evening gown, embellished with a heavy gold chain and other jewelry. They made an absurdly disparate couple, but this time she did not chide him. It was her habit and method to make him miserable with harshness and meanness, and then recapture his devotion with a sudden outpouring of affection and tender attention. She did this often, and it was working once again.

He sat cross-legged, smoking, on the divan. She lay with her large head in his lap, ignoring the occasional ash that fell as she looked up at him, smiling.

"A girl is so terribly happy," she said.

"A boy is terribly happy with his girl," he said. "Otherwise he is quite cross. Where are the others? Why are they taking so long at dinner?"

They were alone in their suite, with only Runcie and a sailor, stationed just outside the door, to summon for company.

"We don't need the others." She reached and stroked his face. He brightened as a pet animal might, but it faded.

"I'm so tired of this voyage," he said. "And we've scarcely been out two days. I'd rather be back in the Paris riots. We'd at least have something interesting to look at. When we get to New York, I'm going on a spree. We might even have Edwina take us up to Harlem."

Wallis would certainly prevent that ghastly occurrence from happening.

"Darling," she said. "I've an idea. Why don't we have a dinner party?"

"In New York?"

"No, darling, here on the *Wilhelmina*. The sitting room is nearly as large as the dining room in my flat at Bryanston Court. We can make it a very special affair. I'll have invitations printed up. We'll get the ship to produce some chairs without arms, to accommodate all the guests. I would also have two sorts of cocktails and white wine as well as vin rosé. We'll hire one of the ship's chefs and extra servants for the night. Do say yes, David. I've been quite as bored as you, except for that horrible experience this morning."

"A boy says yes. A royal yes. But there'll be all the same old dull faces."

"We'll invite others, as well."

"Fruity will forbid it."

"We'll select them carefully, for their discretion. I'll make inquiries as to who's on board. Chips will know. He knows everyone in the world."

"All right, Wallis. We'll do it! And I shall play the pipes."

He was quite happy now. For once, she did not argue with him about the pipes. That would come later.

Somewhat breathless and amazed, Count von Kresse returned from his strange rendezvous the way he had come, slipping out of the other man's cabin and retracing his steps up the ladders that led to the top of the ship and the sports deck. It was slow and painful for him, but much less public than the central corridors. In the gloom, as he passed along in the shadow of the aftmost funnel, he encountered only a couple at the rail near a deck tennis area, and he could barely see them. If they were aware of him, certainly they could not see the bulky envelope he carried.

There was no hiding it from Dagne on his return. She had apparently just come back from Lady Cunard's, and was flushed and happy.

"*Erfolg, liebchen!*" she said, lighting a cigarette and swinging a leg over the arm of her chair. "Despite your unspeakably rude early departure, they were quite taken with us. Pardon my exuberance. The nice Herr Channon told me at the end that he'd laced the cocktails with Benzedrine. He said it always made a party go."

"I think also automobile engines."

"But we've done it, *liebchen bruder.* They confided to me about the Prince of Wales, that he's aboard. They're going to introduce us tomorrow, if it can be arranged. If you can mind your manners."

"My leg hurt. I just had to leave."

"It didn't hurt enough to prevent your going off for a midnight stroll."

"The walk helped. I feel much better."

"What do you have in the envelope?" Her happy expression was gone.

"Nothing. Just some airplane pictures. I met someone on deck and we fell to talking about flying. He let me borrow some pictures."

"I thought you had put flying behind you."

"I can no longer fly, but I am still interested in aircraft. I read aviation books all the time in Ortelsburg, which you'd notice if you ever left Berlin."

She got to her feet and took the envelope from him. He dared not protest.

"These are very detailed drawings," she said, pulling some out. "What aircraft is this?"

"A Messerschmitt 108 Taifun."

"A German aircraft."

"A sport aircraft, Dagne."

"But German nevertheless."

"The fellow I met has just come from Germany."

"And who is the fellow?"

"Just a passenger. But don't worry about sport aircraft secrets falling into the wrong hands. He was given these drawings by Reichscommissioner Hermann Goering himself."

Spencer and Edwina separated from their embrace when they saw the figure of a limping man pass slowly by, but he paid them no attention.

There was a sea breeze, but it failed to dissipate the oily, acrid smell emanating from the funnel.

"You said we would be alone up on the sports deck," Spencer said, his arms close around her waist.

"It's that Prussian count. He's a bit crippled, I think. Something's wrong with him, though he doesn't seem to mind creeping about the deck in the middle of the night. I don't know why I'm worried about his seeing us. You know, I was out on deck completely naked last night. Well, dawn, actually."

"Naked? Completely naked?"

She laughed. "Just an impulse, and a bit too much to drink. And frustration."

"You must have startled the crew."

"Actually, I did, rather. Two of them. A seaman and a maid."

They fell silent, listening to the hissing rush of the ship's passage. The breeze had become a head wind. As they were sailing into it at some twenty-five knots, it blew strong against their faces.

"There are no crew up here now," Spencer said suggestively.

But she turned away from him, her face lifting toward the dark sky. "James. Look at that."

Even as an aviator flying in all the eerie unreality of warfare at night, he had seen no phenomenon such as this before. The ship was below a mass of clouds, for they could see no stars or moon, and it had begun as a hazy moonlit night. But ahead of them, through a widening rent in the cloud cover, there appeared a fairyland. It, too, was a thing of cloud, but white and phosphorescent, curving away from them like a celestial highway. And it was filled with stars, sparkling brilliantly like diamonds on the soft cotton backing of a jewel box. Edwina was transfixed.

He put his hand gently around her breast. Just as gently she removed his hand, her eyes still on the starry path. "My God, it's magic. A blessing from heaven."

"It's only a trick of the moon."

"But it's so lovely. I sailed on a copra boat this summer, as crew, in the South Pacific. There were many extraordinary nights, but never anything quite like this."

He had lost her to this celestial apparition. Her eyes would not move from it.

"Moonlight is not always so lovely. There was moonlight in France, in the war."

"This is true beauty."

"Truth is not always beauty—especially in the moonlight. I know a French writer, Antoine de Saint-Exupéry, an aviator who flies in Africa. He told me once of a young woman in some Berber town. For some small crime she was stripped naked and taken out into the desert. They bound her to a stake and left her."

"Please."

"He wrote me about it, about a father and son who rode out to look upon her after a day in the sun, so the son would learn a lesson. The son wanted to help her, but the father forbade it. He said she was discovering that which is essential. That she was beyond suffering and fear, that she was discovering truth. It's Antoine's concept of religion—and mine."

"Good God, James. How could you?"

Spencer reached for Edwina, but she was walking away, very quickly, making clear she did not want him to follow.

Standing at the forward bridge windows, Captain van der Heyden observed the starry phenomenon in the sky but paid it little attention. His years at sea had been crowded with bizarre sightings, but he had early on learned to concentrate only on what was important to the ship. At the moment he was much more interested in the distant flashes just a few points off the starboard bow.

"Bring me the latest weather report," he said to one of the junior officers.

Because he was so much in view on so social a night, he had confined himself to two glasses of wine with dinner and a small sip of champagne later. He had stopped by the bridge on the way to retiring. Now his quarters, and his nightcap, would have to wait.

The young man handed him the signal. "Deteriorating, sir. Force-five winds predicted."

"Well, well," said van der Heyden. "The North Atlantic is returning to her old self. An end to the idyll." He folded the paper and slipped it into his pocket, as if it were a secret message. "Just as well," he said, moving to the chart table. "I was beginning to forget I was aboard a ship."

He pondered the map. They were far out to sea, but the pencil line marking their progress seemed to have barely intruded upon the vast white space of charted ocean.

"Sir? Do you want to alter course to the south?"

"No. The storm system's too large. We'll take it head on and endure the worst for the shortest possible time. The *Wilhelmina* is in for a real sea trial." He looked about at the youthful faces on the bridge. "I'm going to my cabin now. Wake me when the storm hits."

# CHAPTER
# *NINE*

Reichscommissioner Hermann Goering rose early, his groggy stupor from the overlong party the previous night quickly banished with a large dose of one of his "medicines."

His wife, Emmy, remained in bed, curled up in a protective bear's den made of covers. She was not asleep, but trying to cope with the anger and humiliation she still felt from the night before. One of the women at the party, the wife of a party functionary at the Labor Ministry, had informed Emmy of the scurrilous jokes about the Goerings' love life that continued to plague the Reichscommissioner in social Berlin. The woman even repeated the most current one in circulation, a vile tale in which Emmy came upon Hermann doing odd things with a marshal's baton up his own backside. As the joke went, he explained he was conducting an official ceremony: "I am promoting my underpants to overpants."

The woman likely thought she was being of some service, and thus ingratiating herself with the Goerings by relating this information. But Goering had been angry. He had managed to keep these terrible stories from Emmy for all the months of their marriage. Now this fawning, intrusive woman had let all the cats out of the bag. Just before retiring Goering had telephoned to order her arrest. He had had more than ten people arrested thus far for repeating these jokes, though this had failed to stem them. Their primary source, he suspected, was in high party circles beyond his powers of discretionary arrest.

Emmy had threatened to cancel the dinner they were hosting that evening for Rolf Rienhardt, the most powerful publishing figure in the Reich, but Hermann had insisted they go through with it. Rienhardt had been a friend of Gregor Strasser, a party rival of Hitler's whom the Führer had had murdered in the "Night of the Long Knives" the previous year, but Rienhardt had many skills and other powerful contacts, and so had survived and prospered. Goering would not risk offending him.

Emmy had married Goering only the preceding April—in a mammoth wedding ceremony that was the most celebrated social occasion in Nazi Germany. She would have to learn to perform her official duty like the formidable stage actress she was, and soon. With Hitler unmarried, she was, as the wife of the Führer's principal deputy, the First Lady of the Reich. Malicious gossip, however outrageous, was always attendant upon such high positions.

Still, he likely would have to have many more arrested, and perhaps a few shot or hanged.

He patted her ample backside, then reached to squeeze one of her enormous breasts. She cried out angrily. He left the bedroom feeling jolly.

Goering had two immediate tasks before him that morning. One was to read and approve the latest development report on the Heinkel III bomber, which was his answer to the costly, useless four-engined aircraft being pushed by the fools who were trying to persuade Hitler of the efficacy of long-range strategic bombers. The twin-engined Heinkel III was cheap, easy to produce in great numbers, and ideal for ground support missions, as well. The Great War had proved the long-range bomber to be militarily pointless. How many three-engined Gothas had bombed London to no result but to stiffen popular support for the British war effort? Britain was the only logical target for the four-engined monsters being proposed, and Britain could still be kept out of any continental conflict. Goering remained convinced of that.

The other task before him was to examine a new cache of paintings that had been confiscated from the property of a rich Jewish collector who had recently fled the country. It would have been a perfectly legal confiscation even if the owner had not been Jewish, for most of the works were by officially proscribed artists, including the notorious abstract artist Paul Klee, who had himself fled to Switzerland after Goering had denounced him as a Galician Jew. That had been a lie, but a useful and effective one.

The Reichcommissioner went through the Heinkel report quickly, pleased with the work of his subordinates. Then, pouring himself a morning schnapps, went on to his haul of paintings.

About half of them were by Klee. They had been officially proclaimed "degenerate" by the party and their public showing was
forbidden. Goering would of course comply with that stricture, stor-
ing them in one of his basement vaults rather than burning them.
That they were illegal made them all the more valuable. The Reichscommissioner was convinced he now possessed the most valuable
collection in Europe.

The other works were also abstract but by less dangerous paint-
ers—Wilhelm Lehmbruck, Max Beckman, Max Ernst, and the night-
marish Ernst Ludwig Kirchner, whose garish green-and-red
"German Street, Dresden" had been one of the favorite works of
Goering's wartime flying comrade von Kresse, himself a collector.
Unfortunately "Dresden" had not been in the Jew's cache.

Goering had his servants set the paintings up all around the walls
of one of his larger viewing rooms, deciding he would spend an hour
enjoying them before locking them away from official view.

He did not get his hour. As he stood staring fondly at the first from
the stack, a brown-and-beige two-dimensional study by Egon Schiele
reminiscent of the artist's wonderful Portrait of Gerta Schiele, Goering's adjutant came marching into the chamber. He clicked his heels
so loudly the sound echoed down the corridor. Goering wondered
if the man did this to impress him or to irritate him.

"Herr Reichscommissioner," said the adjutant, a Luftwaffe colonel. "Reichsführer Himmler is here and wishes to speak to you."

Goering glanced at his paintings. "Have him shown into my
study."

"He wishes to speak to you outside, Reichscommissioner. He is
waiting in his car."

"He is in his car? He expects me to come out and deal with him
at curbside? He sees me as a filling station attendant, *vielleicht?*"

"He wishes to speak to you in his car, Reichscommissioner. I told
him I did not think you would find that suitable."

"You go back and tell him it is most unsuitable, and that if he
wishes to speak to me he must come inside. Show him into the study."

"He said he had instructions from the Führer, Reichscommissioner."

Goering glowered. "The Führer instructed that I should go stand
on Himmler's running board? Tell him to come inside!"

"*Jawohl*, Herr Reichscommissioner!" There was another thundering click of heels.

Gesturing at his staff to gather up the paintings, Goering peevishly rubbed at his fat chin. Himmler's impudence was becoming insufferable. As was his ambition. Though it was Goering who had first suggested concentration camps when he was virtual dictator of the state of Prussia, it had been his subordinate Himmler who won laurels from the Führer for so efficiently constructing and filling them. Hitler, Goering, Goebbels, and Hess had agreed that the rowdy S.A. brown shirts had to be smashed and their leaders eliminated if the new Nazi regime was to have the support of the army. But it was Himmler's magnificently disciplined S.S. that had carried out the job and made such a success of the Night of the Long Knives. Since then Himmler had been ascendant. Goering feared to think where his climb would end.

The Reichsführer-S.S. eventually compromised to the extent of coming into Goering's vestibule, but he would advance no farther. At length Goering went to join him.

"What is all this about, Heinrich?" Goering asked. "Why do you refuse to join me in my study?"

Himmler was dressed in a resplendant black "Death's Head" S.S. uniform. The night before he had uncharacteristically worn evening clothes, with his receding chin, beaky nose, and round spectacles looking very much like what he was, a sniveling petit bourgeois would-be snob. On the rare occasions when he wore a business suit, occasions that were becoming rare as the party consolidated its power, he looked like the schoolteacher his father had been. In the forbidding Schutzstaffel uniform, however, he looked quite macabre, a figure from one of the hellish paintings by the mad Belgian artist James Ensor.

He stared coldly at Goering, his nose twitching like a rabbit's.

"Because we have little time," he said finally.

"*Warum?*"

"Because the Führer wishes to see us."

"*Wann?*"

"At once."

"What for?"

Himmler glanced around at the large number of Goering's assistants, guards, and servants who were standing about the large, marble-floored chamber.

"All right, very well, I will come outside with you," Goering said.

They walked down the bricked drive to a loudly splashing fountain.

"It's about Markgraf von Kresse," Himmler said.

"What about him?"

"The Führer knows about his mission, apparently."

"How did he find out?"

Himmler shrugged. "Count von Kresse is considered unreliable and dangerous. Many others are having him watched. Someone else's people may have followed him to the ship, or onto it. And Ribbentrop knows all about the voyage."

"And the Führer is angry?"

"We should waste no more time, Hermann. The Führer is waiting. Come, there is my car."

He gestured to his motorcade, which consisted of a black Mercedes-Benz touring car, two black Mercedes sedans, and about a dozen motorcycles—all with party flags flying.

Goering was not about to become a passenger in a procession so identified with a rival.

"I will join you at the Reichschancellory," he said. "I must prepare myself."

As quickly as possible, he changed into his best blue-and-white gold-braided uniform, while his staff organized a separate motorcade for him made up of his Mercedes limousine, three Luftwaffe sedans, an armored car, and every motorcycle in Goering's motor pool.

Himmler naturally arrived first, but he had not been admitted to the Führer's inner sanctum by the time Goering waddled into the antechamber.

They were made to wait another twenty minutes. Albert Speer, the Führer's young architect, emerged from behind the great wood and steel doors, a roll of what Goering presumed were blueprints or drawings under his arm. He nodded curtly to Himmler and more generously to Goering, but said nothing. A moment later, the Reichs-commissioner and Reichsführer-S.S. were summoned.

Hitler was thus alone less than sixty seconds. He could not stand to be by himself for any period, a consequence of his time in prison perhaps, or of his miserably lonely youth spent as a friendless would-be artist. Goering suspected that Eva Braun's function as the man's mistress had not to do with any sexual acts but was merely to provide him with company while he slept.

The Führer sat exactly at the middle of his elongated desk, his back to the towering windows. The massive black drapes had been drawn to within six feet of each other, leaving most of the vast room in darkness but allowing a shaft of brilliant light to fall on Hitler's head and shoulders and the papers before him. The effect was almost as theatrical as the light shows Speer had engineered at the rallies in Nuremburg.

The Führer was wearing his customary light-brown military tunic, a white shirt, and a black tie. He was hunched and looked tired. He lifted his eyes from the work in front of him, then rubbed them wearily. When he lowered his hand again, he was staring at the two of them darkly. He was forty-six but seemed a decade older.

"Ribbentrop informs me that the Prince of Wales is sailing to America incognito on a Dutch ship," Hitler said sharply, as if Goering and Himmler had personally put the British crown prince aboard. "He says that a Markgraf von Kresse, a known troublemaker, is also on this ship. I am also informed that he is there on your orders." His eyes went from Goering to Himmler and back. "This is true?"

Goering glanced at Himmler, who said nothing.

"Yes, it is true, my Führer."

"True that you put this Prussian count, this colonel, on this ship with the crown prince of England?"

Himmler had turned to face Goering, as well, as if he were as ignorant of this matter as Hitler was.

"Yes, my Führer." Goering had stopped calling him Adolf six years before. "But I would not call him a troublemaker so much as an eccentric. I knew him well in the war, in the Richthofen Jagdgeschwader. He was a great hero, very badly wounded. In the end, he fought in the trenches as a common soldier, as did you, my Führer. He still suffers pain, and it makes him irritable. He says things he does not mean. He is very popular with the old officer corps."

"Yes, yes, very well, Hermann. But why did you put him on the ship? What is he doing there? Is he annoying the Prince of Wales?"

Himmler folded his arms across his chest as he stared at Goering intently. Except for the one's toothbrush moustache and the other's spectacles, the Reinchsfuhrer-S.S. and the Führer resembled each other greatly, even to the same pasty faces and pudgy cheeks. Without their uniforms, they looked petit bougeois indeed. Himmler had been a chicken farmer for some years after the Great War. Hitler had left school at sixteen and worked for a time as a laborer.

Goering, like von Kresse, had been one of the most photographed heroes of the war, though the once-jutting squarish jaw had disappeared into softer flesh.

"His sister is with him, my Führer. She is a faithful member of the party. You have no more loyal follower. And she, like von Kresse, is a true Aryan. You should look into their gray-eyed, fair-haired faces. Dr. Goebbels should use them on posters."

"But why is he on this ship? Why has he been sent after the Prince of Wales, to bother the prince with his 'eccentric' ways? The prince is well disposed toward us. I am told this. I have read his speeches. He's very good for us. Because of him England will yet be with us. Yet there is von Kresse. Why is this, Hermann?"

The Reichscommissioner turned toward Himmler, but the latter's face remained impassive. Goering would have his revenge for this.

"By sailing to America, the prince has put himself at risk," Goering said. "There are many in Britain who are combining against him. I thought we should do whatever we can to protect him; whatever we can to stay close to the situation. I needed someone who could move in the prince's aristocratic circles, who was not too closely identified with our movement, who would do what I told him. And I needed such a person in a hurry. We had only hours to spare, isn't that so, Heinrich?"

Startled, the Reichsführer only stared.

"We can trust him," Goering continued. "I have bought this trust with a threat. He knows I can have his wife eliminated with a single telephone call. We have her under surveillance in Krakow."

"Krakow?"

"His wife is Polish, my Führer. They are separated, but he still cares for her. My threat has meaning."

"Polish!" Hitler said. "So now you tell me this crippled, troublemaking, eccentric Prussian markgrav has a Polish wife? Next you will be telling me he is Jewish." The Führer snorted, leaning back in his immense chair.

"Hardly," said Goering. "In the war he was my best friend."

"I will remember that, Hermann."

"My Führer," said Goering. "A man as loved as you should not be so mistrustful. Was there ever a leader who so possessed the faith of his people? Was there ever a king or kaiser who commanded so much loyalty as you? Von Kresse is a Prussian officer. Every Prussian officer took an oath on his life to you. You saw what that meant in the war. These *Ritteren*, these Prussian knights, they held firm. They fought to the last. As you have made all Deutschland realize, it was the Jews and the bankers who sold us out."

Himmler's gaze was now frankly admiring.

The Führer clasped his hands together in a familiar, bent-wrist gesture that in a lesser man would have seemed effeminate, almost supplicating. He always did this in response to what he took to be affection. Goering had assiduously learned the reason for Hitler's every tic, nod, and blink. He knew more about the workings of the Führer's countenance than he did those of the Heinkel III's in-line engines. As he said to himself, lives depended on it. Including his own.

"*Sehr gut, Hermann,*" Hitler said, leaning back farther and folding his hands in his lap. "I will presume you know what is best. But I want full reports on everything that occurs, everything that this von Kresse does, everything the Prince of Wales does." He lifted a hand and an admonishing index finger. "I do not want the prince annoyed! The English and we, we are the same people!"

"*Sicher rechts, mein Führer.*"

All of them smiled, but Hitler abruptly frowned again and began to shift some of the papers on the desk before him about.

"Heinrich, before you go . . ." He could not find what he sought. "There was a memorandum. To remind me."

Himmler stood very stiffly. It was Goering's turn to fold his arms across his chest and look on as a bemused spectator.

"Yes, yes," said Hitler. "I remember now. The executions."

"Executions, my Führer?" Himmler's doubt was not as to whether there had been executions but to which Hitler referred.

"The executions in Plotzensee Prison!" said Hitler, with marked and sudden anger.

"*Allerdings, mein Führer.* They were carried out yesterday. Six beheadings and thirty-one hangings. This made for difficulty because we bury them two to a coffin, as you know. But we were able to wedge two children in with their mother and make a fit. *Alles ist gerade.*"

"I want to see photographs of these dead traitors. Of their corpses."

"But my Führer, they are all buried."

"Then disinter them. I want these photographs on my desk this afternoon. After lunch!"

"It will be done, my Führer."

Hitler's expression gentled. He smacked his hands against the desktop. "Of course it will. Gentlemen, I think we will go to Berchtesgaden next week. Yes. Inform your wives. We shall have an outing, while the weather is still pleasant."

"Emmy will be delighted," said Goering.

The Führer had turned to something else—a map of Austria.

"When you go out, you will find Hess waiting. Send him in at once."

"Heil Hitler!"

He returned their salute, rendered in unison, without looking. He held a magnifying glass in his hand. He looked much the idle stamp collector.

Neither Goering nor Himmler spoke until they had reached their respective motorcades. The courtyard was filled with roaring vehicles. Goering motioned Himmler closer.

"Heinrich," he said. "You did get someone aboard that ship with von Kresse, isn't that so?"

The pale face beneath the black hat remained impassive, but the lips compressed into a slight, wispy smile that was his only reply.

"I think, Heinrich, that it is best that we end this now, before anything goes wrong. Ribbentrop apparently learns about everything."

Himmler thought a moment, then nodded.

"What I mean," said Goering, "is that I think von Kresse is now dangerous to us. To both of us, and of course to the Reich, as the Führer seems to have observed. I think it is best that he be removed. You can attend to this?"

Himmler grinned, in his face, an expression utterly lacking warmth or humor. "Your war comrade, Herr Flieger?"

"The war was long ago. Do what must be done. *Wiedersehen.*" Goering hurried away, so that his motorcade might leave before the Reichsführer's. He needed to get another message to Dagne von Bourke und Kresse, to warn her about Himmler's operative. As Goering had earlier involved Himmler in the operation's possible success, he had now provoked the Reichsführer into implicating himself in the mission's now probable failure. Himmler's agent was likely to cause trouble now, no matter what Count von Kresse did. The count could lose his life in this, but that could not be helped. Goering wanted Dagne to survive. He needed her. There were times when Emmy was being particularly hysterical or dense that he wished he had married Dagne instead.

# CHAPTER
## *TEN*

In the warm, humid, unnatural calm, the *Wilhelmina* had seemed the largest object in creation, the dominant feature of an empty sea that ran from the edge of the earth to the edge of the earth.

In the sudden, protean tumult of the autumn storm, she'd been rendered the smallest thing imaginable, caught in the colliding marches of thirty- and forty-foot waves and shoved and heaved about like a toy boat in the hands of an impish and violent child.

It was encouragingly manifest that the untried *Wilhelmina* was not frail. Though she shouldered the oncoming seas with heavy shudders, she emerged from every encounter intact and with the triumph of forward movement, sliding into the deep of the following troughs with almost graceful speed, her bow rising defiant to face the next towering wave crest. Yet there was something of the innocent awkwardness of a wild creature's first swim, a young bird's first flight, a foal's first gallop, in the *Wilhelmina*'s progress. She responded instinctively, but it was as if she hadn't quite got the hang of it. The ship wheeled overmuch to port or starboard after each collision with the mountainous water. She heeled excessively. At one point it seemed to van der Heyden that he was looking straight down from the side window by his captain's chair into the swirling, foamy blue-green depths of ocean to the side—the ship but a few inches of movement, a few pounds of balance, from capsizing.

An extremely high wave taken on the starboard quarter came rushing along the working deck, its waters exploding upward against the bridge windows, a slap in the *Wilhelmina*'s face by the god of oceans. Van der Heyden, glaring defiantly, waited for the opaque wall of residual water clinging to the windows to be erased by the wiper blades. The next wave was smaller. He continued about his business.

The captain had endured storms infinitely worse, especially in the South Atlantic and Indian Ocean, and had learned to deal with them in terms of his ship's response, not nature's spectacular threats. The *Wilhelmina* was taking some water forward, a significant amount in Hold No. 1 and somewhat less in Hold No. 2. The pumps had caught up and were prevailing, but the hatch covers were obviously deficient. Van der Heyden made a notation about them on a small piece of paper and added it to several dozen others he had put into a nearby drawer—deficiencies the shipyard would have to correct.

It was clear that the ship's excessive lateral roll could not be controlled adequately and would have to be endured. The ship performed best taking the waves on the bow quarter. Noting the rapid northeastern track of the storm, though its accompanying winds were out of the northwest, van der Heyden ordered a course change slightly to the south—though not so much that the heaving seas and winds would be put to her starboard beam, aggravating the roll intolerably.

Van der Heyden was weary. He had taken two Bols gins before retiring and had had slightly less than four hours' sleep. It was unfair of the old Norse gods who held dominion over these seas to order up this storm the morning after captain's night in the dining salons. They had no respect for the protocol requirements of trans-Atlantic liners. They treated only horny-toed and leather-faced sailors, not dinner-jacketed dancers.

"Should we decrease speed further, Captain?" asked First Officer van Groot, who had been on the bridge since the first sign of bad weather. It was more recommendation than question—even an implied command. It was what van Groot would have done.

Van der Heyden had already slowed the ship to ten knots.

"No," he said. "I don't want to wallow. In fact, increase the speed a knot or two. In the long run, she'll take less punishment with more headway."

"Half speed, ahead one-third," van Groot commanded. A seaman at the ship's telegraph complied, two clangs sounding the movement of the lever.

"Half speed, ahead one-third," the seaman repeated.

Van Hoorn appeared, neatly dressed in a black suit as if reporting for a board of directors' meeting. Respectful of van der Heyden's absolute authority on the bridge and urgent duties of the moment, he did not intrude. Nodding in greeting, he gripped the railing that ran along the rear bulkhead and remained out of the way. The captain wished him a good morning, then turned back to the forward windows and the helm. As the ship mounted another gargantuan crest, he had a view of the relentless procession to come. Some of the distant wavetops seemed a great deal higher than those around them, but that could simply be an illusion. So much at sea was illusion. Decisions based on it were often drastically wrong—and deadly.

Karl Poeder, the junior officer who had gone out onto the bridge wing for an observation of the decks aft, returned through the sliding door. His shoe caught on metal stripping and, tumbling forward, he slid along the sloping deck as the ship heaved into another roll. His back struck a stanchion and he cried out.

Van Groot and a seaman went to Poeder's side.

"I'm all right, sir," the young officer said, but his contorted face contradicted him.

"You may have cracked a rib or something, Karl," van Groot said.

"Get him to sick bay," ordered van der Heyden. "You can stand for him till the end of this watch."

Van Hoorn, the cautious company man, came forward now. "Are we in any trouble?" he asked.

The captain grinned. "Small trouble. There will be a lot of vomiting today, however. We are fortunate we have so few passengers."

Van Hoorn nodded, though he was unhappy with the captain's sense of irony.

Third Officer Kees Witte entered, though he was not yet on watch. He carried a signal from the wireless room.

"A disaster, sir," he said.

The others snapped their heads around. Van der Heyden took the message grimly, but his expression eased as he read it.

"A disaster for a Dutch shipping line," he said, "but not this one." He handed the signal to van Hoorn, turning to his first officer.

"Holland Amerika?" said Van Groot.

"The *Rotterdam,*" said Van der Heyden. "She's run aground on a reef east of Jamaica. Hurricane out of the Gulf of Mexico passing over Cuba. The Rotterdam was carrying four hundred sixty passengers and a crew of five hundred twenty-six. But she's beached, not sinking."

"Four hundred sixty passengers?" said van Hoorn. "That's a passenger list almost as small as ours."

"Bad times, *mijnheer,*" said van der Heyden. "For everyone."

"East of Jamaica," said van Groot. "That's three thousand miles from us at the least."

"For now," said the captain. "But that hurricane is moving due north." A pair of binoculars fell from a shelf and skittered across the floor. "This pleasant weather may not last."

Nora Gwynne awoke as she was being flung violently to the floor of her cabin. She crawled back to her bed, gripping its wooden siding, then sat back against it, feet and lovely legs splayed out before her on the carpeting.

Her head was wobbly, but to her amazement, she felt no more than a little queasy. At dinner she had followed the German count's advice from the previous night, avoiding spicy and unsettling foods and stuffing herself with potatoes and good Dutch bread. Her stomach felt relatively secure.

It might be better, though, if she were thoroughly sick, confined to her bed and aware only of nausea. As it was, she was fully cognizant of every wrench and creak and slam and thud, of every terrifying manifestation of their peril. She wondered why there had been no alarm sounded. With such violent movement, they surely must be sinking.

Rising, grasping at the furniture as she moved forward, she made her clumsy way out into her sitting room, pausing once there to rest in a chair near a porthole. Catching her breath and her equilibrium, she turned to kneel backward on the chair and peer out the porthole glass at the deck.

That was a mistake. The parade of gigantic waves galloping so furiously by the rail beyond overwhelmed all her senses. She could not imagine how they were going to live through the day.

Nora huddled in her thin nightdress, cold hands gripping bare, folded shivering arms. She closed her eyes a moment, trying to keep back tears. She would have been miserable this morning no matter what the weather. The Coopers may have been duchess's daughter and earl's nephew, but he had behaved as grossly and awfully as the most slobbering, filthy-minded, unscrupulous Hollywood creep— and they, at least, usually offered roles in movies.

Duff Cooper behaved as if he had bought her for five dollars in a Maumee, Ohio, roadhouse. While his wife blithefully chattered on, he had shoved his hand beneath the tablecloth up Nora's thigh to the top of her stocking. She was terrified of making a scene over this but didn't know what else to do. Finally she turned vigorously away to talk to the captain, who decorously ignored Cooper's lascivious antics. And then Duff moved his hand to the waist of her backless dress, sliding his fingers down to the base of her spine, one finger wedged between the curves of soft skin.

She had stood up, knocking her chair over. Excusing herself without explanation, she hurriedly left the table, but Duff came in pursuit no more than a minute after, tracking her to the door of her suite, grasping her by the waist and muttering what he must have presumed were endearing and sweet entreaties into her ear.

For all his charm and high bearing, Nora was repulsed. She could think of only one escape, one calling up much of her talent as an actress. She feigned gagging, slipping about within the grasp of his arms as she clutched her stomach. Open mouthed, she made as if to cover the front of his evening clothes with dinner. Startled, gentlemanly apologetic, he backed away and then fled.

Just another rotten night in a holiday that had consisted of little else. Worse was the knowledge that her ploy had surely provided only a temporary respite. He would be back at her as soon as he thought her well enough to jump.

But Duff or no Duff, storm or no storm, she was not going to remain a prisoner in her cabin. She was, as all the world must someday learn, the indomitable Nora Gwynne.

The storm excited Spencer. When he opened the outside door of his stateroom and leaned out over the deck, the cold, wet, furious reality of it invigorated him fiercely. He stood, breathing in the moist, stinging air, listening to the crash and roar and the whistle of the wind, feeling as if the sea had come to greet him, to invite him to come see all its wonders.

He was passionate about the ocean this way, as intoxicated with its scents and intimacy and wildness as he ever was with Whitney. Flying airplanes, he rejoiced in cold, calm, crystalline air, in which he could soar to the greatest possible heights and sit behind his rumbling engine seeing all the universe. With the sea, he loved it crazed and tempestuous—not the dull flatness they had been traversing since leaving Le Havre but the hellish boil that had kept mariners clinging to coastal waters for century after century until the Vikings and, later, Columbus.

He looked down. Amazingly, if somewhat wet, the morning's collection of ship's announcements was at his feet. Spencer picked up the first piece of paper, the picturegram of the day's weather forecast. It was incredible. Of the eight squares, the one with the bright-yellow sunburst captioned "sunny" had been circled. The "expected temperature" was written in as 100 degrees.

He stepped back and closed the door, looking at the weather sheet again and then setting it aside. The one-page "Ocean News" was more compelling, if no less unreal.

Greek President Alexander Zaimis had been voted out of office by the Greek assembly, which had then voted to restore the monarchy.

British Imperial Airways had purchased two huge flying boats to investigate the possibility of trans-Atlantic air passenger service to compete with ships. A United Air Lines transport had crashed near Cheyenne, Wyoming, killing all twelve aboard, including the pilot, H. A. "No Collision" Collison, who had given famed aviator Wiley Post his first airplane ride.

The Nazi government had forbidden the Hohenzollern family to fly the flag of its royal house, stating that the swastika was the only official emblem permitted for the German Reich.

The Russian government had asked for League of Nations intervention in Abyssinia, fearing that the Germans and Japanese would exploit Western refusal to stop the Italian invasion with military aggression of their own.

An Italian admiral had returned a medal awarded him by the British for assistance to their forces in the 1902–04 campaign against the mullah in British Somaliland.

The Italian air force had bombed the Abyssinian fortress of Dagnere on the Webbe Shibeli River.

And finally, actress Dolores Costello had filed suit for divorce against John Barrymore, charging cruelty and desertion and asking for both of their automobiles, two rifles, and a shotgun, as well as repairs to their Beverly Hills house.

Another announcement said that there would be special sales of British woolens and French perfume at the shopping center in the first-class main hall. The movie that day was *Dinner for Three*, starring Cary Grant, Nora Gwynne, and Amberson Hayes. Nora Gwynne.

Spencer put all this aside and looked out the porthole. He was puzzled that Edwina had neither come to him nor tried to contact him, but decided not to telephone her and run the risk of a chat with Lord Mountbatten. He missed her. She had become mixed up in the pain he still felt over Whitney. In an odd way, so had Nancy Cunard.

Edwina had left a small pearl earring on his dresser. He put it in a jacket pocket as he completed his morning preparations, bundling finally in a tightly buttoned trench coat and Scottish wool cap.

The wind was too fierce for him to go far forward, though standing before the bow of the ship had been one of the privileges of first class he had looked forward to the most. But, sliding and slipping, he made it to the rail. Peering over it into a swirling cavity of foam and cerulean blue, the very bowels of the ocean seemingly in view, he felt exultant. The thrilling pleasure remained even as a sudden, unseen wave rushing back from the bow showered him with cold water. He ducked and shouted like a happy boy, then was surprised to hear another voice next to him.

It was a woman, dressed in yellow oilskins obviously borrowed from a crewman, for they were much too large for her. Curly tufts of blond hair stuck out from beneath her dripping hat. Her cheeks were wet and rosy, and she had eyes that were at once the bluest and the grayest he had ever seen.

"*Guten morgen,*" she said. "Excuse me. Good morning."

"*Ich spreche Deutsch,*" he said, recognizing her from the Le Havre railroad station.

"*Ja.* Well, isn't it wonderful, *der zee? Wunderbar!*"

Another passing wave dashed water against their faces. The roll of the ship pulled back at them, but they gripped the rail tightly. When at last the *Wilhelmina* began to shift back again, the woman peered over the side as he had done, holding onto her hat.

"What power!" she said. "*Solch Wut. Das Wut von Gott.*"

"It's very humbling," he said.

"I feel so *furchtsam*—timid," she said. "I ride horses. I fly airplanes. I climb mountains, I shoot big game. But I am a bad swimmer. Here I would drown."

"Here Gertrude Ederle would drown. Do not feel timid. Feel simply human. That's why God created storms. To remind."

The blond woman had been smiling hugely at the sea. She lessened the expression to something more correct as she reached to grip his hand.

"*Entschuldigen sie, bitte,*" she said. "I am the Countess von Bourke und Kresse. Dagne von Kresse will do. *Und Ihnen?*"

"*Ich heisse Jim Spencer.* C. Jamieson Spencer. *Von Paris, und Chicago.*"

"*Entzückende.* I must get back to my brother. He has trouble getting about in this heavy weather. *Wiedersehen.* I leave you to be human with God." She smiled again.

Like the storm, she had cheered him. It hadn't mattered that she was German.

Nora went to the first-class verandah grill for breakfast, making a hard, lurching progress along the corridors, slipping and banging her elbow twice. Her pale skin bruised easily. She feared she'd have to wear long gloves with her evening gown that night. She hated them because they made her hands sweat.

The headwaiter took her to a large table near the side windows on the starboard side. There were only four or five others in the room and there was little chance she'd be bothered, though she was feeling lonely this morning and wouldn't mind company, of the right sort. Not philandering English gentlemen.

She glanced about at the other breakfasters. As she almost should have expected, the damned American was there, the omnipresent slender, handsome man from the Ritz Bar, from the de Mornays', from the train, from the lifeboat drill, from the ends of the earth. He nodded politely as their eyes met but immediately went back to the book he'd been reading.

Perhaps it was she who was haunting him.

"Boiled potatoes and toast," she said to the Oriental waiter when he came. "And hot tea."

"Boiled potatoes, missy? Boiled potatoes not on the menu."

"That's what I want. Boiled potatoes, please. With a little paprika."

As usual, she was being too polite. If for once she started acting like a movie star, she might be treated like one.

"Yes, missy. We try. We try."

As he moved away, she wished she had stayed in her cabin or, indeed, had never boarded the *Wilhelmina.* It was her lucky, lucky day. The storm, the strange American, and now Duff and Diana Cooper, standing in wobbly fashion at the grill's entrance, waiting to be escorted to a table.

Fortunately, they were looking the other way, at the headwaiter, who was busying himself with a steward.

Nora was desperate but helpless. She couldn't just dash past them, but it was the only way out. She had no newspaper to hide behind. If she lingered much longer, Duff would see her and the Coopers would descend upon her table. Nora needed to act at once, and to her dismay, there was only one thing she could do.

Moving quickly, she crossed over to the American's table and sat down in the chair opposite him, fumbling nervously with her hands as she snatched up a napkin. He still made her feel quite spooky with his mysterious and constant presence, but she could say this for him: He might not be an English gentleman, but he had not put his hand on her bare buttocks during the last night's dinner.

"I'm sorry," she said. "May I join you?"

Her expression seemed to reflect so many conflicting emotions, Spencer was as perplexed as he was amused—and pleased.

"You already have," he said gently. "In any event, you're certainly welcome."

"I'm really sorry. I'm trying to avoid someone."

"Obviously not me. For once."

She smiled but looked no less troubled.

"No, that seems impossible." It unsettled her further that she found herself warming to his presence. For all that he had frightened her in recent days, there was something oddly comforting about him. "It's that couple the maître d' is taking to a table. They're English. She's an aristocrat or something and he's supposed to be a very important man in the government. Anyway, he's a masher. He was pawing me at dinner last night, just outrageously, and at the captain's table."

"First class is very small." Spencer set his book aside. "It's hard to avoid one's peers."

"Pardon?"

"A joke. Not a very good one. Like this thing." He showed her the weather forecast form predicting a hundred degrees and sunshine.

"That's crazy," she said.

"I asked a steward. He said someone slipped a bunch of these in with the real ones. The real ones predict fifty degrees and stormy. We have a real comedian aboard."

"This is the strangest trip I've ever taken."

Her eye caught the movement outside the window. It was entirely vertical. There was a glimpse of the horizon. Then, as the ship plunged on in its roll, the line of sky rose upward and disappeared, the window filling with a lifting curtain of green and swirling white that went on endlessly. Finally it stopped. The motion reversed itself until the horizon slowly reappeared and then vanished again, as the view turned to one of dark and angry clouds.

He followed her gaze.

"I used to spend hours this way," he said, "crossing the Atlantic in a convoy during the war. I'd see an escort vessel on the horizon, and then the ship would roll and there'd be nothing but water, and when we righted ourselves the escort would be gone from the stage."

"Not sunk?"

"No, although we could never be sure."

"You were a flier, weren't you? You won a lot of medals. I was told that, that night at the de Mornays'."

"I flew, but there weren't a lot of medals."

"I met Lindbergh once. At a dinner in New York. It was for the governor of New Jersey."

"I wish you could meet him again. Right here, today."

"What do you mean?"

"Nothing. A sort of joke, with myself. Perhaps on myself."

"Mr. Spencer, it's no exaggeration to say I don't exactly understand you."

The Oriental waiter started toward the table she had abandoned, saw her, and changed course toward them.

"You eat here, missy?" he said, setting down her potatoes and toast. "You not like other table?"

He had only half filled her teacup, but the ship's slide caused its contents to slosh over the side nevertheless. A flower vase on the next table tipped over, rolled, and fell to the floor with a loud crash. The table vases were made of expensive Irish crystal.

"They must have been a handsome couple once," said Spencer, looking at the Coopers after the waiter had gone. "It's funny how people become caricatures of themselves as they get older."

"They're still quite attractive," Nora said. "But I'm not attracted. He behaved like a real lug."

Instead of eating, she fidgeted, then lighted a cigarette.

Another waiter was coming toward them, bearing something on a silver tray that was not food. He'd been at the Coopers' table.

It was a calling card. Nora picked it up, then stared at the back of it in fury.

"What a creep," she said. "He's asking us to join them."

"Mademoiselle," said Spencer, taking the card from her. "You are dealing with an English rake, as they like to style themselves. They're hopeless, but something can be done." He handed the card back. "Write this on it: 'If you want to see me, come to the first-class cinema at eleven o'clock.' "

"But I don't want to meet him at the movie theater."

"You don't have to. If you haven't noticed, the movie today is that film you made with Cary Grant, *Dinner for Three*. If he comes, there'll you'll be."

For a moment she thought he was mocking her, but his gaze and manner were quite sincere. He grinned.

"Aren't you clever," she said. She took up a pen and wrote what Spencer said on the card and gestured to the waiter to take it back to the Coopers' table. She was enjoying this, in a way. "I was embarrassed to see that film on the schedule. Now you've made it worthwhile."

"If you want to avoid him the rest of the day," Spencer said, "go over to second class. No one will bother you, and they have movies and other amusements, too."

She reached and touched his hand, a gesture of gratitude and friendship.

"You're actually a kind and funny man. I'm a little surprised. You still frighten me a bit, but it goes away, talking to you. I'm sorry if I've been rude."

"Such flattery. Finish your breakfast and then make a break for it. I'll stage some rearguard action to keep him at bay."

"You're being very nice."

"You set a good example."

"Thanks. Thanks really very much, Mr. Spencer."

Lady Emerald stepped beyond the pale—through the connecting doors that led into second class—to her mind, stepping into the hell that was the middle class. Judging by the nondescript dress of the few other passengers she encountered in this inferior region, it was every bit as degrading as she feared.

Clinging to the passageway railing, feeling old and vulnerable in this storm, Emerald kept repeating her daughter's cabin number over and over in her mind, so she'd make no mistake. She wished to speak to no one else in this place but Nancy.

She might have to spend a large part of the day here, if Nancy wished. Whatever it took, she would make the sacrifice. She had sworn an oath to it. She and Nancy would reconcile. It would not be said that Emerald, Lady Cunard, was without a mother's heart, or *noblesse esprit*.

It would not have done to have kept pressing Nancy to join her in first class. Ultimately, her daughter would have given in only by dragging Henry Crowder along with her, and that would have been the end of all of them.

Emerald came to the correct cabin number, drew up her courage, and rapped on the door. There was no response. She rapped harder, then pounded in frustration. She could not bear to have made this unhappy journey for nothing.

The door was unlocked and, before her thumping, gave way. "Nancy?" she called, and stepped inside. The bedclothes were in disarray and there was a dirty glass or two visible, but otherwise no sign of them—no clothing, no luggage, nothing. "Nancy?" she called again, poking into the closet, and then the bath. There were no toothbrushes, nothing at all.

Someone was standing behind her—the room steward.

"Something wrong, mum?"

"My daughter. The people in this cabin. Where are they?"

"Oh, they move, mum. This morning. Down to third class."

Emerald pushed past him, wanting to shriek. She would pursue Nancy no farther. She had done all a mother could do.

Dagne returned from her morning's vigorous walk, which had included much of the ship's interior as well as some time on the outside deck. The count was up and dressed, again studying his aircraft drawings.

She began brushing out her hair.

"*Mein Gott*," she said, "did you know this ship has a kosher kitchen?"

"Don't worry. I'm sure they won't require you to eat from it."

"I've never heard of such a thing."

"You must spend more time out in the world, Dagne. Civilization has many amenities nowadays unknown in Germany."

"Stop it."

"You stop it, *bitte*. Two envelopes came. One, I think, is a wireless message."

"Didn't you open them?"

"I have no interest in wireless messages, particularly if, as I presume, they come from Germany."

Only one of the envelopes contained a wireless message. The other was large, stiff, and formal, addressed to the both of them. Turning it over, Dagne stared at the royal crest on the back.

"*Liebchen bruder, Ich glaube wir grosse Glück haben.*"

"*Ja, ja, Dagne. Sicher,*" he said.

She opened the envelope carefully. The words "His Royal Highness" jumped out at her, as did "commands me to invite you to a dinner." The invitation was signed by a Major Metcalfe, whom she took to be an aide-de-camp.

Dagne danced about the room, collapsing finally on the settee.

"We've done it, *liebchen!*"

"Congratulations. What have we done?"

"We wanted to break into the royal circle. We're being invited into it with open arms, by the prince himself! It's like sailing unchallenged into the midst of the British fleet off Jutland." She held the invitation up like a downed game bird. "Dinner! Tonight! In his suite! *Auchgeseichtnet!* Lady Cunard and Chips Channon must have told him about us. You see, my charm works its wonders."

"Good for you, Dagne, though I'm sure tonight's will be as insufferable as last night's dinner."

"This time you will have no choice but to mind your manners."

"Certainly. The prince can't possibly be as loathsome and supercilious as those two."

"I am told he is an anti-Semite, *liebchen.*"

"More of your wishful thinking. *Liebchen.*"

Annoyed with him, she opened the wireless message and froze. The joy she had felt upon seeing the royal invitation now utterly vanished. It was from Goering, signed, as they had agreed, "Uncle."

"Sickness at home," it began, which meant there was trouble and danger. "Sister Susan"—Goering's code name for Himmler—"does not want you to return, but you must. Be careful. With love. Uncle."

She swore, to herself. Himmler had learned what they were doing and was trying to interfere. That was clear, just as it was that he did not want them to survive the voyage, that others might not want them to survive the voyage. But how would the Reichsführer-S.S. attend to that? With agents in New York? Where else?

She went to the dressing room of their quarters and took her pistol from a suitcase, placing it in her handbag. She would keep it with her every moment now.

They were always grasping and scheming, those others, those conniving exploiters who had seized upon the Führer's brilliant rise to pull themselves out of the chicken shit that made up their small, mean, grubby lives—ever putting their ambitions over the one glorious goal of restoring Germany to its old power and grandeur. They had no idealism, these grubs. As her brother could never be made to understand, Dagne had idealism—enough for the both of them.

"Is something wrong, Dagne?"

"No, Martin. I'm just trying to think of what to wear tonight."

Spencer went to read in the first-class smoking room, which to his amazement had a working fireplace, though the smoldering logs kept rolling off the grate and a patient steward, like Sisyphus and his rock, had to rush over and restore them every few minutes.

The room remained empty of other passengers for nearly an hour. It was not a place where Edwina could be expected to come—though he had come to realize that Edwina could be expected to go almost anywhere, if she put her mind to it. He had not come here in search of Edwina, or whatever it was she represented in this unreal other-life he now inhabited. It was simply a part of the ship he had not yet visited, and it therefore held out the promise of something new and different happening to him. Like a chance meeting with former army mail pilots from Minnesota.

Nothing new and different did happen. Instead, Chips Channon walked in on him, wearing a tweed jacket and smoking, much the master of an English country house come to greet a guest. He took the chair opposite Spencer's and ordered a whiskey before speaking. Spencer simply watched and waited.

"I've been looking for you, dear boy," Chips said, "having heard you'd changed your accommodations. I wanted to welcome you to our little circle, though I gather you've been welcomed quite warmly already."

"Henry—"

"It's 'Chips' now, Jamieson. To one and all."

" 'Chips,' then." Spencer smiled. "Why did you tell one and all about me and Alice Silverthorne? Hardly in the Francis Parker tradition. *Old boy.*"

"It just came up. Alice is quite notorious down in British East, and everyone here knows about her. It was a way of explaining you. An introduction. You required some explaining, popping up like that. Perhaps you still require some explaining. Why are you here, Jamieson?"

"I'm traveling on business back to the United States."

"No. I mean here. Among us."

"I was in second class. I was content with that. Lady Mountbatten wasn't my idea, though she's a lovely idea."

"Indeed. And what sort of 'business' are you on?"

"Publishing business. Encountering you was completely a matter of chance. Or mischance, as you might put it, or I should. As a matter of fact, it's something of a distraction."

"Though hardly the distraction presented by the inimitable Edwina."

"A very charming lady, as I said."

"And very generous," Chips said, rolling his eyes to include the luxurious chamber as a silent addendum to his remark. "You've caught her in the depths of what's come to be known as her black period, Jamieson. She's flung herself all over the world in recent years, risking her life, struggling to be alone. She was nearly killed in a civil war in Bolivia and has brushed with death in every other godforsaken place. But she's kept coming back. Turns up at all the best garden parties in the South of France, when she's least expected. Lady Edwina, chipper again, brilliant again. Sometimes too chipper, perhaps. She paused overlong in America after her stay in the Pacific. Stayed with Joshua Cosden at his estate on Long Island, but saw quite too much of Harlem. According to gossip, she also saw quite too much of that skirt-chaser Prince Obolensky."

Spencer motioned to the steward. Channon was giving him reason to join in the ritual early drinking of these tribal British people, the same they doubtless gave each other.

The logs had stopped rolling off the fire. The storm was easing.

"Tuppenny royalty, really, the Mountbattens," Channon said. "But the Prince of Wales quite dotes on them." He paused to study Spencer's reaction, but there was none.

"I like them, too," he continued. "And she is quite beautiful."

"As you 'English' say, 'quite.'"

"Well, then," Chips went on. "Since you're going to be with us, let me tell you about the rest of our party."

"If you must."

"Dear boy, I should think you'd be rather intrigued. We're the only 'quality' to be found aboard, I daresay. 'We' includes Emerald Cunard. Emerald, *Lady* Cunard. A dear friend of the Prince of Wales, and a very dear friend of mine."

"An aging salon queen who's past menopause and dies her hair canary yellow," said Spencer. "She carries on with an ex-wine salesman whom Adolf Hitler has sent to London as the perfect ambassadorial representative of the Third Reich. She's a bitter, mean-spirited insomniac of a woman who can't let an evening go by without insulting everyone at least once."

"You're remarkably ill informed, Jamieson. Who said this to you? Edwina?"

"Certainly not. Old boy. Much too decorous a lady. No, I chanced to chat with daughter, Nancy, who seems also to be aboard this social Noah's Ark."

"It was a dreadful mistake of Emerald's, to invite her. An odious, unwashed little communist, Nancy is. It's my hope we'll deposit her in New Jersey or on Ellis Island or some such place before docking."

Spencer took his whiskey from the steward's tray. He wondered what Chips would have looked like in the kennels of Ellis Island when it was still used as a processing center for millions of immigrants. Since the war and the Red Scare of 1919, it had been converted into a deportation facility.

"To get on with it," Channon said. "We also have the Coopers. If you haven't heard of Diana, you must be the most uncivilized man in the world. She's the daughter of the Duchess of Rutland, don't you know. One of the First Families of the Realm. And she's probably the most beautiful woman in the Empire. I daresay half the men in Society are in love with her."

"The other half doubtless in love with her husband."

Chips lowered his eyelids. "You know little of British society, Jamieson. I'm certain of that. Duff Cooper much prefers women. He has a brilliant mind and a brilliant future, if only he'd come to his senses and abandon Winston for Neville Chamberlain and Sam Hoare. I like Winston awfully. And he's a very close friend of the prince. But, like poor Duff, he's much too pro-Jew and pro-French. He doesn't understand quite which way the country's going."

"As much as I admire what you say of Cooper's politics," Spencer said, "I think he's a filthy lecher. Not above schoolboy panting and pawing at formal dinner parties. Innocent American girls as victims. Sweet young things you and I wouldn't be worthy of."

"You disapprove of lechery? You, Jamieson?"

"I disapprove of *droit de seigneur.*"

"How middle class."

"He greatly embarrassed a passenger. Miss Nora Gwynne, who is by way of being a friend of mine now."

"Yes. Poor Edwina. She'll be devastated to hear. At any rate, also with us are the Count and Countess von Bourke und Kresse. Brother and sister, you know, not man and wife, though I'm not certain it makes much difference to them. Very Prussian, yet very charming. You might enjoy him. He was an aviator, too, during the war."

"During the war I didn't much enjoy Prussian aviators."

"Also, we have Peregrine, Lord Brownlow. An intimate of the Prince of Wales, and I daresay the likely candidate to be lord in waiting to Edward once he's become king. Last we have Major Edward Dudley. We call him Fruity. A very dashing chap, rather like you were once, Jamieson. Cavalry officer. Became a friend of the prince's in India. Married one of Mary Curzon's daughters. You'll recall that Lady Curzon—"

"Was from Chicago. Just like us."

"More than that, Jimmy. That's what I'm trying to impress upon you. There was never and never shall be anyone in Chicago like these people. No one so brilliant, no one so highly bred, no one so *saignant*. You must understand, Jamieson. These are the very best people on earth. The very best. They cannot be trifled with, be fooled with. Be embarrassed. Especially by one of my old friends."

"Have you really mentioned them all? I get the sense of frosting without the cake here."

"How clever of you," said Chips. "Something to do with journalist's intuition, no doubt. Very clever, and unwise." He put out his cigarette and became very serious. He leaned forward, his elbows resting on his knees.

Spencer abruptly stood up and crossed to the fireplace, hooking his arm over the mantlepiece. He swirled his whiskey in the crystal glass. He would play the lord of the manor for the moment, while Chips prattled on.

Channon paused uncomfortably, looking up at his old schoolmate, who, though quite thoroughly rumpled, looked easily as aristocratic as he did, if not more so. Spencer had always had this presence. It was one of the things Channon had admired and envied him for. Spencer had ridden better than he, sailed better than he, danced better than he. But he had not succeeded in society. And Chips had reached society's pinnacle. He would make Spencer wary of coming near, if he could.

"Jamieson. Before this conversation goes any further, there's something I must know. Your connection with the newspaper . . ."

"I'll come clean, Henry," said Spencer, after taking a swig of warm scotch. "Nowadays, I'm just a crumbum reporter. I have been for years, as a matter of fact, ever since my father went bankrupt. Completely and utterly ruined, I am. I haven't a cent. Haven't had for the longest time."

"Mother wrote that she kept seeing your name in the paper. I hadn't realized it might have been a by-line."

"I'm on this boat on a story."

Channon sighed, unhappily, as if Spencer had confessed to some great crime. Whatever Spencer did would adhere to him, as well.

"Then you do know about the prince," Chips said sadly. "Edwina told you everything."

"Hell, no. Old boy. It wasn't just Edwina. It's been practically everyone I've met. You might as well trot the royal fellow around the deck in a golden carriage. But you needn't worry. My story has nothing to do with him."

"What? The Prince of Wales is the biggest story in the Western world. Do you know who else is with us? Wallis Warfield Simpson, the Baltimore lady who's become the prince's favorite. We have them both. Her husband, Ernest, a nice but dreary sort, actually, is off in Canada on business. This is raw meat for you newspaper types, Jamieson."

"Not me. I don't give a damn."

"Well, what is this story you are on?"

"Can't say. It could ruin everything."

"It would help if I knew."

Spencer wondered what it would help. "I'm on the *Wilhelmina* to interview Charles Lindbergh."

"Lindbergh? Why, that's ridiculous."

"Of course."

"Then why are you here?"

"To interview Charles Lindbergh."

Channon rose and went to stand next to his one-time friend as he might in the gentleman's lounge of his club.

"Enough bad jokes, Jamieson. This is quite important to us all. The consequences of, well, widespread public knowledge of the prince's presence, and Mrs. Simpson's, on this voyage could be disastrous for him, at least while the old king is alive. Your discretion is paramount. The others have sworn theirs. Will you? For the sake of friendship, and old times? For the sake of honor? You've always been an honorable man, Jamieson."

Spencer shook the other's hand in affable, old-school manner. "Of course. Old boy."

"Seriously?"

"Yes. Seriously. Of course."

Channon smiled benignly. "Well, then," he said, taking an envelope from his pocket and handing it to Spencer. "I have a most pleasant surprise for you."

Spencer opened the envelope, wondering, for a passing moment, if it might contain money. Instead it was an engraved invitation, with an elegant script filling the blanks. "I have been commanded by His Royal Highness . . ."

"As you note, simply black tie. I'm not sure what your relationship is with Edwina at the moment, but it would be appreciated if you would be on your best behavior. Lord Mountbatten will be there, too."

"And how will he behave?"

"Perhaps you'll escort Miss Gwynne. You said you're friends. It would be appropriate. Indeed, most suitable."

"Jolly well suitable."

"I daresay she could use a protector, after what you say about Duff, and I expect she could use some guidance, as well. Some social guidance. There'll be cocktails in the Mountbattens' suite beforehand. Seven o'clock. And, Jamieson. I promise you. Alice Silverthorne won't be mentioned again."

The storm was spent. Though there were humplike swells slapping against the bow and sides, the winds had diminished as the following high-pressure center moved colder, clearer, and infinitely more stable air over them. The angry squall line was moving rapidly on to the east. The violent pitch and roll had ceased. All was well, except for one disappointment. The violent roll had stopped at the wrong moment. The *Wilhelmina* still heaved and shifted, but it was stuck in an irretrievable list to starboard. Every deck was slanted by twenty degrees. One could adjust one's movements to the back and forth of the roll, but this slope made every step a clumsy one. Forgetfully, van der Heyden poured coffee straight into his cup, only to have the stream fall three inches to the side, splattering his shoe.

He laughed. "*Geblokkeerd.*"

"What's wrong?" van Hoorn asked.

The captain shrugged. "That we have to find out. There was a German ship that had this problem before the war. The *Imperator.* They had to refit her, taking weight out of the superstructure, removing the marble baths in first class."

"We already did that with the *Wilhelmina,*" van Hoorn said. "After the sea trials."

"It didn't work with the *Imperator* either," the captain said. "She still lists a little. She's in the Cunard service now, you know. The British confiscated her after the war and renamed her the *Berengaria.*"

"Lady Cunard should feel at home," said van Groot, the first officer.

"We have to do something," van Hoorn complained. "We can't steam into New York harbor this way."

"If the passengers crowd the rail, as they always do, it will be even worse," said the captain. "I fear it's those new ballast tanks they installed, the ones that were supposed to prevent the ship from rolling." A bit of merriment came into his reddened eyes. "Ingenious, those tanks."

"They weren't my idea, Captain."

"They were someone's. Don't worry, *mijnheer.* I'll shift some of the cargo and get as much fuel oil into the port-side tanks as possible. Maybe that will help. But the main thing is to complete the crossing. And anyway, *mijnheer,* the *Imperator* was very popular. What's a little idiosyncracy?"

Flushed and happy as a little girl on her birthday, Nora Gwynne cheerfully welcomed Spencer into her suite, though she kept a careful distance from him.

"How do I look?" she asked. She was wearing a long, low-cut green satin gown, with long green gloves.

"Incomparable. You'll be the most beautiful woman there."

"I can't believe they asked me. I can't believe this is happening. Think of it. The Prince of Wales. I'm going to have dinner with the Prince of Wales!"

"He's just a little middle-aged man, hardly as aristocratic, really, as Ronald Coleman."

"He's the real thing, Mr. Spencer. I've never met a real prince before, and this one's going to be King of England. I wish I could tell people. I'd love to tell my mother."

"Tell your mother. Everything he does gets out sooner or later. I don't think he really cares."

"I promised to say nothing. I don't lie to princes."

She looked into a mirror and pushed at her hair, then picked up her green evening bag. Her breasts bulged slightly against the bodice of her dress as she leaned closer to the glass.

"Well, I'm excited," she said, standing straight. "I'm goddamn thrilled, to be truthful about it. My holiday is finally turning out like I hoped."

"We've four more days to go, and your friend Duff Cooper's still aboard."

"But now I have a gallant escort," she said, putting her arm in his. "It's so funny that you should turn out to be my protector. *If* I can really trust you."

"You can ask Chips Channon. I'm an honorable man."

Edwina herself greeted them at the door, as friendly to Spencer as she was to Nora, no communication of any kind visible in her eyes. He could have been the President of France, or a postman. It seemed all the same to her. He pressed the pearl earring she had left in his cabin into her hand discreetly. She took it without a pause.

"How nice to see you again, Lieutenant Spencer. I'm so pleased that you could join us, Miss Gwynne."

Chattering on about the weather and the ship's peculiar list as they stepped into the noisy room, she brought them to her husband, Lord Mountbatten, who was wearing a dress naval uniform.

"Wonderful to have you aboard, Miss Gwynne," he said, "I saw one of your films today. Top ho." The commander's demeanor went from boyish to correct as he turned to Spencer. "You're Chips's friend. Lieutenant Spencer, the aviator."

"That was a long time ago, on both counts."

"Yes, well. Edwina's told me quite a lot about you. I gather you were one of the more illustrious aces of the war."

"Not at all. I only downed three aircraft, though I killed every man I hit."

Nora, who'd been looking about at the others in the room, gave him a startled glance, as if it had never occurred to her that those in the war killed each other.

"Well, you and Edwina seem to have hit it off jolly well. Miss Gwynne, do you know our good friend Noel Coward?"

Before she could reply, Chips Channon came up, acting the host even here in the Mountbattens' suite.

"You must come meet His Royal Highness," he said, beaming.

"I'm going topside," Mountbatten said, "and see if I can't do something about this idiotic list. If the Grand Fleet had been commanded this incompetently, we all should have perished at Jutland."

"I didn't know you were at Jutland, Dickie," said Lady Cunard, coming up to them in a long yellow dress that matched the color of her hair. She introduced herself, eyeing both of them speculatively, as if restrained only by the prince's presence from making some pithy, ripping remark. Instead she spoke next to Chips. "This dinner party seems a trifle large, don't you think?" She glanced pointedly at the young Mr. and Mrs. Parker who were seated on a couch, content to be awed spectators.

"They're Wallis's idea," said Chips. "She insisted when she learned he's from Baltimore. Now, come along, Jamieson. His Royal Highness awaits."

The prince and Mrs. Wallis were standing in the far corner, he dressed in a Scottish kilt, she in a long, powder-blue evening gown with her wrists and neck swathed in jewels. Nora gripped Spencer's arm tightly.

"I don't know what to say," she said, in a nervous whisper. "How do I act?"

"Don't act. Just be your charming self. He's supposed to initiate all conversation and physical contact. Call him 'Your Royal Highness' the first time. After that, 'sir.'"

"Do I curtsy?"

"No. You're an American. And remember, so is she."

"Come," said Chips. "They're waiting."

Nora did curtsy, anyway, in wobbly fashion. Mrs. Simpson showed her disdain for this awkwardness with arched brows and lowered lids, but the prince was using his working manners and was all impeccable charm. He mentioned the titles of three of Nora's films and discussed her co-stars as if he knew them. In practiced royal fashion, he seemed deeply interested in everything she had to say. Spencer supposed it was the exactly the same with jobless Welsh coal miners and visiting maharajas.

Edward was even more striking in person than in photographs, actually more beautiful than handsome—a girl's face with a man's physique. For all the quick smile and chipper mien, his eyes had a troubled melancholy to them. His visage seemed oddly illuminated from within, a religious light. Spencer felt uncomfortable looking at him.

Mrs. Simpson struck him as at once hard and rough and coolly elegant. Her voice was light and slightly Southern, but decidedly cool. She extended her hand, almost as if he should kneel and kiss it.

Instead he shook it politely, then quickly reached for a glass of champagne from a tray carried by a passing servant. If this was a breach of protocol, it was fine with him.

"We're so very pleased you could join us, Mr. Spencer," she said. "His Royal Highness is very fond of Americans."

"So I've noticed. And thank you for calling me 'mister.' Others in your party have been calling me 'lieutenant.' "

"Whatever for?"

"I used to be an aviator in the military."

Something about this bothered her. She turned to attend to what the prince was saying. Spencer lingered a moment, then slipped away, wanting to talk to Edwina. Instead Chips virtually leapt to his side.

"Jamieson!" he said, in seething, whispered rebuke. "You don't walk away from His Royal Highness while he's speaking! Must you be the Chicagoan all your life?"

Before Spencer could reply, Edwina appeared, taking him by the arm. He thought it was to draw him aside for a quick few private words, but instead she brought him to the handsome German couple.

"I want you to meet the Count and Countess von Kresse," she said. "As fliers, you must have much in common."

The count bowed slightly, stiffly. The woman, smiling in recognition, extended her hand to be kissed. He complied, then recalled their morning encounter. When the Germans spoke, the man did so with a surprisingly American accent, his speech almost Southern. She spoke English well and crisply, but sounded exactly what she was, a Prussian aristocrat.

"I have not flown since the war," Spencer said.

"Nor I. It was certainly enough."

"You were the seventh-ranking German ace. I remember your name well."

"Tied for seventh. All that is unimportant now."

"You killed forty-four men."

"Forty-four aircraft, Mr. Spencer." Von Kresse sighed and shifted his weight painfully. "I don't know how many men died in them. It was too many."

"Mostly British?"

"We never flew patrols in a French sector. It doesn't matter. They were brave men, whoever they were."

"Maybe. I only shot down three planes. Two of the times, they were trying to get away. Observation planes, without escort."

He recalled the observer of one, rising from behind his machine gun with the impact of Spencer's heavy bullets, standing and flinging his arms out Christ-like.

"It was war, Mr. Spencer. We all did something like that, or worse."

"The Richthofen Jagdgeschwader perhaps especially. So many victories."

"The war was such a long time ago," said Dagne. "We shouldn't be talking about it. Now we are all friends."

"Mr. Spencer," said the count. "It was a regrettable war for all concerned."

"Goering was one of your squadron leaders, wasn't he? That explains a lot. There were atrocities, as I recall. Especially after the breakout from Cambrai. The cold, highly skilled, bloody-minded hunters of the Flying Circus. I remember one report about school children being strafed."

The count's face went ashen, the muscles about the mouth and jaw clenched hard.

"You know nothing about it, Mr. Spencer. You were not there."

Nora came to Spencer's side. "I can't believe it," she said. "He's just wonderful!"

"Permission to come aboard the bridge?"

Van der Heyden was surprised to see Lord Mountbatten at the entrance curtain, surprised more to see him wearing a naval uniform.

"Yes, Lord Mountbatten. Certainly. We're just trying to deal with this damned list to starboard. It's proving rather stubborn."

Mountbatten stepped into their midst, halting with legs close together and hands clasped behind his back. His voice was pleasant and friendly, but his demeanor was that of someone in command.

"Did you ship a lot of water in the storm, Captain?"

"Pumped it all out some time ago," said van der Heyden. "No, this list is an old friend. It first showed up in sea trials. The company sent the *Wilhelmina* back for refitting to get rid of it, but now it's back."

"We encounter this problem occasionally in destroyers."

"No doubt, sir," said van Groot, leaning over a large plan of the ship's interior that was spread out over the chart table. "But the *Wilhelmina* is not a destroyer. She's five times the size of a destroyer."

"Size is irrelevant. The physical principles are the same. Have you tried shifting fuel and cargo?"

Van der Heyden coughed, and not too gently. "We are in the process of doing exactly that, Lord Mountbatten."

Dickie nodded approvingly. "You should also drain your ballast tanks."

"These ballast tanks are especially designed to prevent roll, sir," van Groot said. "How can emptying them reduce the list?"

"I'm quite familiar with this new system," Mountbatten said. "I've read about it exhaustively. It's not quite perfected, now is it? It fails in really heavy weather, as your system did this morning. But now it's working, too well. It's preventing recovery from the list."

Van der Heyden and van Groot looked at each other, not happily.

"Go ahead and flush your tanks," Mountbatten said, giving them his best smile. "If it doesn't work, pump them full again. But I'm deuced sure it will work. Soon everything will be all tickety-boo."

With Lord Brownlow and Fruity Metcalfe absenting themselves to attend to duties, official and private, there was ample room for everyone else on the invitation list to dine in the prince's suite. Wallis's cleverness was evident in the table and seating arrangements. She and Edward were at either end. To her left was the young Parker boy from Baltimore, whose mother had once snubbed Wallis at a garden club luncheon in Baltimore's Druid Hill Park—an offense she'd now have reason to forever regret, as Wallis would tactfully make clear.

Seated along that side of the table after him were Emerald Cunard, the crippled but very aristocratic Count von Kresse, Edwina Mountbatten, Chips's friend Jamieson Spencer, and the actress Nora Gwynne. Wallis thought this juxtaposition of Spencer and those two attractive women altogether wonderfully clever. The evening would not flag.

On her right, Wallis put her entertaining champion, Chips Channon, with the rest of that side of the table taken up by the young Mrs. Parker, Duff Cooper, the blond and mysterious Countess von Kresse, Dickie Mountbatten, and Diana Cooper. The prince would have on his immediate right the most beautiful woman of the evening, Nora Gwynne, and to his left the most conversationally gifted and charming, Diana Cooper. Dickie would be both near his royal cousin and directly opposite Edwina and her lover, Spencer. Duff would have two new pretties to paw, while being kept a useful distance from Miss Gwynne, whom the morning gossip had made clear was very offended by his pawing. Emerald, of course, would have another handsome German with whom to flirt.

Wallis took much pride in all this. Hers was an unsurpassed social talent. She was truly born for the society in which she now moved.

With bagpipes skirling, the prince led the procession from the Mountbattens' down the passageway to his own suite and the dinner table, with Fruity, Brownlow, and Inspector Runcie blocking off the corridor at both ends until all were inside and seated.

All had accustomed themselves to the steep list, but the servants and stewards still had trouble with the pouring. When one splashed a few drops of wine on the linen table cloth near Wallis, she called him an ugly name. The others ignored this, beginning their various conversations as if on cue.

Spencer was left much to himself. The prince continued to expend his charm on Nora, and she responded with something akin to rapture. Edwina attended only to the count, talking about French and German painters and refusing even to look at Spencer. Diana and Dickie Mountbatten were engaged in debate over the Abyssinian crisis. The Prussian countess tried to flirt with Duff, who disliked Germans and was having none of it. But he seemed bored with Mrs. Parker, as well. Chips and Emerald performed as brilliantly as always, but this was lost on the young Mr. Parker, who was little interested in the bejeweled Baltimore lady who was his hostess, particularly as she went on interminably about all the Virginia Montagues in her family and how she had been presented to society at Baltimore's famous Bachelors Cotillon, notable, among other things, for the cherished tradition of its officially misspelled name.

Parker had dated many girls who could make this claim. He was much keener on being at the other end of the table with the prince.

Finally Lady Mountbatten looked down at her plate as the count turned to answer a question from Emerald.

"Edwina," Spencer said, quietly. "You haven't spoken ten words to me today. What in hell is wrong?"

"Well, you spoke enough last night, didn't you, Lieutenant?"

"I don't know what you mean."

"I thought I'd made it magnificently clear that I was in a thoughtful mood, not in a mood for *amour*. Yet you responded with the most persistent insensitivity."

"I'm sorry."

"Too right, Lieutenant. And then you told me that perfectly hideous tale about that poor Arab woman staked out naked in the desert. What unmitigated horror that was. How could you?"

"I'm sorry. It's something that's stuck in my mind."

"Well, it's something that stuck in my mind all bloody night, Lieutenant Spencer. Every time I fell asleep I'd see her, that wretched creature, moaning and writhing as she baked and froze to a crisp. I'd see me, and wake up terrified. Good God, I spent the night with Dickie!" Her eyebrows flared as she stared hard at Spencer, then turned to Count von Kresse. "You were telling me about Egon Schiele."

"Oh, yes," said von Kresse. "A magnificent painter. Like so many of our best young people, he perished in the war. He was only twenty-eight."

"He was German?"

"Austrian. But it's all the same. These countries and empires come and go. There was no Germany until sixty-five years ago. There are only Germans. And most Germans, like me, are in large part something else."

"You're not pure Prussian?"

"There is no such thing. Certainly not in East Prussia, where I come from. We're all at least a little Polish. I'm American, as well. My mother was from Virginia. And who knows what else lies back in the centuries? Norse Vikings exploring the Baltic Sea and raiding the coast and rivers. The dark hordes riding out of the East." He smiled at her for she seemed interested and approving. "There are no nations. No pure races. Only culture and language. Those are what survive, what must survive."

"Dickie's part Polish," Edwina said.

"Yes? One of the czarist Polish families?"

"Oh, he's czarist enough. His aunt was the unfortunate czarina. His great-uncle was the Czar Alexander II. But his grandmother on the Battenburg side, the wife of a prince of Hesse, was a Polish commoner named Julie Hauke. Dickie's grandfather met her in St. Petersburg, where he was serving as an officer in the Lancers. He eloped with her to Warsaw and then married her in Breslau. It's the most wonderful thing about his family, I've always thought. Though he never talks about her. He's most tediously inexhaustible in his recountings of all the others."

"Our Führer is German," said an eavesdropping Dagne, "but was born in Austria. Martin is right. It's all the same. *Ein Volk, ein Reich, ein Führer.*"

"*Entschuldigen sie, bitte,*" said Duff, from across the table. "But at last report, Austria was a sovereign nation. Nothing at all to do with your Reich. Or has something transpired since we left Le Havre? Some military maneuvers? No, no. I've got it quite wrong. The Rhineland comes first, then Austria. *Nicht wahr?*"

Dagne, reddening, did not reply. To her right, Dickie Mountbatten asked Duff how he felt about the Italian invasion of Abyssinia.

"You and Diana are so fond of the Italians," he said. "I can't wait to sink as many of them as the *Wishart* has ammunition for."

"I adore the Italians," said Diana.

"Quite as much as Ambassador Dino Grandi adores you," said Duff. They had been given center stage, and he would use it.

"They're not the Germans," Diana said. "We must remember that. But—"

"They killed several hundred women, children, and invalids in that bombing of Adowa," Spencer said.

"Exactly," said Diana. "They cannot be excused. That was barbarism."

"If the government doesn't take a stronger stand against Mussolini in this, Eden is going to resign as foreign minister and I for one shall support him," said Duff.

"By 'stronger stand,' do you mean go to war?" asked the Countess von Kresse.

All conversation stopped. The prince was speaking to them.

"Baldwin asked me to meet with Haile Selassie when he was in London," he said. "Can you imagine? He said it would offend the dominions and the empire if I didn't. I replied it would offend the Italians if I did."

"Germany will not intervene in Abyssinia," said Emerald. "Ambassador von Ribbentrop assured me."

"We were at a dinner party at Venetia Montagu's—" Diana began.

"An assemblage sadly pro-Semite and profoundly out of touch," Channon said sonorously.

"At Venetia's dinner party, a toast was made," said Diana. "It was hardly eloquent, but it bears repeating."

"Crinks Johnstone made it," said Duff. "It was to the death of Ribbentrop."

"Duff!" exclaimed Emerald.

"And I amended it," Duff said. " 'That he should die in pain.' "

Wallis was grim. All this political bombast was going to make a shambles of her party. Why did Duff always have to go out of his way to provoke Germans? Why couldn't such a high-born man have better manners?

"Some circumspection, please, Duff," said Chips, leaning across Mrs. Parker, who looked dazed. "Joe von Ribbentrop is a dear friend of Emerald's. The countess is a friend of Chancellor Hitler."

"I have only met him, sir," she said. "But we are all of us proud to have him lead the nation."

"I met him myself," Diana said. "When Duff and I were at Bayreuth in 1933. In fact, he was staying at the same hotel at the time."

"Almost moved out," said Duff.

"No, you didn't, Duffie," Diana said. "You asked for an interview, but they fobbed you off on that fool ideologue Rosenberg. He invited us to Nuremburg."

"Couldn't get anyone in that damned hotel to make a proper gin fizz," Duff said. "And they want to rule Europe."

Martin could see that Dagne was on the verge of screaming. He nodded to her in congratulation of her remarkable self-restraint, then realized she had only mistaken his gesture for approval of Duff's comments. He did approve of them, of course, but had no intention of expressing that. Certainly not when she was so near the explosion point.

"We did go to Nuremburg," Diana said. "A panoply of beastliness. I actually passed within two feet of the Great Man. Could have killed him, I suppose, if I'd had a bomb. His complexion is quite dark, or it was then. Had a fungoid quality. Our eyes met, the famous hypnotic eyes. To me they seemed glazed and without life—dead, colorless eyes. The silly *mèche* of hair I was prepared for. The smallness of his occiput was unexpected. His physique was on the whole ignoble."

Dagne shot up from her chair, giving her napkin one very hard wring and dropping it with a thud on the table.

"*Entschuldigen sie, bitte,*" she said, looking to the prince. "I'm sorry. I feel ill. It's the ship."

Face flushed, the opposite of seasick pale, she hurried from the room.

"Actually," said Mountbatten, eyeing the level of wine in his glass, "I think the list is beginning to lessen."

The prince turned to Nora Gwynne, as if to reassure her about the others.

"I'm afraid Duff doesn't understand Mr. Hitler, or what he's trying to do," said Edward. He took both of Nora's hands and held them tight together, as if bound. This was extraordinary. One never touched royals. And royals touched almost exclusively by shaking hands. "You see, when Hitler came to power, the Jews held Europe like this. They still do, to quite a large degree, though he's working to change that. All Hitler's trying to do"—the prince flung Nora's wrists apart—"is free Europe from the tentacles of the Jews."

The Coopers and Count von Kresse stared at him—Diana with disgust, Duff with cautious contempt, the count with a sort of sad bemusement. Von Kresse rose.

"Please forgive me," he said, "but I think I should attend to my sister."

"Please stay," said Emerald.

"I'm sorry. Very sorry. But I must see to her."

When he was gone, Edwina drained her glass and also got to her feet.

"I'd just like to say," she said, with a dazzling smile, "that I think you're all a great lot of crashing bores, including you, sir."

"Edwina!" said her husband.

"I was having the most marvelous conversation with that gentleman and I intend to finish it," she said, taking up her evening bag and sidling toward the door. *"Bonsoir."*

They all sat in silence until the door shut behind her.

"Sir," said Wallis to the prince in that plaintive, insinuating whine that crept into her voice when she wanted him to do something. "Isn't it a breach of protocol for others to leave a gathering before Your Royal Highness? I'm just asking for my own instruction."

"Oh, Wallis," he said. "It doesn't matter. Everyone is just a bit out of sorts what with this awful storm and all. I'm sure we'll all be back to our merry selves in no time."

Mountbatten was peering at his wineglass again.

"Actually, David," he said. "I'm afraid I must duck away for a bit myself."

"Don't tell me you're running after Edwina," said Emerald. "That would be something of a first, would it not?"

"No," said Dickie, frowning. One day someone would put Emerald in her place. "Just up to the bridge for a minute. I told them what to do to correct the starboard list and I think they're doing it."

As Mountbatten stepped out onto the deck, a blow caught him from behind, a hard, heavy object striking the side of his head. Stunned, he staggered and dropped to his knees. Another blow was struck on his back, knocking the wind from him and causing him to collapse on the deck. Gasping, he tried to reach for his adversary, but was kicked and sent rolling toward the rail. For an instant he grasped the person's foot, but it pulled away and he was kicked again. He lapsed into unconsciousness just as he was pushed through the rail into the dark void below, just as he was pondering the odd realization that the foot he had briefly held was small, stockinged, and a woman's.

Some of the group went on afterward to the ballroom for some late-night dancing, Spencer and Nora with them. Chips took Nora off for the first dance, however, leaving Spencer with Emerald, the Parkers, and the Coopers. Then a ship's officer cut in, and then some other movie fan from among the other first-class passengers. Nora waved once to Spencer but otherwise was caught up by her circumstances. At one point she had to stop to sign two autographs.

"Celebrity is so time-consuming," said Diana, who was on Spencer's right. She moved closer.

"Quite," said Spencer, trying out the English phrase again and still not liking it. Edwina, the von Kresses, and Lord Mountbatten had not returned.

"I was once a theatrical person myself," said Diana, blond hair falling over weary blue eye. "I did that dreadful *The Miracle*, as you may know. *Tableau vivant*, the lowest form of theatrical art extant. But I did love it."

"I'm afraid I didn't see it."

"That's because you were fortunately off in the Orient or somewhere, darling, while *The Miracle* was packing them in in Cleveland. I made two films, though. One was *The Glorious Adventure*. It was a most foolish fandango about Charles II and the Great Fire of London. I played Lady Beatrice Fair and was abused by Victor Mac-Laglen, boxer cum actor. He played Bullfinch."

"I saw him in *The Informer* last month," Spencer said. "It's hard to imagine you *à deux.*"

"Oh, he was rather sweet, actually, when he was sober. My other film I was rather proud of. *The Virgin Queen*. I played Elizabeth, and had to shave my eyebrows. 'A splendid sacrifice to her sense of art and duty,' the *Daily Mail* said. Other periodicals were much the less kind. The costumes were horrible and I looked grotesque."

"I can't imagine you looking grotesque, Lady Diana."

"You're rather sweet, too, Lieutenant Spencer. Your popularity with some members of our party is not surprising." She leaned quite close, till their arms were touching on the table. She stroked his hand.

"I daresay you won't believe this, but I was offered the lead in the film *Anna Karenina*. It was while I was on tour in America with *The Miracle*. Greta Garbo had walked out of the role and they offered it to *me!* I couldn't make up my mind. Duff was so unhappy about the vulgarity of it all. Finally I decided to take it, but, *quelle domage*, it was too late. The great Garbo had changed her mind. I was never asked again to do a film. I suppose it was all for the best. There was a lot of hostility to my theatrical career, among people I scarcely knew, if knew at all. I once got an anonymous letter that said 'How can you, born in a high social position, so prostitute your status for paltry monetary considerations—you THING!' I half wondered if it was from my mother, the duchess. I doubt it, though. She knew very well that the monetary considerations were far from paltry. Then, strangely and curiously, I lost interest. Dear Duffie began to do so well with the government, and I found the government such mad fun. Had I kept on with it though, I might have been your Miss Nora Gwynne this evening. Would you have found that exciting?"

Nora had vanished from the dance floor.

"Quite," said Spencer. "Lady Diana, are you trying to seduce me?"

She shrank from him, her expression very chill. "You vulgar man, whatever are you talking about?"

"Well, what's going on here? What's the point of all this intimate chatter? We hardly know each other."

"It's true that I do enjoy a flirtation now and then. But nothing more base. I adore my husband."

"Speaking of things more base."

"You're insulting him, and he isn't even here."

"Where is he?"

She placed a hand on his arm. "Oh, please, Lieutenant Spencer. Don't spoil it. Don't cause trouble."

"Awfully sorry, your ladyship. But I simply must."

Spencer caught up with them in a dimly lit vestibule by one of the exits leading to the deck. Spencer had no idea how Duff had persuaded Nora to accompany him to this place, but it was evident she had no interest in remaining. He had his arms around her and was kissing her neck. Restrained by embarrassment and confusion, she struggled weakly and futilely. When she saw Spencer, her embarrassment increased.

Spencer pulled Cooper, a plump rather than large man, back rudely, then spun him about. Without a further word, he hit him in the jaw. Pain tore at the knuckle of Spencer's little finger. His skin had torn on one of Cooper's teeth.

Duff staggered backward, bleeding from the lip.

"You sod!" he said. "What in blasted hell is wrong with you?"

"Do you want me to hit you again?"

"Certainly not!"

"Then good night, sir. Now."

"What?"

"Go away! Go back to your wife. Go now, or we'll have a real fight."

Duff pulled himself up straight, in drunken dignity. "Good night. *Sir.*"

Nora was upset, but calmed by the time they reached the door to her suite. She opened it quickly.

"I get so tired of it," she said. "It happens wherever I go."

A man who followed her through that door could likely lay claim to bedding one of the most beautiful and most celebrated women in all the world. It was the sort of boast to make, at the proper time, in Harry's New York Bar. It was the sort of thing to interest Hemingway, like an elephant shot or a barracuda landed.

He took her hand and kissed it, as decorously as possible. "Good night, Miss Gwynne. A better day tomorrow."

"Will you come back? Will you be with me tomorrow?"

"Miss Gwyne, I'll be with you whenever you wish."

"Not 'Miss Gwynne.' Nora."

"I'll see you in the morning. Nora."

"Good night, then."

"Good night."

Kees, almost groggy now from his long labors supervising the shift of cargo, went to the first-class galley for a cup of coffee. Its heat and strength revived him, but he had had only a few sips when a crewman came up to him.

"Sorry, sir. Lady below asking for you. Down in third class."

"Asking for me?"

"Yes, sir. Sorry, sir. She in quite a state. Very unhappy. I say, frightened."

"A woman with long dark hair?"

"Yes sir. Long dark hair, long dark dress. In third class."

Kees set down his cup, shaking his head. He was so weary his nerves were numb, his limbs worked as though independently from his brain. Dislocated. Disconnected.

"Very well," he said. "I'll go see what she wants."

Olga answered the door at the first knock, her eyes wide, looking quite distraught.

"Captain," she said.

"I am not the captain," said Kees. "I am merely a third officer."

"Yes. Third officer, sir. I smell oil! Is something burning?"

"What? Oh, no. No." He turned to the crewman, motioning for him to leave them. The small dark man did so, happily. "No, miss. But we've been transferring some fuel, to help with the balance."

"I'm afraid. I fear we're going to blow up."

"No, miss. Come with me."

She stepped forward timidly, her eyes full upon him, and wary.

"Come, miss. It's quite all right. I want to show you something."

He took her past two turnings in the corridors, coming to a noisy place with locked doors and large panels set on either side.

"There are two ventilator shafts here," he said. "One vents a fuel tank and the other one of the oil burners. They run right up to the aft funnel. That's what you smell."

"But it's in my cabin."

"Oh, it can't be. You've a cabin on the hull side."

"No. It's true. Come see. Come smell."

He did so. Shutting her door behind them, she took him to her washbasin. There was a slight odor of the fuel oil, but it was minimal, a minor nuisance visited on those who could not afford the accommodations that were well situated to avoid such smells.

Kees sniffed. "It's from that same ventilator shaft. It's nothing to worry about." He leaned close to the wall, putting his hand to it. The surface was cool. "Nothing at all."

He heard an odd rustling sound, and turned to face her.

She had slipped off her dress and was wearing nothing underneath. The bare body on the bed that had haunted his dreams all the night before was now revealed to him again, soft and full and womanly—her breasts as perfect as they were large.

"This time, Captain," she said, "do not run away."

# CHAPTER
## *ELEVEN*

Count von Kresse eased open the door to his stateroom and stepped inside quietly, discovering at once that there was no point to such stealth. Dagne was awake, sitting up in her bed, her cheeks rosy in the first pink light of sunrise.

"*Gute morgen,*" he said, crossing to his own bed and lowering himself stiffly.

"*Morgen wirklich. Allerdings nicht langer nacht.*"

"Certainly not night," he repeated, yawning as he began to undo his tie.

"Which was it?" she said. "The admirer of aviation art or the English Jewess?"

"Will you never stop, Dagne? I have no wish to breakfast on tripe this morning, especially regurgitated Herr Schicklgruber tripe." He pulled off his shoes and leaned back. Despite his sister, despite his pain, he felt happy.

"You haven't answered my question."

"I don't question your liaisons, Dagne, even when they're with one of those Berlin gutter politicians."

"I am not married. You are, *liebchen bruder,* and to a Catholic woman."

"Whom I've not seen in twelve years."

"But married all the same."

"And does the new regime recognize marriages with Polish persons? I thought they'd been declared *untermensch.*"

"The Jewess is married also."

"It's what you would call a modern marriage."

224

"Well, her husband, who is a good German Englishman, was almost killed last night!"

"We learned that a few minutes ago. Edwina's with him now."

"If the ship hadn't been listing to starboard he would have fallen into the ocean. It's extraordinary luck that he rolled onto the deck below instead."

"Extraordinary luck that he wasn't badly injured even at that," said von Kresse, pulling off his dinner jacket. "They say it's just bruises and a slight concussion."

"And where were you when this was happening? In some stairwell? A lavatory?"

"We spent the night in an unoccupied cabin, and there is nothing more about this you need know, *schwester.*"

She pulled her knees up to her chin and wrapped her arms around them. It was only then that he noticed the pistol on the bed beside her.

"I am very worried, Martin."

"So I see."

She picked up the weapon and held it loosely in one hand, the barrel pointing down.

"I received a warning from Goering," she said. "Himmler knows what we're doing. For some reason he wants to stop us. And, I presume, he has an agent on board this ship, maybe more than one."

"Why didn't you tell me?"

"I didn't want to upset you. I wanted you to concentrate on our task. I thought I could handle any trouble. But now he attacks Lord Mountbatten. Why couldn't he go after Mrs. Simpson instead, and save us all this effort?"

"According to that Channon fellow, someone locked Mrs. Simpson in her closet yesterday morning."

*"Ja, aber nichts mehr."*

"We don't know that it was Himmler's people in either case. We don't know for certain if there are any of Himmler's people on this ship. How could there be? Only Goering knew we were sailing on it."

"Goering learned about Prince Edward's plans from Ribbentrop, who talks to everyone."

"I want to give this up, Dagne."

"Too late, Martin. Besides, we may yet succeed. That American boy, Christopher Parker, he told me last night about Mrs. Simpson's background. 'Genteel poverty,' I think that's the term for it. She grew up poor as dirt in some rundown section of Baltimore. Her mother took in boarders. If the prince knew that, he'd drop her fast."

"Dagne, where she comes from, the state of Maryland, it's exactly like Virginia. It doesn't matter how poor you are. As in Prussia, all that matters is who your family is. And I don't think it would matter to the prince if she was an upstairs maid. Not in the slightest. It wouldn't matter if her people were gypsies or, to harken to your obsession, Jews, even though he seems to hate them."

"And Jews her people may very well be. Anyway, Martin, I'm going to find out as much about her as I can. And I'm going to let Lady Cunard and that Chips Channon know everything I discover. Soon the prince will know all about her, as will British society."

"As long as the prince remains so enamored of her, they won't do a thing to harm her. She's their ticket to the palace."

"She's got to be stopped, Martin."

"Dagne, our task, our 'mission,' as the fat Hermann put it, is ridiculous. I'm a broken-down old Junker who can't even ride a horse. Am I supposed to charm her away from him, the Prince of Wales? Am I supposed to seduce her? She's not interested in sex. She's interested in becoming Queen of England. Interested? I'd say she's obsessed. I think she believes it's really possible. Do you recall her at dinner? It was as if she'd already been crowned."

"She will not become queen. It is obviously impossible."

"*Ohne Zweifel.* But he is the same about her. This man would do anything to have her. Give up the throne. Become a bootblack."

"Not a bootblack."

"If she wished it."

"That's a lot to say on the basis of one evening."

"I would say it on the basis of ten minutes with them. We must forget this whole business, Dagne. Learn some secret from these British. Pass that on to der Dicke. Let that be his coup. But forget Prince Edward and Mrs. Simpson. It's a fool's errand."

"You know what's at stake. You and Hermann are in agreement at least on that."

" 'Hermann,' is it?"

"Yes."

"And what about the bountiful Emmy?"

"Oh, don't be disgusting." She threw back the covers and went to the closet, rummaging through a bag. "You will need some protection. Himmler is *sehr verrucht*. He would order our deaths for any reason."

"I don't want a gun. Guns are for National Socialists."

"There's only one and I need it for myself. The chicken farmer seems to particularly enjoy having women killed. But there is this." She held up a stiletto in a narrow leather sheath. "Very sharp point. Very sharp edges. Stab or slash. Your victim's dead. It can be easily hidden in your clothing. An Italian gentlemen gave it to me when we visited Rome last year."

"I don't want it."

She came and dropped it in his lap. "For such a brave, intelligent, and worldly man, Martin, you are sometimes a ridiculous fool." She kissed him on the forehead. "But keep this well in mind. I mean to destroy this royal romance. My contributions to the Reich have been meager. This is my great opportunity and I will not squander it. This woman will not marry the prince."

Major Metcalfe and Lord Brownlow entered the bridge unannounced, finding First Officer Van Groot and several junior officers on duty.

"We want to see the captain," said Metcalfe.

"I'm sorry, sir, but you cannot," van Groot said. "He is in his quarters, sleeping. He was up much of the night. As you see, we have corrected the list. We are sailing level again."

"What was the problem?" Brownlow asked. Sunlight was glinting all across the water in front of them. They were up to full speed, and the bow was churning foam, though seas were low.

"Something to do with the ballast tanks," said van Groot.

"There's another problem," Metcalfe said. "As you know, Lord Mountbatten was attacked last night."

"I know too well. I am so glad that he was not badly injured."

"First Mrs. Simpson, and now Lord Mountbatten, the two people on board closest to the prince. I'm quite convinced Lord Louis was mistaken for the prince, being in naval uniform and all."

Van Groot looked back at his fellow officers, who were following the conversation intensely. "Come with me," he said to the Britishers.

He led them out through the sliding door onto the port side bridge wing, waiting until the door had closed behind them before speaking again. The brisk head wind created by the ship's forward speed made them raise their voices.

"Gentlemen," he said. "What is to be done? Do you want to keep everyone in your party locked in their quarters under guard? We have searched the entire ship. We have armed several officers and crewmen and are conducting patrols. We have the prince's quarters under constant surveillance. What more can we do?"

"Lord Mountbatten said his assailant was a woman," Metcalfe said.

"Yes? *Een vrouw?* How could a woman throw an athletic naval officer like Commander Mountbatten overboard?"

"We should not ignore this."

"Do you want me to have every woman on board interrogated? With whom shall I start? Lady Cunard? The Countess von Kresse? Lady Cooper? Miss Gwynne? Lady Mountbatten? They're the only ones who've had any access to your group."

"That's ridiculous," said Brownlow.

"And they can all be accounted for," Metcalfe said.

"Yes?" said van Groot. "The von Kresses left your dinner party early. So did Lady Mountbatten. Has she been quarreling with her husband? She spent the night with Count von Kresse. And before that she was with an American."

"That's none of your business, sir," said Brownlow.

"Yes, it is. As you requested, I have all of your section of first class under surveillance. I don't know how the attacker, man or woman, eluded our people. But we are doing everything we can, gentlemen, even if it means keeping a log on which unused stateroom Lady Mountbatten chooses to rest in."

Metcalfe sighed. "Very well, sir. I'm satisfied you're concerned about the danger."

"We are very concerned, Major. But may I remind you, your party is not aboard the *Wilhelmina* at the invitation of the Lage Lander Line."

Upon rising, Spencer kissed his photograph of Whitney and set it on his night table, a silly, sentimental gesture that helped to keep his thoughts from Edwina—and Nora Gwynne. They were now more than a thousand miles from Europe, utterly isolated in a tiny steel-and-iron world of their own chosen circumstance, but that meant also that they were a thousand miles nearer the United States and all the decisions he would ultimately have to make.

That morning's "Ocean News" could be dealt with in a glance. The British had ordered the evacuation of civilians from Malta. Canada had imposed a boycott of nickel imports from Italy. The Red

Cross had organized a mission to Addis Ababa to aid wounded and refugees. Hungary was calling up men twenty-two to thirty for emergency military service. It was revealed that Joan Crawford and Franchot Tone were secretly married two days before.

The weather was predicted to be sunny, with temperatures reaching 58 degrees.

That evening there would be a fancy dress ball in the first-class ballroom. Costumes would be available in the starboard gallery throughout the afternoon for those who had not brought any.

He smiled. He had once taken passage through the Strait of Malacca in a tramp steamer in which everyone aboard was in costume—pirate and thief, rum guzzler and Polynesian chief, cashiered British officer and Singapore whore. He and Whitney, whom he had just met in Venice, had gone to a fancy dress ball in Nice in 1931, during the carnival. Most of the guests had been costumed in keeping with an ancient Mediterranean theme—Roman soldiers and Roman slaves, Greeks in togas, Mesopotamians, Hittites, Babylonians, Etruscans. Most of the men had been half clad. At least a dozen women had come entirely nude except for sandals and bizarre headdress.

Whitney had worn a veil and a billowing white gown with nothing underneath. Spencer had submitted to this degradation only to the point of attending the ball in a cheap suit—and a fez. Two naked women had sat on his lap and kissed him, with Whitney watching, amused and intently curious. He had returned the kisses with some feigned ardor but had declined the proferred bare breasts. That night was the first time he slept with Whitney.

The ball this evening would be worth attending simply to see how those in Prince Edward's party chose to bedeck themselves. This ship was hardly Nice. The costumes the Dutch would provide would likely be clown suits and monk's cowls.

A steward brought a note while Spencer was dressing. It was from Nora.

"Thank you for last night," it said. "You are a very nice man. Will you please be my escort at the ball tonight? Your new friend, Nora."

Spencer reread it, then looked to Whitney's photograph again. Whitney was in Paris. He went to the desk and hastily wrote a reply on ship's stationery, scrawling *"Bien sûr, mademoiselle charmant."* Only after the steward had taken it away did he remind himself that the lady from Toledo probably knew no French.

His hand hurt. It was becoming discolored around the cut caused by Cooper's tooth. He administered a heavy dose of iodine from his kit, but otherwise paid the wound no further mind. In the war it would have been a trifle.

Spencer entered the smoking room to find Chips Channon seated in a high-backed chair facing the entrance, almost as if waiting for him.

"Good morning," he said, with a glance at Spencer's injured hand and its crimson smear.

"Good morning. Drinking so early?"

Chips had what looked to be a stinger on the table beside him. "I feel like death today. I wonder if the sands are beginning to run out; how much longer I'll be able to go on racketing about as I do."

"I think you'll make it until the end of this voyage," Spencer said, "though stingers in the morning make it a closer run thing."

"You were in a brawl with my friend Duff Cooper last night."

"Not a brawl. I just hit him."

"Was that really necessary?"

"Yes. It really was. As Nancy Cunard would say, 'quite, quite.' As you would say, the man was behaving with a decided lack of manners. If he'd been a crewman, the captain would have him flogged."

"You are talking, Jamieson, about the nephew of an earl. And, after all, that girl's no special friend of yours. She's merely an actress. And from Toledo." He pronounced the word slowly, with great emphasis on each syllable.

"I guess she should appreciate the great honor Cooper was trying to bestow upon her, but I don't."

Chips stared at him frostily, then his expression collapsed. He looked horribly fatigued, the look of a man who'd just emerged from prison, or hospital.

"Forgive me, Jamieson. I've been a poor friend. You're quite right, and Duff is quite wrong. She's a lovely, sprightly creature, *très vivant.* I'm being churlish. I have this violent headache. I wouldn't be surprised if I had a fever. I should never have come on this antic voyage. You've no idea how terribly I miss Honor and our little Paul. It's an extraordinarily satisfying emotion to meet a white pram in the park that contains one's own son. And we're moving into a new house in January, in Belgrave Square."

"I'm pleased for you, Henry. Er, Chips."

"It's a satisfying emotion seeing you again, Jamieson. It really is. I'm sorry if I seemed distant or rude. It's all very nerve-wracking being around His Royal Highness, especially in such a peculiar circumstance."

"You're certainly a devoted subject."

"And I didn't mean quite to go on so about the Jews. Whatever the awkwardness and vulgarity of their situation in England, what's happening to them in Germany is simply hideous. No one ever accused me of being anti-German, but there are times when I wonder how much longer I can cope with the present regime there. They seem to have lost all sense and reason. They carry the Jewish persecutions to such a fiendish degree. It's shortsighted, cruel, and unnecessary. Utterly unnecessary. And now we're told we shall have persecutions of Roman Catholics, too. Are they mad? How does this help our government's effort to maintain amicable relations with them? I fear Hitler thinks we are an effete, finished race."

"You English."

"My grandfather was English. And now, with me, we are English again. My little Paul will be English."

"Why don't you discuss the Nazis in such strong terms when you're with the others, Chips? Why *do* you go on so about the Jews?"

"Because of Emerald, and H.R.H. We have to humor them, don't you know. Otherwise everything becomes intolerably disagreeable."

" 'Intolerably disagreeable' is a good way to describe what it is you're humoring."

Chips took a sip of his stinger. He paused, waiting for its desired effect. "At all events, Jamieson, you shouldn't have hit Duff. He's going to become minister of war the next year. There's absolutely no doubt."

"What you don't seem to have learned about me, Henry, is that I would have hit him if he were King of England."

"Yes, I suppose you would. Crazed from the war and all that. Also, Jamieson, you should not have gotten involved with Edwina. None of us has, you know. Tuppenny royalty or no, Lord Louis is the prince's cousin."

"As I said, it was entirely Edwina's idea, at least in the beginning."

"I gather you are no longer *éprisé*?"

"Apparently not," Spencer said. It was all the same as when they were in school, talking about girls like Alice Silverthorne. "I'm sorry, too. An extraordinary woman."

"So we've all heard. And now it's the crippled count's turn. What do you think of our Prussian friends?"

"Well bred and arrogant, and probably swine. He was a real killer in the war. She strikes me as something of a beautiful corpse, although I liked her when we first met out on the deck."

"She's very forward and guttural. And not a little fanatical. He, I think, may be quite something else, however. You newspaper fellows sometimes make hasty judgments."

Duff Cooper, moving uneasily, came up to them, swooping up Channon's drink.

"Damned decent of you to have this waiting for me, Chips." He took a large gulp, a deep breath, and then took another large gulp. "Bugger you, Spencer. And good morning."

Duff's lip was as discolored as Spencer's hand, and still slightly swollen.

"Good morning."

Cooper waved frantically at a steward, pointing to the drink and making a circular motion to include them all.

"She's a damned bit of all right, Miss Gwynne is," Duff said finally. "Worth all this morning's discomfort, I daresay."

"I'm going to presume the rest of her voyage will be pleasant and uneventful."

"Right you are, Spencer. Now, I can't stand another insufferably boring day. A game of cards is in order. Poker."

"Oh, Duff," said Channon. "We needn't. It's not as though Somerset Maugham were aboard."

"Only good thing about that stammering poseur, his poker playing. We need more players. Chips, you go fetch Fruity and as many others as you can find. I can't stagger another step."

Major Metcalfe was the only other player they could recruit.

"Thank you, gentlemen," he said as Duff dealt the first hand. "I need to stand down for an hour or two. H.R.H. is particularly vexed this morning, and vexing."

"What's the term?" said Channon. "Stir crazy?"

"Yes, and now I know why jailers are little better off than their charges," Metcalfe said. "Brownlow's with him. And two armed crewmen. I've given Runcie the morning and afternoon off. He'll be busy enough tonight. The prince insists on attending the masked ball."

"Isn't that all right?" Chips asked. "He can be amply costumed. No one would recognize him."

Channon still looked like death, but the mention of the evening's gala party enlivened him. He was the sort of man who would want to attend his own funeral, and make a gay thing of it.

"The prince's costumes," grumbled Duff, "are seldom ample."

Spencer, who was holding two small pair, folded his cards. Duff won the hand with three kings, and gathered up £11. Spencer was using *Press-Bulletin* expense money. He wondered how Chief of Correspondents Carlson would react to an expense report that carried a huge gambling debt and listed the Prince of Wales' equerry and the next British minister of war as persons entertained. Carlson would scream at the expense even if he listed Charles Lindbergh.

Spencer often played poker with Whitney's husband and his friends. He remembered the touch of Whitney's hands on his shoulders as she stood behind his chair in the de Mornays' large, elegant drawing room. Luck for him and never her husband, but it was Monsieur de Mornay who often won the most.

Spencer was the victor of the next hand with two high pair. The next round went to Channon, who held a full house of two queens and three tens, but no one else had bet very much and the pot was quite small.

The game continued another forty-five minutes. Spencer remembered something his father had said about the stock market, the same stock market that had ruined the man: "Bulls win. Bears win. Pigs lose." He played as conservatively as possible, yet managed to win enough pots to be £63 ahead of his expense-money funds. Duff's early luck diminished and then fled, compelling him to borrow from Chips. Metcalfe lost consistently and looked glum, though, like Channon, he was married to one of the richest women in the empire.

Cooper bet heavily on a straight, only to lose to Spencer's heart flush. Channon won the next three hands.

"Now I know why you're called Chips," Duff said, throwing down his cards. "We need more players. An infusion of capital. Fruity, go find that young Parker fellow. He's an American. He must play poker. If he doesn't, we'll teach him."

"Duff," said Metcalfe, who was his friend. "Don't you think you've lost quite enough?"

"The game's hardly begun, old cock. Now fetch this young sport and I'll arrange for another infusion of strong drink."

The major was still gone on his errand when Lord Mountbatten appeared at the doorway, dressed in pajamas, slippers, and dressing gown, his ear and forehead bandaged. He looked about the smoking room, ignoring them at first.

"*Mon Dieu,*" said Spencer. "*Voilà President Deschanel.*"

Duff laughed, excessively. Channon only stared. "Deschanel? Do I know him?"

"He was elected president of France after the war—a handsome fellow, the amiable symbol of the happy times to come. Lost his mind almost immediately after taking office. He fell off a train and was found wandering along the tracks in his pajamas. 'You may not believe this,' he supposedly said to the first railroad worker he came upon, 'but I'm your president.' I think he ended his term of office the next year in a mental home."

"Do you think Dickie's become deranged from the blow he suffered?"

"Not at all," said Duff. "He seems very much himself."

Mountbatten came up to their table looking much like a man reporting a theft to the police.

"Are you all right, Dickie?" Channon asked. "I thought you were still in hospital."

"After the blows you took, old sport, I'm surprised to see you up walking," Duff said. "The old Royal Navy spirit, what?"

"I'm quite fine," said Mountbatten. "Have you seen Edwina? I can't find Edwina." He addressed the last sentence to Spencer.

"I've not seen her since the dinner party last night," Spencer said.

"None of us has, laddy buck," said Duff.

"She was with me this morning," said Mountbatten. "But now she's gone. I can't find my sleeping powders. She put them some bloody place and now I can't find them."

"Try the ship's doctor," said Cooper.

"He's the one who gave them to me in the first place."

"Dickie," said Cooper, with slightly clenched teeth. "Go back to him and get some more. Or send a steward to fetch some."

"Don't patronize me, Duff."

"I'm not patronizing you, Commander. I'm trying to bring you and sleeping powders back together again, if not you and Edwina."

Mountbatten's eyes were cold but a little bleary. He was perhaps not himself after all. No one invited him to join the poker game, but he seemed uninterested in it. Without another word, he turned and marched off, his slippers making a flapping sound.

"To think that man commands a destroyer," Cooper said.

"He told the captain what to do to stop the ship from listing last night," Channon said. "It worked. He may have saved us from capsizing."

The seas had become noticably heavier and they could hear the wind whistling through some nearby aperture.

"Dickie our savior," said Duff as liquor slopped over the side of his glass. "We may need him again."

"It's not a storm," Spencer said. "We've crossed a cold front and have passed into a high-pressure area. Clear skies and stiff breezes."

"And stiff passengers," said Channon. He drank.

Young Parker came more than willingly, but appeared badly disappointed that there was no royal personage at the table.

"Doesn't His Highness play cards?" he asked as Duff ordered him a drink.

"He does, but not in public," said Channon. "On this trip he does nothing in public, as we explained."

"Then why don't we join him?"

"Because, dear boy, we've not been invited."

"Deal," said Duff.

The boy said he had played poker at Harvard, and indeed he showed not a little skill. He began winning almost immediately, mostly by raising bets so extravagantly as to drive others out. Once Duff tried to outraise him, presuming a bluff, but was devastated when Parker laid out four eights to his three jacks. Cooper had borrowed £100 from Chips but now it was gone. He turned to Spencer, who was now quite comfortably ahead.

"I say, old boy," said Cooper, "could I impose . . ."

"Duff," said Channon. "Borrow from me. Then you'll only have to write one check."

"I shan't have to write anything," Cooper said, accepting two stacks of counters. "My luck is going to change."

It didn't. Within the hour he was in need of money again. As all were at least a bit tipsy, it seemed a good time to end the game, but before they could agree to do so they were joined by yet another player. It was Mrs. Simpson, dressed as if for some afternoon's high social function and glittering with rings, bracelets, earrings, and an enormous necklace.

"Wallis," said Metcalfe, glancing about at the other men in the room, "do you think this wise?"

There was no longer the rigid separation of the sexes that applied to many of the public rooms of the old pre-war liners, but even in 1935 women were almost never seen in the first-class smoking room. On some ships it was still called the gentlemen's lounge.

"I can't be penned up in there a moment longer," she said. "And no one's going to make much of a do over a little old Baltimore lady like me. Now will one of you gentlemen bring me a chair, or must I stand?"

Chips lurched from his own to drag one over from the next table. He left it adjoining their own, but not brought quite up to it.

"I'd like to join your little game," Wallis said, her soft Southern speech hardening. "Will you please make room?"

They hesitated, looking at each other, then shifted their chairs obediently. "Why not, Wallis?" said Duff. "You'll change my luck."

She changed Spencer's instead. The hands he was dealt thereafter were never quite good enough and he was compelled to fold time after time. Frustrated, he began to play more recklessly, drawing cards to outlandish combinations. His great horde of chips began to diminish.

Spencer pushed the glass at his elbow aside. Young Parker was now quite drunk and Chips had become a bit silly, prattling on about gossipy matters to which no one was paying any real attention. Major Metcalfe had stopped drinking, as well, and kept glancing at his watch. Duff Cooper had consumed a vast amount of brandy and creme de menthe but seemed sober, even grim.

Mrs. Simpson drank only Vichy water. She was winning quite handsomely with her disconcerting style of play—the fragile Southern lady confused and helpless in the midst of skilled gamblers, taking her cards with much fluttering of fingers and drawled exclamations of "Oh me, oh my." She would look at her cards, and then at the backs of the others' cards, repeating this several times before making her draw and bet. When her mind was finally made up, she had the habit of flicking the bottoms of her cards against one of her rings.

She wore four. In China there had only been one, a wedding ring, though she was then separated from her husband. One night in Shanghai's Palace Hotel, she had beat Spencer out of $225. Spencer remembered the sum exactly. He now remembered this woman, as well, and very well. He tended to remember those he lost to in poker. He had forgotten the names of half the girls he had dated as a young man in Chicago but could recall almost photographically the police lieutenant who had taken him for his every cent the first time he had joined in the perpetual card game that was the principal activity in the press room at police headquarters. Half Greek and half Irish, the shrewd and bullying man had been, with meaty hands too big for his shot glass and an enormous pistol on his hip. It was said he'd killed a dozen or more Negroes with it, usually on Saturday nights.

"Why, I believe I'll raise you a pound note, Mr. Spencer," said Mrs. Simpson. "That's not too daring, is it? A pound note?"

He saw her raise when the bet came round to him and called to see her hand. She beat his three tens and Metcalfe's pairs of kings and jacks with three queens.

It had been a dark and smoky room in the Palace Hotel that they'd played poker in that night in 1924. As now, she'd been the only woman present, and she was the evening's big winner. He'd danced with her once in the Palace bar that night, then lost her to some minor American diplomat from the consulate, who lost her to an Englishman. Shanghai was filled with westerners then. All of China was, except for the hard lands in the west, the lands and fierce, hard people Spencer had found at the ends of the long roads.

She told him, in their brief dance to a badly played jazz tune that might have come from a Paris *thé dansant*, that she had come to Shanghai to arrange for a divorce from her naval aviator husband, a Lieutenant Win Spencer from Chicago. He didn't realize at the time that she was talking about a very distantly related cousin of his, Earl Winfield Spencer, Jr., of Highland Park, an alcoholic philanderer who spent much of his off-duty time in China at the singsong houses. These were honorable places, but highly obscene. In them was practiced every form of sexual sin known to civilization, along with a few new ones the Chinese were working on.

Mrs. Simpson had been much more attractive then, almost pretty, though most Caucasian women in China seemed pretty. She had a warm, friendly voice and was flirtatious. She'd been twenty-seven or twenty-eight then. According to some reports he'd heard, she sometimes accompanied her husband to the singsong houses to enjoy the titillation. She had, it was said, a lascivious mind and tongue. The provocation to divorce came from her husband's drinking. She could not abide drunks, and drunkenness was a fixture in the navy life that Win Spencer had exiled her to.

Jamieson had learned more about her before he'd finally left China. She'd gone on to Peking, where there were many more westerners and an abundance of unattached men. With no income other than her monthly navy allotment, she'd drifted from newfound friends to newfound friends, a perpetual itinerant house guest, surviving with ingratiating charm and a skill at cards. A wealthy American couple named Rogers finally took her in and made her a permanent resident of their luxurious Peking villa. There was talk of a *ménage à trois*.

In later years Spencer had sometimes wondered what had become of that strong, strange, and pathetic woman. Now, here she was before him, bejeweled and the mistress of the next King of England. A hard and aging woman, almost ugly. It was uncanny.

"Mrs. Simpson," he said at length as Duff shuffled the cards. "I wonder if we haven't met before, before last night."

She smiled without looking at him, fiddling with her stacks of chips. "Why, I suppose that's altogether possible, as we're both Americans and friends of Chips."

"No, Mrs. Simpson. I mean long ago, in the Orient. I was in China in the early twenties." He waited, not picking up his newly dealt cards.

She lifted her eyes to his. Her smile lingered, but her eyes were defiant and challenging, masking a cold and terrible fear. She had asked Win Spencer about this other Spencer she had met at the Palace Hotel and he had acknowledged the slight relationship.

" 'There were rich Spencers in Chicago and poor ones,' " Win had said. "We were among the poor ones, and we never ever got to meet the rich ones. I became a flier because of him, though. He was a big hero in Chicago right after the war. He was in all the papers, not just his Daddy's. Then he went off to Europe. I never did get to meet him.' "

Wallis had finally removed Earl Winfield Spencer from her life in America—with a divorce decree granted in December 1927 by a judge in Warrenton, Virginia, after a year's suffocating residence in that Little Blue Ridge county town.

Now he was back to haunt her, in the form of this strange and forbidding cousin, bound to her until the end of this voyage.

"I was in the Orient in the 1920s," she said slowly and sweetly. "And I was for some time in China. But I led the cloistered life of the wife of a naval officer. I doubt that we met there. Surely I'd remember, for you have the same name as the officer I was married to."

"Earl Winfield Spencer."

"Why, yes. However could you possibly know that? You must have read something about me in the Baltimore newspapers."

There was pleading now faintly visible in her eyes, though otherwise her expression had not changed.

"Your draw," muttered Duff.

"Two cards," said Spencer. He kept two aces and a king. The two he drew were a three and another ace. He won the hand and a sizable pot.

Thereafter Mrs. Simpson's game became genuinely confused. She left within half an hour. At the final summing up, Spencer found himself the equivalent of $635 ahead. He could afford passage back to Europe, back to Whitney, without filing a story about Charles Lindbergh—or the Prince of Wales.

The next fire alarm went off with First Officer van Groot in command on the bridge. The captain had gone for a nap and had not returned, though he was overdue.

"Fire alarm, sir!" said one of the junior officers, redundantly.

Van Groot moved quickly to the electrical display board. Only one red light was showing, indicating a fire in the engine room.

"That's where the false alarm was when Kees left the bridge the other night," said the junior officer.

"Are you sure?" asked van Groot.

"Yes, sir. I think so. He checked out that entire system. There was nothing wrong."

"Call up the engine room. And get Kees. He should know where we should look for the trouble."

"But Mr. van Groot, Kees is off duty."

"Send a crewman to find him."

Van Groot leaned over the display board, staring glumly at the red light, waiting for more, waiting for a chain of red lights to flicker on—each tiny glow a silent representation of spreading flame. But there remained only one.

He leaned closer still, then swore.

"*Een ogenblik!*" he said. "You're wrong! Kees's false alarm was in the circulating pumps. This alarm light represents the main machinery supply switchboard. We had two of those units burn out at Le Havre."

"*U bent juist, Heer van Groot.*"

"Only this time we can't put the passengers out on the dock."

The quartermaster at the helm was staring straight ahead out the bridge windows, keeping the ship on the ordered course despite the serious distraction behind him.

The junior officer turned away. He had the engine room on the intercom phone. "It's Chief Engineer Brinker, Mr. van Groot."

"Yes? And?"

"He confirms a fire in the main machinery-supply switchboard. An electrical fire."

"*Ik ben ziek.*"

"Sir?"

"This is not good."

"No, sir. Chief Engineer Brinker says they are trying to put out the fire with extinguishers, but he thinks they should close down the system until they have found the trouble."

"That means shutting down the turbines and stopping the ship."

"Yes, sir."

Van Groot took up the phone.

"Brinker," he said. "This is serious?"

"*Gevaar, Mijnheer,*" said Brinker. "The fire hasn't spread, but it's stubborn."

"Very well," van Groot said. "I'll be down as soon as I can."

"Where is the captain?"

"The captain is . . . sleeping."

He returned the intercom phone to its hook. "Full stop," he commanded. "Rudder amidships."

"Yes, sir. Mr. van Groot? Should I sound the alarm throughout the ship?"

"Certainly not! We're not in that kind of trouble yet. All that burned at Le Havre were two switching units. That's nothing to panic all these people over."

"Yes, sir."

"Turn out the next watch. I want them on duty now. Just in case."

"And the last watch, sir?"

"Let them sleep for now. We may need them soon enough."

"Should I summon Mr. van Hoorn, sir?"

"I'll talk to him on my way below. I want you to awaken the captain, however."

"The captain, sir?"

"Yes. Call him to the bridge. There are times when the captain should not be sleeping. I'm going down to the after-turbo generator room. When Kees shows up, send him to me."

Kees was down in third class, standing outside Olga Maretzka's cabin door. Close to staggering from fatigue, he had gone directly from the bridge to his quarters when his watch was over, but he had not been able to sleep. The thoughts that had kept him so painfully awake had brought him here.

He rapped twice, then two more times. There was no response. He waited a moment more, then rapped again, with more force. If she did not come, he would return at once to his bed. He was sure sleep would not fail him again.

The door opened with a swift motion. He glimpsed a look of fear on Olga's face but it vanished quickly. She held him with her eyes, then led him inside.

She had a book in her hand, printed in a language he did not know.

"Dear Kees," she said. "You've come again."

She was wearing a rough woolen robe. Her legs and feet were bare. She set down the book and pulled him into her arms. She had only one small lamp on. This strange young woman seemed so fond of darkness.

"I can't stay long," he said. "I've been working double watches. I've got to sleep."

She pulled him closer, tight against the great softness of her chest. "Sleep here, *kochany.*"

"No, I can't. I'm on call. I just wanted to see you."

Before this voyage, love for Kees had meant kisses and feels and pats snatched from blushing girls he took for evening strolls and *kaas broodjes* on the quay of his hometown of Schoonhoven. On one call at Le Havre, he had gone with two fellow officers to a famous brothel, from which he'd emerged sick with drink and considerably poorer.

What he had experienced with this mysterious and voluptuous dark-haired woman of the East was to him more exotic and more enrapturing than anything he'd ever heard in the fantastic tales of his shipmates. He'd become instantly addicted to her. He wondered if there was some way he might move her to his own cabin.

She kissed him, then stepped back, pulling away from him. With her haunting eyes fixed on his, she drew loose the ties of her robe. It fell open, exposing both large and wonderful breasts, the soft curve of her belly, and the tempting darkness beneath.

"I can't," he said. "I really can't. I must be where they can find me. I have only a minute or two."

Her eyes fell. She turned away, thinking, then took hold of his arms and moved him to a chair, gently pushing him down into it.

"Just a minute or two," she repeated, and reached for his belt.

"You don't need to . . ."

"I want to. I want to."

He protested no further. He closed his eyes as he felt her lips come over him. The soft, moist heat of her mouth was electrifying. The sudden touch and skillful work of her tongue dashed all thought and feeling from his mind and body but the explosive and consuming passion it so quickly produced.

Fancy dress was one thing in the South of France at carnival time, in the free-spirited company of a suntanned young girl like Whitney. On a trans-Atlantic liner, among the class-conscious and very mannered rich, it was quite something else. Spencer chose his costume with care, avoiding the outrageous and settling finally on something that suited his mood—and, he supposed, his circumstances. It was a French Legionnaire's uniform, complete with khaki kepi, gold epaulettes, blue sash, and the Legion's seven-flamed grenade insignia on the collar. The tunic bore sergeant's stripes. Perhaps tonight they would stop calling him "lieutenant."

He felt awkward going like this to Nora Gwynne's suite, until he passed someone dressed as an Arab in the passageway. He had seen a drunken Legionnaire shoot down an Arab once, a random act in a late-night street in Algiers. The civilizing presence of the French again.

The body had been ignored by the other passing Arabs. Bodies were collected in the morning. The Legionnaire might just as easily have himself been the victim, gutted by another such Arab. Perhaps, on another night, he was. Spencer had reported the incident but had been treated rudely. He'd never heard any more about it.

Nora had chosen the costume of a Renaissance princess, and was breathtakingly lovely in it, a fairy-tale confection. Her gown was cut more to Empire tastes than medieval ones, revealing much of her bosom. Duff Cooper would have to be beaten off with a stick.

"Do you know, I've never been to a costume ball before," she said.

"I thought every day in Hollywood was a costume ball."

"There are a lot of producers and studio heads who look like ogres, but those aren't costumes. Will we have a wonderful time tonight? I'm having such a good time now."

"How could we not? As my friend Chips Channon keeps telling me, these are the best people in all the world."

"Including Duff Cooper?"

"He's not so bad, when he's not pawing you. It's my hope he'll discover someone else tonight, perhaps even his wife."

She leaned forward and kissed him on the cheek.

"Thank you again," she said. "You're so amazingly sweet."

Then she led him quickly out the door.

The others were all gathered at tables in the far corner of the first-class ballroom when Nora and Spencer arrived. Lord Mountbatten was the most prominent figure, costumed as an Indian rajah, his bandaged head swathed in a bejeweled and feathered turban. Edwina was dressed—or more precisely, undressed—as a harem dancer, all bare legs and belly beneath the diaphanous cloth. Emerald was a bizarre, buckskinned cowgirl; Chips a Cherokee chief. Diana, as might be expected from an actress in tableaux, was perfect as a Greek goddess. Her husband had managed to transform himself into a reasonable facsimile of Charlie Chaplin.

Spencer could not find the rest of the party, but after he and Nora seated themselves and ordered drinks, he saw the prince and Mrs. Simpson out on the dance floor, dancing close and much more slowly than the tempo of the music. The prince was nearly naked, disguised as a Roman soldier, his battle garb a minimal ensemble of sandals, greaves, armored skirt, and horsehair headdress with side pieces that masked his face. Mrs. Simpson was costumed as some sort of royal personage, perhaps Marie Antoinette, but she'd overwhelmed herself with powdered wig, elaborate gown, and showers of jewelry. For a woman so meticulously careful about maximizing her appearance, she was excessively and unattractively overdressed. Perhaps His Royal Highness had insisted upon the outfit. She would be his queen, if only for that night.

But the most regal-looking woman of the evening was Nora.

"The band certainly is fond of Cole Porter," she said, holding Spencer's hand. "This is the third Porter tune in a row."

"They may well despise Cole Porter, ruffians that they are," said Chips, who had joined them. "It's Edwina who has the passion for Cole. She paid them an extravagant sum to play nothing else tonight."

The next song was Porter's "Easy to Love."

"Come on," said Nora, rising. "The song speaks for me."

Spencer came into her arms and they moved circling onto the floor. He was actually an excellent dancer, schooled in it as a child and perfected by Whitney, who had demanded it of him. They glided among the other couples effortlessly. Nora slipped closer, pressing her cheek against his. The feel of her skin was cool at first; then became enticingly warm.

"I feel very beautiful tonight," she said.

"As well you should. I don't know why the prince doesn't drop Mrs. Simpson this instant and propose to you. You're the princess on this ship."

"On this ship, you can be whatever you want. It's like the masked ball. Everything is make-believe. I'm very good at make-believe. You can be, too."

"No. I'm very good at the opposite, at grim reality."

"We're still a long way from New York."

The song concluded, the orchestra paused, then picked up with "You'd Be So Nice to Come Home to." Spencer and Nora never stopped dancing.

Duff, cane in hand, hurried out onto the dance floor in mimicry of Chaplin's splay-footed quick step. He nodded to them, then moved on to where the Parkers were dancing, the two badly costumed as Punch and Judy. Grinning roguishly, Duff hooked young Parker away from his wife with the cane and, with a tip of his hat, cut in, whirling her off toward the other side of the room.

"Tonight's victim," said Spencer.

"Actually," Nora said, leaning back to watch the other couple with great amusement, "I'm kind of glad for her."

"*Je ne comprendrai jamais les femmes de la monde,*" he said. "*Pas quelqu'une.*"

"What?"

"I said I didn't understand women."

She laughed. "But you're not supposed to." She pulled close again, her breasts and lower body pressed as close to him as her cheek had been. For a third time virtually in as many days he would be unfaithful to his darling Whitney. There was no stopping it now. There was no wanting to stop it.

The von Kresses arrived at the ball late and, for the moment, took chairs near the entrance of the ballroom. The count had declined the frivolous outfits offered by the ship's costumers. As his "fancy dress," he chose simply his military uniform, the feldgrau tunic and breeches of a Wehrmacht oberst with the elite red stripe of the general staff and highly polished black parade boots. With his two medals, the plain Iron Cross and the imperial Pour le Mérite, topping it all off, he struck just the right note of absurdity for this assemblage.

Dagne had greatly disapproved, accusing him of disgracing his military office. He had replied that the new regime had already accomplished that for him. She had herself broken the bounds of good taste by choosing a valkyrie's robe, round brass breastplates, and horned helmet for herself. He had begged her not to wallow in the Wagnerian in this silly way, but she had insisted. Ever since, he had been addressing her as "Brunhilde." She was quite agitated and nervous.

"*Es tut mir leid,*" he said, "that I cause you offense, Dagne. And that you provoke me so to do it. Why don't you just put on one of those damned swastika armbands of yours and demand that Lady Mountbatten wear a yellow star?"

"Just shut up."

"We should join the others. Then we can ignore each other."

"I want to sit here for a few minutes. To make what you would call a reconnaissance. I am sure he will be here. Yes. Yes, there he is. Over by the bar."

"He?"

"Himmler's man."

"That blond young giant?"

"*Rechts.* I'm sure that's him. Only the chicken farmer would choose a spy on the basis of his Nordic looks."

"The fellow betrays himself by his lack of costume. He is the only one here in black tie."

"He would look the same dressed as a courtesan, brother. All barrel chest and biceps and jutting jaw. He must be six inches over six feet tall. You see, his tuxedo barely fits him. Only the Death's Head uniform suits him. Everything else is—yes—costume."

"Perhaps you are wrong, Dagne. He is much too obvious, even for Himmler."

"No. I've been following him about the ship today. He is in the passenger manifest as Herr Braun. He has sent a number of wireless messages to Hamburg since we left Le Havre I gather all to the same person."

"How do you know this?"

"I became friendly with one of the wireless clerks. It was one of the first things I did."

Captain van der Heyden, reeking of eau de cologne and with tie askew and jacket unbuttoned, stumbled onto the bridge. The second officer, Willem Lodewijk, was temporarily in command. It was crowded, as two watches were on duty at the same time.

"Fire?" said the captain. "Another fire?"

"Yes, Captain. In the after-turbo generator room. Mr. van Groot and Chief Engineer Brinker are down there."

Van der Heyden rubbed his eyes, blinking afterward. "Get me coffee, a large hot strong cup of coffee. What's our speed and course?"

"Full stop, sir. We had to shut down the turbines."

"Full stop? We're no longer under way?"

"No sir. We're stopped. Dead in the water."

"Turn on an emergency generator and get one of those propellors turning, just to make enough headway for steering."

"Yes, sir!"

"Has anyone sounded the main fire alarm?"

One of the junior officers started toward the control panel.

"*Nee, nee!*" shouted van der Heyden. "Not yet!" The young man halted, confused.

"No one's sounded the main alarm, sir," said Lodewijk. "We've just had the one on the panel there."

"Well, wait. We won't panic everyone yet. Get me van Groot on the intercom."

The first officer took several minutes to respond. Van der Heyden took this as impertinence.

"Mr. van Groot, this is the captain."

There was a long pause. "Yes, sir. Have you been apprised of the situation?"

"Yes. Why didn't you have me awakened earlier?"

Another pause. "Captain. I wasn't sure I should wake you at all."

"Damn it, van Groot, there are regulations!"

"There certainly are, sir. Too often broken."

This time the captain hesitated. "How bad is the fire?" he said finally. "Is it under control?"

"It's spread to two other of these motor switchboard units, but it appears containable. The trouble is we're having to hack through the equipment to get at the source of the fire. We've broken one fire axe already."

"Keep at it. Ring me back in five minutes with a report."

He hung up the receiver, then stood a moment, holding onto a stanchion for support. The deck felt to him as if they were in the pitch of heavy seas, though everyone else was standing easily.

"Where is van Hoorn?" he asked. No one spoke, but then a voice behind him said,

"Here I am, van der Heyden."

"We have a fire, sir. Another fire again."

"Yes. I know. Do you think it is very serious? Shouldn't we be getting passengers into lifeboats?"

The captain rubbed his eyes once more, then stared ahead at the darkening skies and waters out the forward windows. "Do you want to do that, sir?"

"It's the very *last* thing I want to do, Captain. But I don't want a catastrophe either."

"Well, I don't think it's too serious. Not yet."

Nora and Spencer returned to their table and drinks. He felt sixteen again, a year of his life full of happy exuberance. It was the next year that he had gone to war.

The band was playing one of Porter's faster numbers. Mrs. Simpson was sitting it out, leaving the prince to whirl a somewhat startled and faltering Emerald Cunard about the floor. Chips and Lady Diana were dancing, and looking marvelous. Duff had still not released Mrs.

Parker. His face seemed so flushed Spencer feared he might at any moment collapse with a stroke or heart attack.

Edwina was suddenly before them, leaning forward with both hands on the table as Nancy Cunard had in the second-class cocktail bar. But she was not there to harangue them. Smiling perfectly, she was performing the role of hostess.

"Dear Lieutenant Spencer. Darling Miss Gwynne," she said, glancing from one to the other of them. "Isn't it a divine party?"

"Divine," said Spencer. He pointed to the sergeant's stripes on his Legionnaire's tunic. "Incidentally, I've been demoted. In fact, as a commander's wife, I'm not sure you should even be talking to me."

"Your humor is always so self-deprecating, Lieutenant. How very American of you."

"We're having a swell time, Lady Mountbatten," said Nora.

"Do call me Edwina. And may I call you Nora? I hope that doesn't seem too forward. You're such a famous and accomplished person."

"Why don't you call her 'Lieutenant Gwynne?' " Spencer said.

"Ah, more wit," said Edwina. "Such an amusing lieutenant. But now, can you tell me please if you've seen our German friends, the count and countess? I don't know what's keeping them."

"They're over there by the entrance," said Nora. "They arrived a few minutes ago. I don't know why they haven't come over."

"I think he needs to rest awhile," Spencer said, "before he can complete the arduous journey to this side of the room."

"That's cruel and boorish, Lieutenant," said Edwina.

"A perfect description of my wartime foe," Spencer said. Edwina walked away angrily. She waited for the orchestra to finish the number, then crossed the dance floor, heading for the von Kresses as purposefully as a cheetah cutting through a herd of wildebeest for the one creature it had chosen for its prey.

"Fancy Edwina developing such a passion for the Hun," said Duff, breathing heavily as he seated himself. Mrs. Parker had gone back to her husband. "There was a German woman killed at our hotel back in Paris, and Edwina found the incident vastly amusing."

"Mildly amusing," said Lady Diana, who had also joined them. "I found it ghastly. It happened right on the balcony, during the riot. It could have been any of us, really. When she heard about it, Edwina thought it marvelously ironic that the filthy Germans who had encouraged the rioting should have one of their own fall victim to it."

"In fairness, Diana," said Duff, "most of that rampage was spontaneous. Good French fun."

"What hotel was this?" asked Spencer. Nora felt his fingers clench.

"L'Hotel Crillon," said Diana.

"She was a blond woman? In a blue evening gown?"

"Yes. You must have been there," said Diana. "It was such an awful mess. They carried her right past us. We were going upstairs, to play bezique."

"And you say she was German?"

"Excruciatingly German," said Duff. "She was the wife of the Reich's military attaché in Paris. Of course, all the Reich's diplomats are military attachés these days."

"How do you know this?" Spencer asked.

"Why, we had cocktails with them a bit earlier," Diana said. "There was a reception. The Boche agents provocateur assembling to watch the results of their handiwork."

"She was very lovely, that woman," said Spencer.

"But I think a horrid person, really," said Diana. "Very cold and forbidding. As if she loathed everyone and everything. How queer that, of all those on that crowded balcony, the bullet should find her."

"Yes," said Duff, nodding toward the von Kresses. "But one goes down and up pops another."

"I say," said Lord Mountbatten, from the next table. "Have you noticed? I think the ship has stopped."

"It's the wine, darling," said Diana. "Have another glass of champagne and she'll start right up again."

"I'm jolly well serious," said Mountbatten. He reached down and put his hand flat against the floor. "And I'm quite right. There's no vibration. They've stopped the engines. We're adrift."

"Utterly my favorite way to be," said Diana. "Come, Duffie. Let us dance."

Nora looked to Spencer, but he was staring at the tabletop, seeing only a dead woman's face. He looked much like he had when she had first encountered him drunk in the Ritz bar.

Edwina placed her hand on Count von Kresse's shoulder. *"Darf ich sie vereinigen?"*

"Please do," said Dagne.

Lady Mountbatten seated herself, but on the edge of the chair, tentatively.

"Actually, I should have thought you'd join the rest of us," she said. "The prince quite considers you part of our little party."

"He's most kind," Dagne said. "My brother and I were just having a brief family discussion. We meant to come over presently."

"I hope I haven't intruded," Edwina asked.

"Only in the most welcome way," said Dagne. "But now I must excuse myself. There is someone it is most important I talk to. I will be with you again in a few minutes."

When the countess had left, Edwina moved closer to von Kresse. "Perhaps your sister does not like me."

"She is just all business tonight."

"Business?"

"She's concerned about something. *Macht nichts.* I like you, *Gnädige Frau.* Very much."

"You're a very dear man, Martin. A very noble man."

"A few days ago we hadn't even met. A few days from now, after we dock and go our different ways . . ."

"Who can say, Martin? I could be anywhere. This year I've been in South America, Australia, New Guinea, the United States, Malta, France, Spain. All in one year. With air travel now, who knows where we will find ourselves?"

"And in five years, where will we be?"

"In amusing places, I'm sure. Now come, my dearest count, and we shall dance. I'm mad for dancing."

He yearned for the touch of the flesh revealed by her costume.

"I'm sorry to say, *Gnädige Frau,* that I do not dance, not since the war. I am happy enough just to walk."

"If one can walk," she said, rising and taking his hand, "one can dance. The music is enchanting. I am enchanting. You will forget all your pains."

"I really can't."

"You can. I will be the one to perform the miracle. I shall restore your powers of dance. Come."

"I can't possibly move as fast as the music."

"*N'importe.* It certainly won't matter to me. I shall in fact rather prefer that."

The warmth of her smile and the merry wickedness in her eyes overcame his last resistance. Lying in a hospital seventeen years before, he had day after miserable day brought himself to accept the bitter reality that he would never again ride, never again dance. Now this magical creature, this will o' the wisp out of Goethe, was offering to restore him. He got unsteadily to his feet and moved into her arms.

Kees was taken by surprise when he came onto the bridge. He had come directly from Olga Maretzka's cabin and knew nothing about the emergency, although he guessed the nature of it as soon as he saw

Captain van der Heyden and Willem Lodewijk poring over a schematic diagram of engine room equipment. There were two red lights twinkling on the alarm panel.

"A fire, sir?"

"Yes, Kees. Yes. A fire," van der Heyden said without looking up. "Someone get me van Groot again. He was supposed to report in five minutes."

"Yes, Captain!"

"Captain, do you want me to go down there?" asked Kees. "I checked out all that equipment when we had the alarm the first night out."

"No. Then you were looking for a fire. Tonight we have found one. Just stand by here, please, until we fully know the situation."

"Yes, sir."

A signal man came up, clutching a wireless message. "A weather bulletin, sir."

Van der Heyden took the piece of paper and studied it blearily. Without another word he went over to the chart table. He shook his head.

"More trouble, gentlemen," he said, handing the message to Director van Hoorn. "The hurricane that foundered the *Rotterdam* is passing in front of us on a course to the northeast." He stroked his chin. "There is this, though. As long as this fire keeps us idled, we may miss most of it."

When the others had gone off to dance again, Nora pulled her chair close to Spencer and put her arm around his shoulders, the solicitous mother attending to the troubled child.

"Are you all right, Jimmy?" She began to stroke his cheek.

"I'm fine, thank you. Just in shock."

"Did you know that woman who was killed at the Crillon?"

"Apparently not."

"Then why are you so sad, about a complete stranger?"

"We should all be sad about strangers once in a while. They may have no one else."

"She sounded like a hateful person."

"And I thought she was a very lovely one. But there's no way of knowing now, is there?"

"You don't think you might meet her one day in heaven?"

"What?"

"Don't you believe in heaven, Jimmy?"

"Nora, just how Catholic are you?"

"I'm not a simpleton. But I believe in heaven."

"I don't believe in that kind of paradise. Such a heaven would have to have dance bands."

"I don't understand."

"Such a heaven," he said, with a gesture to the ballroom, "that would admit that poor woman at the Crillon, that would admit me, it would probably be just like this."

The orchestra was playing "I Get a Kick Out of You."

She took both his hands in hers and turned him toward her, leaning even closer. "Jimmy. Don't be like this. You're ruining my romance."

"Your romance."

"With you. My shipboard romance. I always wanted one, ever since I was a little girl, and now here I am. And do you know what? It's even better than I'd hoped. It's absolutely wonderful. You're wonderful, Jimmy. I love you, I love these people, I love this ship. I love everything."

She kissed him, gently but warmly, her lips parting slightly.

"Now don't spoil it," she said.

"I think you picked the wrong fellow," Spencer said. "I'm just a beaten-up newspaperman with some ridiculous problems. Nothing wonderful about me at all. Just ask Lady Mountbatten."

"Stop it." Her voice was sharp. "I mean it, Jimmy. Everything else about my trip ended up ruined. Don't ruin this."

He was being a fool, behaving more foolishly even than those who believed in heaven. "I'm sorry, Nora."

"Don't be sorry. Be happy. Listen to the music. Look at the others. Everyone is happy. Come dance with me again. I'm particularly happy when we're dancing. Nothing can go wrong as long as you keep dancing, as long as the music goes on and on."

He smiled, an effort, but less of one than he expected. "I will accept that as a profound truth."

"Then come and dance."

And so he submitted. He did as Whitney would have wished, and set aside all his sorrows and mournful truths. He accepted the reality Nora offered, warmth and love and music and a Catholic heaven in which the wives of Nazi diplomats were admitted for muttering the right ritual phrases, or being accidentally shot. For the remaining days and nights of this voyage, it was as good as any other reality. There was as much compelling fact in Nora's soft belly and flawless face as there was in the splattered brains and blood of the blond woman on the Crillon balcony. In the long run, Maynard Keynes had said, we're all dead. This was the short run. "Beauty is the scent of roses," F. Scott Fitzgerald had written profoundly at the absurdly youthful age of twenty-three, "and the death of roses." Spencer would sniff the roses.

Clinging to each other tightly, yet without a moment's stumble or clumsiness, they swept out into the slow carnival on the dance floor. Neither of them said anything more, or wanted to. They would take their fill of this rich and gratifying and illusory evening. They would tumble on into a night of sex and love and warmth and sleep and safety. And they would accept the promise of the day to come, no matter how much they'd been cheated by such promise in the past. They would both be fools.

Nora was humming the dance number, softly and beautifully. He closed his eyes, his senses full of her touch, her scent, her warmth, the soft, fragrant blessing of her hair. But in a moment he opened them again, curious about all his shipboard friends.

They, too, had succumbed to this magic mindlessness. Chips and Emerald circled past, their unheard exchange of brilliant banter revealed in the easy cheer of their faces. Diana Cooper, at that distance, a vision of grace and beauty, swung by, her arms about a chattering and, for all his injuries, agile Lord Mountbatten, revived by the simple ministration of a glamorous woman's attentions. Duff Cooper, his arms enfolding the newly recaptured Mrs. Parker, had been transformed from rogue to swain. She had succumbed, with apparent gratitude. His hand was gripping her bottom.

And, wonder of wonders, the crippled Prussian count was dancing, with stiffness but not stagger, supported by an enraptured Edwina, whose athletic powers provided them with a grace that belied her burden. The German countess had vanished. Her grating presence would have been an intrusion upon all this sentimental bliss. Spencer could not see the prince, but then he did—the man inexplicably but unconcernedly dancing with the young Mr. Parker.

Mrs. Simpson, grim and dark and disapproving as a medieval Spanish dueña, sat at her table, huge hands folded, staring after the dancers. Major Metcalfe, still in his tweeds, had joined her, but she was paying no attention to him.

Nora murmured and pulled him closer still. Two Apaches danced by, and then a Nubian slave clutched by the sun god Ra. Two Greek Orthodox priests, one with enormous breasts, followed, dancing in heavy but lusty movement. Beyond were a gypsy, two Arabs, a pirate and a colonial maid, an Elizabethan lady, a convict, a cave man, a bathing beauty, a gladiator, a gorilla, Ming the Merciless, and Mata Hari. It was a madhouse loosed, but all of them seemed just the same, just as blitheful, as Nora and Spencer.

Of a sudden he felt transported, elevated, rushed a thousand miles into the night sky, looking down upon the daft, revolving circle of dancers till it shrunk into nothingness, and the ship itself, the earth itself, was but a tiny pinprick of light in a vast blackness that was all there was to anything.

In the long run, they would be dead. But for now they could be happy.

Van Groot rang up from the engine room. His voice was full of relief and triumph and a measure of contempt, as if he had just rectified some calamitous error made by the captain.

"The fire," van Groot said, "is out."

"Are you sure, van Groot?" said van der Heyden. "The alarm light is still glowing."

"Captain, reset the board."

Of course, of course. That's how the mechanism worked. That was procedure. Van der Heyden's mind was not working. He needed sleep, or more coffee. Or Bols gin.

"Reset the board," the captain repeated to Second Officer Lode-wijk. "Van Groot says the fire is out." There were cheers. The young man did as he was bidden and the dot of red light vanished.

"You are certain it's out, completely out?" van der Heyden asked. "Or should I come down?"

"No, Captain. You're not needed. It is completely out. But four of these switchboard units are out of commission, damaged beyond repair, I'm afraid. And it may take several hours to rewire the feeder circuits. There'll be a voltage loss. Substantial, I fear. But we'll be able to get under way again. Certainly by morning."

Van der Heyden took in a deep breath. Everyone on the bridge was looking at him, waiting.

"Very well," he said. "Get to work. Get every man you need. Report every half hour."

He hung up the receiver. Van Hoorn was at his elbow.

"It goes well," the captain said. "No injuries. No serious damage. The fire's out. We'll soon be under way." He risked a smile. "But you are going to have to have a serious talk with those shipyards."

"I think I'll stay on the bridge awhile," the company director said.

"Please do, *mijnheer.* I am going out onto the wing."

He stepped out into the cool, moist air, going to the end of the platform and leaning on the railing. High clouds, the vanguard of the passing hurricane ahead, had been drawn across the sky like a curtain, masking the stars and moon and the western horizon. The breeze was stiffening noticeably, the ship behaving clumsily in it without the stability provided by forward motion.

He really did need a drink. It wasn't a matter of want. He did not want another gin, another glass of champagne, anything. But his body screamed for it. He gripped his hands together tightly to stop their trembling. He looked down the long line of the ship's starboard side, at the bright lights of the portholes and windows. He could hear the band music. Sometimes he took pleasure in the blasé contentment of his passengers, so far out in the midst of this dark ocean. Other times he hated them for it. They had no idea what their contentment cost him.

He heard the sliding door open and close behind him. It was Kees Witte. He came to the rail but said nothing. The captain felt the young man's eyes on him, but when he turned to meet them Kees was gazing out into the blackness.

"Well, Kees. As I told you, no voyage is ever the same."

"I wouldn't want another like this one."

"I've had much worse. In my freighter days, off Zanzibar, I was on a ship that burned to the waterline. We were two days in lifeboats, we who survived."

Kees paused. "Are you all right, sir?"

"Yes, I'm fine. The fire is out. All is well. I am good."

"Captain. You know what I mean."

Van der Heyden sighed, rubbed his chin, clenched his hands, and watched the sea. "Yes," he said finally. "I know what you mean. Kees, I do not drink when there is trouble. My problem, if I have a problem, is when all is well."

"Sir, you do have a problem. Mr. van Groot was complaining about your drinking. Mr. van Hoorn is aware of it. The men talk about it all the time now. They call you Captain Fles. Captain Bottle."

"Well, there is nothing I can do about the talk of others."

"Yes, there is, sir. I hope you don't think I'm being insubordinate, Captain. I speak only out of concern for you. But I don't think you should drink anything more on this crossing. Van Groot is ready to shoot you down. He feels it is time for him to become master of a vessel."

"Should I say that he is welcome to this one?"

"He would take it, sir. In a minute. Fires or not."

"Well, not yet. She's a beautiful ship, the *Wilhelmina*, the best I ever commanded. If only they could get her to work."

"She worries me."

"I am always thinking about retirement these days. Juliana wants to go on a driving tour of the United States. And you know, the thought of all that mass of land entices me. It would be such a good feeling. I think of my home at Noordwijk and its view of the sea. It troubles me. Often I turn away from the windows now when I am in that house."

"I will help you all I can, Captain. Anything you ask. But please, sir, not another drop."

"Don't worry, Kees."

The sliding door was wrenched open with a squeal and bang.

"Captain, Captain!" Lodewijk exclaimed urgently. "More fire alarms! Come quick!"

The display board showed two clusters of flickering red lights, one in the forward-Turbo generator room around No. 3 turbo generator, the other beneath the aft stairs of the engine room, apparently in the gear case behind one of the turbines—and above a huge oil drain tank.

"Ring up van Groot!" the captain said. "Tell him I'm coming down!"

Dagne was certain Himmler's young blond giant was very stupid. She had gone to the bar in the pose of seeking a drink and engaged the man in conversation, remarking on the heavy accent with which he spoke English and asking hopefully if he were German. When he acknowledged he was, she all but embraced him, treating him as gladly as she might someone rescuing her from hostile savages.

"Ach, these foreigners," she said, looking back at those on the dance floor. "And I think half of them must be Jews. But what can you expect of a Dutch ship?"

He seemed confused, this physically perfect Reichsführer's male model and clumsy assassin. As she talked, Dagne studied him, wondering if he was a homosexual, as she already had convinced herself that Himmler was.

"We took this ship only because it was the next one leaving," she said. "It was a whim. My brother and I were in Paris and just decided of a sudden to sail across the Atlantic and back. Very self-indulgent, *nicht wahr?*"

"An ocean voyage is very healthful," he said awkwardly.

"And why are you on this ship?" she said. "You, so German a gentleman?"

"I have business," he said. "In Holland, and in New York. I am in business."

"Yes? You seem very young to be so concerned with business. What business are you in."

"Why, export-import."

"Of course." She leaned close to him, studying his face with extreme care. "You're not Jewish, are you? There are so many Jews in export-import."

He reddened in anger and perplexity.

"I am not a Jew," he said. There was threat and worry in his voice.

Dagne stepped closer to the blond youth as two men approached the bar.

"Actually, my brother is an importer," she said. "He imports many art works. But he is a collector. Not a man in business."

"Oh." The young man looked uncomfortable to be so near and intimately engaged with his prey.

"You should meet my brother," she said.

"I would like to."

"Ach. Look, he is dancing. All but crippled in the war, a great German hero who feels pain with every step, but now dancing. The German resolve, *nicht wahr?*"

"*Sicher, Gnädiges Fraulein.*"

"How did you know I am not married?"

"I, uh, you have no ring. Pardon me please if I have caused offense."

"No, none at all. Come. I want to get some air. I would appreciate company. Will you come walking with me on the deck?"

He didn't want to. It was obvious his overwhelming desire was to escape this situation. He doubtless much preferred to murder the von Kresses in their sleep, or in the basement of some Berlin police station. But he was, like all of them in the Schutzstaffel, a man driven overwhelmingly by his notion of duty, and she was offering him an opportunity for duty.

"I should be delighted, *Gnädiges Fraulein,*" he said stiffly. There was a touch of servility in his tone, deference born of what? Himmler recruited these boys from every proletarian quarter, proclaiming them nobility solely because of their hair color and physique.

She smiled as seductively as she could manage.

"Well, then," she said. "Let us go on deck."

Dagne chattered away about Berlin and the latest social doings, receiving in return only nods and grunts as they made their way to the passageway and the doors that led out to the promenade deck. His Spartan existence doubtless did not involve him much with salons and cabarets, or even politics.

She took his arm once they were outside, leading him along the rail toward the stern and the partition that separated them from second class. There was no one about, not even crewmen. They all seemed to have some concern inside.

In a shadowy place between deck lights, she went to the railing and leaned against it, looking at the misty sea. He came beside her, staring at her now. Dagne suspected she had little time.

"Reichsführer Himmler is a little piece of shit," she said softly.

"*Was sagen sie?*" the young man said.

"I said Himmler is a piece of shit, of chicken shit. He is a fool, a dull-witted bourgeois faggot."

She sensed his anger. She could almost feel its heat.

"I don't understand what you are saying, *Gnädiges Fraulein.*"

"He is a clod who thinks he is a great man because someone allowed him to wear the uniform of a German soldier. We should not soil the sacred German uniform with such shit. He ignobles the Führer. The Führer should have him shot."

She turned quickly to look the man full in the face. There was all the proof she needed. He was utterly betrayed, convicted beyond hope of appeal, by his contorted expression.

Before he could move, she leapt back, pulling forth her Mauser pistol from the folds of her gown. His back was to the railing, hers to the bulkhead. No one else was about. There was no use in further words, in delay. She pulled the trigger.

The gunshot was muffled somewhat by the moist air. His outcry was not. He doubled over from the impact and agony of the enormous wound in his belly, but he did not die. He still stood, half supported by the railing. Dagne fired again.

The caliber of the pistol was small but the bullets were heavy load and soft-nosed. This one cleared through what remained of his intestines and smashed against his spine. Its force drove his bent body between the railings, his posterior extending out beyond them, his now-paralyzed legs as akimbo as a marionette's, his feet splayed sideways on the deck, his upper torso and head hanging down.

Yet still he lived. He made horrible groaning, bubbling sounds. The stag Dagne had killed with a knife had made such noises.

She went up to him, pointed the pistol at the top of his head, and fired. This was a mistake. The gore splattered on her costume.

But at last he was dead. After sliding the pistol back into its hiding place, she took hold of one of his arms and pulled. He was heavy, but if she could hang the corpse over the rail and lift his legs, he would go overboard. That would be that.

But he would not budge. Bent in two, he was stuck. The bullet's impact had wedged his huge body firmly between the railings. His thighs and lower back were gripped as if by a vise. How could this have happened? Why had God abandoned her?

She pulled hard again. She tried the other arm. And then both. She leaned over the rail and tried yanking on the cloth of his pants.

Bells began ringing throughout the ship. She heard shouting, and people running about. Were they running after her?

Desperate, sweating profusely despite the cold and damp, she pulled now on the man's leg, slipping and falling backward painfully on her own bottom. Swearing, she rose and tried once more. The corpse mocked her.

She would have to rid her costume of this filth. She would have to get Martin; there was no other way. And she would have to find him quickly. She could only hope the Jewess Mountbatten had not already taken him to her bed.

Lifting her skirts, she ran along the slippery deck. Before she could reach the door, it swung open violently as a small, dark Oriental crewman rushed out, colliding with her.

"Go get your life jacket, missy," he said frantically. "Get your life jacket and go to your lifeboat station. The alarm bells are sounding!"

"Why? What's wrong?"

"Hurry, missy. The ship is on fire. Very bad! Very bad!"

# CHAPTER
# *TWELVE*

"What the hell are those bells?" Duff asked, still clinging to Mrs. Parker as they danced up to Chips Channon's table.

The bells' message was not clear. A few people were leaving the ballroom, but most of the passengers remained. The band continued to play as if these chimes were some sort of planned accompaniment. Only three couples remained on the floor, including the prince and Mrs. Simpson. Mrs. Parker's husband was standing drunkenly on the edge of the dancing area, watching like a small boy waiting for his turn at a game.

"I think it must be another lifeboat drill," said Lady Emerald.

"Damned lot of cheek scheduling a lifeboat drill in the middle of a ball," Chips said.

"Your typically Dutch sense of fun," Emerald said.

"It's not a drill," said Spencer, his arm around a still-blissful Nora. Her mind was elsewhere, rejoicing in another girlhood fantasy about to be fulfilled, and she wasn't attending to their words.

"I daresay you're quite right," said Mountbatten, rising. "They've got this ship into a spot of trouble again. I'm going up to the bridge."

"Wait," said Duff. "Here comes the head Dutchman."

Van Hoorn, looking severe and shaken, his dinner jacket unbuttoned and shirtfront smudged, went to the microphone at the bandstand. The orchestra stopped in midnote.

*"Het is dringend,"* he began. *"Er is een ongeluk gebeurd."*

As he proceeded with his brief, unhappy speech, more couples began to hurry from the room. One large Dutch woman, costumed as a milkmaid, shrieked at something van Hoorn said and began running.

"Why in blazes can't that fool speak in English?" Duff said.

"Ladies and gentlemen," van Hoorn said, as if in obedience. "This is important. There has been an accident. There is a small fire in the electrical system. We do not believe it is serious, but as a precaution we would like you now to get your lifejackets and report to your lifeboat stations. Please, go at once."

He turned to leave, quickly. The evening's celebrants crowded around him, asking questions he answered only with shakes of the head. The band resumed playing, virtually where it had left off. The band on the *Titanic* had played until the end, when the deck was sloping at so steep an angle the musicians could no longer stand.

Nora's bliss had gone to fear, and her wide eyes were fixed on Spencer. He held her tightly around the waist. "It's all right," he said. "These things happen all the time. It's all part of the adventure." He kissed her forehead, but she seemed little comforted.

"Now, now, everyone," said the prince, joining them with a most unhappy Mrs. Simpson in tow. "Let us maintain our imperturbability. We are, after all, British. Now let's be on to the lifeboat. I shall lead the way."

"My jewels!"

"Wallis, don't worry yourself over your jewels. Runcie shall get them when he fetches our life jackets. I'm sure there's plenty of time. Now follow me."

And so they moved off, a gypsy carnival of a procession led by a half-naked Roman centurian and his overdressed lady, a pack of lunatics heading with great seriousness to some appointment in their asylum. Nora was trembling, but the most agitated person in their group was Lady Cunard, whose acerbic, worldly façade had cracked and who had begun clenching and flailing her hands about like someone performing an odd and primitive ritual.

Mountbatten strode proudly along just behind his royal cousin, his outlandish turban as good as a ship captain's cap. Duff had abandoned Mrs. Parker for his own wife, who held to Chips Channon's arm, as well. Chasey Parker pulled her terrified husband along. Edwina was in another part of the ballroom, helping Count von Kresse, whose limp increased with their haste. His sister the countess was not to be seen.

As they passed in ragged file into the passageway behind a crowd of other passengers, Fruity Metcalfe came up to them, joined a moment later by Lord Brownlow. Both looked like men returning to headquarters from a tour of beleaguered front lines.

"Well, Fruity," said Prince Edward. "An ocean voyage, you said. I never realized it would be such fun."

"You idiot!" said Mrs. Simpson, presumably to Metcalfe, but it was hard to be certain.

"Now, Wallis," Edward said. "Fruity's forte is horses, not ships."

"I don't believe the situation is all that serious—yet," Metcalfe said. "The important thing is to get to the lifeboat. We're assigned to one of the steel accident motorboats, remember. They're the best rescue craft aboard."

The fearful passengers ahead of them were packed tightly together in the narrow corridor, moving along steadily but with frustrating slowness. A scream or shout or other precipitate of panic would have caused a violent trampling.

"This is 1935, after all," said Edward. "The wireless can bring help wizard quick. I'll wager there are probably a dozen ships within an easy sail of us."

"My jewels," Wallis repeated, her voice now more quavering than shrill.

"Yes," said Edward. "Where's Inspector Runcie?"

"He was at the ballroom door," Metcalfe said. "But he's disappeared."

"It's my fault," said Lord Brownlow. "I sent him to the bridge to find out what's gone wrong."

There was now an acrid smell of burning oil and paint in the air, but it was impossible to tell if it was rising to reach them. The crowd pushed on at a more rapid trudge. An elderly woman stumbled and went down. Her husband turned and shoved his way back, kneeling to protect her.

"My jewels," said Wallis. "You said you'd send Runcie for my jewels."

"Wallis," Metcalfe said. "Let's get to the lifeboat first. Then worry about jewels."

"You don't understand," she said with unrestrained anger. "My charm bracelet is in my bedroom. I'm not leaving this ship without my charm bracelet!" It was an imperial decree. The world would stop in the meantime.

It had been a gift to her from the prince the year before, his very first. The premiere ornament commemorated their initial meeting. He'd added another since. It was a totem of their relationship, the two extant charms trophies of her success, the many remaining empty spaces signifying promise. She would not abandon it, not for anything, certainly not for any hazard to Runcie's wretched little life.

Wallis was utterly furious that this could be happening. She was certain it was due to her failure to perform the ritual of attending the ship's first lifeboat drill. She would kill the crude attacker who had locked her in her closet.

"Well, Fruity," Edward was saying. "Since Runcie's not available, and you're all off to your cabins, I'd be deuced glad if you could run up to our suite and fetch the jewels and our lifejackets. The jewels really are most important to Wallis."

Metcalfe patiently controlled his temper. "As soon as I can," he said. "Until we get clear of this passageway, I've no choice but to struggle along with this lot like the rest of you."

After three slow turns of stair, they squeezed through a narrow doorway and burst in twos and threes out onto the deck. The air was cool and heavy with moisture, but the odor of oil and smoke was even stronger. Spencer could see no flame, at least not in that part of the superstructure looming over them, but there did seem to be a great many sparks dancing out of the aftmost of the three funnels.

A voice over the twelve exterior Loudaphone speakers of the public address system, six to each side of the boat deck, was urging calm and the quickest possible movement to lifeboat stations. As the prince's party hurried along forward, clusters of others—second- and third-class passengers who had made their way through unfamiliar passages from below—bundled along in the opposite direction, their faces pale and ghastly in the gloomy light.

As with the earlier drill, many of the lifeboats they passed had crewmen standing by them but no passengers to attend to. Here and there they came upon another anomaly: busboys and stewards, waiting for instructions but for the moment without anything to do, leaning against the bulkheads or sitting on deck chairs, smoking and chattering like street idlers.

Other stewards and crewmen, with sternly ordered tasks to perform, dodged, shoved, and jostled their way through the passengers. A cabin boy who bumped into Spencer and Nora, little more than a child, was crying. Two seamen who parted to let Spencer and Nora pass were laughing. They might just as well have been strolling some street in Batavia.

Someone, somewhere in the command system of the troubled vessel, threw a switch and instantly the decks were bathed in bright light. The white superstructure sparkled in it, but the glare made the sky and surrounding sea darker still.

The ship seemed so huge, a firmament of strong metal, the feel of deck and cold touch of painted steel rail hard and invulnerable. This vast and mighty thing could not possibly be harmed by any threat within it. There was no iceberg, no huge guns as at Scappa Flow, no silent, deadly mines. Only the free and easy sea and the hugeness of this floating city. Spencer hugged Nora as best he could with the two of them wrapped in Kapok. When they reached the steel motorboat designated as their salvation, she smiled weakly.

Their motorboat and the twenty-three other survival craft the *Wilhelmina* possessed were suspended from gravity davits to be lowered either manually or with electric winches. It was an elaborate and expensive system, and one much tested. A ship's officer had told Spencer that a lifeboat had deliberately been dropped all eighty feet to the water line without a single sign of damage.

The regular lifeboats were thirty-six feet long, weighed nineteen tons fully loaded, and were each fitted with eighteen-horsepower diesel engines capable of producing six knots in calm seas. The two steel motorboats were slightly smaller but were driven by gasoline engines that could attain speeds equal to the ship's.

Brakes limited the descent of any boat to no more than sixty feet a minute and a special release mechanism freed each craft from its lowering cables the instant any part of it struck the sea. Javanese Kapok buoyancy material superior to cork had been fitted within the boat's sides and bottoms. Every imaginable safety feature had been thought of, improvements paid for at the price of knowledge gained from previous maritime disasters.

Yet the crews were having difficulty even lowering the boats to the level of the deck for boarding. The bow of the steel motorboat was at that moment a good two feet higher than its stern. While the officer in charge yelped at them, two crewman were working on the winch at the forward davit. A third was in the prow, holding uselessly to the cable and watching the others at their unproductive labors.

The officer, whom Spencer recognized from the dining salon, turned to greet the prince's party. He smiled, in practiced, engaging fashion, but it was clear he was near panic himself.

"Ladies, gentlemen," he said, wringing his hands. "You need not worry. Everything is under control."

Captain van der Heyden clambered in haste down the steel staircase leading to the No. 5 boiler room, the site of the worst of the two fires. He still felt weak and wobbly, but his mind had cleared. Van Groot was lecturing him about oil fires, but the captain wasn't listening. He was thinking hard. When he put his hand to the entrance door, it was warm to the touch.

Stepping into the chamber was the same as stepping into a furnace. Men were playing streams of water from the fire hoses onto the flames, but they kept spilling out of the junction of boiler and oil pipe. A curtain of fire was now dancing around the steel plating at the base of the boiler. The heat made the captain gasp. He clambered down more metal steps leading to a flooring slippery with water and oil. Slipping and sliding, his entourage followed after. Van der Heyden barely concealed his gratification when van Groot fell bottom first, sprawling.

Kees Witte helped the first officer up, then rejoined the captain.

"It's bad now," said Brinker, the chief engineer. "I think you should order abandon ship. At least for the passengers."

He was no alarmist. It was his habit to describe all difficulties in the most objective and mechanical terms, leaving conclusions to his commander. His dark eyes showed no fear, but there was worry.

Van der Heyden looked from burning boiler to ceiling, picturing their location in a map of the ship. Immediately forward of them was the after-Turbo-generating room where the previous fire had occurred. Behind them stood the forward engine room that was Brinker's headquarters. Above them were the port and starboard oil filling stations. Just behind those was the oil tank whose contents were feeding the flames.

"We've got to get to the main circulating discharge valves and turn them off," the captain said. "Then we'll have to drain that oil tank into the sea and refill it with water. I want this chamber flooded, as well."

"But the fire has reached the circulating pumps, sir," said van Groot, using the respectful "sir" for the first time that night. "We can't get through to them."

"Yes, we can," said van der Heyden. "We have to."

"I'll go," said Kees.

"No, you won't," van der Heyden said sharply. "I have a job for you, the most important one there is right now. I want you to take charge of the party at the starboard steel accident motorboat."

"The prince's party, sir?"

"Yes. He must be kept safe at all costs. If the ship sinks, so be it. He cannot be lost. If that happens, the Lage Lander Line is lost. We cannot permit it. You are my best junior officer. If we have to abandon ship, I want you in command of that boat, of that party!"

"But, sir. Someone assigned that boat to Maansteen."

"And it was a fool thing to do. Maansteen, damn it, is a maître d'. I'm not going to trust the life of the most important passenger in the world after our own beloved queen to an arranger of tables even if he was a seaman once."

"Yes, sir. But what about our other special passenger?"

"Don't worry. He'll turn up. When he does, I'll get him into the other steel motorboat. I'll hold it in reserve. But the prince is more important. He is royalty, Kees. English royalty!"

"That makes him more important?"

"Not in the world I would make but certainly in this one. Now go. Go!"

"Yes, sir!"

Kees hurried away, moving over the oily wet floor and up the metal stairs as nimbly as if they were dry and made of rubber.

"Who shall we send in to turn off the pumps, sir?" van Groot asked.

"We'll send no one," said van der Heyden. "I'll go."

"But sir!"

"Quiet! I want to make sure this job is done! Until I get back, you'll be in command. That's what you want, isn't it?"

"Captain—"

"I'll go with you," Brinker said. He turned to van Groot. "Have those men keep hoses on our backs as we go through there. I want to keep my skin. Ohms—get us some heavy oilers' gloves!"

The subordinate hurried away, glad he had not been assigned this suicidal task but wanting to help. "We'll do everything we can," said van Groot. "Good luck."

"Luck," said van der Heyden. "You've got the wrong ship for that."

Most of the prince's party were at the steel motorboat by the time Kees got to them. Lady Cunard was extremely agitated and the young American, Parker, was crying, but the others seemed calm, if frightened.

"It's all right," Kees said. "We are getting the fires put out. We see no need yet to abandon ship. Please don't worry."

"I want my daughter, Nancy," Emerald said. "I want her with me. I want her now."

"She'll be fine," Duff said. "There are more than enough lifeboats for everyone."

"I want her with me."

"Shouldn't we be getting into the boat?" Edwina asked.

"Not until it is ordered," Kees said. "We get into the boats only when they are to be lowered. We must follow the rules."

"I thought I was in charge here," said Maansteen, the maître d', his voice a tremulous whine.

"No," said Kees. "I am now. Captain's orders. Our special passengers."

"Should I be here? What should I do?"

"Go to the kitchens and bring some food. Hurry."

"I *insist* on having Nancy here." Emerald was at a loss to speak as they all might have expected. She had lost her wit as completely as if it had been removed in a surgical operation. Channon had never ever seen her in this way before. The woman who had terrified Britain's greatest artists and aristocrats with her tongue was acting like a vulnerable, helpless child.

The Countess von Kresse, her face ashen, came up to them, clutching at her brother though Edwina had her arm around him.

"Is the ship going to sink?" Dagne asked. "Should we leave the ship?"

"Not yet, Countess. Please, stay calm. Everything is under control."

"I see flames!" said Lady Diana. "Coming from the funnel, the third funnel. How bloody Greek. It's like the fall of Troy."

"Wallis as Helen?" said Duff, *sotto voce.*

Major Metcalfe ran up to them, Brownlow and Runcie following. He was gripping a large canvas bag.

"Here you are, Wallis. The lot. At least all I could find."

Mrs. Simpson jerked the bag away from him, tearing the closures open and peering desperately inside. She pawed through it frantically.

"You fool!" she bellowed. "You didn't get my charm bracelet!"

"I looked everywhere."

"It was in my closet. In a small velvet box in the pocket of my dressing gown!"

"Wallis, I'm sorry. You didn't tell me."

"You damned fool!" she cried and, pulling away from a startled

Prince Edward, ran stumbling toward the entrance way to the main first-class corridor. The prince, startled, hastened after, as did Metcalfe and Lord Brownlow. But she would not let them restrain her. When the prince caught her arm as she was ascending the carpeted interior staircase, she called him a filthy name.

Though soaked, van der Heyden was gasping from the heat as he groped his way through the lateral bilge well that led to all-important pumps. The water from the hoses arrayed behind them seemed to boil away from his skin. Brinker bumped against him, making him stumble.

"I don't think the fire hoses are helping!" Brinker shouted.

"We're alive, aren't we? But it's too dark. We should have brought an electric torch!"

"There's fire up ahead. We'll soon see clearly enough!"

He was right. The small chamber, encased in shiny metal sheeting, was aglow with the flame around the pump mechanism. It was much like crawling inside a bright lamp.

Brinker had brought a wrench. He lunged for the small metal wheel that controlled the flow of oil through the machinery.

"No," said van der Heyden. "Let me. I'm the stronger."

He clutched at the chief engineer, but instead of halting the man, he caused him to fall. Brinker's head, arm, and shoulder struck the flaming metal, and he cried out, horribly, as from a death wound, his hair above his right ear disappearing in sparks.

Van der Heyden dragged him away, beating at the crackly flames on Brinker's jacket with his gloved hands until the burned threads were no longer aglow.

The blows caused Brinker to scream.

"Wait, Jan. I'll get you out. But the pump. We must turn off the pump."

The metal of the wheel seemed to quiver with fire. When van der Heyden touched the wrench to it, the heat shot through the tool's length and through the thick material of the glove to his hand. His skin might as well have been bare. With a cry, he dropped the tool.

His life, his future, all their fates, they were all reduced to this. It was a simple matter. There was no doubt to it, no uncertainty. An uncomplicated choice. To live, for all of them to live, he had to turn the valve. To die, to perish horribly in flame or in the cold darkness of the sea, he had merely not to turn the valve. To live, he need simply burn the flesh of his hands. To evade the pain, he need only die.

He pulled off his jacket and wrapped part of it around the wrench. It took two or three attempts, but he got the bite of the wrench's jaws around a spoke of the valve wheel. He swore from the agony that came to him despite the folds of cloth, then took a deep breath and pulled.

Nothing budged. His jacket had caught fire. Swearing continuously now, he pulled again, with all his might, with all his hate, with all his fury. He begged God for forgiveness for all his life's sins. He begged for mercy. He begged for the metal to move. He promised never to touch alcoholic drink again in whatever remained of his life.

The valve wheel moved.

The public address system announced insanely that the stores had been opened in the main hall's shopping center so that passengers could obtain sweaters and other warm clothing.

"Are they going to charge for them?" Duff asked. "Are we going to stand in line signing chits while the bloody ship burns to the water line?"

Kees Witte, the only person who could answer him sensibly, had gone below to find Nancy Cunard for Lady Emerald. It had meant abandoning his post and his orders, but he had decided of a sudden on a different set of priorities. The prince's was not the only life of value aboard.

"Chips," said Spencer. "Let's you and I go. We'll bring back things for the others."

Channon looked at him with as much panic as Nora did, and she was holding onto Spencer as if he were a life preserver.

"I'll go with you," said Duff. "It shouldn't take but a minute. Edwina's going to perish of pneumonia before we even get into the boat if we don't find her something warmer. We would have lingered longer in our cabins to change, if they hadn't panicked us."

Spencer kissed Nora's cheek, then pried her hand from his arm. "It's all right. I'll be back in a moment. I will."

"Are you my friend?"

She had a wonderful sense of the irrelevant.

"I love you madly. I'll be back. I'm not leaving the ship, after all."

Leaving the princess behind, the Foreign Legionnaire and Charlie Chaplin disappeared into the crowd.

Half supporting and half dragging the heavy Brinker, van der Heyden emerged from the bilge well staggering with his burden and his pain. Crewman took the chief engineer from him, laying the semiconscious man on the deck. Van Groot rushed to his side.

"The valve is closed," the captain said. He was relieved to see that the flames around the boiler had already lessened.

"Captain. Your hands!"

"Yes," said van der Heyden, with an odd calm. The palms of the gloves had largely burned away and his smudged and dirty skin was puffy with dirty white blisters. He now had the hands of a circus clown. "Get Brinker to hospital. I am going back to the bridge."

"But you should go to hospital also."

"Not yet. I'll leave you in charge of this, van Groot. Get this fire out. What about the new fire, the smaller one forward?"

"I don't know. It was under control."

"We'll deal with it. Now you put this one out." Van der Heyden looked at the oily, slippery metal staircase he had to ascend to return to his proper place in the ship. He could not touch the railing with such injured hands. "I hate to take a man away from you, but I need help up to the bridge."

Elbowing their way past greedy passengers loading up on perfume and jewelry, Duff and Spencer reached the clothing section and began gathering up woolen goods—sweaters and skirts and scarves—taking more than their party's fair share perhaps but not wanting to stop to count the items.

The insanity of the voice on the public address system intensified. Having invited them to the stores for looting, it now ordered them to take to the lifeboats and prepare to abandon the ship. It spoke in a heavily accented monotone. "Ladies and gentlemen. Please now board your lifeboats. Passengers may be required to leave the ship. Ladies and gentlemen. Please now board . . ."

On impulse, Spencer snatched up a bottle of Worth perfume. He had the strange notion that a gift of it would make Nora happy.

The ship's doctor, busy tending to Brinker, sent his assistant and the ship's pharmacist up to the bridge to deal with van der Heyden's hands. The captain was just as pleased, for he knew the doctor to be a drunkard. Seated in his chair by the windows with his arms outstretched, he paid the medics and his injuries little attention.

"Now who ordered them to the lifeboats?" van der Heyden asked. "Who did this?"

"Mr. van Hoorn, sir," said Ladewijk.

"Mr. van Hoorn is not an officer of this ship."

"No, sir. But you were gone, sir. The fire aft has spread to the aft funnel hatch and the ventilating units at the expansion joints."

"The principal source of the fire has been put out. We have cut off the flow of oil. That's how I did this to my hands."

"Yes, sir. But there are flames coming out of the funnel, apparently feeding off the interior paint of the shaft. Mr. Van Hoorn was afraid there'd be panic."

Van der Heyden took in a very deep breath. He exhaled slowly. The others on the bridge were very busy. There was constant conversation over the intercoms, and signals staff kept bringing in weather bulletins.

"Did you order all hands or just the passengers into the boats?"

"Only the passengers, sir. And their lifeboat crews."

"Very well, Ladewijk. We probably should have gotten the passengers off at the first alarm. I don't know who we're trying to fool. This ship is a disaster. We should probably all abandon her."

The young officer said nothing, unsure what was spoken thought and what was order.

"The fire forward?" the captain asked.

"In the gear casing? It's out, sir."

Van der Heyden looked to the ship's telegraph. As he had ordered, the *Wilhelmina* was making headway, though at the slowest possible speed.

"Ladewijk," he said wearily. "You cannot lower boats when the ship is moving, no matter how slowly. Order full stop."

"Yes, sir! Is there anyone in the engine room to respond?"

"Full stop, damn it!"

"Full stop!"

The crewman at the telegraph obeyed instantly.

Van der Heyden could hear cries and screams and the formless sounds of fear and confusion down on the boat deck just below. On the bridge, all was seemingly under control. For the moment, he really had nothing to do.

One of the medics began bandaging his hands. "*Mijnheer Dokter* says I should give you morphine and send you to bed," he said. "Don't you feel pain?"

"Yes, by God. Massively. It makes me want to beat my hands together to make it stop." He looked down at the two big bandaged lumps. Carefully he touched them together palm to palm. The dressing was thick and he felt little. The agony in his skin raged with or without pressure. He wondered how terrible the pain would be if he were to end up in the cold, salty sea. "But no morphine."

"Are you sure, Captain? Mr. van Groot is not injured. He can take command."

"Mr. van Groot is busy dealing with the damned fire in No. 5 boiler room. I want no morphine. Now go attend to the others. Brinker is not the only one burned."

When the medic had left, van der Heyden called Ladewijk over to his chair. "In my cabin, in my chest, are several bottles of Bols gin. Fill a cup and bring it here."

The other hurried to comply. This was not a spoken thought. This was a crisp, clear-cut order. Ladewijk guessed it would be repeated many times throughout the night.

By the time Spencer and Duff returned to the steel motorboat, nearly all the royal party were aboard, including the prince and Mrs. Simpson, huddled in the boat's middle. Kees had not come back from his third-class search for Nancy Cunard, and Emerald was leaning over the gunwale, calling out, pointlessly. Dumping their cargo of woolens into the boat, Duff and Spencer clambered over the side onto the wooden seats. They began handing out the warm clothing.

"His Royal Highness first," said Mountbatten. "He hasn't a shirt."

"His Royal Highness last," said the prince. He took two sweaters from Duff and handed them to the Parkers, as if performing a monarchial gesture of self-abnegation—Henry II accepting the lash for Thomas à Becket's murder, the Pope washing the feet of the least among them. The famous Prince of Wales' common touch.

"There are plenty of sweaters to go around," Spencer said.

"And there are scarves and wool skirts," said Duff. "Diana, you'll need one. Edwina, darling, I daresay you could use several."

"I'll take one myself," said the prince. "To cover my knees. Not much different from a kilt, what? Too bad I haven't my pipes."

"There's a vision of hell," said Duff. "At sea in a lifeboat with a man playing bagpipes."

"Keep up our spirits," said Edward, sounding insulted.

"We have blankets, missy," said one of the East Indian crewmen to Mrs. Parker. "You cold. You take blanket."

"There are blankets on this boat?" Duff said angrily.

"Yes, *mijnheer.* Under seats. With rations."

"Why the hell didn't you tell us?"

"You not ask, *mijnheer.*"

"Damn you!" thundered Mountbatten. "Break out those blankets, man!"

"Yes, *mijnheer.*"

"I say," said the prince. "Wait just a moment. Where's my valet? I assumed he was here. He's always where he's supposed to be. But now he's not. We can't leave without him."

"It's my fault, sir," said Fruity. "I sent him to send a wireless message."

"How can you send a wireless message?" Channon asked. "Aren't they busy sending an S.O.S.?"

"A ship like this has a half-dozen wireless sets," Mountbatten said.

"A message to whom?" asked the prince.

"To the palace, sir," said Metcalfe.

"Buckingham Palace?"

Metcalfe sighed. "Yes, David. To inform Their Majesties that you are alive and well."

"Well, how the devil would they know I was in any danger?"

"I'm afraid your man has been sending messages to the palace since we left England. I just found out this afternoon. Lord Brownlow and I were sifting through the day's lot."

"Damn and blast!" said the prince, furious. "I'll have the man sacked."

"He was ordered to do so, sir."

"By bloody whom? That damned Major Hardinge?"

"By your mother, sir."

"My mother?"

"I'm not certain the king knows. Given the state of his health, she's likely been keeping it from him. But apparently she's been following your progress since you arrived in Paris."

"Spied on by my own manservant. What damnable cheek. Well, bugger him. I don't want him with me an instant longer. We'll cast off without him."

"No!" shouted Emerald. "We're not leaving without Nancy!"

The braking mechanism on the forward davit cables slipped, causing the bow to drop a good three feet below the level of the stern and sending several of them tumbling forward onto the decking and adjoining seats. Emerald and Chips fell, as did the drunken young Parker. Nora slipped from her seat, accidentally kicking Count von Kresse in the leg as she went over. He said nothing, though it must have hurt badly.

The Parker boy was whimpering. Channon looked utterly terrified, but he eventually managed to get a glib smile on his face.

"You little bastard!" Edwina shouted at the crewman in the lowered bow. "I don't want to die because you don't how to launch a fucking lifeboat!"

"I touch nothing, lady. Nothing."

Spencer pulled Nora up and close to him on their seat. She moved numbly, without speaking, without looking at him. Instead she put her head against his shoulder as he drew her sweater more closely around her. Remembering, he placed the perfume in her hands. She took it but paid no attention to what it was.

"I love you, Jimmy," he heard her say. "Save me, Jimmy." Her voice was faint and wispy, a vague prayer, missent to him instead of God.

All he could do was hold her more tightly. He sensed the dark water beneath them; it made him aware of how precariously they were suspended above it, how close they were to being plunged into its depths. The motorboat was banging against the davits with the pitch and roll of the now-drifting ship.

Death had visited him so many times. Each he had presumed to be the final call. For a long time, for endless, sleepless nights at miserable, muddy aerodromes all over eastern France, he was certain he'd die in a long, final plunge, a leap from a burning aircraft. Having survived all the menace of that war, and so much else, he wondered if God was toying with him. His wish was that his demise could come in the uneventful, stoic manner of the old man seated cross-legged at the edge of that road in China, resting awhile in the peaceful circumstances of surroundings as familiar as one's own fingers, observing the occasional passing farmers and oxen, certain, at last, of the inconsequence of man in a universe in which individual stars were insignificant among their infinite billions of fellows. Then he'd fall over, life turned almost imperceptibly to death. The most minor possible incident in the history of time.

He reminded himself of the warmth and beauty and affection of this celebrated woman beside him, of the bonhommie of their glamorous company, but it would make no difference. She and they would all vanish the moment his drowning body gave up its breath.

"Should we get back aboard the ship?" Chips was saying.

"Are you mad?" Duff said. "That funnel's a tower of flame. It must be roaring out of the belly of the ship."

"Christ, this wool itches," said Edwina.

"It's Icelandic," said Diana. "The warmest but coarsest kind."

"Should we order them to lower the boat then?" Channon said. He was wearing one of the sweaters over his Indian costume.

"No!" said Emerald.

But the seaman on deck fiddling with the gravity davit control caused the motorboat to drop another foot or more, steepening the angle of the lowered bow.

"Damn and blast!" said the prince.

"Perhaps we really should get back on the ship," Duff said.

"Be patient," Count von Kresse said sternly. "God is not through with us yet. He teases us. You see, little by little."

His sister the countess was laughing hysterically.

"They're here!" said Chips.

Kees Witte appeared at the railing, a wild-eyed, dark-haired woman beside him. Nancy Cunard, looking drunk, stepped next to her. Then came Henry Crowder.

"No!" shrieked Emerald.

"Emerald, darling," said Diana. "Do shut up."

"I won't have him!" Emerald said. "No! I said Nancy! Just Nancy!"

"We've been hanging here, young man," Channon said, with a pointed look at the dark-haired woman, "while you've been recruiting refugees from steerage."

Kees ignored them. He helped Nancy aboard, and then the other woman. Then he turned to Crowder.

"No!" screamed Emerald.

There was a sudden *thwack* as Nancy hit her mother full in the face. Everyone ceased to move. It was as if they'd been instantly petrified.

"There is room for all," said Kees, his voice stern and serious and making him sound much older than his years. "We will take these people with us and lower the boat." He turned to the seamen at the davit controls. "Do not use the gravity device. Lower the boat with the electric motor. When I say so."

He climbed over the railing and slid down into the motorboat. Ignoring his passengers, he pushed his way past them to the small wheelhouse in the stern that enclosed the helm.

"All right!" he commanded the seaman. "Now!"

There was a snap and then a whirring sound. The boat began to ease rapidly and smoothly down to the water, but with the bow still pitched forward. It went splashing underwater when it struck the sea, rising suddenly as the stern crashed down, sending cold seawater rolling over their feet and legs.

Kees had the engine started. "We have a pump. It will get rid of this in a few minutes. Hold to your seats."

He revved the engine. They had only one other crewman aboard.

"Release the cables forward!" he shouted to the man. "I'll get these aft."

It took several minutes of hard and frequently unsuccessful effort to get all four of them free, with Kees calling the man vile names in Dutch and Javanese and finally coming forward himself.

The pump did little to empty the water, and in a moment it stopped. So did the engine. When they were at last clear of the cables, Kees hurried back and restarted it—with some difficulty.

There were many lifeboats in the water behind them, though they seemed to contain few people. Holding down their speed in the rising swells, Kees steered the motorboat in a circle to starboard, then headed along the side of the ship through the milling, white-sided rescue craft.

"Get us away from the ship, damn it!" Mountbatten shouted. "She could explode!"

"I want to make sure there's no one in the water," Kees said. "This lifeboat procedure did not go well."

"Damn it, man! We've the Prince of Wales aboard!"

"Shut up, Dickie!" said Edward. "Carry on, Third Officer. We've certainly room for more aboard."

Kees nodded. There was a small searchlight mounted atop his tiny wheelhouse. Leaning out with his hand on the steering wheel, he played the light on the waters ahead.

Nothing was to be seen but the flick or smear of foam. Rising and falling with the swells, they rumbled and rattled on, the people aboard the other lifeboats staring at them warily, or stupidly, as if wondering what they were about—curious at their showing so much purpose while the other boats merely drifted about.

As they passed the section of the ship by the aft funnel, the flames appeared mountainous. They could feel the heat a hundred feet below. Reaching the stern, Kees steered to pass beneath it, as if for a look at the other side of the ship.

Spencer found himself gazing up at a tall, thin figure standing at the railing of the after promenade, a man in a raincoat, seemingly unconcerned about the danger and despair all around him. The bright deck lights had gone out but the fire made everything visible. The man was staring down at them, as if idly curious as to who they might be. Spencer knew the face. It was the same haunting person who had appeared on the deck that first misty dawn at sea. It was Charles Lindbergh.

Van der Heyden moved randomly about the bridge, restless with his pain, frustrated by his inability to touch and hold things. He could gingerly lift his cup of gin using both hands and sipping carefully but little else. He had to have Ladewijk hold the intercom phone for him when van Groot finally reported from below.

"The fire in the No. 5 boiler room is out," Van Groot said. "I'm calling from the forward engine room. We flooded No. 5 boiler room as you ordered. And the oil tanks above. As a consequence, we've also put much of this room underwater. A lot of other places."

"Close the watertight doors that separate you from the after engine room."

"I did, Captain. Of course."

"Good. Secure things there and get up topside. The ventilator shaft fire's penetrated some bulkheads and is into the second-class cabins. Also, the galley of the first-class dining saloon. The galley's full of combustibles. I have men fighting it but I can't be there."

"How are your hands, sir?"

"Bandaged. Useless. Get up there. If you think it might be too bad for us to remain aboard, I want to hear from you, quickly. *Vlug!*"

"*Ja. Oktober aan zee.*"

One of the junior officers took a just-delivered weather bulletin to the chart table.

"Captain," he said. "We're going to have a brush with that hurricane."

Van der Heyden hurried over, studying the intersecting lines the young man was drawing across the wide expanse of paper.

"*Ja,*" said the captain. "That storm must be five hundred miles across."

"It's shifting course from north northeast to east by northeast. Sir. We'd have trouble outrunning it if we headed back for Le Havre at full speed."

"It's still at some distance. It may change course again." Van der Heyden spoke with his arms held behind his back.

Ladewijk was holding the intercom. "Sir, it's the doctor. Chief Engineer Brinker is dead."

"Dead? He wasn't that badly burned!" The captain went to the phone, which Ladewijk held for him. "What is this, Doctor? What happened to him?"

"He went into shock. Bad heart, I suppose."

"Damn! Damn! It's my fault. I made him stumble into the fire down there."

"The burns were not so serious. His ear, yes. But it should not have been fatal. Just shock. It happens. How are you?"

"I have been tended to well, but I hurt like hell."

"You declined morphine."

"I have a fire at sea, *mijnheer.* Save your dope for the other casualties. I fear you will have many."

"Only seven others so far, Captain. None really serious. We are lucky."

"Ah, yes. What glorious luck we are having. Mevrouw Brinker will be so pleased to hear about it." He had Lodewijk hang up. More red lights were twinkling on the fire alarm display board, a bright cluster of them showing behind the aft funnel.

Company director van Hoorn appeared from behind the entrance curtain. For once van der Heyden was glad to see him.

"The passengers are all evacuated," the captain said. "The engine-room fires are out but one in the ventilator shaft has spread to some aft cabins."

"Should we be here, Captain? Shouldn't we put to sea in the remaining boats?"

"And abandon your beautiful new flagship?" van der Heyden shrugged, wincing. "I'll know more when van Groot reports in. I sent him to deal with the new fires. If they can be put out, we should try. There is a bad storm approaching. I'd rather confront it in this than a lifeboat. No matter what the fire damage."

"A bad storm?"

"A hurricane. The same one that drove Holland Amerika's *Rotterdam* aground."

More fire alarm lights appeared, farther and farther aft.

A seaman who had entered was speaking agitatedly to Ladewijk.

"Brinker's dead," van der Heyden said. "He was with me down at the oil pump. The doctor says it may have been a heart attack from the shock. But I caused his burns. I made him stumble."

"Surely it was an accident."

"All of this," said van der Heyden, gesturing with his bandaged hands, "has been an accident." He turned to the steward who had just brought coffee. "Go to my chest and bring me a bottle of Bols gin."

"Gin?" said van Hoorn. "Now? Of all times?"

The captain waved his hands about again. "Especially now! If you want me functioning."

Ladewijk came up. "This fellow is saying something crazy. He says there is this big blond man, a dead man, with his ass stuck in the railing on the boat deck."

"Dead? From a fire? Have we a fire on the boat deck?"

"No, Captain. He says the man's brains have been blown out. He's been shot, sir."

"Shot? That's crazy."

"This man's not crazy, sir."

Indeed, the seaman did not look crazy—merely bewildered by all the madness about him. "Get back there," van der Heyden said to Lodewijk. "Make sure there is such a man, and that he's dead, and that he's been shot. If so, get him off the boat deck and into one of the empty cabins."

"Shouldn't I find out who he is, sir?"

"If you can. But don't take overlong. I need you up here. We can worry about dead men when we're sure we're all not going to be in such company."

"Yes, sir."

He vanished behind the entrance curtain that shielded the night vision of those on the bridge from the bright lights of the corridor. Van der Heyden wondered why he had kept it up. They'd all lost their night vision in the glare of the flames.

The curtain moved again. A tall, slender man stepped from behind it, but stood shyly, without moving further. He wore a rumpled raincoat and a suit with a tie much too short for his long body, but his was a commanding presence nevertheless.

"Sir," said van der Heyden, drawing himself up to parade-ground attention. "Why aren't you in one of the lifeboats?"

"Are you trying to save the ship?" the man asked. He pulled at a curl on his high forehead, keeping his eyes from van der Heyden's. It seemed to pain him to speak.

"Yes," said the captain. "With not much success, but we're trying."

"I'd like to help," said the man, his clear blue eyes now meeting van der Heyden's. "I know about electrical circuitry and fuel lines. I know about engineering."

"My God," said van Hoorn. "Every alarm light on the sun deck is showing red from the aft funnel to the Verandah Grill!"

On the steel motorboat, now two hundred yards or more from the burning, stricken *Wilhelmina*, Kees made a decision he hoped was right but sensed was probably wrong. He allowed the passengers to break out some of the liquor ration. There were two bottles of rum in the wheelhouse under lock and key, but the alcohol available beneath the seats consisted entirely of beer and wine, including several bottles of champagne.

The company brochure contained the idiotic line "Even in our lifeboats, you travel first class."

"Well played, Third Officer," the prince said, pouring himself a tot of red wine into a tin cup from a ration pack. "Your shipping line has redeemed itself."

There were also large containers of fresh water, condensed milk, bread, tinned fish, and tinned cheese beneath the seats. These Kees would not allow to be disturbed until morning. For the moment, he wanted his passengers amiable and, if possible, asleep. The wine would help.

He had Olga sitting on a center seat by the entrance to the wheelhouse. He reached and touched her shoulder. Despite her heavy clothing and the thickness of the blanket she'd been given, she recoiled as if he had stabbed her, her eyes filled with malice when she turned her head. Slowly her expression eased, but she did not smile.

They all felt they were near death, he supposed. But not all. When Mrs. Simpson had gone back to their suite for her all-important charm bracelet, the prince had fetched his ukelele. He pulled it out of her canvas bag, strumming idly a moment, then sliding into a boisterous version of "Yes, We Have No Bananas." Some of the others began singing along with him.

Spencer held Nora with both arms, one hand inadvertently resting against her breast. She was fully cognizant of him, but was murmuring a prayer to herself. The Parker woman was looking intently at him.

"What do you think?" she said.

"I think it is better not to think," he said. "That's the virtue of prayer."

"You're very cynical, Mr. Spencer."

"I'm very cold," he said.

Except for Mrs. Parker's husband, who was drunkenly asleep on an empty seat up by the bow, all the couples aboard were hugging each other. Channon even held Lady Emerald, keeping her turned away from the sight of her daughter and Nancy's companion.

While the prince played his trivial instrument, however, Mrs. Simpson hugged only her bag of jewelry. She had put the charm bracelet onto her wrist. Everything else was now in the bag and she clutched it tightly, watching with vacant eyes and frozen countenance the dancing, distant light of their burning ship.

# CHAPTER
## *THIRTEEN*

Sometime after midnight, the burning *Wilhelmina* passed from view, lost to them even when the steel motorboat was at the height of the wavecrests. It was impossible to tell whether this was because of an intervening curtain of mist or because they had drifted too far distant. It was possible that the ship had burned or exploded and sank.

They could not know. The small wireless set in the motorboat's wheelhouse was not working. Kees had fired a flare from one of the Very pistols aboard. It had illuminated a large area of empty, heaving ocean, but there had been no response from the ship. All they could do was wait until morning. Everyone presumed they would be rescued by morning.

They made do. From her canvas bag, Mrs. Simpson produced, of all things, a much-used Fanny Farmer cookbook, and had made of their tinned rations of tasty antipasto, which they consumed along with tin cups of cool white wine. They bailed out the boat, and so afterward were able to lie down between the seats and sleep in some comfort, though several, over Kees's protests, removed their life jackets to attain this state.

Nancy Cunard and Henry Crowder were at the bow, as far as they could get from her mother. Nancy was drinking wine almost continuously, her sips punctuating a profane jabber. The Parkers, life jackets removed, slept on the floorboards nearby. Except for Metcalfe, who had stationed himself back by the wheelhouse near Kees, the prince's party lay in blanket-covered lumps about the center of the boat, some of them snoring loudly.

Both the Prussians remained awake and huddled together, the count in worsening discomfort, the countess looking a little crazed.

Spencer was unable to sleep, though Nora, clinging tightly to him, was blissfully unconscious. Needing to relieve himself, he gently disengaged himself from her arms and crept aft. There was a toilet under one of the two seats in the wheelhouse. The dark-haired woman Kees had brought aboard was sitting by its doorway, wide awake with a bellicose expression on her face, but Spencer paid her no mind. She looked as if she had heard the sound of men pissing before.

When he emerged, she turned her eyes up toward him, as wary as she was hostile.

"Nice night for a boat ride," he said.

"Don't be a fool," she said, speaking with a rough accent.

"These motorboats are built very tough," said Kees. "Don't worry. We'll survive the night."

"Jolly right," Metcalfe said cheerily. Spencer had come to like this tall, bluff, well-intentioned fellow. He wondered how the man could have become such a boon companion to such a petulant and self-centered middle-aged child as the prince. Perhaps that was just the way with well-intentioned fellows. Spencer hadn't known all that many in his life.

When he finally made his way back to his place by Nora, Edwina sat up, awake. They were but three feet apart.

"Was your copra boat in the South Pacific anything like this?" he asked.

"A damn sight bigger."

"Would that we could go back to our night with the cloud full of stars."

"That was a thousand years ago, darling." She stretched, then pulled her blanket more tightly about her. Before Spencer could speak again, she suddenly clambered over the seat and went to Count von Kresse's side.

"You must be in agony," Spencer heard her say.

"It is nothing," von Kresse said.

"Let me massage your leg," Edwina said.

"Leave him alone!" screamed the countess. *"Geht weg!"*

Her shouting awakened several of the others, but it didn't matter. Her words were followed by the first drops of what quickly came to be a deluge of rain.

Except for the Parker boy, who was dead drunk, all now awakened, some of them swearing, including Wallis Simpson.

"There's a tarpaulin," said Kees. "Possibly two. I'll break out what

I can find. They're up at the bow." He struggled forward over the now-slippery floorboards. "Bail! The pump's not going to cope with all this, if I'm even able to restart the engine."

Duff and a few others reached for buckets or their tin cups and began the dreary labor as requested. Others, most notably the prince, just sat there, shivering.

"This won't do," said the prince. "Absolutely not. Wallis is getting soaked."

"We're all getting soaked, sir," said Diana.

"She'll get pneumonia," Edward complained. "I won't stand for it. I want her inside the wheelhouse."

"That's our toilet, sir," said Diana.

"We'll make arrangements," the prince said. "Now, Wallis, go to the wheelhouse."

Stumbling, her dripping hair flat against her skull, Wallis complied with the command with great willingness, avoiding everyone's eyes as she made her difficult way aft. Kees's dark-haired woman stared at her with much contempt but made no attempt to obstruct the prince's favorite.

"You, too, Your Highness," Lord Brownlow said.

"Oh, no," Edward protested. "Certainly not. I'll weather this with the rest of you."

"That's foolish, sir," said Brownlow. "Need I remind you that your father is seriously ill? You are heir to the throne. If you should become ill yourself you'd be placing the stability of the country—of the entire empire—in great jeopardy."

"Nonsense. There's my brother Bertie."

"Sir, your brother is not prepared to become king. You simply cannot endanger your health this way."

Metcalfe said nothing. For all his friendship with the prince, he thought Brownlow wrong in this.

"For God's sake, sir," said Duff. "Your staying out here isn't going to make the rest of us any drier."

"Oh, very well," the prince said abruptly, and he quickly darted up to join Wallis. Once inside the small chamber, they closed the door, all snug, their faces two pale featureless ovals behind the rain-covered glass.

"*Scheiss,*" said the countess. "*Wie sie sind Schwein.*"

Kees and the Oriental crewman came aft with the two tarpaulins. They were large and quite heavy.

"We'll form bailing parties of four, to be relieved every hour,"

Kees said above the thundering rain. "The rest of you get under these. They'll keep you dry."

Metcalfe, Spencer, Duff, and Mountbatten volunteered to take the first bailing detail. The others crawled under the shelters, the crewman having to drag the sleeping young Parker under the forward canvas. The count remained on his seat, insisting that his anxious sister join the others under the tarp. Moving stiffly, he began to bail, as well, accomplishing much less than the others but working his best.

"It's a pity we have to keep all this secret," Duff said. "I've half a mind to denounce the damned Dutch government from the floor of the Commons."

"Not just the Dutch government," Metcalfe said. "Every Dutchman who ever lived."

"This was your idea, after all, Metcalfe," said Mountbatten.

"It wasn't my idea to start a fire," said Fruity. "And certainly not for you to come along on this trip."

"Bail, buckos," said Duff. "Bugger off quarreling."

Spencer contributed nothing to this exchange. He felt more cold and miserable than he could ever remember being in the war. The thick wool of his Legionnaire's costume was heavy with water and rough against his skin, and every movement was a terrible ordeal. But he didn't complain. No one did.

He was near the section of the tarpaulin where Nora had sought shelter. She was sitting up. He was sure she was praying. By the time they were rescued she would be a nun.

Edwina emerged from under the canvas. Cursing, she groped her way back to the wheelhouse. When the door didn't open, she banged on it.

"I have to pee!" she said.

The prince opened the door wide enough to lean his head out. "I'm sorry, Edwina darling, but I can't expose Wallis to these elements a second longer."

"Damn it all, sir! I have to pee!"

The prince pulled the door closed again.

"Use one of the buckets, Edwina," Duff said. "Like the rest of us."

Ultimately she did, in relative good cheer. But in time cheer or misery ceased to matter. It was all the same being under the blankets and tarpaulins or out in the storm as the rain filled the boat. Their movements became mechanical, then numb. The four men kept bailing long past their appointed one hour, but they progressively slowed. At length, the rising level of water sloshing about the bottom began to outpace their best efforts. Kees tried twice to start the boat's motor so he could get the pump working again, but with no success.

The rain slackened, but the wind and seas were rising. The boat took water over the side.

"Everybody up!" Kees shouted. "I want everyone bailing except for four men on the oars. We've got to keep the bow into the wind and ride these waves on the quarter."

"Oh, go to hell," said Chips.

"That's where we'll all go if you don't get up and help. We can't let the boat get swamped!"

Most of them struggled out from under the canvas and did as bidden, though Parker and Emerald remained beneath. Lord Mountbatten and Henry Crowder took up the forward oars; Spencer and the count manned those amidships. Spencer could not imagine von Kresse lasting at this effort more than a few minutes, but the Prussian insisted that he could manage it. He claimed the work would help ease his discomfort.

"I've lived with this pain for nearly half my life," he said. "Why should I not embrace it in this moment of great need?"

To Spencer's amazement, the count proved good to his word, matching Spencer almost stroke for stroke. Spencer could not decide whether it was a matter of Prussian stoicism or some source of inner strength that could be called up *in extremis.* He had encountered a few German soldiers like that in the war—not supermen but mortals who had simply put out of their minds that they were human, that there was any reality other than what they were required to do. He had seen the shot-up pilot of a Fokker triplane, its engine streaming smoke, keep fighting until he had shot down two Frenchmen, carrying on until his own plane exploded.

The German fliers had been issued parachutes by that time, yet inexplicably the man had failed to use his. Perhaps he had been wounded so badly he was beyond escaping his cockpit. Perhaps he had realized he was as good as dead and was making this extraordinary effort simply to exact revenge.

It was at that moment in the war that Spencer had at last found himself capable of feeling hatred for his enemy. The two Frenchmen had not needed to die.

He had hatred enough for his own countrymen, as well. The United States Congress had decided to forbid American fliers to use parachutes. The politicians, none of them aviators, feared pilots would sacrifice valuable aircraft at the slightest sign of trouble just to save their own skins. The idiots had not realized that the worth lay in the pilots, not the machines. A flier who managed to survive three weeks of combat and could thus count himself a skilled veteran was worth a dozen pursuit planes.

And at the end of the war the army had found itself with thousands of aircraft that had never even made it across the Atlantic. Some of them were later used for the experimental air mail service. A mail pilot named Charles Lindbergh had lost three of them bailing out on the Chicago–St. Louis run in bad weather.

"Fucking bloody bastard!"

It was Nancy Cunard. Spencer looked over his shoulder to see that she was swearing at a wave that had just soaked her.

By dawn the rain had dwindled to a patter, but that development brought little cheer. The cold gray light revealed the full extent of their predicament and peril.

There was no ship or lifeboat to be seen on any point of the horizon. The waves had become mountainous. In the troughs, they were thirty or forty feet beneath the wavecrests. Kees, steering from his command position at the now-open door of the wheelhouse, kept the bow pointed up into the fierce wind, ascending the steep slope of each great advancing wave with only the most adroit seamanship as others struggled with the oars.

At each summit, they'd catch a grapeshot of wind-whipped foam and then the boat would careen into its next descent, plunging tumultuously into what appeared to be a widening hole in the sea.

It was this way with every wave. Each required a miracle to surmount and survive, and they came on relentlessly, endlessly. They were infinite. This was a hell invented by the most fiendish devil imaginable, a hell far worse than one of mere fires.

A coconut floats. That was the comforting platitude told to Spencer when he was first taught to sail small boats in Lake Michigan.

"But I am too big to sail in a coconut," he had said. He said it again now.

"What was that?" asked Count von Kresse.

"Nothing." Spencer felt an impulse to call him a Hun bastard. He was thinking too much of the war in all this misery.

The count looked at him curiously but showed no anger. He just kept pulling at the oar. How could this be? The man had been barely able to help with the bailing—a different motion, a different pull of muscles, to be sure, but an infinitely less vigorous one. Why hadn't he torn his crippled back apart? Why wasn't he in agony? Or dead? Why weren't they all dead?

A wave suddenly loomed over them from abeam. Kees spun the helm to turn the boat toward it as quickly as he could, but not soon enough. A huge, heavy wall of water came over them, splashing across and down through the boat and thudding against the wheelhouse windows, almost knocking Kees overboard. It was a stupefyingly amazing discovery that they were all still aboard, that the little craft still floated.

"Keep rowing!" said Kees. "The rest of you bail. When we're a bit drier, we'll get some breakfast together. And something to drink."

This was nonsense. They were barely able to hang onto their seats. He was saying it only to keep up their morale, such as they had any.

"Duffie," said Diana. "I forgive you for absolutely everything!"

"Darling," he shouted back. "You don't know about everything!"

"I daresay I can guess!"

"Pity His Royal Highness isn't king," Chips said, seated just in front of Spencer. "As Defender of the Faith, he'd have some considerable influence with God."

"I've never heard you speak of God before," Spencer said.

"Dear boy, I move with the times."

"Bail!" shouted Kees.

It was Nora who noticed young Parker get to his feet at the bow. He had not been helping in any way, and had barely been conscious. But now he stood, looking unhappily about. He seemed to want one of the buckets, but they were all well in use.

Nora had meant to warn him to be careful, but she instead turned away as he unbuttoned his fly and prepared to relieve himself, climbing onto a forward thwart.

Nora turned her back completely to him, hunching forward in fear of what might come in the spray. An instant later she heard him cry out, a sound followed by that of a splash.

Everyone stopped, most in disbelief. Their peril had been brought infinitely nearer. Could their doom be that close at hand—a matter of inches? A simple matter of taking a piss? Was death just the other side of the gunwale? Was all this great vastness of ocean around them a colossal manifestation of the inevitability of death?

"Man overboard!" shouted Kees. "Get the grappling hook! Why in hell isn't he in his life jacket?"

The Javanese crewman scrambled for the pole, slipping on the floorboards. Young Parker, his eyes wild, his mouth wide open but speechless, was barely able to keep his head above water. His hands flailed about. It seemed to Spencer that he probably did not know how to swim, or was too drunk to remember.

There were those aboard who did. Spencer and Edwina had talked of distance swims they had both completed. The countess had set swimming records in Germany. But no one moved. Except one. There was another splash. Mrs. Parker had kicked off her shoes and flung herself after her husband. Her dark head appeared beside the boat and then slipped beneath the surface. A moment later it reappeared, as she began attempting a painfully slow breaststroke toward him. A moment later Parker himself disappeared in the water. When he became visible again, he was even farther away. Another huge wave was rising over them.

"Get that damned grappling hook!" Kees shouted, his voice screeching with hoarseness.

His poor crewman was trying, but the long pole with the hook on it was hopelessly caught in some coiled line.

Mrs. Parker vanished again. Spencer, gripping the count's shoulder, turned and stepped onto the seat and then vaulted over the side. He heard von Kresse hiss with pain and then at once he was immersed in the shockingly cold sea, its size and depth and supremacy suddenly awesome. Its frigid temperature was overpowering. He had kept his life jacket on, but it was impeding his progress. He supposed he had only a few minutes to live if he did not get back in the boat.

The water filled his clothing and dragged against him. He fought against the pull, his eyes fixed on the woman's beautiful head. She was sideways to him but did not look back. She was intent upon her husband, who appeared to be drifting away swiftly.

Spencer took the deepest of breaths and pulled hard. He had only a few feet to go, but they were as good as miles. He was as consumed by fear now as purpose. He did not turn his head but was worried that, behind him, the motorboat could be moving away—miles and miles away.

It took a dozen, and then two dozen painful, exhausting strokes to reach her. He thrust his right arm under hers, then caught her up hard and, leaning backward, held her above the surface. Turning his head back to the boat, he discovered it was only two or three feet away. Kees and the men at the oars had kept it near.

Clutching the gunwale, Spencer found he could scarcely breathe without strenuous effort. But the strong arms of Mountbatten and Metcalfe reached past him and grasped the woman beneath her shoulders. She was struggling, muttering and protesting in anguished cries, fighting to remain in the water.

Spencer seized her thigh and shoved. With the other two men pulling, they got her over the side. The three disappeared from Spencer's view, and then Metcalfe and the crewman appeared, pulling him up by his arms, wrenching his back painfully as they hauled him into the boat.

He lay motionless, staring upward, listening vaguely as he heard Kees shout, "Try for the husband!"

Spencer, breathing deeply and with great effort, was amazed that he could become so fatigued from a brief minute or two in the water—another surpassing discovery of life. Amazing, too, was that he no longer felt the cold or wet. It was as if the nerves that ran to his skin had been somehow disconnected. His perception of time had also vanished. He stared at the huge and malevolent gray clouds above as they raced past in great, ponderous swirls, trailing ragged edges. He could mark their extraordinary speed. His ears were filled with the strangely pleasant music of the howling, whipping wind. But there was no time.

A human form interposed itself in his view of the true universe. He felt his head being lifted, cradled. The face that came near his was Nora's, still exquisite despite the abuse of her hair by the storm and her lack of makeup.

She stroked his cheek, saying nothing, her lovely eyes full of sadness, tenderness, and caring. He could hear someone else—a woman—screaming. It was Mrs. Parker.

Spencer sat up. They were all looking out to sea, their faces blank with horror and disbelief. Mrs. Parker's husband was nowhere to be seen. He had vanished on the other side of one of these liquid mountains, into the maw of a watery valley beyond. He would be sinking now, a slow, tumbling, endless fall through hundreds of feet of petrifying cold and darkness—until the undersea pressure and the gas within his body combined to hold him in suspension. In time, if he was not eaten by the fierce, cold creatures below, this combination would serve to return him to the surface as a dreadful corpse. But by then the boat would have been carried far, far away.

"I want everyone in life jackets!" Kees said. "Now! This must not happen again."

A few of them began to comply, but most simply sat stupidly.

"People, please!" Kees said. "I want no more lives lost! Put on your life jackets!"

Olga watched as the others, prince and count and lord and lady, dumbly complied—small sleepy children dressing on mummy's orders upon awakening.

One life. All she needed, all she asked, all she required of this awful sea voyage was the loss of one life, a wasteful, redundant, pointless, and intolerable life. Instead this idiot boy had drowned, as simply and easily as an expended breath.

She had her pistol in a pocket of her heavy wool skirt. It was as useless on this little boat as a Japanese lantern or French pastry. All she had needed to do was to get her victim over the side and into the sucking sea. She could have done it in the night in the midst of the rain. A bashing rap on the skull and then a shove and he would have been gone, and the Union of Soviet Socialist Republics would have been free of the ugly, incipient menace he represented.

There would be another night. They did not seem near rescue.

Reichscommissioner Goering was at lunch, an enormous *Mittagessen* of *Leberknödelsuppe*, smoked *Forelle*, *Bratwurst*, *Gefülte Kalbsbrust*, *Kartoffelsalut*, and *Rotkohl*, washed down with Riesling and to be finished with *Blätterteiggeback*. But he did not get to finish. A servant entered, carrying nothing.

"Oberst von Glaube is here, sir," the man said.

"I am not to be disturbed while eating. Never!"

"*Jawohl, mein herr Reichscommissioner*. But he insists it is a matter that requires breaking that rule."

Goering had been in such a good mood. The Führer had informed him that morning that he was to become colonel general of the new Luftwaffe.

As usual with the Führer's telephone conversations, Goering had not actually talked with Hitler himself. A secretary spoke the leader's words into the telephone for him as he sat nearby and related Goering's responses. The Führer never talked directly into the telephone. He feared that the mouthpieces of these devices were acrawl with germs.

When he suspected he could no longer trust a secretary's discretion, the Führer would have him or her sent to a camp or shot. The secretary who somehow managed finally to achieve and maintain his full trust would likely become one of the most powerful persons in the Reich.

"What does the oberst want? Why does he disturb me?"

"He did not say, *mein herr Reichscommissioner.* He said only that he must."

"Go ask him why." When the servant left, Goering took advantage of the delay to devour the rest of the stuffed breast of veal. Then he drained another full glass of wine.

The servant returned. *"Mein herr Reichscommissioner,* the *oberst* wishes . . ."

"More wine!"

*"Jawohl, mein herr Reichscommissioner."* The men leapt to his duty, then set down the bottle, standing at attention. "The *oberst* wishes to say that it concerns a Dutch trans-Atlantic liner."

Goering dropped his fork onto his plate. "Send him in at once!"

The colonel was one of Goering's most able intelligence aides. He had been one of the first members of the old German Air Service to join the party, and had served on Goering's staff when the Reichscommissioner was prime minister of Prussia.

Goering motioned him to a chair and then dismissed his servant. "Take a glass of wine, Erich, and then tell me everything."

The colonel poured a glass, more in obedience than thirst for it. He sipped, set down the wine, then looked at Goering calmly in the face. The Reichscommissioner had not told anyone on his staff of von Kresse's mission, but had alerted his intelligence people to watch for news of the ship, saying it was of the utmost importance.

"The Dutch liner *Wilhelmina* is in distress, sir," said the colonel. "Specifically, it is on fire. In the middle of the Atlantic. I have the coordinates."

"On fire?"

"Yes, sir. Possibly sinking. It has lowered its boats and sent distress messages."

*"Mein Gott!* Do you know who's aboard?"

"No, sir. You did not tell us that."

"Certainly not. Are there any ships in the vicinity?"

"The naval ministry reports three vessels within eight or ten hours' sail of the *Wilhelmina.* One French, one Greek, one Italian. The Italian ship may be as close as six hours. It's a military vessel."

"Any German ships?"

"No, sir."

"No German submarines?"

"That I do not know, sir. Their positions are secret."

"Get me Admiral Canaris on the telephone. No, wait. I'll go in person. Get me a car. At once!"

"*Jawohl, mein herr Reichscommissioner!*"

The man stood, saluted, smacked his heels together, and was gone. Goering stuffed some more food into his mouth, then hurried after.

When his motorcade was ready, the Reichscommissioner thought upon it and sent it back, requesting instead a small, black, inconspicuous sedan with curtained windows. On this quick trip, he had no interest in advertising his presence, nor his destination. When they reached the headquarters of the Abwehr, the Reich's principal military intelligence service, Goering had his driver proceed into an interior courtyard so he might enter the building by an obscure entrance.

Canaris had been chief of the Abwehr since the previous January, an appointment the Führer had made with deliberate disregard for the fact that the admiral had failed to support the Nazi movement in the revolutionary days of the first putsch. An opportunist and something of a dilettante, the son of an extremely wealthy Westphalian industrialist, the slick Greek-German master spy had a pathological fear and hatred of the Soviet Bolsheviks and had been among the loudest cheerers when Hitler finally came to power in 1933.

Goering had no great faith in the man's loyalty. Canaris had an aristocrat's loathing of the S.A. brown shirts and other party street units, and Goering suspected him of a sentimental sympathy with Jewish intellectuals, indeed with intellectuals of any stripe. But the two of them shared a dread of being forced into another war that might pit them against both the European democracies and Russia. A war that might again enlist the United States as one of their foes was utterly unthinkable.

They also shared a taste in art. Canaris was very fond of the works of Egon Schiele.

The Reichscommissioner had some doubts about the admiral's talents for spying on the Reich's presumed enemies, but he was very, very good at spying on Germans. And he had kept the much-feared S.D. intelligence service at bay through the simple expedient of blackmail. The S.D.'s blond, blue-eyed Aryan model chief, Reinhard Heydrich, was half Jewish, and Canaris had documents to prove it. Heydrich had once been a protégé of Canaris's until forced out of the navy by Admiral Raeder for raping a shipyard owner's daughter. Now Heydrich was lieutenant general of the S.S., and desirous of maintaining that rank, and his life. He was very deferential toward Admiral Canaris. So was Goering.

"My dear Hermann," the admiral said, rising as Goering was ushered swiftly into his office virtually unannounced. "A pleasant surprise. And congratulations on your forthcoming promotion."

"How do you know about that?"

"Hermann, please."

Goering sat down in a chair much too small for him. The admiral was fond of fine French furniture.

"Wilhelm," Goering said. "There is a Dutch ship in trouble in the Atlantic. Do you know anything about it?"

The admiral replied first with a quick, capricious smile. He fetched a slip of notepaper from a neat stack on his desk.

"The *Wilhelmina?*"

"Yes. The *Wilhelmina.*"

Canaris glanced over the notepaper and then looked to Goering, his eyes lingering. "About the *Wilhelmina*, Hermann, I know not only anything, I know everything."

"That is something I should always presume. What do you know?"

"That it is on fire and probably sinking. That you, Herr Himmler, and the Führer have an interest in it. That the crown prince of England and a very prestigious entourage are on board it, along with the Count and Countess von Kresse representing yourself, a Herr Braun representing Herr Himmler, and an assassin named Olga Maretzka representing the charming Comrade Beria of the charming Union of Soviet Socialist Republics. The *Wilhelmina*'s last reported position was forty-three degrees forty-six minutes north, thirty-six degrees fourteen minutes west."

Canaris had commanded U-boats in the Great War and later had served as captain of the battleship *Schlesien*.

He returned the memorandum to its neat stack and sat back in his chair, his hands folded carefully in his lap.

"Who else have you informed of this, Wilhelm?"

"Not Herr Himmler," said the admiral. "You know that I find him difficult. I have made a report to Admiral Raeder, informing him only that the ship is in distress and that the royal British party and our dear friends the von Kresses are aboard. I said nothing of Her Himmler's gentleman, or the von Kresses' reason for being there." He smiled, a silky expression on his dark face.

"And?"

"Unterseeboot 283 is proceeding toward the *Wilhelmina,* on the surface and at flank speed. It will be there within a few hours. Raeder's instructions to it are to assist in any rescue effort, with particular attention to the royal party. It would be a dramatic gesture of friendship to the English, and a triumph for the Reich, would it not?"

"Apparently I need not have come, Wilhelm."

"As usual, Hermann. But it is always a delight to see you. May I offer you a glass of schnapps?"

# CHAPTER FOURTEEN

As the rain stopped, the wind quickened. It didn't seem to affect the size of the already gargantuan waves that had been marching their way from many miles distant and still threatened their hapless little boat, but it tore at their faces with bitter cold and stinging salty spray. They huddled together under their blankets and canvas in small clusters, with women the dominant figures, especially the still-sobbing Mrs. Parker. Thinking of Lady Diana's remark as they had left the burning ship, Spencer was reminded of Euripides' *The Trojan Women,* these forlorn and noble ladies of their lifeboat party standing now for Agrippa, Cassandra, Helen, and the other forlorn figures of that fifth-century B.C. tragedy, each with her own wretched tale to tell, each with her own separate fate to confront.

Cassandra's curse, aside from her own violent murder, was to foretell the fall of Troy yet not be believed. Was Nancy Cunard Cassandra? And who was the unfortunate Mrs. Parker, deprived of her husband for no sensible reason? There was kingdom involved here, as well, and a woman stolen from her husband by the son of a king. Certainly there was tragedy enough, and flames as terrible as those that had consumed that noble city two and a half millennia before. Hector's son had died by being thrown from the highest wall of Troy. The Parker boy had perished taking a piss. Both deaths were equally pointless.

And who were the treacherous, infiltrating, and ultimately triumphant Greeks? He, C. Jamieson Spencer, was good for one. So were Chips Channon and the Germans. The most dangerous Greek of all, Spencer supposed, was Mrs. Simpson. They were all here looting the

English, but she represented most the soldiers in the wooden horse who would take and destroy the kingdom.

Spencer's own possible spoils would not be inconsiderable. If they survived this disaster, his would be the greatest newspaper story of the decade, perhaps any decade. He had been writing and rewriting it over and over in his mind all night and all morning, amending it only to accommodate each new preposterous development. If the world did not yet know of the prince's dalliance with this plain, coarse, and scheming woman, a person whose singular worthlessness was equaled only by the prince's own, they would shortly. Spencer felt no reluctance in doing this, no compunction whatsoever. With Lindbergh—if that mysterious figure in the raincoat was Lindbergh—he'd been constrained by a genuine guilt, a distaste for his profession's penchant for pawing through the sordid tragedies of others. His mind had been full of the image of the Lindbergh's little boy lying dead in a ditch. But the outrage and scandal that would fall upon this pathetic royal figure was probably the most deserving fate one could wish upon him—if only because they had made Edwina pee in a bucket. Spencer would be in the service of a cause, the cause of providential irony. With every seamy, sensational word that would come from his typewriter, he could be striking a blow far more devastating than any revolutionary's. And he would feel a kind of joy. One of his aerial kills in the war had been like that. His last.

Nora was holding his hand. She was smiling at him. She had totally calmed now, as if she had received some answer to her hours of prayer.

Actually, there was a cheering element in this mean, chill wind. It seemed to be blowing the storm away from them. Spencer turned and saw to the west a faint, pale-pink line drawn across the horizon that grew wider and brighter with each passing minute. The storm had arrived as a harsh, Wagnerian opera curtain; its retreat now took the form of a soft coverlet being pulled off the earth. The pink at the edge of the sky became a light and then intensely cerulean blue. The margin between stormy cloud and clear air was a sharp demarcation, a crescent reaching from horizon to horizon. With amazing rapidity, it passed over them and moved swiftly away to the east. They were left in bright if not warm sunlight. The wind was growing ever brisker, but the huge waves actually seemed to be diminishing.

"I think we just had a brush with the tail of the hurricane," Kees said.

"What bloody hurricane?" Major Metcalfe asked.

"There was a hurricane on our course," said Kees. "It must have shifted to the north. We hadn't time to inform you."

Duff Cooper swore and laughed, both rebukes.

"I speak truly," said Kees. "It was very busy on the bridge. On the entire ship. In any event, our situation improves. Excuse me."

He left his seat and went to the wheelhouse, making Mrs. Simpson move so he could retrieve his Very pistol and a box of flares. With much indignation at being moved, she left that sanctuary and took a seat outside near the others, rewrapping herself in her blanket. Spencer recalled that someone, Chips, probably, had told him she was highly claustrophobic. She was probably relieved to be out of the box that was the wheelhouse, now that it was day and the sun was shining.

Kees loaded the pistol and fired it with a loud report. The flare arced into the limitless blue and exploded in a ball of flung spark and flame. In such clear air, it could doubtless be seen for miles and miles.

"I will fire one every half hour," Kees said. "We have two boxes of flares. I think, with this improving weather, they will not all be necessary."

Count von Kresse had gone to talk to Edwina Mountbatten. Neither his sister nor Edwina's husband objected, or paid much notice. The countess, staring down at the floorboards, seemed quite oblivious to everything. After Parker's drowning, all aboard the motorboat had become subdued.

Dagne, however, little moved by Parker's pathetic passing, was feeling bitter and frustrated, made as unhappy by the improving weather as the others had been cheered. Rescue would mean an end to everything—a different ship, different circumstances, doubtless separation from the prince and his party. Their task would be impossible. And depending on what happened to the *Wilhelmina*, bearing Herr Braun's blond body, she might shortly find herself being locked away in a jail cell.

She could at least still succeed in their mission. Their only hope lay in the few hours that likely remained before they were found, if even hours there were.

It made her so furious. The whole future of the Reich could be decided here in this small boat—indeed, perhaps, *had* to be decided here. But she could do nothing. She could think of nothing that could be done. Her brother was no help at this point. He was more an obstacle than an ally. She had her pistol, with five shells still in the magazine, but to even think of using it was madness. Look what had happened the last time she had resorted to this weapon.

She envisioned herself, standing with the gun, ordering Mrs. Simpson over the side as some American western movie badman might order passengers out of a stagecoach. Dagne began to laugh. It did not ease her anger.

"I think we should have more of the wine," Spencer said, "and try to be as cheerful as we can."

"Jolly well right," said Duff.

"Is there something better than that dreadful swill we had last night?" asked the prince, who had joined Mrs. Simpson. "It was Belgian, wasn't it? Flemish stuff. Is there nothing French? The French are all a pack of Jews, but they have mastered the art of the grape."

Duff and Spencer hauled out a box that proved to be a case of red wine, the last aboard, though there was some brandy and several cases of Dutch beer. When it came turn to fill his tin cup with wine, the prince made a face but accepted the stuff. He drank thirstily enough.

Mrs. Simpson had none of it. She looked up with much irritation when the Countess von Kresse took a seat beside her.

"Did you know poor Herr Parker in Baltimore?" Dagne asked.

Mrs. Simpson looked both offended and alarmed.

"No," she said. "My mother knew his mother. She's quite prominent. As was my own family. In Maryland."

"Yes," said Dagne. "Your family was in the hotel business?"

"What?"

"Didn't you own a hotel? Or a *Gasthaus?* Excuse me, a guest house?"

"I don't know what you're talking about!" Mrs. Simpson looked about frantically. The prince was sipping his wine, thinking upon some absorbing matter, inexcusably inattentive to her. There was no place Wallis could go on the boat without the countess following her if she wished. There was no escape.

"Didn't you have paying guests in your house?" Dagne persisted. "Boarders? Herr Parker said this."

The prince remained distracted. The countess's gray-blue eyes had a wild gleam to them. Wallis could not understand what had provoked this assault.

"My mother was a very good cook," Mrs. Simpson said icily. "One of the best in Baltimore. A number of prominent gentlemen of the city came to our house to eat, and they left money with my mother to compensate her for her grocery purchases and her efforts."

"I see," said Dagne, glancing to the still-impassive prince. She was sure he had heard. It would come to him shortly.

"Why do you ask?" Mrs. Simpson demanded. "What concern is it of yours?"

"Oh," said Dagne, with her wickedest smile. "It is because we have something in common. My family owns a number of inns. They are the central part of the many villages on our estate."

"How nice," said Wallis, a sweetness and heavy drawl returning to her speech. "You are in Poland, are you? You're Polish?"

"We are German! *Wir sind von Ost Prussen!* And you? You are Jewish, yes? You have an Uncle Solomon?"

"Wallis is certainly not Jewish!" the prince exclaimed suddenly.

"Dagne!" said the count. *"Komst du hierher! Jezt!"*

Smiling gleefully now, Dagne did as bidden. She was sure she had done it. With just a few words, a brief but potent exchange, she had revealed what she was certain was the Simpson woman's most horrible secret. She had planted the seed in the prince's mind. He was as much an anti-Semite as anyone in the Reich. The seed would flourish and grow. His passion would turn to wound. It would fester.

Von Kresse had left Edwina, to draw Dagne away from this awful exchange with Mrs. Simpson. The countess pursued her brother, moving awkwardly along the center aisle of the rocking boat, the clever smile still in place.

"I have administered the poison," she said in a heavy whisper when they finally took a seat. "I should have thought of doing this days ago."

"What poison?"

"She's a Jew. Or she could be. He must come to believe this. Her dark hair. Her large nose. Even if she isn't, he will come to think so. I've planted it in his mind."

"Don't be ridiculous. She has the bluest eyes I've ever seen."

"Unlike your darling Jewish Edwina."

"Be quiet!"

"We have triumphed, Martin. It took only a moment. I just went up to her and said a few words and it's done. They will never be married. He will never leave the throne."

"Are you mad, Dagne? Look at them. You upset her and his response is to comfort her. She could be wearing a yellow star of David and he would only pull it off like some offending piece of lint. You could have the word 'Jewess' or 'Negress' branded on her forehead, and he would kiss it. Can't you see that? If we are to perform any service for our disgusting government, it will be to report that they are inextricably attached, that the German nation must accommodate itself to this reality and plot its foreign adventures accordingly. Germany and Great Britain will never be allies."

The countess's triumphant expression turned to one of confusion and worry, but she would not speak such feelings. "You are wrong, Martin. You have been wrong about what is happening in Germany and you are wrong about this."

"I don't want to hear any more. You make me want to get up and jump into the sea."

He rose stiffly and went back to Edwina. Dagne stared after him coldly, then asked Duff for some wine. She took a cupful, drank it in a few gulps, and then asked for more.

If Martin was correct, she would try again. She would find some way to provoke this Mrs. Simpson into a self-destructive act. She would not let glorious opportunity pass unused. They still had hours left, perhaps another day, trapped together on this tiny boat. If Dagne could not accomplish what had been asked of them, everything she believed about herself would be wrong. She was a superior person. She and Martin were the best. Mrs. Simpson was cabbage.

Kees fired off another flare, then set the Very pistol back into its place in the wheelhouse.

"Is there anyone here who knows about engines?" he asked, coming forward to the center of the group again.

"I know everything about engines," Lord Mountbatten said.

"I need some help with the motor," Kees said. "Now that the weather's cleared, I want to take out the spark plugs and distributor—all the electrical parts—and dry them. I think our trouble may be simply that they got wet in the storm."

"I'll be more than happy to undertake this," Mountbatten said. "Do as I instruct you and we can have it done in twenty minutes."

"*Quel sangfroid,*" said Diana. "Our dashing Dickie."

Nora moved closer to Spencer, leaning her head against his shoulder. In private, in some warm and comfortable intimate surrounding, it would be cuddling. Perhaps it was even here.

"You seem happy," he said.

"I am. I am thinking happy thoughts."

"Happy thoughts? In the middle of the sea in this little boat? Happy thoughts of what?"

She grinned, holding him more tightly. "Of our children."

Without their ever having been to bed, or even come close to it, she had progressed from goddess to nun to wife. His life had taken him to this small, forsaken boat and this beautiful but worrisome woman. Where were they bound after this?

"Mother!" Nancy Cunard shrieked. "The sea is calming! We're going to live! Isn't that quite quite wonderful! Don't you just hate it?"

"Shut up, Nancy!"

"You look quite quite awful, Mother. You look a sight. Actually ugly. Quite, quite. That's how you're going to live the rest of your life. And then you'll die, Mother! We'll all die! Not today. This is just a reprieve. But soon enough, Mother!"

"Oh, Nancy," Diana said wearily. "Do give it a rest."

Captain van der Heyden sat like a great lump in his bridge chair, legs and arms hanging limp with his extraordinary fatigue. The blood that swelled his hands and fingers filled them with pain, but his sense of it was dull and bleary, like his vision. He was tired of frustration, tired of his continuing effort, tired of the unending threat and danger, tired even of drink. If he were to die now it would come as a great relief. To die, to sleep. And not to dream.

Van Groot's square face came into the captain's vision.

"They're out," he said, in a slow voice as weary as the captain's.

"What are out?"

"The fires. They're all out. Every one. Every single damned one."

"You've said that before during the evening."

Van Groot spoke not in triumph but in fact. "The evening is ended. It's cold daylight and it's true. All the fire control stations report everything out. It's something of a miracle, I admit, but it's true."

The captain sat up, with great effort, his hands held ridiculously up in the air beside him, his eyes blinking against the harsh sunlight. "Every single one, Mr. van Groot? It's actually all over? I'm not having a dream?"

"Not about the fires, Captain."

"Yes, it seems to be true," said van Hoorn, coming forward from some shadowy part of the bridge. "I think we're over it."

The quartermaster still stood at the helm, one hand resting on the unused wheel, but the officers on the bridge slouched and slumped. One sat on the floor, back against the bulkhead, snoring.

Van der Heyden heaved himself further erect, leaning forward with his elbows on his knees.

"I want a complete damage report," he said.

"That's relatively simple," said Van Groot. "Boiler Rooms No. 4 and No. 5 are burned out. Most of the upper second-class cabins were destroyed, along with the second-class galley, dining room, and lounge. The aft funnel and ventilating shafts are burned out; the first-class galley and the after-turbo generating room, too. But the forward three boilers are undamaged. I think we can get under way." The first officer's face was blackened from the oily soot and smoke.

"What about casualties?"

"Amazingly," said van Groot, "only Chief Engineer Brinker and two seamen are dead, and that mysterious man who was shot. Perhaps two dozen are burned, at least ten so badly as to need hospitalization. Including yourself, Captain."

Van der Heyden coughed. "Nonsense." The remark made him feel the pain in his hands more strongly. "At least not yet. What about the electric?" he asked.

"We're rewiring what we can. Enough to restore power to the turbines."

"The weather is good now," van Groot added. "Improving."

"So?" said the captain, looking at the other's face quite clearly now. They had not ever really been friends, but they had long sailed together.

"So the possibility exists that we can continue to New York."

"To what purpose?"

"Captain, to complete the voyage," van Hoorn said. "Your only purpose."

The captain looked over at the chart table, but was doubtful of mustering the energy to walk to it.

"What's our position?" he asked.

"The storm drove us about sixty nautical miles to the northeast, and we're drifting farther north in the Gulf Stream."

"But not much?"

"Not yet."

"And the passengers?"

"We have all the lifeboats in view except three. The passengers appear to be all right, though they may have lost some overboard during the night."

"And the starboard steel motorboat?"

Van Groot cast his eyes down. "I am afraid, Captain, that the Prince of Wales' party is one of the three that are missing."

"You can't lose him," said a voice from across the bridge. The tall, curly-haired man had removed his raincoat and was standing in shirt-sleeves, his too-short tie askew. He came up to the group gathered around the captain. "You have to go after him first."

"I will retrieve them all," said van der Heyden, rising clumsily. He touched the chair back for support and winced with the hurt. "Every passenger. But you are right. That one first. If possible."

"I'll help you with the navigation," said the tall man. "I know something about drift."

"I guess you do, sir," said van Groot.

His steps dragging, the captain went to the sliding door that opened onto the starboard bridge wing. When Ladewijk shoved it back for him, he stepped into the cold, reviving, brisk air, his eyes burning from the dazzling dancing light upon the sea. Turning slowly, he looked toward the stern. From the aft funnel to the second-class promenade, the superstructure of the *Wilhelmina* was a blackened ruin. In many places the steel had been twisted by the heat and there were still small, wispish columns of smoke rising here and there, blown back by the wind.

"Have we taken on any more water?"

"Only from the fire hoses. Otherwise, no sir. The hull's not damaged."

"You're sure?"

"Yes, sir. We have the water from the hoses to pump out, but there's been no significant leakage."

"Very well. As soon as you have power, get the pumps going and see if you can get some steam up."

"There's an Italian warship within forty miles of us, sir. Coming as fast as she can."

"*Luister naar mij.* I did not become master of this vessel to be hauled off the ocean by the Italian navy. If it comes to that, we'll wait for the Dutch navy."

The others laughed, including the tall, curly-haired American.

It took nearly an hour, not the twenty minutes Lord Mountbatten had boasted, but he and Kees managed to dry and reassemble the engine parts with great precision and, after several coughs and sputters, get the motor started again. After running it at high revolutions for several minutes, Kees then turned it off.

"What the hell?" Duff said.

"I don't want to waste fuel," Kees said. "We're not going any-where until I can get a fix on our position and have a reasonable idea there's a ship in our vicinity."

"The *Wilhelmina* should be just to the northwest," Duff said.

"We don't know where she is," Kees said. "We don't know if she's even afloat."

"He's quite right, don't you know," said Mountbatten.

Kees fired off another flare with the Very pistol, the sound startling a number of those aboard the motorboat. Their mood had diminished from cheer to solemnity as the horizon continued to remain empty.

Spencer found Mrs. Parker suddenly kneeling before him, her tears dried but her eyes still full of sadness—and a little craziness. She placed her hands on his.

"You saved my life," she said. "I must thank you for that. You're a very brave man. I might have drowned. You might have drowned."

He moved his hands to take hers. They were extraordinarily beau-tiful hands despite all the wind and salt water, lovelier even than Nora's. Her face was reddened, though. She'd been thoroughly beaten, by more than the sea.

"I'm glad I was able to help you."

"But we killed him, you and I," she said. "By saving me, we abandoned him. We made him drown, you and I." She began to cry again.

"It was an accident, Mrs. Parker. It was no fault of yours. Or mine."

"We might have saved him," she said, sobbing. "We could have. We could have."

Nora, transforming herself from wife to mother, reached and drew Mrs. Parker up on the seat beside her, putting both arms around her.

Spencer took himself away. The only available seat with easy reach was by Count von Kresse. Edwina had gone aft to the wheelhouse.

"*Wozu,*" said the count.

Spencer had not heard the term since the war days. It was the German version of the phrase that had come to be the theme of 1918. The French talked of "*la Gloire*" and "*la Victoire.*" The British and Americans in the trenches said "What's it all for?" And their German foes said "*Wozu?*"

Not all the French talked of "*la Victoire.*" When the armistice came, Spencer had been flying near the French sector east of Verdun and landed by their war-worn trenchworks to view the awesomely quiet front. There'd been a grizzled old poilu standing atop a breast-work and gazing solemnly out over the cratered moonscape that was no-man's land. The old soldier shook his head and uttered just one word. He said it softly:

"*Merde.*" It was much the same as "*wozu.*"

"What was your worst day of the war?" Spencer asked the count.

Von Kresse shrugged, his left shoulder twisting as he did so. "A day? A single worst day? I suppose I could say it was a day in October 1918 when I was more or less blown apart by a seventy-five–milli-meter shell. There was a bloody awful day—two days, during the Meuse-Argonne when I had to kill three Americans in a shell hole with a rifle and bayonet and then spend that night and the next day with them while they died—one slowly after another. I could name a hundred days but they now seem all the same—they were all the worst."

"You fought as an infantryman at the end, yes?"

"For a time, yes."

"But you were one of the leading aces of the war."

"I gave up the war in the air after—after that unfortunate incident we discussed earlier. The 'atrocity.' "

"The schoolteacher and the children. The only atrocity attributed to the German Air Service."

"Yes," the count said gravely.

Spencer stared down at the floorboards. "You were that pilot?"

"Yes." Uttered with the longest of sighs, this affirmative was almost a philosophical statement. "We were strafing an advancing British column that we caught in the village. I was making a firing pass as I came around a church steeple. I thought it was an infantry file. When I made the second pass, I—I saw what I had done. There's been nothing more horrible in my life."

"But you shot them up again!" Spencer restrained himself. "I'm sorry. That's how the story went."

"The story is true. They were in terrible agony, thrashing about on the ground. It was almost as if I could hear their screams, their terror. I wanted to leave them in peace."

"Some might have lived."

"I had only a few seconds. I was coming apart in pieces over what I had done."

The two sat silently for a long moment, listening to the wash and slap of the water against the rocking boat.

"I've never been quite put back together," Count von Kresse said.

"I strafed a trench once," Spencer said. "I killed sleeping men."

"War."

"Fucking war."

"*Wozu.*"

"And you went into the trenches," Spencer said. "To get rid of your guilt. To expiate your sin. Maybe to kill yourself."

"Possibly. I have never been rid of that guilt. I simply didn't want to fly any more. I wanted no more fighting against those I could scarcely see. I realized how 'unclean' the pristine 'knight's war' in the air really was. If I had to kill, I wanted my enemy directly in front of me. I wanted my hands on him. I wanted him to be able to kill me. But you know, with those three Americans in the shell hole, it was just as bad as the French schoolteacher and her children. In a way, worse. I killed those three men with great intent, to save my own life, but then I tried to save them—two of them anyway, the last two—but I could not. They went one, two, three. And when the last one went, it was the worst. I remember the look in his eyes. His eyes are great holes in a musty hunk of bone somewhere, but the last look in them still lives with me."

"You fought as a private soldier? You gave up your rank?"

"In my family, this rank is hereditary. I can never be rid of it. It's my curse now. In 1918 I simply decided to ignore it." He pointed to his Pour le Mérite. "This I was awarded after my twentieth kill in the air. I sent it home to my father, knowing it would please him." His finger moved to the plain Iron Cross beside the more princely medal. "At the end I wanted no medals, of any kind. But they gave me this—for killing in the muck and the filth, when my squad captured an American machine-gun post. I was the only one left of my squad when it fell, so they gave me the simple soldier's Iron Cross. I think they were handing them out to every other man by then. Corporal Hitler got one, for carrying dispatches in a gas attack, I think. Mine was a pitiful, pointless feat. There were hundreds and hundreds of other American machine guns to come, and tens of thousands more Americans, but my battalion treated this small success like the fall of Sedan in the Franco-Prussian War. In all, I think our counterattack in that sector delayed the ultimate German collapse by three hours."

"*Wozu.*"

"*Wozu.*"

"My worst day," said Spencer, "was when Raoul Lufbery fell out of the sky: May 19, 1918. I was there. I saw it. I was one of his wingmen."

"You were friends?"

"I was one of his wingmen. Many, many times. We flew together with the French before the United States got into the war. He told me about his days flying in China. He's why I later went to China. We weren't really friends. We were comrades, we were wingmen, and I admired him very much."

"Yes, like our Oswald Boelke. We were all devastated when he fell."

"Raoul didn't fall. He jumped. His Nieuport had been set on fire. We were not issued parachutes, as you were. Our Congress thought it would lead to our wasting aircraft. So Raoul, with seventeen victories, chose to jump instead of burn."

"Our parachutes didn't always work."

The others were beginning to show signs of excessive stress. Nancy Cunard and her mother were still exchanging snarling insults. Mrs. Simpson was complaining bitterly to the prince about seemingly everything that had been inflicted upon her, as if it were all his fault—and none of hers. Diana, for the first time on the voyage, was talking of seasickness. With the calming seas, the waves had grown smaller and the troughs shorter. Consequently the motorboat was rocking with much more vehemence.

Duff ignored his wife. Chips Channon began to feel seasick himself. Fruity Metcalfe and Lord Brownlow were arguing about something, perhaps over which of them was to blame for this ultimate predicament.

Only Nora, embracing another human being in love and comfort, seemed at all happy now.

Edwina emerged from the wheelhouse and went to her husband, who was standing near Kees. Despite his ridiculous Hindu costume, Mountbatten had posed himself, head high, Brendan the Navigator, Leif Eriksson, Cristoforo Colon.

"Are you all right, darling?" Edwina said, shivering. She had a skirt and sweater on and a blanket over her shoulders, but her legs were bare to the wind.

"Of course, darling," he said. "We'll soon be out of this."

The count smiled sadly. "The perfect couple," he said quietly to Spencer.

"I don't understand their marriage," Spencer said.

"Their marriage is perfectly understandable," von Kresse said. "It's their relationship that's not."

"Any of her relationships."

Spencer sought the other man's eyes but was denied them. The count was staring at his sister.

"She's drinking a lot of wine," Spencer said.

"She's very unhappy," von Kresse said. "Perhaps the wine will be of some help."

Kees fired off another rocket. It was amazing how bright the burst was in such a brilliant sky and in such shimmering sunlight.

"People are drinking everything they can find," Spencer said. "Another night out here and there'll be nothing left."

"If we have to face another night out here, it will be a very good thing to have the alcohol gone," the count said. "There is not much civilization remaining with these people."

"My friend Chips Channon would disagree with you. He thinks we're all the best humanity has produced."

"He's a fool. The world would be much better off if this motorboat were to sink. I would save some of the ladies if I could, but the rest of us are no treasure, including two or three of the ladies. We're far from the best humanity has produced. I daresay we're quite the opposite."

"I'm not disagreeing. I'm just curious why you wouldn't save yourself, or me."

"You know why, Mr. Spencer."

Spencer looked about the boat, as if the answer lay with someone else. He could provide his own reasons, but he did not know whether the count's were the same.

"And your beautiful sister?"

The count turned his head to gaze upon her a moment. "She is a flawed thing. I love her very much, perhaps more than I have loved any other woman, including my wife. You have no idea what a wonderful woman she can be, what a wonderful woman she was."

"But?"

"But she is one of Goethe's villainnesses. It isn't that she is evil. The awful thing is that she isn't evil. She is herself, yet she is one of them. That's inimical. Antithetical. Impossible. But the improbable truth asserts itself constantly. She's sick inside. *Vielen krank.* The beautiful princess transforms herself into a monster. A self-imposed curse. What you must learn about the Nazis, what is most important about the Nazis, is that they are sane. They're just ordinary people. You have to learn that. That's why they're so awful, and what they do is so dangerous."

"Your sister is dangerous?"

"*Sehr richtig*. But she is not mad. I keep saying this. The most terrifying thing about the Nazis is that they are perfectly sane, perfectly normal. You can find them in any country, on any street corner. Ordinary people."

"I would like to think you're wrong."

"You've traveled, Mr. Spencer. You've been in Europe these last few years. You're a journalist. You know I'm right."

"How do you know I'm a journalist?"

Nora was staring at them. So were Mrs. Parker and Channon. The count pretended to uncoil some tangled line, a pointless effort because it so obviously pained him and he accomplished nothing.

Finally he dropped the rope. "Edwina told me about you."

"Edwina is indiscreet."

Von Kresse laughed, the first time Spencer had heard him do this. Several of the others looked at them, including Edwina. Then she returned her attention to Mountbatten, who was arguing with Kees. She was trying to intervene, though it wasn't clear on whose behalf she was doing so.

"She is afraid," von Kresse said.

"Of what I might write?"

"No. She knows what you're going to write. She's afraid of what may happen as a result. She feels it's her fault you've come among us, not your friend Mr. Channon's. She thinks you may serve to keep the good Prince Edward from his throne."

"And so what? You've just said you'd be happy if he went down with this motorboat."

"Jimmy!"

It was Nora. "Jimmy. Something's wrong with Mrs. Parker. She's shaking like crazy."

Spencer motioned to Kees. "Get another blanket for this woman! And some brandy!"

Kees hurried forward, leaving the helm with the Oriental crewman.

"What are you going to write, Mr. Spencer?" the count said.

"I'm going to write about the prince."

"That's what Edwina thought."

"I hope my story will bring him down. He's a goddamn Nazi."

"That's what I think Edwina hopes, too. But she's frightened about what will happen to her husband."

"Then her concerns are trivial."

"But my concerns about her are not trivial," the count said. "What else are you going to write?"

"In my business, you write everything you know. I'll write about all of us, everything that's happened."

"Is this a threat? A promise? Idle talk? What?"

"It's simply a fact. Like Lindbergh."

"Lindbergh?" The count seemed startled.

"Yes. The Lone Eagle. He's aboard the *Wilhelmina,* or in one of the lifeboats. I've seen him, twice. The crown prince of England and the Greatest American Hero, together on a sinking ship. And some of the richest aristocrats America and England have ever seen, and some of the most beautiful women, certainly the most beautiful actress in Hollywood. And one of Germany's greatest flying heroes, and his sister, the eminent party member. Hell, I'll have everyone but the Queen of Rumania and Laurel and Hardy in this."

"Now you know why I would make no exception for you, why I'd have you sink with the rest of us."

"No, I don't. Why?"

"Because you are a parasite, Mr. Spencer."

"I write the truth."

"And what good that does serve? Look at the prince and his married lady. What good does the truth do them?"

"Speaking of parasites."

"You're speaking of royalty, Mr. Spencer."

"Royalty, nobility, aristocracy. Parasites. All the same."

"You were once an aristocrat, Mr. Spencer. Yes, we live off our ancestors. You journalists, you live off the living."

"And who does Charles Lindbergh live off? The great pathfinder conquers the Atlantic and then becomes rich endorsing wristwatches and automobiles."

"Charles Lindbergh is not with us."

"And we are here. On this little boat. This doomed little boat. Fuck you, Herr Markgraf."

"I say!" shouted Lord Mountbatten, rising to his fullest height despite the poor footing. "A ship! It's a ship!"

Duff Cooper turned to look in the direction of Mountbatten's gaze. They all did. Few saw anything, at first. Then the slim pencil line of black became more visible on the horizon.

"It's a fishing boat," Duff said.

"There's no mast," said von Kresse. Spencer had read that the count had better eyesight even than that perfect hunter von Richthofen.

The Oriental crewman pulled out a pair of binoculars from a box by the wheelhouse. Kees snatched them up, then handed them to Mountbatten, while reaching for the Very pistol. Another flare went up; then another.

"It's a submarine!" Mountbatten said.

"English?" asked Duff.

"No."

"American?"

"Not American," said the count. "German."

Mountbatten looked back at von Kresse, amazed, for the man hadn't even the use of the binoculars.

"That red flag," von Kresse said. "You'll find a white circle with a swastika in the center."

"We are saved!" Dagne said. She was ecstatic, but there was a craziness in her eyes.

Kees gave orders to the crewman, who hurried back to the wheelhouse. The engine started.

The submarine had stopped. Kees gave more orders, and the sailor spun the helm, turning the motorboat toward the larger vessel. It occurred to Spencer how absurd they all must look in their blankets and sodden costumes. He wondered if he might pass himself off as an actual Legionnaire.

"If it is German," Diana asked, "what will they do with us?"

"We're not at war," Mountbatten said. "At least I shouldn't think we are. If you wish to worry, be glad she's not Italian. Abyssinia, don't you know. Who can say whether we've declared war on Rome?"

"I'm quite sure she'll take us to the nearest port," Channon said. "Though I haven't the foggiest as to where that might be. The Azores? Iceland?"

"Newfoundland," Kees said. "We're the closest to Canada. Given the importance of some of you, though, they might take us directly to England."

"What a catastrophe that would be," said Metcalfe.

"Nothing could be more catastrophic than this," Emerald said.

"You see, Mother," Nancy said, an odd calmness to her voice. "We are going to live. You'll get to be old. Truly old."

The submarine appeared to be moving. It's silhouette narrowed. It was turning. Apparently toward them.

Kees again spoke in Javanese. The crewman increased their speed. The motorboat's bow began to kick up spray as they cut more rapidly through the water.

"My God," said Duff. "An embarrassment of riches."

"What?"

"Look!"

There was smoke on the western horizon.

"What's that?" asked Diana. "What could be burning out here?"

"A ship could be burning," Duff said. "If I may remind you of the circumstances under which we so disagreeably parted from the *Wilhelmina.*"

"It's not burning," Kees said. "It's a ship under steam."

"Well, for God's sake let's not press on toward that submarine," Channon said. "They're the most uncomfortable craft afloat, I'm told."

"As cramped as coffins," said the count.

Kees shouted a command, and the crewman put the boat into neutral. Their headway ceased immediately. They floated at idle, the boat's motor bubbling and snorting. Everyone was staring at the increasing smoke on the horizon. In a moment, a dark shape appeared beneath it. It grew to be several times the size of the submarine.

"It's a passenger liner," von Kresse said.

Spencer marveled at the man's eyesight. He would have been terrified to have come upon the count in combat in the skies over France. He would have been dead before he knew it.

"We'll be sipping stingers in a trice," Channon said. "And munching the good Beluga."

"No!"

It was the countess.

"Go the other way!" she said to Kees. "Go on to the submarine!"

Kees once more gave orders in Javanese to the seaman, but, instead of carrying out Dagne's commands, the crewman continued to turn the motorboat toward the approaching liner. He pushed the throttle forward. They began to pick up speed.

"No!" said the countess. "The submarine!"

"Dagne! Stop it!"

"The submarine!"

Kees ignored her, but then could not. She had taken out her pistol. She aimed it at the seaman, jabbing her arm in the direction of the submarine. The Oriental man looked terrified, turning his wide eyes to Kees, who violently shook his head and repeated his command.

"Go to the submarine!" Dagne shouted.

"Dagne! Stop this! You're going to cause trouble for everyone! Including your stupid Führer!"

The gun went off. Whether it was deliberately or accidentally fired was irrelevant. The bullet's impact slammed the seaman against the wheelhouse wall. It passed through his body, putting a large hole in the rear window. His body slumped to the floorboards, leaving a bloody smear. Mrs. Parker screamed. Several others began to cry.

Kees moved. The countess jerked the pistol around to confront him, but he moved past her, to the helm. He kept the motorboat on a course for the liner.

Dagne fired again. Kees, spinning around, clutched his thigh, then fell.

The countess shifted the pistol once more, aiming it directly at Mrs. Simpson's head. Unshaken, the American woman stared back with cold fury. Spencer was surprised and impressed.

"Dagne!"

The count was on his feet. A man without his infirmities could barely stand in a boat moving so fast through such water, but von Kresse was perfectly erect. He moved forward and to the side, interposing himself between the pistol and Mrs. Simpson.

The bullets that had struck the crewman and Kees had passed just alongside Olga's head. She was scared and angry, but sat quietly. Her own revolver was at hand in her long skirt. She would probably have opportunity to shoot the countess without the woman's even seeing her movements. But that would of course be a ridiculously stupid thing to do. Whatever was going to happen to them in this little boat, Olga would have to be passive, to await another opportunity.

Of course, there was always the chance the countess might do her work for her—a chance bullet, perhaps a deliberate one, eliminating Olga's target with no effort, and no risk, on her part. The von Kresse woman was waving the pistol back and forth, trying to sight at Mrs. Simpson again.

But her brother was coming for her. When he got too near, Dagne lifted the weapon to aim at him. Lifting it a few inches farther, she fired a bullet over his shoulder.

He came closer. She raised herself in the seat, lifting herself onto the gunwale, thrusting the pistol at him, her eyes full of her desperation and hate. She fired again, once more missing him, intentionally.

Von Kresse struck her with great violence. Spencer was startled by the man's strength. There was a splash. He had knocked his sister overboard. Her legs flew into the air and then she was gone. She was not wearing a life jacket. She had been one of those who had defied Kees's orders despite young Parker's death.

Mountbatten, Spencer, and Duff Cooper rushed to the side of the boat. With no one at the controls, it sped on, leaving the countess farther and farther behind. They saw her wet blond head, wide angry eyes, gasping mouth. She was shrieking in German.

Kees struggled to reach the controls.

"No!" shouted Count von Kresse. "It's too late!"

"She'll drown!" Kees said.

"My God, man, that's your sister," said Duff.

"She is already dead!" von Kresse said.

All sat staring in horror as in a brief moment the blond head disappeared in the dark-blue water.

The count gripped the gunwale, his face and hands ghostly pale. Then he collapsed in the seat behind him and began to sob. Edwina rushed to his side, holding him close.

"Christ," said Diana. "Why didn't we stay in the Paris riots?"

The prince was comforting Mrs. Simpson, saying, "Wallis, Wallis, Wallis." But she needed little comforting. Her face bore the same irritated expression it had before the incident. It was he who seemed the most distraught. He was uncertain whether the German woman meant to kill him or Wallis. The thought of possibly being assassinated had never entered his mind before and he could not come to grips with it.

But then he found a way. They'd been spared. He and Wallis were alive and the countess dead. It was a sign. He and Wallis were meant to be.

The submarine came no nearer. It stood off as the big liner approached, its blue-and-white colors clear. Smoke was coming only out of the first two funnels.

"Good God," said Duff. "It's the *Wilhelmina!*"

"The ever reliable Dutch," said Diana.

"We have to decide something quickly," Metcalfe said. He looked about the boat, glancing into people's faces, his eyes settling the longest on Spencer.

"You're quite right," Brownlow said. "We have to agree on a story."

"What do you mean?" said Duff. "There's been a murder." He looked over at the count. "Possibly two."

"It's not simply murder, Duff," Metcalfe countered. "It's a nasty international incident—one that could cause His Highness a lot of stinking trouble. Unless we find another way of dealing with the matter."

There was a loud, sudden splash. The dead crewman had been thrown overboard, by Olga Maretzka. She eyed them all defiantly.

"There," she said, in her thick accent. "Now you have three drownings. Accidents. In the storm."

Kees stared at her in unhappy amazement. "You can't do that."

Olga shrugged. "It's done. See. He slips beneath the surface."

"Who are you?" Diana asked.

"It doesn't matter," said Olga, turning away slightly to observe the approaching liner. "Just someone who has no more interest than you in being interrogated for hours or days in a New York or Canadian police station."

After a long silence, Metcalfe was the first to speak. "Well, there we are."

"Is everyone agreed?" Brownlow asked.

No one answered him, but he took that for an affirmative response. Kees was troubled by the situation that now confronted him. If he filed a complete report on what had happened, he would have to implicate Olga—perhaps involve her in serious trouble. She was obviously very afraid of that.

"What about the officer's leg?" Mountbatten said.

"Injured in the storm," Brownlow said.

"And the bullet hole in the wheelhouse window?"

Metcalfe rose, picking up an oar. He went to the wheelhouse and smashed the oar against the rest of the glass. "It was a very bad storm," he said, returning to his seat. "Someone hand me a bucket. We've got to wash away all this blood."

Olga went up to Kees and examined his leg, taking up the cloth of his pants where the bullet had gone through. With a sudden ripping, it gave way. Mountbatten came up to help her.

"Find the first aid kit," he said to no one in particular. Diana rose and crawled over them to search for it in the wheelhouse.

Kees's leg was bleeding badly. The bullet had torn through skin and muscle. But the bone had not been touched and the wound looked like a long gash.

The *Wilhelmina* was bearing down on them. The submarine, in the way of such craft, had quietly disappeared.

"And what will you do, Lieutenant Spencer?" Edwina asked. She was holding the count's head close to her breast.

"I will get some brandy," Spencer said.

# CHAPTER
## *FIFTEEN*

After being examined by the ship's doctor once back aboard the *Wilhelmina,* the group divided according to mood and circumstance. The prince, Lady Emerald, Chips Channon, and the Coopers, feeling the nervous effusion that often accompanies survival of a life-threatening ordeal, went to the prince's suite for celebratory drinks, though Mrs. Simpson took a hot bath and went directly to bed. Mrs. Parker was given a strong sedative and sent to her cabin to sleep. The Mountbattens went to their quarters to change out of their ridiculous fancy dress clothing, but Edwina left quickly after to join Count von Kresse in his cabin, where she found him seated in a chair staring mournfully at his sister's empty bed. Mountbatten thought of joining the prince's party, but first made himself a pink gin. He took it to an armchair and picked up one of his European genealogy books, but quickly fell asleep with the book and the drink falling untidily to the carpet.

Nancy Cunard and Henry Crowder vanished belowdecks, going immediately to the third-class bar. Metcalfe and Lord Brownlow held a brief reunion with Inspector Runcie, who had been left to another lifeboat, informing him in cursory fashion of their misadventure, noting that three people had died accidentally but giving no details. Then they dispatched him to the door of the prince's quarters and held a quiet conference between themselves in the major's stateroom.

"We have two problems," said Metcalfe, pouring them both whiskies. His hands were slightly unsteady.

"Only two?"

"Two significant problems. One is His Royal Highness's safety.

Though I'm certainly glad to be off that wretched motorboat, I've no great confidence in the *Wilhelmina*'s completing this voyage."

"I quite agree, I'm afraid," said Brownlow. "The after-superstructure looks like it's been shelled. I shouldn't be surprised they end up having to scuttle her."

"We have simply got to get the prince onto another ship."

"And it will have to be British. I was going to inform the palace of the prince's rescue in any event. I'll have them dispatch a naval vessel at once."

"The captain is going to make for port. He won't put up with any delays for a rendezvous," Metcalfe said. "Damn stubborn Dutchman."

"He does seem to have done a bloody good job of keeping this firetrap afloat, though. I'm certain the Admiralty can dispatch a destroyer or cruiser out of Canadian waters soon enough to intercept us. What's our other significant problem?"

"Some corpses at sea, Perry. I've been thinking about how bloody serious a business it will be if we don't report those two murders. Obstruction of justice is a felonious act, and we'd be involving His Highness. At the least, he might be called upon to testify or make a deposition in some Dutch maritime court. Unthinkable."

"But we've all agreed, Fruity. And think of the alternative. Better to involve him in a felony than in a screaming public scandal," Brownlow said.

"I'm not sure we can get away with it," said Metcalfe, sipping the warm whiskey thoughtfully.

"Think of all the other things that have been managed for the prince. Thelma Furness in Africa. That pregnant woman in Chicago. Good God, man. We managed to help him get away with Mrs. Simpson."

"For now."

"It's worth a try, Fruity. If the real story were to get out, we'd all be in the slops."

"Edwina and Dickie are certainly safe," Metcalfe reflected, "as I'm sure are Emerald and Chips and the Coopers. They're all loyal to a fault. And the count won't talk. He committed one of the murders."

"I'd hardly call what he did murder. It was bloody marvelous. The prince was nearly killed."

"We could have rescued the countess. We all just sat and watched her go under."

"Now don't you start feeling guilt, Perry. This was something between them. Deuced strange people, the Germans."

"What about Nancy Cunard and her, uh, gentleman?" Brownlow asked.

"They wouldn't be believed," said the major. "Especially Nancy, but we'd better have a bit of a chat with Crowder. I'm sure he can be bought off."

"What about Mrs. Parker? She can't be bought off," Brownlow said. "She's now a very rich widow."

"It's no matter to her, is it? Her husband wasn't murdered. His death was entirely accidental—his own bloody fault, at that. But I'll have a talk with her when she's calmer. She seems a decent sort, and I'm sure would be glad to serve the interests of the British Crown. I'll simply tell her we're taking care of all the official reports. And not to talk to the newspapers."

Brownlow rose and began walking about the stateroom. "That young third officer will be making an official report, and he certainly can't be bought."

"He's smitten with the Polish woman, or whatever she is," Metcalfe said. "And she's already part of our little conspiracy. I think he'll be looking out for her, but I'll have a chat with him just to see where matters stand."

"I shouldn't worry about the actress," Brownlow said. "She has her career to think about. She won't want to get involved in a lot of nasty muck about murders when she can walk off this ship such a glamorous heroine. I suppose, however, she might make a confession to some priest. Irish, you know."

"I'm Irish, as well, Perry, and I can assure you that the sanctity of the confessional is just that, though I've had no personal experience with it."

"So we're left with just one other question mark," said Brownlow, pausing at a porthole. "Chips's newspaperman friend. He's a correspondent, don't you know. I had that checked. He's the Paris bureau chief for his father's newspaper."

"He seems something of a gentleman," the major said. "Perhaps Chips can obtain his word of honor on it. To protect Edwina's reputation or something like that."

"Edwina's reputation?" Brownlow laughed nervously.

"He also seems a little down on his luck," Metcalfe said. "Possibly he can be bought off, as well."

"What if he's neither a gentleman nor can be bought?"

"Perhaps we can have Edwina prevail upon him in some fashion. She has a number of fashions. Now let's go join the others. I fear the prince may do something outlandish now that we're back aboard. We'll have to keep him as circumspect as possible before we get him onto a British vessel."

"That reminds me, Fruity. We have a third significant problem."

"What?"

"Mrs. Simpson."

"She's certainly not going to talk," Metcalfe said.

"I know, but what are we going to do with her? We can't have her sharing the prince's quarters on a Royal Navy warship."

"We'll have to arrange something," said Fruity. "He won't leave without her."

"Dear, dear, dear," said Lord Brownlow, draining his glass. "There are times when I fear that's going to be a permanent condition."

Kees knew that his first duty was to report to the bridge and then to see to his wound, which was painful, though not disabling. But he wanted to see Olga safe and comfortable in her quarters first. She was, however, unwilling to go to them.

"Kees," she said as they reached the ship's main stairway. "I don't want to stay down there. I will never be able to sleep. I want to be up here, near the lifeboats."

"But this is first class," he said.

"Yes? So? The ship has been on fire. They've moved many to new quarters. I am afraid to be down there."

He paused, biting his lip. The bleeding had stopped quickly and the bandage around his thigh was tight, but he was beginning to hurt awfully. He thought again of going first to ship's hospital, but again decided to wait.

"You can stay in my cabin," he said. "It's against regulations, but it's a regulation that is broken often."

"Your cabin, is it up here? Is it in first class?"

"Near enough. One deck below. I'll come get you in a few minutes. Now I have to report to the captain."

She kissed him. Their lips and faces were rough from the sea and weather, but they held each other tightly.

"Thank you, Kees. I am grateful to you. For everything. But promise me something. Please don't tell anyone what I did on the little boat. I don't want to get in any trouble with authorities. Too much in my life have I been in trouble with authorities. Please, Kees. Promise."

He looked into her face intently, smiling, then kissed her again.

"If I told them what you did, I should have to tell them what all of us did, including me. Don't worry. I'll take care of this. Now gather your things together and we'll move you in with me."

He kissed her forehead. Her hair badly needed washing, but he supposed his did, too.

When Kees had left the bridge the eternity ago that was the previous night, it had been a dark, crimson hell with the light from the flames aft playing fiendishly over the shadowy windows and bulkheads. All had been madness and confusion, with charts, maps, rescue equipment, and life jackets scattered everywhere.

Now it had been restored to perfect order. The windows had been scrubbed clean and the handrail that ran beneath newly polished so that it gleamed in the bright afternoon sunlight. The chart table was as neat as a draftman's board. The officers and crewmen stood at their positions almost at attention. Van Groot, like the others, had changed into a crisp, clean uniform and stood stiffly just behind the quartermaster, his arms folded behind him so exactly that the gold braid on his sleeves seemed run together in unbroken lines. They might have been sailing out of port for the very first time.

But, of course, they were not.

"I saw them bring your boat back aboard," van Groot said, gruffly but not meanly. He turned to note Kees's arrival.

"Yes, sir."

"Are you all right?" van Groot asked, though with little benevolence in his voice.

"I cut my leg, Mr. van Groot. But not so badly. I'll be all right."

"You are missing some of your party."

"Yes, sir, three."

"But not our royal guest? I was unable to tell with all of them in costumes and blankets."

"No, sir, and none of his companions or entourage. We lost the American Mr. Parker, the Countess von Kresse, and a crewman, the only one I had aboard."

"And how did these misfortunes happen?" Van Groot still had his hands folded behind his back. Kees sometimes wondered if the man hoped to become captain simply by acting like one.

Kees returned the first officer's gaze steadily but said nothing, gathering his thoughts.

"Mr. Parker fell overboard while trying to relieve himself over the side in heavy seas," Kees said finally. He was drunk. His wife tried to rescue him but had to be rescued herself, by Mr. Spencer, the American whom Lady Mountbatten had moved into first class."

"And?"

"And Mrs. Parker and Spencer are fine. They were only in the water a minute or two."

"And what about the Countess von Kresse?"

"Yes, sir. She fell overboard also, climbing up on the gunwale while quarreling with her brother. She was quite hysterical. She went under before we could get to her. I was prevented from turning the boat in time."

"Prevented?"

"I—I was not at the helm, sir."

"No one was at the helm?"

Kees had a great craving to lower his eyes, but he kept them level. The glittering sun on the sea was beginning to make them hurt. Van Groot's face was virtually a silhouette, his blue eyes faint glimmers within it. Kees was reminded of a police interrogation, which in a way he supposed this was.

"No, sir," Kees said. "I was attending to one of the passengers and my crewman was by then already dead."

"How so?"

"He was slammed back against the wheelhouse and suffered a serious hemorrhage, sir. A window was broken. There was blood all over the floorboards, though we cleaned it up. ."

"I saw no crewman's body carried off, Kees."

"He, too, went overboard, sir, when we were trying to deal with the countess."

"In heavy seas."

"Yes, sir. Very heavy. It was very bad back there, in a small boat."

Van Groot stared at him for a long time without speaking, then sighed and went over to the captain's chair, seating himself gently.

"Very well, Kees. Make out a report as soon as you can. Leave out nothing that is pertinent."

"Yes, sir," Kees retreated, then hesitated. "Mr. van Groot, where is the captain?"

"The captain," said the first officer, in practiced fashion, "is sleeping."

"Sleeping, sir?"

"Yes. Very deeply. And I think for a very long time. His hands were burned in the fire. In the meantime, I will be in command. I have returned the vessel to a course for New York. To my amazement, we are making fifteen knots. We will not win the *Bleu Ribband* for fastest Atlantic crossing, but I think we will complete our voyage without much further delay. All the fires are out and all is secure."

"Yes, sir," said Kees, but he got no farther than the doorway.

"Kees," Van Groot said. "With so many deaths involved, I think we should have statements from witnesses as well."

"Yes, sir. I'll get them from Commander Mountbatten and Major Metcalfe. All in proper military fashion."

Van Groot nodded. "And have that leg attended to. I need every officer."

Kees limped down the corridor as fast as he could. He would have to leave the frightened Olga in her quarters deep down below and deal with this all-important paperwork without delay. He went searching first for Lord Mountbatten.

Spencer and Nora sat quietly in opposite chairs in the sitting room of her suite. She looked pathetically sad, a child who'd been abandoned by everyone she loved. Spencer was merely weary, but deeply so, into his bones. He went to make drinks, but she would have none.

"Oh, God, Jimmy," she said, looking down at the carpeting. "I feel so awful. I fear I'm going to feel this awful the rest of my life."

"It'll get better, Nora. Just give it time."

"Every time I close my eyes I see those people in the water. I see them when my eyes are open. I see those horrible waves. I don't know how I'm going to sleep."

She raised herself slowly, tilting her head back over the top of her chair. She stared up at the ceiling, then closed her eyes, pounded her fists down once on the chair arms, and gave out a long primal scream. Then she hung limp, as if the effort had taken all of her energy.

He rose and poured brandy into a glass, adding water. He knelt before her, placing the glass gently into her hand. Slowly, with trembling fingers, she gripped it, perhaps gripped it too hard.

"I think this will help. We've all been in shock. Now it's wearing off and we're confronted with the reality of what we've been through. It was as bad as anything I saw in the war." That was a lie, but not by much.

She looked down at him, her sad eyes still forlorn, but more trusting. She raised the glass hesitantly and took a long sip. Making a face, she set the brandy down on the table beside her as if it were a loathsome object. After rising with great effort, her arms hanging slack at her sides, she walked wearily toward her bedroom.

"I'm going to take a bath, Jimmy," she said weakly. "A long hot bath."

"Do you want me to leave?"

"No, Jimmy," she said, disappearing through the doorway. "I don't want you to leave."

He wondered what she did want, and what he really wanted. His greatest desire, much as he had any, was to be off this damned boat and in New York. He had an urge to give birth, as a long-pregnant woman longed to give birth—to be in the New York bureau of the *Press-Bulletin* and writing and filing this long, sordid, tragic, magnificent newspaper story that would change his life.

He listened to her brushing her teeth as she ran water into the bath. It would be nice to be clean again, utterly clean everywhere, to have skin as fresh as flowers, hair soft and cleansed of brine, a mouth sweet.

But instead of returning to his own stateroom to accomplish this sublimely imperative task, he remained where he was as she had asked. He tried rewriting the story in his mind again, tried thinking of the perfect lead. But nothing useful came. There could no lead until the story had an end, until the voyage was over.

Nora finally emerged, wrapped in a thick terry-cloth robe, drying her hair with a large towel. Some color had returned to her face and her eyes seemed less haggard.

"Now you, Jimmy. Go in there and take yourself a long, hot bath."

"But I need to shave, and . . ."

She seemed puzzled by his reluctance. "There's a razor in there. And shaving cream and extra toothbrushes and everything you need. There's even a rose in a vase above the toilet. This a first-class suite, Jimmy. Indulge yourself."

He fell asleep in the tub, but she did not disturb him. When he awoke some minutes later, sensitive to the cooling of the water, he finished his ablution quickly. When he had at last completed his metamorphosis into a civilized man, he looked down with repugnance at the pile of soiled clothes he had left on the floor—the absurd, salt-stained Legionnaire's uniform. He had no wish even to touch it.

Wrapping a large towel around him, he stepped barefoot across the soft carpeting and into the sitting room.

Nora was on the divan. She had brushed out her hair and, he noticed, had consumed most of the brandy and water he had poured for her. Her cheeks were quite flushed. The front of her robe had fallen open slightly, revealing much of her breasts.

"I'll get a steward to bring me some clean clothes from my cabin," he said. "And take away my costume. I think I'll have him throw it over the side."

"No, Jimmy. Don't call a steward." Putting the drink aside, she gracefully got to her feet and took a step toward him. The robe came completely open, and Spencer felt a stronger temptation than he could ever remember.

Nora held his eyes with hers and then, with the barest movement, slipped the garment off her shoulders and let it fall to the floor. She struck an artist's model's pose, a statue for a garden fountain. Her body was as flawlessly beautiful as her face.

Glancing down at the front of his towel, she smiled almost innocently, blushing, then slowly came toward him, pulling the towel from his waist.

"I'm twenty-eight years old," she said, "and I have made love just four times. Never once was it really love. I thought the first time it might be, but afterward it wasn't."

She lifted his arms around her waist and then slid hers up the muscles of his back, pulling him close.

"Now it's going to be for love," she said. "It's more than time."

The prince's suite was filled with chatter. Their costumes notwithstanding, they all might have been on a country weekend at Edward's Fort Belvedere retreat outside London. The prince's valet had been banned to the lower decks for his treachery in making reports to Buckingham Palace, so an East Indian steward had been brought in to serve cocktails and keep the gramophone going.

Edward seemed almost joyful, a small boy who had beaten every opponent at some game.

"We've come through riots and now we've come through this," he said. "Well played all. The English kings are indestructible, what?"

"At least since Charles I," said Duff, but regretted the remark, which was as untoward as Edward's presumption of kingship while his father lay ill.

In the uncomfortable moment that followed, Diana rode up in rescue.

"You were superb, sir," she said. "An example to us all. I shall remember forever your reminding us to be British with that hellish storm breaking all around us."

"Hear, hear," said Chips.

The prince beamed. "Tonight we must have a party, in celebration of our saga and its triumphant conclusion." He stuck a cigarette in his mouth as Chips leaned to light it for him.

"Sir," said Lord Brownlow. "I'm not sure how many aboard are in the partying mood. There's been some loss of life, and people are still in shock."

"I mean a *small* party," Edward said, the cigarette still in his mouth and tilted at a raffish angle. "Just those who were aboard our motorboat."

"David," said Metcalfe. "Not everyone's up to it. Certainly not Mrs. Parker or Count von Kresse."

"Just us then," the prince said, still cheerful. "Please. I just want a bit of fun."

The door opened, as Inspector Runcie admitted a sleepy-looking Lord Mountbatten. Behind him stood Kees.

"Sorry to disturb you, David," Lord Louis said to his cousin. He looked over at Metcalfe. "This officer would like to speak to us in private, Fruity. I rather think it's important."

"Very well," said the major, rising, knowing exactly what the subject of their discussion would be. "When I get back, sir, we ought to talk a bit about making arrangements for a return to England. This ship won't be making another crossing for a bit."

"Oh, Fruity. Not now. Please."

"Very well, sir. But soon."

"Fruity's gotten so dreadfully serious of late," Edward said, when the major had gone. "All right. Who's for another drink? Here's luck. Chin chin."

"Thank you, sir," said Lady Diana, rising with a slight curtsy. "But I for one need to change out of this costume. I never thought the day would come, but I must say I'm tired of being a goddess."

There was laughter and then the startling sound of a door being slammed back against a wall. In the doorway to her bedroom stood Wallis, wearing a shimmering long blue dressing gown and for some reason clutching loops of diamond jewelry in each hand. Diana guessed she'd been taking inventory of her collection, making certain no piece had been lost. The prince had given her a hideous diamond-encrusted flamingo that certainly deserved to have been lost.

"Will you all shut up!" Wallis bellowed, her Southern accent briefly disappearing. "Will you all go!"

No one spoke. Quietly they left their chairs and began to file out the door.

"Wallis," said the prince. "These are our friends."

"I can't sleep! I can't think! Damn it, why must I be abused this way!"

He turned away, his eyes almost tearful. The steward left his station at the bar and hurried out the door after the others.

Wallis went back to her bedchamber, slamming the door again as she closed it. Her thin chest still heaving in anger, she looked down at the array of sparkling jewelry spread out on the counterpane. She realized suddenly she had made a serious mistake.

She found the prince in the sitting room's largest chair, drinking, and pouting. Wallis leaned and kissed his forehead.

"A girl is sorry," she said. "She loves a boy very much. A girl has just been through a lot."

His blue eyes turned upward, uncertain but less unhappy.

"Come with me, darling," Wallis said. "I think this is a very good time for a girl to make a boy very, very happy."

He followed her docilely into his bedroom and stood contentedly as she removed his Roman soldier's costume and set him back gently on the bed, easing him further back onto the coverlet. Thelma Furness and others of the prince's previous ladies had failed him sexually because they had misunderstood his needs. They had thought of his inclinations in the most conventional of terms, not minding their own lack of satisfaction but presuming he would achieve his own by exerting at least some effort, however briefly. What Wallis had quickly come to realize was that this was a man whose desires could be fulfilled only when he was completely passive. His satisfaction had to come entirely through the efforts of his partner.

Removing her gown—he did appreciate that, at least—she once again employed the curious skills she had learned long ago as a spectator in the singsong houses of China. To Wallis, sex had long been a matter of doing what she felt she had to do. It was like her life.

Spencer and Nora awoke to a soft darkness. A glint of moonlight was coming through the porthole. He leaned over her and felt her reach with the back of her hand to stroke his chest.

*"Bonsoir, mademoiselle."*

*"Bonsoir, monsieur."*

*"Tu es heureuse?"*

*"Heureuse?"*

"Are you happy?"

"Oh, yes," she said. "Very."

"What are you thinking about?"

"Won't say."

"Are you thinking about the names of our children?"

"Oh, no. Not that."

"Or what we'll do when we get to New York?"

"No. Nothing so far in the future. I'm not even thinking about tomorrow, or the next hour. I'm thinking about love, about *being* in love."

"And?"

"It's so much different than I thought."

"Oh, dear."

"No, it's much more wonderful." She lifted herself on her elbow and pulled his head down to kiss him.

"Are you hungry?" he asked, after. "Should we get something to eat?"

"No, I don't want something to eat."

"Would you like another drink?"

"No, no. And not you either."

"Well, what would you like?"

"What I'd like I don't think I can have for a while, but let's try."

As they lay back again against the pillows, they could hear the ship's engines and the sound of the sea wind. It was wonderfully comforting.

# CHAPTER
## SIXTEEN

Dr. Goebbels's gala party for two thousand was held at Berlin's Schloss Charlottenburg, an imposing ancient fortress situated between Spandauerdamm and a wide sweeping curve of the Spree River. The occasion was the first screening of Leni Riefenstahl's breathtaking motion picture rendering of that year's historic Nuremberg Rally, *Triumph des Willens*, subtitled for the English diplomatic guests at the gathering as *The Triumph of Will.* It was easily the most awesomely powerful propaganda film that had ever been made or ever would be, surpassing her own Nazi apologia *Reichsparteitag* released a few months earlier and making Goebbels's own efforts at cinema look like newsreels or home movies.

A film crew of more than one hundred had worked on the Nuremburg project, including thirty-two cameramen and camera assistants operating thirty-six different cameras and employing hundreds of enormous spotlights. It was a massive work that used heroic Teutonic imagery to subordinate the individual into the mass and glorify the authority such a mass represented. She had borrowed from both the stark, dramatic techniques of the German film pioneers of the 1920s and the grand stagecraft of Wagnerian opera. Though few in Berlin had seen it, *Triumph des Willens* was considered certain to win a gold medal at the next Venice Film Festival.

Without any doubt, it would establish Fräulein Riefenstahl as the Reich's preeminent film maker. Hitler had appointed her the film chief of the party shortly after coming to power in 1933, but the hierarchy had accorded her only that respect due a useful creative talent and minor party functionary. After *Triumph,* she would enjoy a prominence, prestige, and inviolability on a level with that of the Führer and his chief lieutenants.

Goebbels was proud rather than envious. He was too smart to be otherwise. She had made it clear publicly and privately that she remained his protégée and had evidenced no other interest than in serving Hitler and the Reich. Certainly she made Goebbels's work enormously easier.

Fräulein Riefenstahl, after the Führer, was the guest of honor. Neither, of course, had yet arrived. Both electrifying entrances would wait until the rest of the two thousand were in place.

A continuous parade of automobiles and motorcycles roared and rumbled into the long driveway leading to the Schloss, the debarkation process much less efficient than should otherwise have been the case because so many of the arriving personages traveled in huge motorcades. Goering had deliberately planned on arriving late and was pleased to encounter further delay at the entrance. When at last he and Emmy pulled up before the great castle gate, he emerged from his limousine dressed in his grandest uniform ever. Though his promotion to colonel general of the Luftwaffe had not yet been proclaimed officially, he had decked himself out in appropriate plumage. His blue-green Luftwaffe tunic was adorned with Prussian blue, gold, and crimson facings, and his breeches were striped along the sides with the same colors. In addition to the standard general's oak-leaf collar and gold cap insignia, he was draped with so much gold cord he seemed encased in ship's rigging. At his throat he wore his World War I Pour le Mérite medal, and over his shoulders a long, flowing cape lined in white. All he needed to complete the ensemble was a marshal's baton, and he supposed that would come soon enough.

With the statuesque Emmy following like an ocean liner under tow, he ascended the steps as grandly as his bulk would allow, carrying himself almost as if he and not the drab Führer were the master of the Reich. That would never be unless the Führer were to perish, but in that unhappy event Goering would make certain the crown would go to no lesser personage than himself. He had been wounded at Munich, after all. Not even Hess could boast that.

They swept inside, greeted effusively as they made their interior progress by swarming sycophants, subordinates, bootlicks, and influence seekers. Goering left Emmy among them, admonishing her to ignore any chance remarks or overheard jokes, and sought a waiter and refreshment. To his disgust, he discovered that Himmler had not yet made his appearance. The chicken farmer had likely arranged to arrive just before Hitler.

Admiral Canaris was there, however. He had noticed Goering's triumphal progress into the castle hall and now discreetly made his way toward him. His admiral's uniform was nearly as grand as Goering's, though strictly regulation.

"I have news," he said, suavely lifting a glass of champagne from a passing tray.

"You always have news, Wilhelm. That is why you are such a cherished servant of the Reich."

Canaris stood sipping his wine, watching a tall blond woman sweep by on the arm of an S.S. colonel.

"Wilhelm! What is it?"

The admiral turned back toward Goering with a clever smile. "Why, it's good news, Hermann. The Dutch liner *Wilhelmina* did not go down. She is proceeding to New York under her own power with nearly the full complement of passengers, officers, and crew aboard."

"The word 'nearly' means what, Admiral?"

"Unfortunately, there were some fatalities, two of them German."

"The von Kresses?"

"One of them a von Kresse. Your beautiful protégée, the countess. She has apparently drowned."

"And the other?"

"I believe it was the mysterious, or not so mysterious, Herr Braun. He was burned to death in the fire. They found him in one of the cabins."

"How do you know this?"

"Wireless messages. Some intercepted, some received directly, others received indirectly. That fool Cunard woman sent one to Ribbentrop in London. It was virtually in the clear: 'I am safe. Edward is safe.' Remind me never to employ her as a spy. Or anyone who knows her."

"Including Ribbentrop."

"Especially Ribbentrop."

Emmy was looking furtively about the crowded room for her husband, her expression anxious. What had she heard that upset her now?

"What about Mrs. Simpson?" Goering asked curtly.

"Apparently alive and well. Were it otherwise, I'm sure Lady Cunard would have messaged Franklin Roosevelt, the King of England, and the Führer, too."

"Hmmm," said Goering. "Then all is as we would wish, *nicht wahr?*"

"*Vielleicht. Vielleicht nicht.* Your friend the Count von Kresse is presumed to be alive. Whether all is well depends much on what you told him to do."

"I told him merely to serve the interests of the Reich."

"Well then, Hermann," said the admiral, his eyes quite twinkly now. "All must be well indeed."

There was a sudden demonic flourish of what sounded like several hundred trumpets being played at once. Uniformed servants began to urge and usher the guests out of the hall, deeper into the castle. Despite the cool of the evening, they were being made to go outside again, out onto the castle grounds to the rear that overlooked the river. Goering reached Emmy and put his arm around her waist, nodding angrily to two of his following aides to help make a path for them. He was not going to mush along with the crowd like some railroad passenger.

"I thought this was going to be an evening of cinema," Emmy said.

"It's going to be an evening of Dr. Goebbels."

Beautiful young girls dressed in theatrical costumes and suffering from it in the chill greeted them as they stepped out onto the vast lawn, the lights of the city shimmering in the river beyond. Tables had been set up in great number, laden with drink and food. Goering and Emmy hurried toward one, but barely had they bit into their roast peafowl when Goebbels's sound and light show commenced. Cannon set atop the castle battlements and along the river were set off in furious fusillades, firing blank but rattlingly fearsome charges. Joining the cacaphonous din were more aerial pyrotechnics than had been seen and heard in the bombardment of Fort Douamant at Verdun, and the effect of the immensity of light and sound was mindnumbing. People stood about motionless, unable to speak or hear and having to blink rapidly to be able to see. This was kept up for an interminable half hour.

"*Mein Gott,*" said Emmy, when silence abruptly came upon them in the wake of rolling echoes.

"*Nicht Gott,*" said Goering. "*Gotterdammerung.*"

There were more trumpets, and then spotlights flashed from below and above to the small balcony on a battlement above the rear gate to the castle keep.

"Emmy," Goering said. "Hitler will be there and we will be here.

Come. We must hurry. See, Hess and Himmler are already there, just below. Speer also."

The crowd was pressing toward the battlement but a way was made for Goering and his wife. The Reichscommissioner pushed himself into a place between Hess and Speer, studiously ignoring Himmler.

Goebbels came forth to only moderate applause, though it sounded noisy enough given the huge size of the assemblage. The doctor gave one of his shorter speeches, ending with his always effective *"Ein Volk! Ein Reich! Ein Führer!"* blasting from the loudspeakers set up throughout the grounds. The applause then became thunderous, and louder still when more spotlights began to play amid more cannon firing from the ramparts.

Hitler stepped forth from darkness into incandescence, wearing his huge bulletproof military hat, familiar brown tunic and black breeches. He raised his right hand, bent backward at the wrist, in familiar salute, as Goebbels led the crowd in a dozen *"Sieg Heils!"* The thought passed Goering's mind that this sort of thing presented a wonderful opportunity for an assassin. All eyes were on the Führer, and a sniper's rifle shot would never be heard in all the noise.

With a curt wave of his arm, Goebbels brought both the crowd and cannon to swift and obedient silence. The Führer then stepped to the microphone. It was really quite cold and Goering feared his master was going to treat them to another of his hour-long speeches. But apparently he was cold, too. He spoke briefly about the destiny of the German people and the Reich and of how magnificently its unrivaled spirit had been captured by Fräulein Riefenstahl's cameras. He spoke of greater glories to come, starting with the victories of German athletes in the Berlin Olympics the next year and followed by the march of Deutschland to fulfill its divine mission in Europe.

Another dozen or so *"Sieg Heils!"* followed and, as he almost never did, the Führer stepped deferentially aside in courtly fashion. Fräulein Riefenstahl then made her appearance—to more ear-splitting applause and cheering—pausing for a moment like a leading lady taking a curtain call. Then she turned to Hitler, gave the Nazi salute, curtsied low, and straightened to hand him a rose. The two thousand below greeted this moment with the hysteria due a religious happening.

Goering and Speer looked at each other, amazed. By the time they returned their attention to the balcony, the Führer and his co-star for the evening had gone back into the warmth inside.

"Come, Emmy," Goering said, returning to his wife. "That's where we belong, as well."

Movie screens had been set up throughout the great castle hall and in many of the wide passageways. Guests gathered in groups before them as waiters passed throughout serving more champagne. At a cue, the lights were dimmed, and then went out. At another, the projectors were started. It was supposed to be a simultaneous commencement, but the timing varied enough for the images and soundtracks throughout the great chamber to be a second or more ahead or behind one another. After a while it began to sound like a madhouse.

There was a presence at his elbow and Goering didn't need to look to know it was the chicken farmer. Who else would wait for the dark for a conversation?

"Good evening, Heinrich."

"Good evening, Hermann. The Führer looks well."

"*Sicher.* A heart-warming sight."

"I have had a full report, Hermann."

"On the Führer's health?"

"On the occurrences aboard the Dutch ship *Wilhelmina.*"

"A report from whom, Heinrich?"

"From my own organization. From Ribbentrop. From the S.D. And from Admiral Canaris."

"Everyone's faithful servant, the admiral," Goering said. He glanced around circumspectly, to make certain they were not being overheard, though that seemed unlikely in the grinding insanity of the competing film projectors.

"The man I put aboard has been killed," Himmler said sharply. "He was one of the best agents I had in France."

"The ship caught fire," Goering said. "A number of passengers were killed, among them the beautiful Countess von Kresse. It's all so sad, *nicht wahr?*"

"The Count von Kresse did not perish."

"No, Heinrich, but neither did the Prince of Wales."

They stood close together without speaking for a moment as the screen showed the gigantic swastika that was the centerpiece of the Nuremburg rally, so bathed in light it seemed afire. It was a masterstroke, that swastika of Speer's. No wonder he stood so close to Hitler.

"I warn you, Hermann," Himmler said finally. "The instant that Prussian traitor of yours steps foot on German soil I will have him arrested. If you object or try to interfere I will go to the Führer."

"Don't be so hasty, Heinrich. You are always so hasty."

"Why didn't you come to see me yesterday?" the ship's doctor asked. He was a friendly, sentimental man with kind eyes and a florid face, and he asked the question out of a genuine deep concern.

Kees was staring down at the long ugly wound drawn in a straight line across the side of his thigh. It had gone purple and yellow at the edges. There was obvious infection.

"Is it bad?" Kees asked.

"Not too bad. Not yet," the doctor said. "But you can't fool with these things."

"It doesn't hurt that much."

"It will in a moment. I'm going to clean it out thoroughly and apply some antiseptic."

Kees shrugged. He had been treating his wound as irrelevant. The doctor knew his business. By turning any and all worries about his condition over to the doctor's judgment, he could continue to ignore the injury.

The doctor began his work. The wound was no longer irrelevant. The pain was such Kees almost kicked and cried out. Gripping the sides of the examining table tightly, the flesh of his hands turning white, he somehow kept himself from doing either thing.

"How did you say you got this?" the doctor asked.

"On the steel motorboat. I fell backward during the storm. Caught it on a sharp piece of metal."

"Fell backward? This laceration begins at the front, Kees. The tissue was plowed through like a furrow."

"I must have turned when I fell. I can't quite remember. It was very confusing. I was very busy. I had just one seaman with me and we had forty-foot waves."

The doctor peered closely at the deep cut as he continued his cleaning.

"Kees," he said, "this is a bullet wound."

"Doctor. How could it be a bullet wound? We were at sea in a small rescue boat."

"I am telling you what I see medically. I treated enough of them in Belgium during the war. This is a bullet wound."

"I fell on the boat," Kees said. "Everything is in the written report I made out for the captain. Or rather, for Mr. van Groot."

"Get ready," the doctor said, reaching for a swab and a small brown bottle. "I'm going to apply the antiseptic."

Kees once more gripped the table, but when the doctor touched liquid to tissue, it didn't help. Kees swore loudly against the agony.

"What in hell is that? Lavatory cleaner?"

"It's even stronger," said the doctor. "We want to avoid amputation, don't we?"

"I'm not sure this is better."

The doctor smiled. "There are no peg-legged captains on the Lage Lander Line."

"Is there really some danger of that?"

"I was joking. But it won't be a joke if you don't tend to this. That means changing the dressing every day and going through this nasty routine."

"For how long?"

"I'll know better by the time we reach port."

He began to wrap Kees's leg in a dressing.

"I'll do as you say. I can take it."

"I've no doubt. You'd already gone a day with it festering. I wonder you didn't fall down."

"It feels better already," Kees said as he began to pull on his pants.

The doctor had gone over to a wall cabinet. He took out a bottle of brandy and two glasses.

"Here," he said, pouring some out for both. "Pain killer."

They drank in silence.

"How bad off is the captain?" Kees said, at last.

The doctor smiled again, but sadly.

"He'll survive. The burns on his hands aren't as serious as they first looked. But I suspect this is his last voyage. I think Mr. van Groot will see to it."

Kees set down his glass, testing his leg as if it were a new shoe.

"Our conversation about your wound," the doctor said. "That's just between you and me. Whatever happened, well, I'm sure you've dealt with it in your report."

"Every word of it the truth."

"Come by again tomorrow. Tell van Groot I want you to rest in your cabin today. And get some sleep. You can't fight infection banging around the bridge.

"Thank you, Doctor."

"You're a good officer, Kees. I'm glad you weren't hurt any worse."

\*     \*     \*

Olga sat in the only chair in Kees's small cabin, looking at the sky through the porthole and thinking hard about her chances while Kees slept. She hadn't counted on his presence for the day. It was worse than an inconvenience. Kees had said they had improved their speed and were making nineteen knots. She had little time left in which to strike. If Kees spent the afternoon asleep, he'd be wide awake all night, making sexual demands of her and preventing her from leaving the cabin. Perhaps she could persuade him to go back to the bridge.

He was snoring gently, lying on his back, his injured leg propped on a pillow. He was a handsome, gentle boy, with a too-small nose but cheerful Dutch blue eyes. She liked him. She hoped she would not have to kill him.

Their stateroom telephone jangled them from their sleep. Nora murmured but did not stir, though the phone was on her side of the bed. Spencer reached across her, his arm lightly touching the flesh of one of her breasts, causing her to murmur again.

He was in no way aroused. Their endless lovemaking had filled her with love and contentment but had drained him of sex. He was tired and sore and not a little hung over. The clock said it was just past nine in the evening. It had been morning such a short time before.

Spencer picked up the insistent telephone clumsily, dropping the receiver and leaning heavily over Nora's chest and stomach to retrieve it. She groaned. Sitting up with the receiver secure in his hand, he put his fingers to his lips and then touched them to hers by way of apology.

He heard the voice on the other end with disbelief. Spencer sat there dumbly, while the other party waited for him to respond. When he finally did, it was as if he still had not comprehended who had called him. It was the other party who should have been halting and incoherent, Spencer the one who should be calm and in control.

The strange, brief conversation stumbled along. At the end Spencer agreed to the other's request. He couldn't think of a way not to.

Spencer walked around the bed to hang up the phone, not wanting to discomfit Nora further, then stood a moment in the center of the room, naked, his hands behind his back.

"That," he said, "was the Count von Kresse."

Nora sat up and yawned.

"That poor man," she said. "I feel so sorry for him, and yet he scares me. Any man who could do that to his own sister."

"She'd just killed a man. She was trying to shoot Mrs. Simpson. She'd gone stark, raving mad."

"He still frightens me."

"Well, he wants to see me."

"See you? When?"

"Tonight. At ten o'clock. He's invited me to join him for brandy."

"He drowns his sister and now he wants to celebrate? He really scares me."

"He sounded very serious."

"What does he want with you? Share old war stories or something?"

"I don't know, but I'm going to see him."

Nora yawned again and stretched, the movement causing her breasts to thrust forward. Now Spencer did feel at least some small arousal, but kept his mind from it. He sat down on the edge of the bed and took Nora's hand.

"Do you mind?"

"No. I'm a big girl. I can manage by myself for an hour, if you can promise me the ship won't sink or someone won't start shooting."

He kissed her hand. "I promise you. Are you tired?"

Her smile was dreamy. "Happily tired. I can use some sleep."

He started to rise, then sat back.

"The count may want to ask me whether we're going to turn him in," Spencer said. "What shall I say?"

"I don't want to stir up any trouble, Jimmy. We've all had enough trouble. What happened was awful, horrible, but it did end with some kind of justice, didn't it? It was like that Madeleine Carroll film about the Russian civil war, when the countess got shot. I just want to forget it, get to New York, and start rehearsing my play. But you're going to write a news story, aren't you?"

"I'm going to write about the prince and Mrs. Simpson, and the fire, and the rescue. I haven't decided what else to put in, or whether to say who all was on that boat."

"Are you going to lie?"

"Of course not. I don't work for a New York tabloid. But there are things I could leave out. There's never room for everything. There are some things I should leave out, that wouldn't stand up in a libel or slander trial, even though they happened."

"Are you going to leave me out?"

He kissed her. "I'll simply remark on the good fortune that the ship's most beautiful and glamorous passenger was among the rescued. I'll note that she gave this correspondent an exclusive interview."

Nora blushed. "You bet, exclusive." She rubbed his back softly. "You go off now and see this strange German man. I'm going back to sleep. Sometime tonight, wake me again."

The count had returned to civilian dress and was wearing black tie, signifying that he had dined in one of the first-class public rooms rather than remain in his stateroom in a manifestation of grief or mourning. As arranged, he was on the promenade deck, standing at the rail opposite the entranceway that led to the main ballroom.

He greeted Spencer with a solemn nod, then returned to looking out over the dark sea. He had seemed so natural, so soldierly, in his gray uniform that it was something of a shock to see him out of it.

His eyes appeared old and weary. At least he was not getting any sleep.

"Thank you for joining me," he said, his voice as sad as he looked. "I appreciate your company tonight."

"What happened to Edwina?"

"Lady Mountbatten is very tired," he said.

Spencer wondered if this was euphemism, if Edwina had by now found yet someone else—a traveling businessman, a Javanese porter, another in the prince's party.

"She constantly pushes herself to the edge in life," the count continued. "An experience such as we just survived can be very damaging. I fear she'll not live a normal lifespan."

Dagne von Kresse had lived no normal lifespan. Neither man spoke. The vibration of the turbines could be felt beneath their feet. The ship was driving very hard.

"I think also she is tired of me," the count said. "Since our rescue I have talked to her only of my sister, and this I think disturbs Edwina. She seems now in a mood for different company."

"What did you want to see me about?" Spencer asked. "To talk about your sister?"

"No. I talk now only to God about my sister. And to myself." The count smoked. "You are going to write a newspaper story about this voyage," he said. It was not a question, merely a statement of fact.

Spencer confirmed it. "I thought that's what was on your mind. Yes, I'm going to write a story. Of course. Why wouldn't I?"

"I am very interested in this story, in what you are going to put into it."

"You're afraid I'm going to write about you and what happened to your sister."

The count had frowned at the word "afraid." It was one never used in association with him—except by himself, in his darkest, late-night thoughts.

"I am going to return to Germany, Mr. Spencer. Sooner or later, but eventually. What appears in American newspapers is of no consequence in the Reich. What appears in German newspapers is of no consequence. They are not believed anymore. In Germany I will be beyond the jurisdiction of Dutch maritime authorities. The Reich is beyond the jurisdiction of all authority, save its own. So I'm not afraid that you will expose my desperate act. In a way, as a matter of fact, it might help."

"How?"

"Help me to understand. To see what happened through your eyes. I would be grateful."

"You saved lives. You killed your sister. You wouldn't let us rescue her. You let her drown."

The count's expression did not change. It disturbed Spencer to look at the man's eyes, to imagine all that they had seen.

"Actually," Spencer said, softening his tone, "no one really tried to rescue her. We're all as guilty as you."

"I didn't mean for her to die," the count said. "I hit her with great violence, but I wanted only to stop her. Yet once she was in the water, well, suddenly there was a simple answer to what for me has been vexing and very complicated problem."

"I can't tell if you're sad."

"Sad? You've no idea the depths of my despair, Mr. Spencer. I am as sad as you are cynical and Miss Gwynne is beautiful. As Edwina is promiscuous. I have more grief than blood in my veins, and it has been that way for years. Especially since Dagne joined the party. It was so easy for her. She returned from a social engagement one evening and announced she had become a Nazi. I could not imagine anything more horrible, more unlike her. The most profound sadness came when I realized that, after all, it was quite like her."

"Are they really as bad as all that?"

"They are worse. Surely you know that."

"Yes. I do. I suppose I was posing a rhetorical question. You're the first German I've met in three years who's spoken against them."

"You will meet more, Mr. Spencer. Those who aren't dragged away in the middle of the night."

Spencer glanced back along the deck. They were alone. He could hear dance music coming from the ballroom.

"I don't know what I'm going to put in the story until I sit down to write it. All I know for sure is that Prince Edward and his girl-friend will figure prominently."

They watched the small dark waves parading by. Finally von Kresse stood erect.

"I believe I said brandy, Mr. Spencer. There is a small, pleasant bar a deck above, adjacent to the gallery overlooking the ballroom. Let's go to it, if you don't mind walking slowly."

They appeared to be the only customers the Oriental barman had had that evening. He was very generous with his pouring. The count was also very generous with the tip he added to the total when he signed the bill. At his suggestion, they declined stools at the bar or a table and instead went out onto the gallery above the ballroom, leaning over the railing as they had out on the deck.

There were only a few couples on the dance floor, moving in a slow fox trot to the band's halfhearted "The Very Thought of You." An earnest attempt was being made by everyone aboard to return to normal, but it wasn't quite succeeding. Passengers had been going back to the second-class promenade all day to examine the grotesque damage, until van Groot had finally had the area roped off.

"Hell, there's Mrs. Parker," said Spencer.

She was dancing with one of the younger ship's officers. Not gaily; there was no merriment about her. She was somber and dignified, and danced with much formality. But she was fully participating in the evening. She wore a long crimson gown that set off her fair complexion and dark hair. Red and black. Colors of death. Also, as Spencer recalled, the colors of Prussia.

"No one believes in mourning anymore," he said.

"She is in mourning," said the count. "You may be certain of that. Her sadness is serene, but it is genuine. I think she also feels guilt."

"He wasn't much of a man, though, was he? What would we have done with such a boy in the air war in France?"

"He would have died as quickly as he did out in the boat," said von Kresse. "He wouldn't have lasted a single patrol."

"I don't think she loved him."

"She was fond of him. She is also very loyal. One of her many qualities. I think she is quite beautiful, though not so beautiful as Miss Gwynne."

"Yes." Fact was fact.

"The most beautiful women on this ship are American," said the count, shifting his weight off his bad leg. "It makes the British ladies very envious."

"Mrs. Simpson isn't very beautiful."

"She makes the British ladies envious for another reason, yes? But I think Mrs. Simpson must be a little envious of Mrs. Parker. She is young, and so beautiful, and of such high social standing. And now she will be quite rich."

"She won't be Queen of England."

"Neither will Mrs. Simpson. But even if she were to be, I think that would be another reason for her to envy Mrs. Parker."

The music faded away and, apparently at her request, the young officer escorted her off the dance floor. The table he took her to was presided over by Mr. van Hoorn of the shipping line. His attentions were very fatherly. The company was extending Mrs. Parker every kindness and courtesy.

"She is fluent in Greek and Italian, in addition to French," the count said. "She fences, writes poetry, knows calculus, and has read Aristotle and Nietzsche. She said she wants to learn how to fly an airplane."

"Mrs. Simpson?"

"No. Of course not. I mean Mrs. Parker."

"How do you know so much about her?"

"She came to visit me today. To console me, about my sister Dagne. She was very—what is the American word? Ah yes, sweet. She was very sweet. I felt very sad for her."

"And how did Edwina feel?"

"Mr. Spencer, you are not being a gentleman."

"No, I'm not."

The band had struck up "A Room With A View," a Noel Coward song. The young officer leaned toward her, but Mrs. Parker shook her head and remained seated, her hands folded neatly in her lap. She stared down at them.

"I'm sorry," Spencer said to the count. "I've been stupid with you about Edwina. Edwina is . . . Edwina."

"She's fond of you, if it matters. But then, she's fond of all of us."

Mrs. Parker had lifted her head. She saw them up on the balcony and, after a moment, nodded in recognition, though Spencer could not tell whether it was to him or von Kresse.

The count shifted his weight again, wincing. He sipped his brandy, glancing back through the doorway to the tables and chairs in the little bar, but made no hint of movement in that direction.

"Mr. Spencer," von Kresse said, looking back to Mrs. Parker, who was talking with van Hoorn. "When I talked with you about what you are going to put in your newspaper story . . ."

"I told you, Herr Rittmeister. I don't know what I'm going to put in it."

"You said you were going to write about Charles Lindbergh."

"Yes. I saw him. I haven't found him again yet, but he's aboard this ship. If I don't catch him here, I'll get him when he gets off the boat."

"Why?"

"Look, I feel sorry about what he and his wife have gone through. About their son. I don't feel that good about what I'm doing. But whatever Lindbergh does is big news. Edward and Mrs. Simpson are news, or they certainly will be when I get through with them. After Hitler and Roosevelt, I can't think of anyone who's bigger news than Charles A. Lindbergh and the prince and his doxy."

"Why do you do this? Are you bitter, resentful? Your father lost his fortune, and now you will have your revenge?"

"I'll do it for the same reason I crawled from my cot every morning and climbed up into the cold at ten thousand feet to shoot down you Huns. I'll do it because it's my job. It's what I do."

The count was looking at him now full in the face, his haunted, hunter's eyes seeking some truth, some fact about Spencer.

"I don't know that we were special," von Kresse said, "we who flew. I think probably the men in the trenches who endured the gas and the slime and the shelling, I think they were probably much more special. But we are different, aren't we? There is a bond between us who climbed every morning to ten thousand feet in the cold air, who drank brandy to freeze our intestines so the castor oil fumes from the engine wouldn't make us shit in our pants. We are brothers, aren't we, even though we tried to kill each other?"

"Why don't you want me to write about Lindbergh?"

"Are we brothers?"

"Yes, we are brothers. *Les frères de la guerre. Kampfbruderen.*"

"Don't you feel this same bond with all airmen, with the brave ones? Don't you feel you owe them some honor for what they are? For what we all are?"

Spencer gave von Kresse a grim look. He stood up, taking a large sip of brandy. He set down the snifter.

"Herr Rittmeister, Count von Kresse, your excellency Colonel sir," he said. "Charles A. Lindbergh never fought in the fucking war."

# CHAPTER
## *SEVENTEEN*

On board a ship, one always noticed the light. It spoke of the world beyond the interior spaces of the vessel, which so quickly become familiar and confining. Like the weather, the light was always changing. The light presented the only real measure of passing time, otherwise marked just by the schedule of meals and social events. The light represented reality. All else around one on a ship was contrivance.

Olga lay awake, uncomfortable but very still on Kees's narrow bed, watching the first light of day make a gray, glowing circle of the porthole above her head. She had been dreaming just before, and remembered the sequence now only as a vague confusion of horses and shooting—an attack on a farm, some battle in the woods, she wasn't sure. The images had nothing to do with her present life.

Earlier in the night she'd had her rat dream again, for the thousandth time, and it caused her to thrash about and cry out, awakening Kees. He had lain there, watching her with great seriousness, for a long time thereafter. Now she listened to the quiet sounds of his own contented sleep.

She had provided that contentment. She had done everything imaginable to please him and, though gratified by the obvious success of her efforts, she was now tired of sex. Like the danger she was facing, she wanted to put that behind her for a long while.

There was something very odd about the light. It had been growing steadily brighter, but now this increase had strangely stopped. It was as if time itself had stopped.

She had decided on her plan. Like all her best plans, it was utterly simple. She would slip into the man's room and shoot him. Just like that. Bang. Dead. Then she would wipe the pistol clean of fingerprints and drop it in the Count von Kresse's stateroom, quickly opening his door with the master key she'd stolen when she took the maid's uniform from the storage room on the lower decks below, days before. The Prussian had already killed on this voyage, before some of the most prominent witnesses in the world. He'd murdered his own sister—a bitter, crippled war veteran obviously capable of any desperate act. Olga's weapon, conveniently enough, was of German manufacture, a cavalry officer's sidearm from the war that Olga had specifically requested because of its excellent quality. The count had a logical motive for murdering this victim. And an added benefit of her plan was that she would not only be taking the life of her assigned target—as she had never failed to do before—but she would also assure the doom of a Prussian aristocrat who had killed many of her countrymen in the war and who stood for everything the Soviet revolution had been created to destroy.

Best of all, by fixing blame on the count, she would infuriate the British people against the German Reich. It would be a masterstroke, though the result of only a few minutes' peaceful thought upon waking at dawn.

The light still did not increase. She was mystified. It remained half night, half day.

If there was a flaw in her plan it was that it must be executed very, very swiftly. She could be gone from Kees's cabin only a few minutes. If he was not on duty when she carried out her mission, if he was still in this bed that he so stubbornly refused to leave, her intention was to hurry into his tiny bathroom the moment she returned, awakening him with the shower and toilet flushes and thus providing herself with an unbreakable alibi. She couldn't have done it, Captain, sir. She was in my cabin, in the shower.

She could afford only a minute or so in her victim's quarters—just a few seconds, really. It would be easy to gain entrance. She'd done that before, twice, so carefully and expertly she'd made not the slightest sound except for the gentle click of her pass key turning in the lock. The first time she'd been scared off by the woman's most unexpected presence. In the second instance, despite the extremely late hour she'd chosen, she'd found him up, doing exercises, in the nude, fortunately facing away from her. She could have killed him right then, actually, but she'd been too startled by his being awake, too distracted by his nakedness.

Olga had tried a third time, out on the deck, but she'd made a mistake and the opportunity had failed her.

This time she'd be deliberate and resolute. She would cross the quiet carpeting from sitting room to bedchamber, put the pistol to his royal head, and fire, once. If the woman were there, she'd take the time to fire one more bullet. The woman's death would fit into the damning story she was preparing for Count von Kresse.

Now the light at the porthole appeared to be fading—time moving backward. She ignored the phenomenon, concentrating her thoughts.

The risk would come making her escape, complicated by her need to pause at the Prussian's door. But she could minimize that risk now. She knew exactly when watches were changed, when stewards could be expected in the corridors, when seamen might be out on the deck. In and out, one gunshot, possibly two, muffled with a cushion. The staterooms and suites on the top first-class deck were spacious, the sleeping quarters far apart. She could do it. She'd learned from her mistakes. She'd undertaken more difficult missions at greater risk. She had always thrived on risk. It was the reason for her celebrity in Dzerzhinski Square.

But she'd have only a few seconds. She hungered for more. She wanted to talk to him, to make him understand his death, to understand her mission, her function. Perhaps she could carve out a few seconds more, enough to awaken him, to speak into his ear three simple words—a royal title and a person's name. That's all that was needed. That would bring understanding enough. Then she'd fire. It was a heavy-caliber revolver. She was excited at the thought of the big bullet's savage impact.

There was one other flaw in the plan. She'd have to wait through this day. She could not strike until night, and it might well be the ship's last night at sea. They could make port by the afternoon or evening of the day after that. Then she'd be confronted with the enormous problem that was New York. The city had something that did not exist aboard ship—a police force with a long history of expertise at hunting down radicals and fugitive foreigners.

She sat up suddenly, staring fiercely at the porthole. Kees murmured and moved slightly but did not awaken. She waited a minute, then, remembering the disciplines of her profession, several minutes more. When she was certain Kees had fallen back into deep slumber, Olga eased herself off the bed.

Standing naked by the porthole, she smiled, quite joyfully. There was no mystery to the aborted light. They were in fog! A dead, impenetrable blanket of fog so thick she could scarcely see the wave-tops directly below.

It would be an hour or more before people even began stirring for breakfast. What crew was on watch would be much preoccupied with the weather since there were few emergencies at sea requiring more concentration than heavy fog. If they started sounding the foghorn, the deep, shuddering sound would obscure the report of even the largest firearm. She couldn't understand why they were not sounding it.

She could strike now, immediately. The archenemy would be dead very, very soon, in less time than it would take most of the passengers to prepare for breakfast. With a quick glance at the sleeping Kees, she went to her discarded clothing from the previous day, pulling on a sweater and her heavy skirt. The wool scratched, but that would help keep her alert. She wouldn't bother with underwear. Once back, she wanted to be naked in the bathroom as quickly as possible. She certainly wouldn't bother with shoes. She didn't intend to be seen, and bare feet would help assure that she would not be heard.

Kees had been respectful of her privacy, enough so that she had felt sufficiently confident to keep her pistol in her large shoulder bag, wrapped in another sweater. Moving quietly, she pulled it free, then shoved it into a pocket of her skirt.

With equal silence, she slowly turned the knob and opened the door. There was no one in the corridor, no sound behind her. After closing the door as someone might gently ease forward the cocked hammer of a revolver, she took a deep breath, and then began her run, her feet making only a mushy padding sound on the carpeting. She would be done with this in five minutes. Justice was not always so swift.

Captain van der Heyden found the bridge under the command of Marius Tor, who after himself and the head chef was the oldest member of the crew. He was a tall and very thin man whose uniforms never quite fit and who spoke in nervous squeaks. The injured captain's sudden appearance on the bridge at dawn startled him. Tor preferred the late night watches and avoided his superiors as much as possible.

"G-good morning, sir," he said. "Bit of fog, sir."

It was so thick they could barely make out the bow from the forward bridge windows.

"What's the speed?" van der Heyden asked.

"Eighteen knots, sir," said a crewman.

"Much too fast," the captain said. "Reduce to ahead one-third. I want it down to ten knots."

"Yes, sir. Ahead one-third," said Tor.

"Ahead one-third," repeated the crewman.

Van der Heyden, who'd been walking unsteadily, lowered himself into his chair with a groan. He was unshaven and, though he tried to speak as crisply as possibly, his speech was a little slurred. But it didn't matter. They were in conditions that required the presence of the vessel's master, and so present he was. He stuck his bandaged hands under his arms at the armpits and pressed hard against the itching and pain.

"We're in sea lanes approaching the coast of North America, Marius," he said. "Why aren't you sounding the foghorn?"

"We tried, Captain. I'm afraid the fire burned out the circuitry."

Van der Heyden sighed. He felt so groggy. He wondered if he'd be able to keep from passing out.

"Marius," he said. "All that's required is to depress a lever and open a steam valve. All you need to do is to send a seaman up the forward stack with a rope."

"Uh, yes, sir. But-but the blast will deafen him."

"Marius. Have him stuff his ears. With Kapok, if necessary, but get him up there. Our lives depend on it. I want no more disasters. I mean to complete this crossing."

"Yes, sir."

With his voice now nearly as high-pitched as a woman's, Tor gave out the orders.

"Where's van Groot?" the captain asked.

"Asleep, sir. He worked six consecutive watches."

"I'll return the favor. Let him sleep."

Van der Heyden glanced about the bridge. The bottle of gin he'd had there during the fire was gone.

"Steer a steady course at ten knots," he said. "I'm going back to my cabin for a few minutes. I-I need to shave."

By the time he'd finished that task, a clumsy and tedious endeavor with his bandaged hands, and consumed a large cup of gin, the foghorn had begun its long, resounding blasts—declarations of the ship's intent, and his.

Wallis had been awake for hours, fitfully turning in her bed, but had not heard him push the note under her door. She never did. The discovery of these missives always gave her a somewhat creepy feeling. Swearing softly, she went to fetch the latest. Her impulse was to rip it up unread. But she opened it, tearing at the expensive paper and cutting her finger in the process. This time she swore more loudly.

"Good morning, my sweetheart," it began.

> A boy's heart beats faster as we draw nearer to the wonderful country of a wonderful girl. In New York, a boy will be able to buy more of these little presents that a boy hopes will speak of his love far better than his eanum words. WE forever. Love, David.

The present, obviously, was outside the door. They were usually left there like bottles of milk or shoes polished by a hotel porter.

She opened the door and there was a neat package on the carpet, tied with a royal-blue bow. Wallis snatched it up, holding it a moment to feel its weight. The heft was most eloquent. The first blast of the ship's foghorn caught her by surprise. She waited for it to end, as one might stand motionless for a national anthem to be concluded at some public event.

Stepping back inside her room, Wallis tore the package open. The velvet-covered box was from Van Cleef & Arpels in Paris. Catching her breath, she opened it slowly, almost gingerly. It was a ruby and diamond bracelet—a half-inch wide and made of large connected squares with a huge oblong ruby the centerpiece of each. She could only wonder at the cost. Had it come into her possession back in the 1920s, when she was married to Win Spencer, they surely would have seen it as worth enough to support them for the rest of their lives.

The thought of an entirety of life spent with her drunken naval aviator of a first husband sickened her, but she was almost equally disturbed by the import of these extravagant gifts. This was the third he had bestowed on her on this holiday, if such a horrible odyssey could be so described. He had bought them all up in advance, obviously. Indeed, he seemed to have had them designed to order. How many more of these priceless trinkets was he carting with him? Did he intend to dole them out to her like treats given a circus animal who performed well?

She had returned her other jewels to their proper place in the chest she carried. She took them out again, laying them upon her bed as if she might be arranging a museum display. At the center, she gently set down the new bracelet. It was the grandest piece of them all, though she much more favored the diamond charm bracelet with the sentimental little inscribed dangling crosses that did for charms.

If she left him, could she keep these? How much of a gentleman was the next King of England?

Wallis lowered her head to the bedspread, pressing her face into it. She began to cry again, though her sobs were weak and dry. It amazed her how much she yearned for her husband, Ernest. He was dull and stolid, more upper middle class than aristocrat, just another Englishman in striped blue suit and mustache. But he had been so warm and loving, so strong and safe and secure, so predictable and stable. She was nearly forty years old. What in hell was she doing with what remained of her life? To what ridiculous risk was she putting her middle years and old age?

Wallis sat up, taking a deep breath. She looked a long moment at the jewels, then rose and went to the mirror of her dresser. She did not look good. She never did in the morning. But she did look regal. Enormously regal. She had realized that very early on in her relationship with the prince. She could admit to herself that there was something of the aspect of Snow White's wicked stepmother in the countenance that stared and often glared back at her, but it had a royal presence. She was ever so much more the queen than the dowdy, dumpy, frumpy Elizabeth Bowes-Lyon, wife of Edward's younger brother Bertie. If Edward did not become king, Lillibet, as the current king and queen so obnoxiously if adoringly called the woman, would be queen as consort of a stammering George VI. The absurdity of that possibility amused Wallis. She laughed in the gentle Southern way that had proved so engagingly charming at London dinner parties, but her melancholy remained near. She took another deep breath, then retrieved the new bracelet and put it on, holding it up in the mirror.

She would have to thank him. She would hang on at least until this holiday was over. The most important thing was to get off this awful ship. Her pursuit of social success—and certainly at that moment in history she was the most socially successful woman in the entire world—had almost gotten her killed. She had thought hard upon it. She had been closer to death than she had ever been even in China.

She left her bedchamber and crossed the hallway to his, hesitating after opening the door, for he was snoring in a very loud and ugly way, the consequence of another night of too much drink. She'd cure him soon enough of that. In China, with Win Spencer, she'd damn well had enough of that.

A sudden snapping sound caught her attention. The door to the sitting room was opening, without knock or announcement. It wasn't Runcie or Fruity Metcalfe or Lord Brownlow. It was a woman.

The fog had absorbed Lord Mountbatten's attention from the instant he'd awakened. It was about the thickest he had seen in his years at sea. Excited, he showered and shaved with even more efficiency than usual, then quickly dressed in his naval uniform, pausing only to flick off a few specks of lint. His place, as always, was on the bridge. He'd received a commendation from the admiral of the Mediterranean fleet for his ability at handling destroyers in foul weather. After all that the officers of the *Wilhelmina* had been through, they'd be appreciative of help, especially when it came with such expertise.

Squaring the visor of his gold-braided cap, Mountbatten started out of the suite, but then paused as he passed by the door to Edwina's bedroom. To his amazement, she was in it, fast asleep.

Leaving the suite, Mountbatten started up toward the bridge, then recalled something and turned the other way, heading down the passageway for the exit to the deck. Even so high above the engine room, he could detect the odd vibrations of the propellor shafts. It was a dropped beat—a bar of waltz music missing a note. Something, he was sure, was wrong. Before reporting to the bridge, he would go out to the fantail and observe the propellor function at firsthand. Such a malfunction ought to be visually and audibly obvious.

He stepped outside onto the moist planking of the promenade. The fog was actually rather frightening. He wasn't sure that, if he were master of this vessel, he wouldn't order it to dead stop.

Olga crept toward her goal, bare feet now making no sound whatsoever, but halted abruptly, startled by the sound of a door opening. She pressed herself back against a wall. Far down the hall, she watched a man step forth and was furious to see it was her intended victim. Worse, he turned in her direction and started up the passageway. If she showed her pistol now, his first act would be to shout, alarming this entire section of first class.

Yet he seemed greatly distracted, so preoccupied by whatever thought that he scarcely noticed her shadowy figure. Suddenly he stopped, turned, and began retracing his steps, heading down toward the other end of the corridor. She waited until he had turned the corner, then hurried after, feet swift and silent.

He was going out on deck! Excited, happy, she paused before the exit door after it had closed behind him. Gently placing her hand against the cold metal, she eased it open, slowly extending her head afterward into the mist that filled the open air beyond.

He was striding briskly away from her along the promenade, heading toward the burned-out aft section that had comprised most of second class. Like a will o' the wisp, Olga scampered after, ducking behind a stanchion or bulkhead whenever he seemed about to glance back, though he never did. He was serenely purposeful. He was wearing his naval uniform as if for some reason, though she had no idea what it could be.

Coming to the rope the crew had strung across the decking, its dangling DANGER, KEEP OUT sign swaying with the ship's movement, he paused, then swung a long leg over the barrier, his other following nimbly. He was going back to where no one would now be. He'd be all alone, and the fog was so dense she could barely make out the gold braid on his sleeve. She quickened her pace, feet pattering along on the cold, wet deck, but making no noise he could notice. He moved along as if she didn't exist.

After ducking under the rope, she scurried on a few more yards, then paused to pull the long-barreled revolver from the deep pocket of her thick wool skirt. The automatic pistols now favored by the heirs to Felix Dzerzhinsky who ran the OGPU were malevolent looking enough, and easily hidden. But they were about as accurate as a rock thrown backhand. With its seven-inch barrel, this revolver could drop a man at fifty yards. Its huge bullet would strike wherever she aimed the sight.

She lifted the pistol, taking a deep breath and holding it steady. Though he was moving away, a squeeze of the trigger now would send the screaming piece of lead into his lower back, shattering his spine and cleaving out large chunks of intestine and abdominal muscle. She raised the barrel slightly, then lowered it altogether. She hurried on. She would have her brief speech.

When he reached the point where the rail began to curve toward the stern at the second-class grill and verandah, she shouted his name, in German:

"*Prinz Battenburg!*"

He stopped and turned slowly to face her. He showed no fear whatsoever. His eyes were dead calm.

"What do you want?" said Lord Mountbatten.

"You are the nephew of the bitch despot mistress of the devil Rasputin?"

"What?"

"You are the nephew of the Czarina Alexandra, executed by the people's justice at Ekaterinburg?"

"I am the nephew of Her late Majesty. Yes. Who are you? What in bloody hell do you want?"

She raised the pistol higher, aiming at his head. "I want your death, Romanov pretender!"

"Olga!"

She whirled about, revolver pointing the way. There was Kees, running toward her, just a few feet away. He must have awakened and followed her. He must have seen her take her gun. She didn't know what to do, but of course she did. A pull on the trigger and he'd be out of her way. Then another pull to put a bullet through Lord Mountbatten. Then she'd be done. A toss of the gun into the sea, or possibly still into the stateroom of Count von Kresse, and all her cares and worries would be over. Just a pull of the trigger.

Mountbatten's kick was brutal. He swung his foot with all his might, striking Olga square in the rectum, an explosion of pain spreading up from the base of her spine. She went sprawling, sliding along the wet deck, but held tightly to the pistol. Another kick came, exactly in the same place, and even more painful. She cried out, the anguished voice of a child, fighting to remain conscious. Whether the revolver was still in her hand she did not know. Another blow struck, a foot coming down hard on her wrist. It went numb, possibly broken. If she had been holding the gun, she did no longer. And now both her arms were rudely pulled back and yanked upward behind her back.

"Damned Bolshevik assassin," she heard Mountbatten say. "What else is going to happen on this cursed ship?"

"Olga," Kees said sadly. She felt his hand on her head. Her cheek was pressed into the wet wood of the deck. Mountbatten was using some cloth to tie her hands. He tied them excessively tight, bringing a shot of pain to her wrist.

"Olga," Kees said, his voice so sweet. "Olga."

They had said at Dzerzhinsky Square that a woman would ultimately fail in this profession, that she would succumb to glands and passion and weakness and make some stupid emotional mistake. In response, Olga had killed with more viciousness than all of them to prove the foolishness of this arrogant male attitude. But now she had proved them right. Two quick pulls of the trigger and she would have killed Kees and her mission target, exactly what was expected of her. But she had hesitated. She had remembered love, or at least sex. It was the only love she had ever known.

The captain had viewed it all from the port bridge wing, where he had gone to listen for the sound of other ships between the blasts of the Wilhelmina's horn. When he saw Olga take out the long black pistol from her clothing, he had rapped on the door to the bridge and called urgently for a crewman to bring one of the rifles from the gun case by the chart table. But now that she'd been so quickly subdued by Mountbatten and Kees, he bade the man lower the weapon.

As they brought the woman back along the promenade, each man gripping one of her arms, van der Heyden called to Kees. They moved her faster than her feet could manage, Mountbatten shoving her rudely at intervals. When they reached the bridge wing, they stopped, Kees looking up as the captain leaned over the railing, resting gingerly on his elbows. The woman glared at him defiantly, fury in her eyes, a beast caught in a trap.

"This woman was going to kill me," Mountbatten said, almost as if complaining about some lawn pest. "Damned bolshevik!"

"I saw it all," the captain said. "You owe your life to my young third officer here. And he owes me a substantial explanation."

"Yes, sir," Kees said.

"Later," said the captain. "Put the woman in one of the third-class cabins. Strip it of all furniture. Draperies, everything. I want two, not one, but two armed guards posted at the door, around the clock." He looked at Kees with deliberate scorn. "And if she offers them sexual favors, they are to shoot her."

Olga cursed him, in several languages.

"Get her below!" said the captain.

When he returned inside, van Groot was on the bridge, looking displeased.

"Are you well, Captain?" van Groot asked.

Van der Heyden ignored him. He went to his chair and stared out the forward windows into the gray wall through which they were moving. He inhaled deeply, a sort of sigh. Van Groot watched the crewman take the rifle back to the case.

"What happened out there?" van Groot asked.

Van der Heyden took another deep breath, then exhaled slowly. The damp air was bothering his lungs. "We caught the woman who attacked Lord Mountbatten the other night. She tried again, this time with a pistol." The captain paused. "This is my last voyage, van Groot, if I get to complete it. If you want command of this jinx ship when it's repaired, you're welcome to it."

The door to the prince's suite opened fully, revealing one of the first-class maids entering with a stack of freshly pressed sheets in her arms. She seemed startled to see Mrs. Simpson in her nightdress, but no less startled than Wallis.

"What are you doing here?" Mrs. Simpson demanded.

The girl was frightened. She almost dropped the sheets. "Ma'am. The sign."

"Sign? What damn sign are you talking about?"

"The sign on all the doors in this part of first class, madam." The maid retreated to the door. Opening it, she pulled forth a large printed card dangling from a golden cord. "Make Up Room Early," it said.

"But it's hardly morning!" Wallis said.

"These signs are all up and down the hall, madam," said the maid. "We thought you all had some special early plans."

Furious, Wallis strode to the doorway and peered out, frowning. There were indeed other signs like this one, hanging from doors in both directions. Farther along the passageway, through an opened door, she heard Duff Cooper swearing as a maid backed out of his room with a stack of sheets.

The commotion had awakened Edward, who came forth in bare feet and dressing gown.

"What deuced, damned trouble have we now, Wallis?" he asked sternly, as if it were somehow all her fault.

"This serving girl just waltzed into our suite," she said, with even more severity than his. "Someone has been hanging 'Make Up Early' signs on the first-class doors, a stupid little joke."

"Well, I won't have it," said the prince. "Where in hell is Runcie?"

They heard the sound of a toilet flushing behind them.

"Here I am, sir," said the inspector, straightening his suit jacket. "I was just using the loo."

Spencer, restless, had been walking about Nora's suite while she slept. Not wanting yet another drink—he was wearying of alcohol on this voyage the way he was wearying of the heavy, rich, and endless heaps of expensive food—he browsed among her possessions, particularly the handsome, silver-framed photographs. He wouldn't have thought

such totems of the upper class would have easily found their way into
the life of a daughter of Toledo, Ohio. But then, she had acquired a
number of attributes that would not have come naturally to her—
from reading books, he supposed, but in larger part from her movie
roles.

She was always being cast as the postdebutante or rich girl. When
she wasn't being likened to Constance Bennett or Mary Astor, it was
to Katharine Hepburn. Nora hadn't quite their acting skill, nor their
wealthy accents, but was certainly more beautiful, and much funnier
in comedies.

Most of the photos were of Nora and well-known Hollywood
personalities with whom she had acted—Cary Grant and Gary
Cooper, Nora standing arm in arm with Myrna Loy and William
Powell on the afterdeck of someone's immense yacht. One photograph was of Nora with the great British actor Leslie Howard, the
two of them playing croquet. She certainly looked the part of an
English lady, more so even than Edwina or Diana Cooper. The
setting, complete with Tudor mansion in the background, was certainly English, except for the palm trees that so loudly proclaimed
California.

But two of the pictures stood out from all the others. One was a
black-and-white studio portrait of Nora in three-quarter view, infinitely more an artist's effort than a mere publicity still. Employing
the now-stylish dramatic highlights that had become *de rigueur* for
Hollywood's major personalities, it showed her with much longer
hair than she now wore, a wave of it falling across her brow almost
to her eye. Her slight smile was sophisticated and knowing, and her
eyes had the same delicious, dreamy quality he had seen in them after
they had made love. In fact, the photo made him wonder somewhat
at the circumstance of its making.

The other picture that struck him was much more startling. It was
of common people, a handsome if overweight man dressed in an
ill-fitting black Irishman's Sunday suit, an attractive woman in a
cheap, light-color dress, and a little girl in a white blouse, plaid
jumper, long white stockings, and patent leather shoes. They might
have been posing in Ireland—behind them was a storefront with
curtained window beneath a sign that said "Reilly's Saloon and Grocery"—but it was Toledo.

Spencer felt an onrush of admiration for Nora—for keeping such
a photograph, for displaying it in an upper-class silver frame among
all the others of her with famous swells.

The noise he heard at the door was almost imperceptible—heard the way he had seen specks in the dangerous skies over France that had become Fokkers and Pfalzes—the hushed sound of feet on the carpet, the slightest turning of the knob. Too many dangers had presented themselves on this trip. He leapt at the door and yanked it open. Someone had hung a cardboard sign on the outside knob, something about maid service. He heard now the *thump thump* of running footsteps, and leaned out to see a tall man in a raincoat hurrying away down the corridor, pausing just once to sling another sign—apparently his last—on a final door.

Spencer pounded off in angry pursuit. The man was the same pernicious jokester who had plagued them all this voyage. Spencer raced around a turning in the corridor, nearly catching up to the fellow as he struggled to open an exit door to the boat deck. The man then turned to look at him, and Spencer stopped stock still in his tracks. There was the famous curly hair, though not so much as Spencer remembered from the newspaper photographs. Indeed, the forehead was quite high. But the clear blue eyes, the Nordic nose, the thin lips, and hero's chin were exactly the same. Spencer was looking at Charles Augustus Lindbergh, "the greatest man in the world."

"You haven't any clothes on," Lindbergh said.

The exit door came free. The man grinned, then vanished outside, looking not a little embarrassed. It dawned on Spencer that he'd run from Nora's suite without a shred of clothing on.

He retreated, hurrying back the way he'd come, surprising a maid and causing her to give out a terrible shriek.

"Sorry," he said. "Going the wrong way."

The door to Nora's suite had closed behind him. He pounded on it furiously until she came to his rescue.

She looked astonished, but as he stepped inside, began to giggle.

"A little habit you picked up from Lady Mountbatten?" she said.

Spencer scowled, but then began laughing himself. He sat down in a chair, his laughter becoming uncontrollable.

"It's not all that funny," she said.

"It's not me," he said. "It's Lindbergh. Nora, that practical joker who's been bedeviling us is Charles Lindbergh."

"What?"

"Charles Lindbergh, conqueror of the Atlantic. It's true. He's on this ship. I knew a pilot who was an instructor of his after the war. He taught Lindbergh how to fly, the military way to fly, down at Kelly Field in Texas. He said Lindbergh used to do crazy things like put itching powder in the pajamas of his fellow cadets. He put a snake into the bed of one fellow, and moved another fellow's bed up on the roof of the barracks. He even poured kerosene into the coffee cup of my friend when they were both mail pilots a few years later. I'd forgotten all about it. I should have realized it immediately. Nora, the Great Hero is—is a card. He's the biggest practical joker in aviation."

He laughed more, crazily. She wondered if he'd been at the liquor again.

The door opened and yet another maid stepped in. She saw Spencer naked in the chair and screamed, fleeing.

"You don't know how glad I'll be when we finally do get to New York," Nora said.

He went to her and put his arms around her. He was no longer weary of sex.

They took a late lunch in the smaller of the first-class dining rooms, contenting themselves with just a single cocktail beforehand. Then, returning to the suite to dress in warm clothes against the cold mist, they set out for a brisk walk about the deck.

"My hair," Nora said, with as much concern as a soldier who'd discovered he'd been wounded.

"Your hair is beautiful."

"It's going to stand out like a clown's."

"New England girls have hair like that all the time. I find it very attractive."

"Well, I'm a Lake Erie girl, and I'm going to wash it before dinner and put some hairdressing on it."

"Nora. I'd love you bald."

"I wouldn't love you bald."

"What will we do when we're old?"

"You won't get bald. You'll just get gray. I can tell."

They kissed, gently and sweetly. They had gone toward the bow, and the wind was a presence. Pausing at the rail, they looked at each other possessively.

"What will we do in New York?" he said.

"Why, we'll stay together. I have a suite reserved at the Plaza Hotel."

"You have a play to begin. What will I do?"

"Just stay with me. After we finish the rest of the auditions, we'll move down to Philadelphia for the tryout run. But then it's back to the Plaza. We could be there a year if it's a hit. I don't want to do more than a year. I can't stand being away from California more than that. I've got a film to do. But I hope it's a year. I hope it's a hit."

"I'm sure it will be a hit." He fought back a frown. "Nora?"

"Yes?"

"Nora, do you want to get married?"

"I don't think it's time to talk about that, not yet."

"On the lifeboat . . ."

She moved away from him slightly, but then realized the effect of her action and placed her hand atop of his on the rail.

"A shipboard romance, Jimmy. Just what I wanted. As for more, let's wait and see."

"Are you worried about something?"

"Actually, I'm worried about someone."

"Edwina? That was nothing at all."

"I'm worried about the blonde."

"The blonde? You mean Diana Cooper? That was nothing, period."

"No, not the faded British beauty. I mean the girl back in Paris. That Whitley."

"Whitney."

"Whitney. What about her?"

"She's back in Paris. And I'm here."

"There are other ships on the sea. They go back to France. You've got Paris in your blood."

"Let's try New York."

"But let's not talk about marriage."

They were interrupted by another thundering blast of the *Wilhelmina*'s horn. There was another immediately after, but it was not the *Wilhelmina*'s. At first it seemed an echo of their ship's sounding, but it came again from off the port bow. The *Wilhelmina* bellowed back. The deafening dialogue went on, almost a contest. The blasts from the other ship became louder.

"Oh, Christ," Nora said, "Are we going to collide?"

The phantom ship's blasts came nearer still, almost as loud as the *Wilhelmina*'s. The thick gray fog was thinning and had become suffused with a falling touch of golden light.

"Jimmy. I see it. I see the ship!"

Another horn blast. Vaguely they saw motion, then the ghostly form of black hull, white superstructure, and single funnel. A freighter, perhaps a coaster. They were very near land.

There was another, shriller sound, such as might be heard from a lighthouse or coastal buoy. Spencer put his arm around Nora's waist. The sea began to widen. The mist was being pulled away. Behind them they could now make out the *Wilhelmina*'s wake. Forward, the fog was a thicker presence, but they could see another shadowy form, much smaller than the single-funneled freighter. In a moment the shape began to draw abreast, and they could detect the color red. It grew brighter and brighter. All at once their eyes were caught by a flash of light, a revolving glare that turned away and swung back again. The shrill sound repeated itself.

"Welcome to America, Nora darling," he said.

"What do you mean?"

"We're off Cape Cod."

"How do you know?"

"It's the lightship *Nantucket.* We're off Cape Cod. We'll be in New York tomorrow."

A telephone call from Chips Cannon awakened Spencer and Nora from a nap in the late afternoon. Sounding exceedingly friendly and solicitous, he invited them to cocktails in the prince's suite. They accepted happily. A bit of society was in order. They would shortly be returned to the real world. It was time to prepare for it.

Everyone was there save Edwina, the count, and Mrs. Parker. The prince, dressed in a loud checked jacket, gray flannels, and a blue tie with an oversized knot, leapt up to see to their drinks. He was unusually cordial—indeed, extremely charming. It was the royal skill, this charm, the secret to his immense popularity in England. If the Windsors could maintain it in succeeding generations, they would sit in their thrones long after the dictators had toppled all the other royal houses of Europe.

Edward was particularly attentive to Nora. After a few minutes he led her away to search for the coast of Long Island from the sun deck with a pair of binoculars Metcalfe had borrowed from the ship. Mrs. Simpson, wearing a pale-blue cocktail dress and too much jewelry, sat in a corner somewhat glumly.

Chips, maintaining a crisp banter and sounding more English than ever, pressed Spencer in the opposite direction, over toward a painting on the wall that depicted Hendrik Hudson discovering the river that bore his name. It was an elaborate and expensive work, but uninspired.

Duff Cooper came up to them. Chips had been talking about the raffishness of New York society, but Cooper changed the subject to politics and the failure of the League of Nations to deal with the Abyssinian crisis. It was as if they had never been through their ordeal, as if Parker, the countess, and the young seaman had not gone into the sea. It was all too blitheful.

Channon nodded toward Mountbatten, who was standing with great dignity next to Lady Emerald and Diana.

"You'd never know he was almost murdered this morning," Chips said.

"Murdered?" Spencer said. He thought of Count von Kresse.

"It was the Polish woman," Chips said. "Or Russian. Or whatever she is. Some filthy eastern tribe. In any event she tried to shoot Dickie right on deck. In the fog. That young officer she took as a lover intervened, and Dickie subdued her. Dickie is nothing if not a man of action."

Spencer shook his head as if in amazement. He was trying to work it out in his mind where he would fit this bizarre incident into his already otherworldly tale.

"One could write quite the book about this voyage," Cooper said.

"Or quite the newspaper article," Channon said.

The prince had gone off with Nora. Mrs. Simpson rose and walked slowly to her room. Everyone else's eyes were on Spencer. The conversation diminished, and suddenly there was silence.

"Sit down somewhere, Jamieson," Chips said. "We'd like to talk to you."

Spencer glanced around the room, at all the faces. Some, like Diana's, were friendly. Others, like Emerald's, decidedly not. He turned and settled onto the couch beneath the Hudson painting. Everyone else took a seat. The cocktail party had suddenly been rendered into a scene from a lawyer's office, with Channon playing the attorney.

"Jamieson," he said carefully. "Everyone here knows what happened to your father—that you support yourself as a journalist."

Spencer wondered if there was some social problem involved in this. He felt defensive about his status in their eyes.

"So, I believe, does Winston Churchill."

"That's not the point," Channon said. "Winston would not for any reason even think of doing what we're afraid you intend to do, which is to make all that's happened to us public in the American press."

"It's a deuced sensitive matter," said Major Metcalfe. "His Royal Highness intended this to be a very private holiday. If he—if we had thought there was a chance of your making professional use of what's transpired, well . . ."

"His Royal Highness would not have extended the hospitality he has to you," snapped Lord Brownlow.

"I am here as a passenger on this ship," Spencer said. He feared he sounded surly.

"Yes, but certain considerations, certain generosities were extended you," Chips said.

Spencer saw Lord Mountbatten color markedly. He wished Edwina were among the group. He felt certain she'd be defending him—indeed, calling for an immediate halt to this embarrassing confrontation.

"It's a difficult time for England," said Duff Cooper. "We've millions out of work. The king is seriously ill. There's the war in Abyssinnia. A public controversy over the prince's, er, social life, is hardly the ticket just now."

"If it's a matter of finances," Chips said. "I mean, I understand how difficult it's been for you since your father's ruin—I mean, reverses. I, we, we're prepared to compensate you for whatever financial loss you fear you might suffer for not—for not being able to carry out what you feel to be your, how shall I say, professional responsibilities."

Now Spencer colored, more darkly than Mountbatten. He started to rise from the couch.

"Look, old sport," said Metcalfe. "I rather think this is hardly the way . . ."

Channon had taken out a checkbook. "Would a thousand pounds be appropriate?"

"Mr. Spencer, I'm sure this isn't necessary," Metcalfe said. "All we'd like is your word as a gentleman that you won't write about this."

"And if we don't get it," Brownlow said, "we can only assume that you are not a gentleman."

With that, Spencer was out of his seat and out the door. He wanted to slam it violently behind him, but the English police inspector was there just outside, and Spencer wasn't half sure that he wouldn't be treated like some dangerous criminal if he did.

He and Nora had just finished dressing for cocktails, to which they'd been invited by Mr. van Hoorn of the shipping line in his suite, when a steward knocked at the door. He bore a neat envelope with Spencer's name written on it. Spencer tipped the man, then opened it. Inside was a check for £1,500 and a note that said "Jamieson, please"—and nothing more.

Spencer tore the lot of it into very small pieces.

"I'm going to write the most searing, sensational story that American newspapers have ever seen," he said. "That the Associated Press, United Press, INS, Inter-Ocean, and Reuter have ever seen."

"Jimmy, what are you talking about?"

"I'll leave you out of it," he said. "Out of the bad parts of it, at any rate. But I am going to raise a lot of hell."

"Why don't you just forget them?" she said, coming to him and putting her hand on his shoulder. "They're all so sad and dull. I have to say I was really impressed at first, but after the fire and all . . . Why don't we just let them go on their way?"

He put his arm around her.

"I won't do anything to hurt you," he said. He had, he later recalled, said the same thing to Edwina.

They had what could only be called a pleasant time at the cocktail party, where Nora was the star of a rather crowded affair, though no member of the prince's party made an appearance. At dinner, they sat at Mr. van Hoorn's table, steadfastly ignoring the English group at the captain's, where First Officer van Groot presided in his place. Young Kees, limping, came by to say good evening and inquire after them. The sad Mrs. Parker was with them, though she spoke little. The count was not present, but Edwina was there with Lord Mountbatten.

Toward the end of dinner, Edwina came up to them, putting a hand on Spencer's arm.

"I heard about all that rot, Lieutenant Spencer," she said in a voice both quiet and brittle. "That bloody inquisition. I rather think you should tell them all to go fuck themselves."

She gave a quick, friendly smile to Nora, then returned to her husband.

There was another envelope awaiting them when they returned to Nora's suite after a long after-dinner perambulation of the deck.

The note was for Spencer. It was from von Kresse.

"His Excellency the Count requests another rendezvous for brandy," Spencer said. "At eleven o'clock this time."

"Jimmy. Forget him. Forget all of them. I have a much better idea on how to spend our time. It's our last night. Aboard ship, anyway."

"There'll be time enough for your better idea," he said, patting her bottom. "There's time now, in fact. But I think I should see him. I suspect the Prussian and I are not done with each other yet."

She reached to unhook the back of her dress.

Spencer and the count met at the same dark place on the uppermost deck. Though he spoke in a pleasant tone, von Kresse looked even more somber than before. In fact, he turned his face away after greeting Spencer, keeping his eyes on the unseen night horizon of the sea. For the rest of his unhappy life, von Kresse would see things no one else would when he looked out to sea. Dagne von Kresse would haunt every ocean, every shoreline. As he thought of it, Spencer felt the more wrenchingly sorry for the scarred and crippled Junker aristocrat. The words the man had spoken about the brotherhood of the air were beginning to take on some meaning.

"We'll have our brandy later," the count said. "There's someone I want you to meet, someone who wants to meet you."

"Who?"

"You'll see. Just come with me. Please. It won't take long, though I'm afraid that once again we'll have to walk slowly. It's a long way. Third class. Far astern."

Spencer made two attempts at conducting a conversation during their transit, but the count replied in desultory fashion and fell silent both times. Spencer then decided to keep quiet. Finally they reached a plain door on one of the lowest decks.

"It's Lindbergh, isn't it?" he said.

The count did not reply, except to knock sharply on the door, five times in quick succession. It opened swiftly. There was only one dim lamp on in the narrow chamber, and the tall figure who greeted them stood in silhouette. Without a word he motioned them in, then shut the door behind them as quickly as he had opened it.

"This is Lieutenant Spencer, Colonel," von Kresse said.

The tall man shook Spencer's hand, fidgeting as he did so and averting his eyes. Dropping his arm then, he glanced about nervously and then retreated to the other end of the cabin, where a small desk was positioned below a closed porthole. There were aircraft drawings and blueprints piled in disorganized fashion upon it.

"I guess we've met," Lindbergh said. "Informally." He gave out a high-pitched laugh, almost a giggle. "Sorry," he said more seriously. "Just having some fun there. Haven't had a lot of fun much, recent days, recent weeks. Not much fun at all."

He had been through the worst imaginable hell for three years.

Spencer could think of nothing to say. To his amazement, he found himself in awe, dumbstruck, cowed by this extraordinary man's presence for all his earlier foolishness. And Spencer was a man who had not only been in a lifeboat with the Prince of Wales but had interviewed Stalin, Mussolini, Mao Tse-tung, and the goddess who was Greta Garbo.

"Good evening, sir," he managed finally.

"Good evening, yes. Good evening. Colonel von Kresse here says you were one of our better fliers in the war."

"I only downed three aircraft, sir."

"Don't call me sir. If you have to, call me colonel or something. We're all military flyers, after all. But, hell, not sir."

Spencer smiled weakly. What was this all about? What would this conversation mean? What was he going to do about this confrontation?

Von Kresse was staring at him with great intensity, though Lindbergh still could not bring his eyes to meet Spencer's.

"But you were a good pilot, the longest surviving American pilot of the war, right?" Lindbergh said. "You flew with the French before America got into the fighting. You were a squadron leader with one of the lowest casualty rates of any American squadron, even though you were in a high combat sector."

"We were lucky."

"It wasn't just that. I was chief pilot of the Chicago to St. Louis air mail service in 1926. Our boys . . . what I mean to say is that leaders, good leaders, well, that good leaders help save lives."

He was blushing. He seemed very much to regret the favorable reference to himself, the comparison of his mail pilot operation to the aerial killing in France.

"Colonel von Kresse here says that, well, that you've got good judgment. He thought it would be a good idea if I were to talk to you about this plane here. He's told me all he can think of. I'd like to hear from you, too."

He shifted the drawings, pulling forth one of a twin-engined aircraft shown in profile and cutaway.

"This is a Messerschmitt long-range fighter," Lindbergh said. "Bf 110-AO. Wingspan fifty-three feet four and three-quarters inches. Length thirty-nine feet eight and a half inches. Two six hundred ten horsepower Jumo 210 B engines. Armament, five seven point nine–millimeter machine-guns. The count here says they're going into production with it next year. It's all real secret."

"I've heard some talk about it," Spencer said, moving to stand next to the hero. This was as unreal as his conversation in a cave with Mao after a thousand-mile walk into the west of China. But he'd recently been talking on the very same subject, with the rich French publisher who was Whitney's husband, in Whitney's kitchen. De Mornay published many books on aviation. It was through him that Spencer had met Saint-Exupéry.

"What do you think they'll do with it?"

"It would make a good night fighter," Spencer said. "If they added cannon to the armament, they could blast the hell out of enemy bomber formations—*our* bomber formations, if we ever have bomber formations—flying outside machine-gun range."

"Exactly. That's what I think. If they added fuel injection, these ships could outrun anything we have now. Right?"

"I'm not sure what we have now. I've been writing about not much more than French politics for three years."

Lindbergh nodded. "Well, they could. Believe me. This is a hell of an airplane. But look at this one. This is the ultimate fighting aircraft."

He pulled forth a drawing of a plane Spencer had seen vaguely drawn and described in at least two French aviation magazines.

"The Me-109," Spencer said.

"Bf 109 B-1," Lindbergh said. "Wingspan, thirty-two feet four and a half inches. Length, twenty-eight feet six and a half inches. A six hundred thirty-five Jumo 210D engine. A twenty-millimeter cannon firing through the propeller shaft and two seven point nine–millimeter machines guns. It's got a service ceiling of twenty-six thousand feet and a top speed of two hundred ninety-two miles an hour. It's in production as we stand on this ship."

"It's their masterpiece," said von Kresse. "It's a very basic aircraft. They can improve it to perfection."

Spencer leaned close over the draftsman's excellent rendering, moving the light slightly to see better. Oddly, he felt almost back in uniform again, though it had been nearly twenty years.

"I wouldn't be surprised if they even managed to double the speed. A better engine, more guns. They can probably adapt it in all kinds of configurations," Spencer said.

"They sure as hell can," Lindbergh said. "It's a brilliant airplane. And what do we have? The Grumman F3F-1, a goddamn biplane. And we're selling it off to a half-dozen countries. What do the British have? The Gloster Gladiator. Another goddamned biplane. There's another Brit machine in the works, a monoplane. Can't tell you about it though it's damned good. But they're dragging their feet on it. The Germans are ahead of all of us. Especially us Americans. If there was war now, they'd kill us in the air."

Spencer didn't know what to say. Lindbergh's eyes flickered, then turned to Spencer's. The shy, nervous, reclusive celebrity of the century suddenly became extremely direct. He was lecturing to Spencer.

"We can't get dragged into another war," he said. "We can't."

"Not now," Spencer said at last.

"No. Not now. Not until we're prepared. And we're far from that. Years and years from that."

"He's quite right, Spencer," said von Kresse, who had lowered himself to a seat on Lindbergh's small bed. "Germany is preparing for war. You are not. The western democracies are not."

"I got these drawings in Germany," Lindbergh said. "I don't understand why they gave them to me. Maybe to impress me. Maybe to scare us. I don't know. But I'm turning them over to the War Department in Washington as soon as I can get there. I don't think the Roosevelt administration is going to do much about it, but we can get something going in the military. I have some friends in the Army Air Corps. Colonel Eaker. Colonel Arnold. I'm going to get them copies. I'm going to keep doing this as long as I can get a hold of things like these."

He put his hand on Spencer's arm. "Do you agree with me?" he asked. "Do you agree these German crates are the best the world's ever seen?"

"I-I couldn't possibly disagree with you."

Lindbergh turned Spencer toward him and gripped both his shoulders. "I don't like reporters, Lieutenant. And you've got to agree that I've got a good reason."

"You haven't had an easy time, sir."

"But I am a pilot. Flyers are the people I like best. You were a really good flyer. The count here says so. He likes you. And you fought each other."

"I suppose so."

"Well, I hope you understand."

Nervous again, Lindbergh dropped his hands and turned away. He pretended to be staring at the drawings, but he was obviously waiting for Spencer and von Kresse to leave. The count, with difficulty, got to his feet.

"Good night, Colonel," he said. He looked to Spencer. "*Und jetzt, ein cognac, Herr Leutnant Spencer?*"

Spencer did as bidden. As they went out the door, a new, extraordinary, and perhaps brilliant lead for his story occurred to him. When they subsequently came out onto the boat deck, into the cool night air, the count stopped.

"Why have we come out here?" Spencer asked. "Why not use the inside stairs?"

"Because, very briefly, I want to say something that I don't want to say in a place of corridors and alcoves. Listen to me well, Leutnant, and please understand. Colonel Lindbergh meant what he said about taking these things to your War Department in Washington. He is going back to Germany in December or January, for a long stay, at the government's invitation. He can obtain more of these drawings and draftsman's work. Plans, blueprints. That fool Goering has even asked his advice."

"What has this to do with me?"

"I'm going to help him. I'll get him what I can. There are others who will do the same. We want your country to be fully aware of what you're up against. We want something done about it. Do you understand? Do you see what this is about?"

"You don't want me to give you away."

"I hope you won't, Leutnant Spencer. I will have faith in my brother pilot. I've dedicated what remains of my awful life to revenge. Don't ruin it for me." He then spoke almost cheerily. "Now, for that brandy."

They paused at the same little bar adjoining the balcony that overlooked the first-class ballroom. The dancing this evening was well attended, the merrymakers impelled by the urge to arrive in New York and the urge to linger out here beyond the reach of such dull civilization. They felt celebratory; glad at the proximity to safety and normality, but not wanting to give up the licentiousness granted by all ocean voyages, particularly this one. Most every woman aboard would be making love this night, possibly even Lady Emerald Cunard. Nora, too.

Spencer and the count, as before, sipped their brandies as they looked down at the dance floor. The band leader, as his orchestra ended a long but vibrant remdition of "Dancing in the Dark," announced that there would be just one last song, one last dance. It was nearly midnight.

Mrs. Parker was again present, again at van Hoorn's table, still somber and very, very correct.

Spencer took von Kresse's free hand, gripping it with firmness and friendship. He sought the man's eyes. It unnerved him to have such piercing vision focused so closely upon him, but he returned the strong, steady gaze.

Spencer's lips parted. He smiled.

"I like you," he said. "Hun bastard. I respect what you're doing."

"*Sehr gut.* I ask no more."

"Good-bye. *Auf wiedersehen.* I must leave you now."

"*Wiedersehen.*"

Spencer wondered if they *had* fought each other sometime in the war. But it didn't matter. He gave a salute of sorts, then departed, heading to the stairway that gave onto the ballroom floor. As the band began "I'll See You in my Dreams," he reached van Hoorn's table. He bowed slightly before Mrs. Parker, who was looking extremely beautiful and gracious, but much older than her years.

"It's the last dance aboard ship, Mrs. Parker," he said. "I'd be very, very grateful if you'd dance it with me."

She rose without speaking, glancing quickly at van Hoorn but ignoring the disapproving expression he gave in return.

Mrs. Parker slipped into Spencer's arms when they reached the polished dance floor but moved woodenly. He pulled her closer.

"We're going to part tomorrow," he said. "All of us. I wish there was something I could do."

"Do, Mr. Spencer?"

"I feel so sorry, Mrs. Parker. I want to help you. In any way I can."

"You saved my life. What more could you possibly do?"

"Your husband . . ."

"My husband drowned, along with others. Can you bring him back? Could you have done anything about him?"

He thought of all the young men he would like to bring back. He thought of Raul Lufbery, leaping from a burning Spad.

"No. I can't do that."

She pressed her cheek against his. It was moist as if from sudden tears.

"Mr. Spencer, no one's been good to me for a very long time. You've helped. A lot. But good night. Good night."

She moved out of his arms and hurried away, heading for the opposite exit.

# CHAPTER
## *EIGHTEEN*

Something was wrong. At the least, something had changed dramatically. Spencer opened his eyes. Nora was lying diagonally across him, her chest flat against his, her fragrant copper hair soft against his cheek, her breathing quiet and gentle. She had nothing to do with what had disturbed him. He stroked the back of her neck a moment, receiving a purring murmur in return. Then, with great care, he reached with both hands to slip out from under her. She settled onto the sheet without stirring. He sat up.

What was wrong was simple and obvious. The ship had stopped once again. The turbines were quiet.

Again with care, he rose and went to the porthole. They had more than stopped. They had arrived. The mad captain and crew of this beleaguered vessel had sailed on at full press through the night, and now the *Wilhelmina* was at Sandy Hook, just off New York harbor. It was first light, and he could see the hazy forms of refinery tanks on the murky western horizon—a well-remembered sight from previous voyages.

He pulled on his white shirt and a pair of gray flannels, slipping his bare feet into the cold leather of his patent leather evening shoes.

Nora still slept. Out the porthole, he could see the pilot boat approaching—and something else. A small warship sitting perhaps half a mile off. Rolling up his sleeves, Spencer went out the door and down to the boat deck.

The pilot boat was coming at high speed, planing somewhat and throwing up a spume of wake. Just beyond it, traveling more slowly, was another small craft, a naval launch, apparently from the warship. As it drew nearer, Spencer saw the British Union Jack flying from the stern. The boat was white with varnished wood trim and the crewman aboard it were standing at attention, very formal and dignified.

What with the stiff morning breeze and the noise of the boat engines, Spencer hadn't heard the woman approach. Resting her elbows on the rail beside him, she startled him.

"Good morning, Your Ladyship," he said, "You're up early."

"Good morning," said Diana Cooper. "Wouldn't miss it. That's a destroyer there. The *Fury*. They're taking him away."

"The prince."

"Yes, the prince. And a few of his loyal retainers, though not, thank God, me and Duff. We've a bit of a bash planned for New York. My producer from *The Miracle* sent a wire. We're going to have a jolly good reunion. Would you like a squiff of vodka, Lieutenant Spencer?"

She handed him a silver flask.

"Gets the day going, what?" she said, giving him the sort of smile that made it clear how she was once known as the most beautiful woman in the world.

"Thank you," he said, accepting the flask, putting aside his memory of her conduct in Duff's attempted seduction of Nora. "In celebration of our safe arrival."

"Precisely," she said, with a bit of a wink. "And the prince's safe departure. God speed, God bless, and thank God."

She watched the launch with some fascination, allowing him to study her face in profile. Hers was a unique yet perfect profile. It was a pity what age was about to do to her.

"What do you mean?" he asked.

"We should all be very, very nice to Mrs. Simpson," said Lady Diana. "I think she's going to do the world—certainly the empire—a very great favor."

"With the prince? I don't understand."

"Of course you do, Lieutenant Spencer. Don't be obtuse." She took a deep breath of the morning air. "What a wonderful day. I think we'll ride up Fifth Avenue on one of those open-top, double-deck buses. I don't know why ours are enclosed, really. One's always bumping one's head."

The pilot boat was alongside now. A door had been opened at the side of the ship below decks, and the pilot, a gray-haired man in a tweed suit, stepped nimbly from the bobbing boat into the *Wilhelmina*. An instant later the bow of the boat swung away and it roared and rumbled off toward the shore, the helmsman throttling the engine up to full power.

The British naval launch, which had been standing off, came up, much more sedately. Two lines were tossed to crewmen of the *Wilhelmina*, who tied them fast, pulling the launch snug against the ship.

The prince and Mrs. Simpson appeared almost immediately. He, dressed in a vested suit, leapt aboard the launch ahead of her, then turned to help her over the gunwale. A crewman helped, as well, but still she stumbled. Spencer, six stories above, could hear her swear.

Edward took her to the rear of the launch and held her close. She put her head on his shoulder, as if apologizing for her outburst. It was a poignant scene.

"Pathetic, aren't they?" Diana said. "A prime case of sadomasochism, if you believe the psychologists, and, these days, one certainly must."

More people came aboard the launch. The Scotland Yard inspector Runcie, Major Metcalfe and Lord Brownlow, Lady Emerald and Chips Channon, of course Lord Mountbatten, though not Edwina. As soon as the prince and Mrs. Simpson were seated and a huge amount of luggage taken aboard, the seamen cast off the lines.

"Good-bye, darlings!" Diana shouted. When they looked up, she waved. Spencer found himself waving, as well, wondering if he would ever encounter Chips Channon again, or would want to. As the boat pulled away, the prince waved back.

"Lieutenant Spencer," said Diana. "There's something I should like to say. I want to apologize, and Duff wants to apologize, for that grubby little scene in His Highness's suite yesterday. It was quite beastly, and you should pay no attention to it. If you want to rush hotfoot into writing your little story, you go right ahead. If they don't know the risks of traveling abroad so infamously like this, well, they'd bloody well better learn."

"The American press is going to be onto them, sooner or later. They'll have no compunctions."

"Quite. I daresay the British papers will restrain themselves only for a time. And, just between the two of us, I think it's a bloody good thing."

She took Spencer's hand and shook it. "Well, I'm off, Lieutenant Spencer. We're booked on one of Emerald's liners departing in two days' time, and we've got lots planned for New York beforehand. I must get ready. Haven't done a thing, really."

She looked at him carefully, squinting against the early-morning sun.

"You're not a bad sort, really," she said. "We absolutely adore Chips, but you deserve better friends."

"I have them."

"Yes. She's lovely. You're a lucky chap. Well, off I go. In a few days we'll be back in Europe and all that horrid Abyssinia business. Do enjoy yourself. I hope we shall meet again sometime."

She walked quickly away. She was beautifully dressed, all in white.

The motor launch was nearing the British destroyer. History was in motion. Spencer could be part of it. Just one long, fascinating story. By now he'd worked it all out in his mind.

He lingered at the rail a moment longer, then started back for his quarters. As he made a turning in the corridor, he heard murmuring voices. Continuing on, he saw that it was Edwina and a ship's officer, in an embrace—a morning's farewell. He retreated and waited a moment. When he made the turn again, they were gone. The officer had been young Kees, who after the past night was likely quite a bit older.

Perhaps she was just showing her gratitude for Kees's saving the life of her husband. Spencer started to laugh in his mind at that notion, but caught himself. Instead, he would believe in it. This was, after all, a quite beautiful morning.

Nora was still packing, a travail that she'd abandoned the night before to accommodate her passion—and his. There was no passion now. She was very fussy and businesslike as she moved about their—her—suite. Every dress and gown was a major concern. She'd called in a maid to help. Once again she was Nora Gwynne, star of stage and screen.

"The captain has invited us to join him on the bridge when we sail into the harbor," she said. "It's a great honor."

Arriving at New York on the deck of a ship, more particularly standing on its bridge, is perhaps the only way to reduce that sprawling, gigantic slag heap of a metropolis to human dimension, or to increase oneself to its. One feels a giant, as well, able to reach out to either shore. After the immensity of the nearly limitless sea, the New York harbor seems a small and confining place, certainly impossible to navigate without ships' pilots and all those darting, chuffing tugboats.

The Chrysler and Empire State buildings rose towering above the smaller structures of Manhattan as they approached the Narrows. The upper harbor was filled with every manner of craft, ferry boats moving in every direction, freighters at anchor, fireboats, and more tugboats racing to meet them.

"Steer two ninety degrees," said the pilot, his gaze fixed on the channel ahead.

"Steer two ninety," said van der Heyden, standing with arms carefully folded just beside.

"Steering two hundred ninety degrees," repeated the quartermaster at the helm.

Spencer, Nora, and the other invited guests stayed back against the rear bulkhead of the bridge area, keeping out of the way. Out the port windows, they saw the figure of the Statue of Liberty. It had been four years since Spencer had been in the United States.

"You can step out onto the bridge wing, if you like," said Mr. van Hoorn of the Lage Lander Line. "We won't be needing it until docking at the pier."

It was a glorious place to observe their arrival. Other ships and boats were saluting them with blasts of horns and sirens as they passed, honoring their maiden voyage, the sound echoing off the metal of the *Wilhelmina* in the now-crisp, clear air. The fireboats shot up sprays of fountaining water, like spuming whales. The tugboats nestled close, like little lovers. The full ship's orchestra was on deck, playing an American military march with unrestrained enthusiasm. All the ship's flags and bunting were flying from the rigging. Streamers were sailing through the air. People were drinking, lifting celebratory glasses, bottles, and flasks. The blackened section of the superstructure aft of first class did not seem to matter, except perhaps as a symbol of their triumph over disaster. They had crossed the ocean. They were alive. Lives had been changed by this voyage, Spencer's immensely. He put his arm around Nora's waist. She placed her arm around his.

"We have a corner suite at the Plaza," she said. "Overlooking Central Park. It's supposed to be enormous."

"I'm all for it, but it'll be a couple of hours before we can get clear of quarantine and customs," he said.

"I still love you," she said into his ear. "Even though our shipboard romance is over. I'm told hotel romances can be even nicer."

"Not in Toledo," he said.

"What?"

"A joke. It depends on the hotel."

"There are nice hotels in Toledo."

"I'm sure there are, but let's be grateful for the Plaza."

An American warship, a small aircraft carrier with a dozen or more large biplanes on its deck moored along the New Jersey shore, sounded horn and sirens as they came past, sailors waving hats and cheering. The *Wilhelmina* responded with its own horn, the thrill of its reverberations passing up Spencer's and Nora's legs and backs. She held him tighter.

"Such a happy ending, after such sadness," she said. "I almost didn't expect a happy ending."

The bridge door slid open as they passed the Battery. Van der Heyden, van Groot, the pilot, and a crewman stepped outside, rendering the bridge wing very crowded.

"If you'll please excuse us now," said the captain, who was looking purposeful but cheerful. In a few minutes he would no longer ever again have to be responsible for a ship, its passengers, or crew—let alone female assassins. He had also had three Bols gins.

"Let's go up to the bow," Nora said. "I don't want to miss a minute of this."

A crewman that chained the entrance to the companionway leading down to the forward deck at first hesitated when they asked to be let by, but then relented. He, like all the crew, now knew them to be important and famous.

There was a breathless moment as the ship turned into the slip and nosed toward its pier. A line was tossed to a man on the dock and he and several of his fellows pulled on it until it drew out the heavy main hawser. When it was secured, two of the tugs on the other side began pressing at the stern of the *Wilhelmina* until she was flush with the pier and more lines were dropped over the side. The engines stopped. Their silence and the lack of motion beneath their feet were strangely unsettling. Spencer kissed Nora's forehead.

"Congratulations," he said.

She smiled. "I've still more packing to do. Come help."

"In a moment. For some peculiar reason, I don't feel in a great hurry to leave the ship."

As soon as the *Wilhelmina* was cleared through quarantine, a horde of reporters and photographers swarmed aboard. Moving in a pack, they paused to ask information of officers and crewmen, then fanned out through the ship, a small mob of them gathering noisily outside Nora's door.

She opened it a few inches.

"Wait for me in the first-class lounge," she said to them.

"We need pictures, Nora!" one of them shouted.

"I have a deadline!" another protested.

"Wait in the first-class lounge!" said Spencer. He shut the door on them. Was he like them? Had he been like that at the first sailing of the *Normandie* from Le Havre?

"A pack of beasts," Nora said, "as Lady Diana would say."

Olga had been waiting. She stood by the wall beside her locked door. In her hands was the heavy lid from the top of the toilet tank from the cabin's small bathroom. Her swollen right wrist hurt from the effort, but she steeled herself to it. This was vital. It meant her life.

The door opened and a crewman stepped in. He got out the word "Miss" just before Olga banged the porcelain weight down on his head. The loud sound made her wonder if she had killed him. He dropped to the floor instantly. She had no time to worry further about him, for another crewman was just behind him. Olga struck him in the face with the toilet top. She was certain she broke his nose. Blood came spewing forth from it as he staggered back.

She had only one chance—just one chance left in all her life—and she took it, leaping past the injured man and up the stairs, running madly and panting heavily as she reached the promenade deck. Without pausing, she bolted out onto the planking and clambered over the railing. She heard someone shout as she dropped to the water.

Nora was the center of attention at the press carnival in the first-class lounge, but some of the reporters began to drift away when, in response to so many shouted versions of what amounted to the same question, Nora began to repeat herself. She had hoped they would ask her about her new play, but they were treating the *Wilhelmina*'s crossing as a disaster akin to the *Titanic*'s and Nora as the principal heroine. They were not at all interested in anything else.

"How scared were you, Miss Gwynne?"

"Is it true Lord Mountbatten was aboard and that he was the hero who steered your lifeboat back to the ship?"

"How did those people in your lifeboat get killed?"

"Will you ever go to sea again, Miss Gwynne? Will you ever go back to Europe?"

A photographer pushed through close to the settee where Nora was sitting, followed by others.

"Our turn now. Hey, Nora. Can you cross your legs?"

Spencer moved away. This was part of the business of being a movie star, a glamour goddess, and there was nothing he could do to make things easier for her. The vulnerable little girl from Toledo would have to revert to her public persona now. And she seemed well disposed to do it.

Someone clutched at his arm. "Spencer! I thought you were in Paris. What were you doing in her room? Did you get aboard early for an interview, or were you on this ship?"

It was a reporter from the *Chicago Tribune* named Henry Pullen, whom Spencer had not seen since they'd covered a prison fire together in Columbus, Ohio, in 1930. Built for 1,500 men, the penitentiary had housed 4,300, and 318 of them had burned to death. Pullen had won a prize for his story.

"I thought they'd sent you to South America," Spencer said.

"They did. Now I'm in New York. Were you on this ship? What were you doing in Nora Gwynne's stateroom? You don't seem to be asking any questions."

"Yes. I was on this ship."

"You want to give me a fill?"

"The ship had electrical problems. It caught fire. A few people burned to death and some drowned when the lifeboats were put to sea in a storm. Now if you want a personal account, there are several hundred people aboard who I'm sure would be glad to give you one. Don't ask for it from the competition, Henry."

Pullen, a heavyset man in a thick wool suit, leaned closer.

"We got word out of our Paris bureau that the Prince of Wales might have been aboard," he said, with lowered voice.

"Why would Prince Edward be aboard a ship like this?"

"It sounded crackpot to me, too, but then we heard that his cousin Louis Mountbatten was on her, and maybe some friends of his." He lowered his voice still further. "There's talk about a woman, too, from Baltimore."

"The Prince of Wales and a woman from Baltimore. That would be a hell of a story. You fellows are drinking too much."

"Haven't touched a drop today, but let's go get one. I've got enough stuff from Nora Gwynne."

Spencer glanced back at her. She had crossed her legs again and was arranging her skirt higher on her knee. She smiled brilliantly. The camera flashes began exploding.

"Okay, Henry. A drink. Just one."

Nearby, Diana Cooper was posing for a lone photographer, looking flattered.

Then came the shouting—no one could tell from where: "Woman overboard! Woman overboard!"

The newsmen began pulling away from their interview, jostling each other. There was a commotion down the passageway. People were rushing to get to the starboard side, out onto the promenade deck. By the time Pullen and Spencer reached it, so many were packed against the rail that the *Wilhelmina* went into its famous list, causing two or three people to cry out.

Down far below, swimming away from the ship in a struggling arc, was the woman, dark hair spreading out on the grimy surface. She gave up the crawl and went into a slower breaststroke. Dark clothing was visible, including a long skirt. It must be heavy with water, working against her progress like an anchor, Spencer thought. She could not know her peril.

The crew was trying to lower the starboard side rescue motorboat to pursue her, the same one that had kept her and all the Prince of Wales' party alive through the fire and storm. The crewmen were being thwarted by the list and malfunctioning davits. The officer in charge was again Kees, the fugitive in the water his Eastern European woman.

She was slowing. After the enormous openness of the sea the slip between the two confining piers must have seemed a narrow place, a short swim to freedom. Down there, in the cold, greasy water, it must have looked like miles to the other side, which was why she was swimming in an arc. She had given up her attempt to reach the opposite pier and was now trying for the dock ahead of the ship. Could she be so oblivious to the passengers and crew at the railings and in the rigging watching her every stroke? Could she not see the several policemen waiting along the pier for her approach?

Someone threw a life preserver toward her from the bow, and then another. They both fell far short and anyway she ignored them, concentrating on her slow, painful, weakening swimming strokes, her face dipping more and more into the slimy water.

They had the motorboat sliding downward now, Kees at the helm. It struck the surface with a heaving splash and the engine started with a puff of smoke bubbling out of the exhaust. Kees drove the craft hard, steering to the side a few times to make certain that he was not about to strike her, that she was still there. The final time he did this, she had disappeared. As they could see from the deck of the *Wilhelmina*, she slipped under the surface when the motorboat was still fifty feet or more from her. It was like the Parker boy and the Countess von Kresse. Olga simply ceased to be.

Nora had joined Spencer and now turned into his arms, pressing her head against his shoulder, away from the scene below.

"I don't understand," said Pullen. "Didn't the first officer say she was a murderess or something? Didn't she try to kill Louis Mountbatten? Why all this effort to save her?"

"Jimmy," Nora said. "I want to get off this ship! Right now! I don't want to look at it ever again."

The taxi scarcely had room for the two of them what with Nora's trunk and the rest of their luggage. They sat close together.

"The Plaza Hotel," Spencer told the driver.

Nora was holding his hand. "We'll stay here only about a week, I guess," she said.

Spencer said nothing, listening to the rattle of the taxi over the bricks of the pavement, the sound and feel of solid land, of the United States, of New York, one of his favorite cities.

"You do want to come to Philadelphia with me, don't you? You said you did," she said.

"Sure I do."

"Good. Because I'm really going to need you."

When the cab swerved up to the hotel's 59th Street entrance, a doorman and two porters leapt forward at the sight of so much luggage. Spencer lingered in the seat as she started out the door.

"You settle in," he said. "I want to keep the cab."

"Where are you going?"

"To the seedy little office in the *New York Times* where the Chicago *Press-Bulletin* has its bureau here."

"But what for?"

"I have to do something, something I promised myself I'd do. At the moment it's the most important thing in my life. Don't worry. I'll be back well before time for dinner."

"The most important thing in your life?"

"After you."

"Is it your story? About the ship, and the voyage?"

He leaned to kiss her cheek. "Don't worry. I'll be back soon."

She touched his face with her gloved hand as she returned his kiss, but her eyes were troubled when she withdrew.

There was a brief rain shower while Spencer was gone, and the streets and sidewalks were still glistening with its remnants when he stepped out of the Times building. There was time for a drink and he decided to walk over to have one at the Algonquin, pausing to buy a late edition of one of the afternoon newspapers. It was a splashy Hearst paper, with the front page full of stories about the *Wilhelmina*'s arrival and its difficult passage. There was also a four-column front-page photo of the *Wilhelmina* taken from the side and showing the dramatic extent of the fire damage.

He went into the small bar off the lobby to the right of the hotel's entrance, took a seat at the only available table, and ordered himself a large congratulatory drink in honor of what he had just accomplished. Then he began to read the stories. For all its length, the main one was rather sketchy, and padded with reports of other ships' misadventures during the hurricane, including the foundering of the *Rotterdam.* The sidebars were more fleshy, filled with vivid writing. One was about "the hero captain" who had badly burned himself trying to put out the fire with his own hands. There was another about Mountbatten's assisting in the navigation and his other heroic exploits. It noted he'd been transferred to a British destroyer off Sandy Hook to sail for duty in the Abyssinian crisis. A breathless piece told of Nora's brave endurance of the perils, and was accompanied by a photo of her and her charmingly arranged legs. The casualty list described all the deaths and injuries as accidental. The passenger list was rather incomplete. Spencer's name was not on it, nor was Lord Brownlow's or Fruity Metcalfe's.

There was no mention of Lindbergh, of course. Spencer was certain he'd remain in hiding on the ship and then slip off to his home in New Jersey sometime during the night.

There was no mention of the prince or Mrs. Simpson, not even the wispiest gossip or vague unfounded report.

The "biggest goddamn sonofabitching scoop of the century," as the *Press-Bulletin*'s managing editor, Charles F. Duffy, would doubtless gracefully proclaim it, belonged to no one—yet.

Finishing and paying for his drink, Spencer folded the paper, knowing that Nora would read every word raptly, and stepped out onto 44th Street, humming to himself. He had not felt so gloriously happy in years. He could not think of when he had felt so much accomplishment, so much freedom, so much independence—so very much his own man.

Alone at last late that night in Nora's twelfth-floor suite, both flung themselves into their lovemaking with a furious passion—and more abandon than they had ever experienced on the ship. A long, sleepy, happy interval followed, but at length she sat up, trembling.

"I'm scared, Jimmy. I can't go to sleep. I keep remembering things."

"Come with me," he said, extending his hand. "Come to the window."

He turned off the lamp nearest it and pulled her close. They leaned forward, the better to see through the darkened glass to the scene below.

Central Park stretched from the few hansom cabs still lingering on 59th Street below past ponds and zoo and out in a vast expanse of blackness laced with necklaces of tiny street lights. Great and extraordinary buildings extended northward as boundaries, those along Fifth Avenue immediately to their right the most bright and colorful. A parade of automobile headlights, seeking destinations they could not imagine, moved along the boulevard, north and south.

"This is your place, Nora," he said, softly. "This is the most stylish, elegant, beautiful corner in this entire city. It represents everything that is classic and great about New York. Scott Fitzgerald wrote about this place. John Dos Passos wrote about it. Henry James wrote about it endlessly. This is your place, Nora. You belong to it, and it belongs to you. Put everything else out of your mind. Forget what we've been through. You're home now. You're home—with me."

She leaned her head forward until it touched the cold glass of the window, still with an arm around him.

"It is so beautiful," she said. "So very, very different from what I saw out my window when I was a child."

"It's yours, Nora."

"Are you mine, Jimmy?"

"Of course. Here I am."

She took him back to the bed. They made love again, with much less ardor but with much more tenderness, and eventual contentment. Within the hour they were asleep.

It was not much later—still well into the dead of night—that First Officer van Groot, now in command of the *Wilhelmina* and the skeleton crew remaining on board, acted to carry out the decision made by the Lage Lander Line that afternoon. With passengers, injured, dead, and cargo all removed—and special passenger Charles Lindbergh taken quietly across the river on a launch sent by the governor of New Jersey—with stores removed and trucked off to be sold to New York restaurants, the wounded ship was set loose from its moorings and pulled slowly out of the slip by tugboats nearly invisible in the darkness.

The destination was Brooklyn's Erie Basin and the shipyards there. If the *Wilhelmina,* which had performed so ably and nobly in the last dash to port, could be repaired and refitted without astronomical cost and losses to the company, the assessment would be made there. If it was decided that their only course was to scrap her, that could be accomplished in the same place.

With all lights out except for those on the hauling tugs, and with considerable assistance from the Coast Guard and New York City police marine units, the new, magnificent, incomparably beautiful, and now much-mutilated ocean liner made its ghostly progress downriver and then across the southern tip of Manhattan. As the macabre waterborne procession, remindful of the medieval gangs who dragged away the dead during the Black Plague, approached the lights of the Brooklyn Navy Yard, there was a rending groan of collapsing metal along the waterline by boiler rooms 4 and 5. The great vessel began to sag and settle at the stern. Then, as water rushed into the rupture, she capsized fully and finally in shallow water. All hands were saved but two—Oriental crewmen whose names were not even mentioned in the morning newspapers, except for *The New York Times.*

# CHAPTER
## *NINETEEN*

The restaurant in Philadelphia's Barclay Hotel was a gloomy, high-ceilinged room, hardly made more cheerful by this gray, drizzly January day. Spencer had arrived first and taken a table near one of the windows. She was late, which surprised him, as she had all of two blocks to come, from just across Rittenhouse Square.

He had gone through most of his paper by the time she arrived, looking as striking as he had remembered, a beautiful dark-haired, brown-eyed woman with pale skin, that day wearing a black coat, hat, suit, and gloves, with a single strand of pearls around her throat. She appeared rather older than she had on the ship, but perhaps they all did.

"I was afraid you weren't coming," he said, rising to greet her. She shook his hand somewhat gingerly, almost as if taken aback that he had offered his first. He'd not remembered that from the ship.

"I almost didn't," she replied, as the maître d' seated her. "I wasn't certain what this was all about."

"Would you like a cocktail?" he asked.

"No, thank you. I haven't had much taste for them since Christopher died."

"Do you mind if I do?"

"No. Not that it would make any difference."

"It would." He ordered a very cold and dry martini, despite the clammy January weather.

She pulled off her gloves, glancing at the headline on his newspaper.

"Good God, there it is," she said. "The old king finally died. Our pathetic little shipmate is king."

"*Le roi est mort; vive le roi.* Do you really feel that way about the prince?"

"If he weren't the prince, Mr. Spencer, who of us would have sought out his company?"

"I don't recall any of us going belowdecks to search for more charming company. On a ship, you take what you get. He's nobody I'd pick to drink with in Harry's Bar, but he wasn't really a rotter."

"Except on the lifeboat."

"I'll grant you that."

"Do you suppose Mrs. Simpson is still with him? I haven't seen her name once in the papers."

"I've no doubt that she is. I'm told she's written about all the time in the London society columns. She and Mr. Simpson are mentioned pointedly as guests at the prince's parties."

"How convenient for her and the prince. She must really have her clutches into him."

"As Edward has his into her."

"I've never understood social climbing like that. It's always seemed to me that there are greater concerns in life than one's social status."

"I used to think that, back when I had some."

She leaned back slightly and folded her hands in front of her, challenging him. "And now?"

He realized how little he knew about this woman, despite all they'd been through, in such close proximity.

"I still think that," Spencer said. "Probably more than before. But grant that Mrs. Simpson has had a hard life. I didn't tell anyone, but I encountered her once in China, back in the twenties, when she had left her rummy of a first husband and was supporting herself gambling and mooching. She had a rotten childhood. She must see all this splendor now as fitting compensation. Certainly revenge."

The elderly waiter came with Spencer's drink. "Would you like to order now?"

"Just tea for me," she said. "And perhaps some biscuits. I've already had luncheon, with my mother."

"Nothing more for me," Spencer said. He waited. "May I call you Chasey, Mrs. Parker?" he asked when the man had gone.

"I don't see why not. We've been about as intimate as two people can be, haven't we?—without actually being intimate. You saved my life." She blushed, a faint coloration of her very white skin. "You hauled me out of the water with an arm around my chest. The toilet

arrangements alone on that lifeboat qualify us for informal address."
The last sentence had some bitterness to it.

"They also caused your husband's death."

"Oh, let's not bring that up, shall we? It's bad enough that he's
gone, without going on about the wretched way he went."

"I'm sorry."

"All right. Forgiven."

They were silent a moment. Spencer noticed several ladies in the
room watching them.

"I chose the wrong place," he said.

"Don't worry about it. I knew where I was going."

"I daresay you were the best of us on that terrible little boat,
Chasey. Certainly the bravest. They shouldn't have treated you so
shabbily."

"They?"

"Some of those in the prince's party. My dear old 'friend' Chips
Channon."

"No one treated me shabbily. Everyone was under a lot of stress,
that's all."

He reached to touch her hand. "Well, I think you handled yourself
wonderfully."

She gently removed her hand and leaned back even farther. "Are
you staying in this hotel, Mr. Spencer? Jim."

"Yes. I've a room overlooking Rittenhouse Square."

"And is it your intention to get me up to it this afternoon?"

She might as well have struck him in the face. He really did not
know her. He had thought her more naive even than Nora. But then,
Nora hadn't proved so innocent herself.

"Why, no. Of course not. Why would you think that?"

"Because you went through practically every woman on that ship.
It's not unreasonable to suspect that you might be making a last stab
at one you happened to miss."

"I'm not a womanizer, Chasey. I'm just . . . all right, I've been on
the rebound."

"From someone you were really sweet on."

No one, not even his mother, would have described his relationship
with Whitney Ransom de Mornay as being "sweet on." He presumed
Mrs. Parker was being sarcastic. She must really be bitter, even tor-
mented. But why not?

The waiter brought her tea and asked again if Spencer was interested in luncheon. He shook his head.

"I didn't go through every woman on the ship," Spencer said. "I had a shipboard romance. They happen."

"And that crazy Nancy Cunard and Lady Mountbatten?"

"Not romances. And Nancy Cunard's not really crazy. She's a militant leftist and an alcoholic. That's all. I saw her later in New York. She's sobered up a bit. She's got a job and going back to Europe. To write for the Associated Negro Press. From Spain."

"The Associated Negro Press. I'm afraid I'm not familiar with it." She glanced away, then turned her head back quickly. "Oh, dear. There's my mother's best friend, not four tables away."

"I don't exactly look like an Apache dancer."

"No, you don't, but I shall have to explain you to Mother anyway."

"Just tell her I was one of those with you on the *Wilhelmina.*"

"Then I'll have to explain you even more." She fidgeted with her wedding ring.

"Why did you come today?" he asked.

"I suppose I'm still not thinking clearly. No, that's not fair. I'm thinking very clearly. I've been thinking very clearly all winter. I came because I owe you something. Because you were one of those who was very kind to me after—after the accident. And because I actually do like you—in something other than an intimate way. Essentially I wanted to know what had happened to you, and to Miss Gwynne."

Outside, the drizzle became heavy rain, blurring the window glass. He was glad of it, for it would discourage her from leaving soon.

"Miss Gwynne is in California."

"Why?"

"Because her play folded. It proved to be a comedy without many laughs."

"The reviews here weren't very good."

"In New York they were awful. The play lasted the full four-week tryout run here, but they killed it in less than two weeks in New York. Nora said she'd never go on Broadway again."

"I came to see it one night when it was here. I couldn't tell if it was good or bad. I just wanted to see Miss Gwynne, in another context than aboard that ship, alive and well and happy after what we'd been through. I thought it might help me as a sort of example. Perhaps it did in a way."

"I wish I had known. I'd been hoping to run into you, knowing you lived here. I thought of you often."

She lighted a cigarette. He'd not seen her smoke at all on the *Wilhelmina.*

"Somehow I hear the sound of your room key turning again," she said with an edge to her voice.

Spencer ignored this. "Nora was devastated for a few days. But she got over it. She's going to make another movie. A comedy with Roland Young and Billie Burke. I'm sure it will restore her reputation."

"Why didn't you go with her?"

"I couldn't make up my mind what I wanted to do, Chasey. I quit my job as soon as we got to New York, my job with my father's newspaper. I hung on with Nora afterward, probably for too long. But I couldn't go to California with her."

"Why did you quit? Jobs are hard to get."

"Because I wouldn't give them what they wanted from me if I was to keep it."

"The story about what happened on the voyage. You never wrote it, did you? I was sure you would. I looked through the *Inquirer* and *Bulletin* every day, but there was no reference to anything you might have written. I have to say I was quite surprised. I was betting you were going to let them have it good. A real sock in the nose."

He finished his martini.

"Are you going to have another one of those?"

He looked down at the empty glass and frowned. "No," he said.

"Good," she said. "Why didn't you write the story? You could have made quite a name for yourself. Those people had it coming. They still have it coming. You owe nothing to them. Why didn't you?" She seemed almost angry with him, as if she had been looking to him as an instrument of vengeance.

"I had a lot of reasons. Some lofty and noble. I wanted to protect some people, including you and Nora. And someone you don't even know about. I didn't want to ruin the reputation of that poor captain, who went out such a hero, and who I think was a hero, even if in the end he was probably responsible for the sinking of his ship. I had some ignoble and craven reasons, too. I didn't want Edwina to think I was trying to get back at her that way. I was also afraid I might not be believed. And that I might get sued. That they'd find some way to get me.

"But, honestly, really honestly, in the end I put all that aside. I would have done it anyway. It would have made my success, and I've needed some success. What stopped me was how worried they all were about me. If people as important in the world as they are supposed to be could be so concerned about what a beat-up, inconsequential man like me might do, then something was terribly wrong. It came down to the fact that I really didn't want to interfere with, well, I suppose, history. The shape of things to come. The fate of the kings of England, the fate of Europe, it's nothing a person like me should be deciding, especially with what's happening, the way everything's going to hell. A newspaperman shouldn't go crashing around in matters that important. Long or short, Edward and Mrs. Simpson's romance will run its course. I don't want to see it aborted by a scandal worked up by some fellow like me, someone who's probably just looking out for himself, looking to make a big personal score, certainly not now that Edward is to be king. To do something like that would scare the hell out of me. There have been newspapermen who've done things like that in the past and they've caused all kinds of terrible trouble. The thought of it scared the hell out of me the one time I sat down at a typewriter to see what I could write about them, about everything."

"But it will get out about them, eventually, if they keep on the way they have been."

"That's true, but that's up to them. Not me. I was just an uninvited guest."

The waiter was hovering. Spencer motioned for the check. She stubbed out her cigarette.

"May I see you home?" he asked.

She laughed, a brittle sound, as Edwina might have laughed. "Certainly not."

"How about across the square?"

She sighed. "To the center of the square." She looked out at the rain. "But it's ridiculous. You shouldn't soak yourself just to go less than a block."

"I only need to get my hat and coat from my room. I won't be but a moment. You can wait for me in the lobby."

She looked at him pointedly. "I'd rather avoid any more encounters with my mother's friends. I'll tell you what I'll do, Mr. Spencer. Jim. I'll be bold and brazen and accompany you to your room. Just long enough for you to get your coat and hat. If that's well understood."

He was confused, but tried not to look it. "Understood."

No one but the desk clerk and a bellman saw them go into the elevator and no one but a grumbling, distracted maid noticed their entering his room. Chasey Chatham Parker went directly to his window and stood looking down at the rainwet pavement below while he fetched his coat. She did not move when he shut the door to his closet.

"This wasn't the room you had with Nora Gwynne while you were here, was it?" she asked, still looking out the window.

"No. As usual, she had a very spacious suite."

"You haven't told me why you didn't go on to California with her. It's a lovely life out there, I'm told."

"It's the land of buccaneers and barbarians. The dictators in Europe at least act out of some small degree of political motivation, some principle, however evil. Those sleazy tyrants who run Hollywood are only interested in greed and self-indulgence. I'd rather work for Marshal Pidulski or Mussolini, much as I despise them both."

"You don't really mean that?"

"No, but I enjoy saying it."

She laughed. "And so it was au revoir, Nora. Only there will be no 'revoir.' "

"As I say, as she used to say, it was a shipboard romance. I'm grateful for the time we had afterward, though, here and in New York. It taught me what it would be like to be a kept man. I was offered that prospect, back in Europe—as a means of staying there."

"By the woman in Paris. That Whitney."

"How do you know about her?"

"There's a lot of gossipy talk that goes on with all that idle time aboard ship. You told Edwina Mountbatten about her and Lady Mountbatten can be a very chatty lady. I just listened. I didn't say anything, but I listened."

"Her name is Madame Whitney Ransom de Mornay. Her husband is as rich as I'm not. It was her idea to institutionalize our ménage à trois by maintaining residences with both her husband and me. I was to quit my job and devote myself to the more romantic of her many needs. Flaubert, Verlaine, flowers in the Tuileries, and strolls along the Seine."

"Is that her picture on your bureau?"

"Yes."

"She's quite lovely."

"Yes."

"We should go now, Mr. Spencer. But first I want you to come here."

Entirely confused now, Spencer came to stand before her. She studied him a moment, then reached to hold his shoulders with her hands and lifted her head to kiss him, once, gently, without opening her lips. Holding him firmly to prevent this encounter from becoming a full embrace, she then stepped back.

"That was not an invitation, Jim," she said. "That was a farewell. I did it to show you that I take you as a man of your word and that I trust you. I did it to show you gratitude and affection and friendship. But I'm not interested in an affair. I'm that way. I came to your room to kiss you because I couldn't think of any other place that would be seemly to do it."

"*Entendu.*"

"Now let's go, please. I've been here much too long."

But at the door to the outside corridor, she paused again.

"Jim. Do you need any money?"

"No."

"I've so damned much money now. You tried to help us. You saved me. I'd be glad to help. No strings. No involvement. I'd really like to."

"Chasey, no. The whole point of this, of what I'm doing, is that I don't plan to need money ever again, not the way I've always needed money. Please don't be offended. I'm grateful, I'm flattered. I'm touched. I feel even more warmly toward you than I already did. But no. No, and thank you very much."

"Then let's not say another word about it."

As they waited for the elevator, she lighted another cigarette, somewhat nervously.

"What are you going to do?" she asked.

"I'm going to Spain," he said. "It's the next big crisis in Europe. There's an election there next month that could tear the country apart."

"You're going as a correspondent?"

"Yes. It's what I do."

"But I thought you said you quit your job?"

"I did, with a great deal of pleasure and relief. I'm a free man now. I'm going to work for myself. I'll sell my reports to whoever will buy them. You can do quite well with that if you've got good stuff. I've talked to the *Chicago Tribune* and they're interested. They've read my work for years in the *Press-Bulletin,* and my father and Colonel McCormick were kindred souls. Belonged to the same fox hunt, don't you know. I've also talked to NBC. There are easy ways now to broadcast news reports from Europe over the wireless. I really find it exciting. I'm almost cheerful."

"Imagine you cheerful."

The elevator arrived, empty but for the attendant.

"This has nothing to do with Nancy Cunard?" she asked as the doors closed.

He laughed softly. "Heavens, no. If I see her in Madrid, I might buy her a drink. If you run into her anywhere, you've no choice but to buy her a drink."

"And Whitney, will you see her again? Will you go back to her?"

The elevator operator tried to feign inattention, but was listening intently. Spencer wondered if he knew who Chasey Parker was and decided he probably did. She was putting her reputation at some risk.

"No, I won't go back to her. And I probably won't ever see her again. She'd have to be willing to give up her life in Paris and come to me in Spain, or wherever else I go."

"And what are the chances of that?"

"About the same as your coming away with me to Spain right now."

The back of the elevator operator's neck was reddening.

"Then I feel very sad for you," Chasey said, "because there's no chance of that, now is there? But will you at least ask her?"

"No. What's done is done. *C'est fini. Tout fini.*"

The elevator doors opened. They turned down the Barclay's ornate main hall and crossed the narrow lobby, pausing at the door to raise coat collars and arrange hats.

"You haven't told me what you plan to do," he said.

"Why, Mr. Spencer, I plan to go on being what I've always been, a respectable young lady of Philadelphia."

They stepped outside. The rain had lessened from the downpour but was still coming down hard.

"Everything is so gray today," she said as they crossed the narrow street in front of the hotel and entered the park. "The sky, the street, the buildings—even the trees and grass."

"It's January that's the cruelest month."

"All this grayness reminds me of that poor Count von Kresse. I feel so sorry for him. It was for different reasons, but he and I did much the same thing out on that boat, didn't we? We bear the same kind of guilt."

"Don't say that."

"I won't then, but I think it. All the time. What do you suppose happened to him?"

"He said he was going back to Germany."

"And?"

"If that's the case, then I think he's probably dead."

They reached the fountain at the center of the square, full of water from the rain, but not functioning, its stone circle as cold and gray as everything else.

She turned to look at him one last time. He moved as if to pull her close, his own gesture of farewell, but she held him off by taking his hand, stiffly and formally. Her eyes were sad, but she offered him a weak smile.

"It was very good seeing you again, Jim," she said, giving his hand a slight squeeze. "Do look me up next time you're in Philadelphia."

Then she turned and hurried quickly away down the walk that led diagonally out of the square to the row of elegant townhouses opposite, a sad dark figure, eventually disappearing into the gloomy mist.

Von Kresse was escorted into the special chamber of the Reichschancellory by six members of Goering's most elite Luftwaffe guard. They moved in exact, perfectly timed military step, and the count had to extend himself painfully to keep up with them, but he managed it, remaining as proudly erect as any of them, willing to go through the worst possible agony to do so.

He had remained in the United States until December 21, when Lindbergh and his family secretly took ship on a United States Lines freighter with passenger accommodations and sailed to England. Von Kresse had met with the American again in London, on one occasion attending a small dinner party with Lindbergh thrown by the man who had become King Edward VIII. Then, knowing that his American friend would be following after, the count had gone on to Germany. He was received by a contingent of Goering's guards, Himmler's Death's Head S.S., and several Gestapo agents at the dock at Hamburg, and now he was here in Berlin, at the very center of the Reich's power.

In a few moments would come the most dreadful, ugly, and painful experience of his life, a life in which so much had been dreadful, ugly, and painful. But he had steeled himself to it, vowing to conduct himself through the agony of this ordeal with all the dignity he could summon. He would restrain himself from any outburst—somehow hold his tongue still when his soul's greatest yearning was to curse them all with every vile name he knew. He would keep himself from weeping when they brought up his sister Dagne. He would carry on through this as he had vowed to do, as a Prussian, as a man who loved his country, his people, as a man who must always do what he must do.

It would be over soon enough. All things came to an end.

Helmeted guards with automatic weapons opened the huge twin doors that led to the dark, shadowy, cavernous chamber beyond. At the far end, the malevolent waiting figures stood in a circle, bathed in bright light, the Reich's principal murderer at their center.

Von Kresse hesitated, and felt himself pushed firmly on by one of his Luftwaffe escorts. He continued further, step by echoing step, closer and closer, until at last he stood before them. As he had promised his now-so-important friend he would do, he then did what he had for years sworn he would never do. He clenched his stomach muscles to keep from vomiting, clicked his heels as smartly as his afflicted legs would allow, and shot his right arm into the air.

"Heil Hitler!" von Kresse said, so sharply the paneled walls reverberated with the sound.

They were all there—Goering, Heinrich Himmler, Admiral Canaris, Joachim "von" Ribbentrop, and Herr Shicklgruber, Der Führer. It was one of the highest-ranking ceremonial functions held in the Reich in months, though it was being conducted entirely in secret.

Hitler came forward, his eyes somewhat glassy, a boyish smile on his puffy face. He clasped von Kresse's arms with both hands, and for a moment the count feared the hateful little man was going to kiss him.

"My dear, dear Colonel," Hitler said, never a man to indulge the nobility with their titles. "I can't tell you how glad I am to see you. Or how badly I feel."

He stepped back and began walking about, as he liked to do when giving vent to his well-known hyperbole.

"Never have I been so wrong about a man," he said. "I, perhaps the most astute judge of moral character in the history of the world. I, who have perceived the weaknesses of every European leader arrayed against the Reich. I ignored your record of courage and gallantry in the war, your long years of loyalty to Germany in commanding forces defending our eastern border against the barbarians despite your painful infirmities."

He paused and swung about, his hands clasped behind his back.

"I thought you a traitor!" he suddenly bellowed. "An enemy of the Reich! An enemy of your Führer!"

His fierce expression melted and mellowed, and he recommenced his pacing.

"But look what you have done, and I have a full report now from all these gentlemen on everything that happened on that Dutch ship. Minister von Ribbentrop here even talked to an eyewitness, the Englishwoman, Lady Cunard. Well, my dear colonel, you have been nothing less than magnificent. You sacrificed your very own sister— your own flesh and blood—to save the life of the greatest friend the Reich has in England, the man who is now King of England! Your very own sister! With your very own hands!" He whirled about, startling the others. "Who among you has done as much for the Reich?"

Goering, Canaris, and Ribbentrop stood there silent, with vacant, stupid expressions on their faces. Himmler looked as if that very moment he would be happy to sacrifice his sister, mother, father, and wife to elicit the same adulatory remarks from his Führer.

Hitler calmed himself, motioning to an attendant to come forward with a small wooden box.

"And so you shall be rewarded," the Führer resumed. "In the war you were one of just six hundred eighty-seven brave fighting men, just eighty brave airmen, to win the Pour le Mérite. Fighting in the trenches, you won, like me, the Iron Cross. But now, Colonel . . ." He reached into the box and pulled out a bejeweled black cross hanging from a crimson ribbon. ". . . for your bravery, loyalty, and sacrifice, I award you the Knight's Cross of the Iron Cross with Diamonds."

As Hitler hung the ribbon around his neck, the others applauded. Von Kresse flinched when the Führer's hand brushed his cheek, then prayed that the man would not notice.

He didn't. He beamed. The others gave out a "Sieg Heil" in unison. Von Kresse stepped back as would be required in a parade-ground awards ceremony, clicked his heels awkwardly, and once again saluted, gritting his teeth as the words "Heil Hitler" once more came out of his mouth.

He knew that, in his own country, Charles Lindbergh would soon be making a similar sacrifice, and would pay a similar personal price.

# CHAPTER
## *TWENTY*

The spring rains had ended and the long season of dry heat had begun for the Spanish capital. By midsummer, it would make explicable every madness and dark passion of these smoldering-tempered Moorish Latins, so famous for their homicidal pride.

But this particular morning was strangely cool—a bright and sunny day full of light air and frequent breezes. It might have been Paris in May, or New York in October—not this sprawling pueblo on the plateau of Sierra de Guadarrama, this city of white buildings and women dressed in black, this place of dust and donkeys and death.

Spencer's idol Hemingway called this a sun-hardened country. Its harsh mountains and climate had been enough to defeat Napoleon, and the Duke of Wellington who vanquished his generals did not linger long. The Franks had defeated the Spanish Moors—but at Tours, not here. And if the Franks had won, they had not conquered. More an extension of North Africa than Europe, the Iberian peninsula had produced a people hard and cruel enough to conquer nearly all of South and North America, handfuls of sweating, helmeted men with muskets wiping out in a few years powerful Indian empires that had taken centuries to build. They had nearly destroyed France and England.

And now they were bent on destroying themselves.

Spencer and his workmates, like theater critics at a Roman arena, military historians counting the corpses at the battle of Canae, were there with their ledgers and notebooks, ready to record the debacle for history on flimsy, thin pages of newsprint that their stirring accounts would share with advertisements for new fur wraps available at Saks Fifth Avenue and Marshall Fields and reports of Alice Marble winning the U.S. lawn tennis women's singles championship.

The reporters who had been earliest on the scene—in time for the wrenchingly polarizing elections that had seen the militantly left-wing Popular Front seize power by the narrowest of margins—had taken the best rooms in the grand, sprawling Palace Hotel on the Plaza de las Cortes. Occupying a full, huge Spanish block and enclosing a thousand chambers, this Iberian version of Beaux Arts Parisian splendor could at least claim four vital necessities of life for the American and European correspondents—telephones that worked; usually running water; periodic electrical power; and a continuously open bar and wine cellar.

Spencer had taken a suite as an accommodation to those among his colleagues who were his friends. It was relatively early in the morning, as the Spanish went about daily life, but his associates had been out pounding hard for an hour or more. Dick O'Brien of the Irish *Times* and Ronny Batchelor of Reuter were working at typewriters, one set on a desk and the other on a room service table still holding spoiled fruit. Robert Rowley of the *Boston Globe* was puzzling over a communique from the new government, with glass of Tio Pepe and Spanish-English dictionary readily at hand. Jan Cawley of the United Press was talking to someone in the United States over one of the telephone lines in the suite; Nancy Cunard, sitting on the window sill, swinging her legs and swigging from a bottle of Paternina, was prattling on over the other phone with some editor in Harlem. They were disagreeing over some point in her story about the Negro antecedents of Spain's Moorish kings, the editor disputing any association with the sub-Saharan peoples most closely identified with bringing the joys of slavery to those who became American blacks, Nancy ragging him for some reason about Othello. Adding to the intensity of the dispute was the fact that it was just after four A.M. in New York. No one minded that Nancy went on so over the phones. She kept the lines open, and she was paying all the phone bills.

Bill Laingen came in, boisterous and cheerful, if utterly fatigued. His face was reddened and moist with sweat, despite the strange morning coolness.

"I come directly from the office of His Excellency the People's Premier Manuel Azana," he said, causing everyone in the room but Nancy Cunard to pause in what they were doing. Laingen took a sip of Rowley's Tio Pepe. "The office of His Excellency, et cetera, et cetera, wishes to announce that it has nothing to announce. Off the record, though, one of His Excellency et cetera, et cetera's secretaries discreetly informed me that there would be nothing to announce tomorrow, either."

There was laughter, and curses, and shaking of heads, then they all resumed what they had been doing, except for Nancy, who hung up her phone, took up her wine bottle, and went out into the white bright sun of the balcony. She sat down on its flooring and leaned against the railing, looking down on the street.

Spencer was by no means as amused as the others. Azana was feckless. The Popular Front, like Kerensky's provisional socialists in the first Russian Revolution of 1917, clung to a center that was rapidly vanishing. The militant socialists were pushing them to the left, the communists were pulling them violently in the same direction, and the anarchists who had so recently held so much power were standing off in contempt of all. The army, abetted mightily by the Church, was reacting with unexpected swiftness, emerging as the most potent foe of a Republic besieged from every ideological quarter. Attempts had been made on the life of the Right's most able political leader, Calvo Sotelo. Spencer was planning to write a piece—that day, if possible, certainly that week—warning of a right-wing revolution and the disaster of civil war. Ronny Batchelor was writing one at that very moment.

Laingen stopped by Spencer's chair, resting a hand on the back. He nodded to the main door of the suite.

"Someone in the lobby wants to see you, Jimmy. Won't go away until you come down."

"If it's that damned Colonel Cavello again he can go fuck himself. I don't want to go to Morocco—or devote my time here to getting Francisco Franco's name in the paper."

"It's not Cavello. It's nobody I've ever seen here before."

"I'm busy. I'm thinking. I've got a long piece to write, Bill."

"Long pieces. Long Spanish days. Take the time. Who knows?" Laingen finished his drink, then smiled. He was happy here.

Spencer leaned back in his chair, then flung out his arms and yawned; he ran his hands through his now sun-bleached, graying hair and sighed. He would investigate. The diversion would help distract from the tension.

The huge, airy lobby was filled with people sitting or moving about beneath the slowly revolving ceiling fans, many of them in uniform and most of them Spaniards. None of them paid any attention whatsoever to Spencer, however. He walked about the room, glancing into faces, receiving nothing but curiosity or hostility in reply. Then, to the side, he glimpsed a blur of white. He paused, closing his eyes a moment, taking a deep breath, calming himself and trying to concentrate his senses against what might be hallucination derived from fatigue. When he felt restored to normal, he turned, and looked again.

When they had first met in Paris in 1931, and shortly afterward had an unhappy dispute, he had written her a long, ardent, and fatalistic letter, telling her that the quarrel was compelling evidence that they were badly suited for each other and that she would be wise to continue with her husband and certainly to find a friend more worthy of her than he had been. It had been a cynical letter, disapproving of romance and human trust, laced with more than a little self-pity, and utterly calculated to make her wish not to have anything to do with him again. It also made clear that he deeply loved her, but that was phrased bitterly, so that she would understand that he expected nothing of it.

A day later she appeared in the lobby of his cheap hotel in Montparnasse, perched atop a radiator by the entrance stairs, having waited for him perhaps for an hour or more, unannounced, unsure that he would soon descend or even that he was there. When he had seen her there, an aristocratic blond apparition in that grimy green-painted squalor, seen her eyes so steady on him and her expression so full of the need to convince him of her fairness and decency and affection, he fell in love all over again. He fell in love forever.

And now there she was again, not on a radiator, but in a deep chair. Again she wore white, but this time a thin cotton dress, and sandals. She was tanned. She may have been in Madrid for several days looking for him.

But he had no words for her. None would come. He hesitated. He was oddly dressed in desert boots, wrinkled white cotton trousers, a dark-blue shirt, and a khaki bush jacket. She, as always, was so fashionably perfect. Spencer rubbed his chin. He had, at least, remembered to shave.

When he came before her, all he could say was "Dear God."

She stood up. "How about 'dear Whitney?' "

" 'Dear Whitney,' " he repeated.

"That's not much, is it? Let's try, 'dearest Whitney.' "

He took both her hands as she offered them. "You look marvelous. You're so tan. I thought it'd been raining in Paris."

"I stopped for a week in Biarritz. I wanted to think, on my own, about what I was doing."

This hotel lobby was not the place for the conversation that was coming next.

"Let's go someplace," he said, taking her arm as they started toward the hotel's main entrance. The touch of her bare skin thrilled and upset him.

He had no idea precisely where to go. The plaza was very bright with sunlight, and wonderfully pleasant. There was now a strong breeze, swaying the tree tops in the Parque del Retiro to the left. They stood a moment. He stared into her face, feeling like a child who had discovered he'd been given a present at Christmas he'd been yearning for all year. He wanted to touch her finely boned cheeks, to kiss those extraordinary blue eyes, run his hands through the long blond hair that was falling over her brow. This was the most beautiful woman in the world. He stood still, feeling awkward and uncomposed, but greatly excited.

"Why are you here?" he asked.

"Because you're here."

"How did you know where to find me?"

"Bill Laingen told me before he came down."

"Good old Bill."

"I asked him to. I'd been after him for weeks to find out for me where you were."

Spencer looked about again. A file of troops was marching along the far edge of the square. Nearer, some politician or agitator was haranguing a small crowd. Spencer found himself thinking of the riot in the Place de la Concorde the previous fall.

"We should go somewhere," he repeated "Have you ever been to Madrid before?"

"I've never been to Spain. Charles said there was only the bullfighting, and he despises bullfighting."

"There's more. Come on. I'll take you to the Prado."

"Jim! I didn't come all the way down here to go to a museum. I came to see you. I need—*we* need to talk."

"Just one painting." He took her hand. It was like their first time together, going to the Louvre.

They entered the cool, cavernous, echoing building as the Spanish did, reverently, as if they were going into a cathedral.

"What is it, this one picture?" she asked, keeping her voice low. "A Velasquez, a Goya, an El Greco?"

"No," he said. "It's Hemingway's favorite painting."

When they reached it, he watched her face. A look of surprise came and went, and then her hand went to her chin as she studied it.

"She's very beautiful," Whitney said.

"It's called 'Portrait of a Woman,' by Andrea del Sarto. Hemingway told us once in Harry's Bar that this was the only woman for whom he ever had any lasting love."

"Having read his books, I believe it," she said. She stepped back. "Well, it's quite wonderful, but it's not the greatest painting in the world. Now, show me your favorite painting."

"My favorite painting isn't here," he said. "It's in the National Galleries of Scotland. It's John Singer Sargent's 'Lady Agnew of Lochnaw.' If she had blond hair and blue eyes, she'd be you, except she's not quite so beautiful."

"Is that why it's your favorite? It's a facsimile of me? I've given you photographs."

"It's my favorite because you have sometimes looked at me the way she is looking at the artist. You still do often, in my dreams."

"Jim, please. Let's find a place to talk."

"All right. I know a café on the Calle Del Santa Isabel."

They walked through the botanical gardens, holding hands like youthful lovers. She looked about at the flowers as they passed, a bemused expression on her face, which suddenly clouded.

"All this beauty," she said, "but such ugliness here, too. They've painted slogans all over the walls, in blood-red paint."

"A lot of that's from the elections, but they put on new ones every day. I'm afraid the elections aren't really over."

"There was a dead man in the street by the railroad station. They were dragging him away as I came out. He had a sign around his neck. And in the cab, I glanced down a side street. There was a crowd of people chasing a nun, with sticks!"

"Do you remember the riots last October in Paris? I know you didn't pay much attention to them." He paused, regretting that. "I mean, you weren't there. But as awful as they were, what's going to happen here will be infinitely worse. That's why I've come. That's why I'll be here a long time."

She dropped his hand and they walked along in silence. In fact, she did not speak again until they were seated at their shaded outdoor table and he had ordered them each a chilled manzanilla.

"You said we had to talk," he said with an amiable smile. "But you've said nothing."

She was staring down at her hands.

"I love you, Jim. That's what I've come down to say."

"You said that the night before I left."

"Well, you left and were gone for months and I still love you. More than that, I know how much I love you. Your going away made me measure it, or try. It's really more than I can measure."

"Then you must know how much I love you."

"Even though you went away."

"Even though I went away. Perhaps especially because of that. I went away because I loved you so much and I couldn't go on, I couldn't accept what you were proposing."

Their drinks came. She ignored hers. He sipped his. When he set down his glass, she put her hand on his and looked searchingly into his eyes.

"There's something else I came down to say," she said. She paused, glanced away, then back. "I can't divorce Charles. Not if I want to stay in France. He simply won't permit it and his church won't permit it. He wants me to remain his wife, under any circumstances. And even if it were possible, I'm not sure I'd be able to go through it. I am so fond of him. He's been so kind to me. He's my family."

"Well, my dear. That leaves us precisely where we were when I took ship for America."

"No, it doesn't, Jim." She took his hand in both of hers now. "I was trying to create my own perfect little world and put you in your perfect little place inside it. I was thinking like a spoiled little girl. I wanted everything exactly my way, as Charles always arranged it, as my parents always arranged it for me. I'm so sorry for that."

He only sighed.

"Jim, I've changed. I've changed a lot. The only fixed thing in this for me is that I can't get a divorce. Otherwise, I want you on any terms, on your terms. Charles understands all this. Like a proper French gentleman, he has a mistress, for heaven's sake. I don't want to be your mistress, Jim. I want to be your love. For life. I want to be with your whenever I can. Whenever you can."

"Whitney."

"I'm not going to say 'please,' Jim. I'm not going to beg, or cry. I'm not that kind of woman. I know it's not enough, but it's all that I can offer. It's more than I would offer to any other man, including Charles. It's all we have, Jim. But it could work. We could have our love this way—forever."

"There is no forever."

"Please, Jim. Oh, dear. I've said it."

She released his hands and sat back, as though relaxing from the completion of some enormous task. She took a sip of her manzanilla, now gone a little warm, and then sought his reply with her eyes. He could see her age now in her face. The young girl was gone and she was fully a woman. She had never looked more beautiful. The most beautiful woman in the world. Yet she had never looked more vulnerable. He could see the self—the gentle, loving person—behind the beauty.

He drummed on the tabletop, then finished his drink.

"I'd like to think about all this," he said.

"Of course," she said. "I plan to be here a week, unless they start rioting and shooting. Unless you decide to say no."

"I have to get back to the hotel. I'm trying to set up a broadcast connection to New York for tonight."

"I couldn't get a room in your hotel. I'm in the Wellington."

"It's nearby. I'll walk you there."

They went back this time through the park, ignoring the sidewalk and instead strolling over the grass. They passed children playing and an old man asleep against the trunk of a tree. A small bird cried out and in darting flight passed in front of them, alighting for one brief instant on a branch, then flitting away to a higher one in another tree. The coolness was so unreal beneath such a bright and clear Spanish sky.

He did not take her arm or hand and she did not offer either. Because their conversation was still incomplete, because the great problem between them was so unresolved, physical contact was suspended. Everything between them was suspended.

"Jim," she said. "If there is a revolution here I'm so afraid you'll get hurt or killed. That's what's been on my mind most."

"It's on my mind once in a while, too. I don't do this because I love the sound of bullets, the way George Washington once said he did. And you can killed anywhere. I was almost killed just crossing the Atlantic on an ocean liner."

They walked on.

"All right," he said. "Just for you, I promise not to get killed."

They walked on still further. He paused, then led them on a few more paces, then stopped again, for good.

He took a deep, sighing breath. There were tiny tears at the edges of her eyes.

"All right," he said. "I guess I've thought about all this long enough."

"And the answer is no?"

"The answer is yes. Of course, damn it. *Certainement. Absolument.* Your terms, my terms, however we can do it. We're the best you and I are ever going to get. You're the—"

She didn't let him finish, and he probably would not have in any event. They came together shamelessly, thigh to thigh, chest to chest, arms enfolding each other so tightly they seemed as one. Her kiss was as warm and sweet as any he had had with her in his dreams. He was dizzy from it, yet he could feel the breeze and hear the sounds around them in the park with almost supernatural clarity.

They swayed slightly and turned slightly, their eyes still closed, their lips and bodies still together. An unwanted image crossed his mind of this same sylvan loveliness piled high with bloodied corpses in months to come, but as long as they held each other, as long as there was the scent of her, the feel of her, the brush of her golden hair against his cheek, then indeed he and Whitney and what they had would go on forever and ever.

She stepped back, her hands moving to his arms. She looked at him deeply.

"Everything will be all right," she said. "There is nothing in the world that's going to happen that can hurt us. Not here in Spain, not anywhere. We're going to go on as I said and everything will be all right. It will be wonderfully and perfectly all right."

And then she came close and held him tightly again, and the breeze came and ruffled their clothes and hair. He stopped listening to the sounds of the park.

# EPILOGUE

Edward Albert Christian George Andrew Patrick David Windsor was proclaimed King Edward VIII in the ceremonies attendant to the Proclamation of Accession at St. James Palace shortly following the death of his father in January 1936. Wallis Warfield Simpson, her husband conveniently in America, stood at his side. Within months, the story of their romance broke in the American press, favorably so in the newspapers of her admirer, William Randolph Hearst. When Mrs. Simpson later that year filed papers for divorce, and it was granted, allowing her to remarry by April 1937, the British press took up the story, forcing a constitutional and political crisis that resulted in the king's abdication that December. His brother, Albert Frederick Arthur George, the Duke of York, took the throne as George VI. Edward dined with him the night before, drinking whiskey while having a pedicure. Edward left the throne with a personal fortune of at least $32 million and an agreement was negotiated that guaranteed him an annual income of about $1.2 million a year.

He and Wallis Simpson were married in France in June 1937, with Fruity Metcalfe as best man. Part of their honeymoon was ironically spent in an Austrian *schloss* lent them by the famous French-Jewish de Rothschild family. In the fall of that year, they journeyed to Nazi Germany as stellar visiting guests.

Edward and Wallis spent much of their remaining lives as exiles living in Paris and New York. In 1940, after the Nazi conquest of France, they stayed for a time in Portugal, where they were a target of then–German Foreign Minister Joseph Ribbentrop, who planned to capture them and enlist them in a plot to restore Edward to the throne of England once the Nazis had conquered Great Britain.

Prime Minister Winston Churchill persuaded Edward to leave Portugal and become British governor of the Bahama Islands, an assignment at which the by then Duke and Duchess of Windsor proved abysmal failures.

After the war the duke devoted himself largely to golf, his garden, his wife, and her social life, creating a sort of cardboard version of a royal court both in Paris and New York. Though he returned to England for royal funerals and other official occasions, he was never again embraced by the royal family. Queen Elizabeth II paid him an obligatory and strained visit in Paris shortly before his death in 1972.

Wallis Warfield Spencer Simpson Windsor never received a royal title, though other nonroyal spouses, such as Edward's sister-in-law Elizabeth, wife of his brother King George VI, had received one upon their marriage. Edward persisted in calling Wallis "Her Royal Highness" after their marriage, but even such loyalists as Chips Channon and Lady Diana Cooper blanched at that.

The Duchess of Windsor devoted herself to her role as queen of what was called "café society" in the 1940s, 1950s, and 1960s, and to acquiring jewelry and expensive clothes. By the time of his death, the duke's fortune was much dissipated. In the 1950s her most frequent escort on her social rounds was not so much the duke as a wealthy and notorious homosexual named Jimmy Donahue, though the three of them were also frequently together. She later dropped Donahue after he began making public remarks about her sexual skills.

On the occasion of the duke's death, the Duchess of Windsor was invited to be a guest at Buckingham Palace for the funeral, but the royal family was absent during her stay. Later in the 1970s, the duchess's mental and physical health deteriorated rapidly. By 1979 she was bedridden and unable to communicate coherently. For much of the rest of her life, she was a virtual vegetable. Among her last lucid remarks was one expressing her fear that the royal family would not allow her to be buried next to her husband. It proved to be unfounded after she died in 1986 at the age of ninety.

Her jewels were bought up by actress Elizabeth Taylor, Arab speculators, and others for more than $18 million the next year at an auction held by Sotheby's in Geneva. Sotheby's hyped the sale by proclaiming the baubles that English high society had found so gaudy and tasteless as totems of "the love story of the century."

\*     \*     \*

Lord Louis Mountbatten went on to a distinguished naval career, ironically serving as the captain commanding the destroyer squadron that rescued the Duke and Duchess of Windsor from Nazi Europe after the fall of France.

Renowned as an inventor, innovator, and military reformer, Mountbatten was eventually promoted to Supreme Allied Commander, South East Asia, and won the noble title Earl Mountbatten of Burma. After World War II, he achieved a lifelong ambition by attaining his father's old job of First Sea Lord, and subsequently became Chief of the Defence Staff.

His greatest recognition came as postwar Viceroy of India, when he oversaw the independence of the colonial subcontinent and its partition into the separate countries of India and Pakistan. Though millions of Hindus and Moslems were killed in the violence that accompanied partition, many credit him with averting an even worse disaster.

Prince Edward had been the best man at his wedding, but Mountbatten remained somewhat distant from his royal cousin after the abdication. He became a favorite of the rest of the royal family and, after George VI's death in 1952, served as its patriarch. After Edward's death in 1972, it was Mountbatten who represented the royal family in making a visit to France to secure the crown property of Edward's still in Wallis's possession.

Lord Mountbatten was assassinated in 1979, when Irish Republican fanatics blew up his fishing craft off the coast of Ireland, killing also a grandmother and young boy who were aboard.

Lady Edwina, Countess Mountbatten of Burma, suffered a fate common to many of her hedonistic bent. Her beauty vanished by the time she turned forty in 1941. Though she did not completely abandon the bright society of which she had been such a luminescent member, she devoted most of her subsequent life to good works, throwing herself into and assuming command of a number of wartime and postwar relief, medical, and welfare efforts.

A friend of Indian intellectual Krishna Menon before the war, as Vicrene of India she, and her husband Dickie, became an intimate of Hindu leader Jawaharlal Nehru, the first Prime Minister of India. There is considerable debate as to whether their intimacy included that of a sexual nature, but they were beholden to each other for the rest of her life. She died in 1960 on a charity mission to North

Borneo, formerly part of the Dutch East Indies, of exhaustion and heart failure at the age of fifty-nine.

Duff Cooper was made minister of war the year following the *Wilhelmina* disaster, and he resigned in 1938 to protest Prime Minister Neville Chamberlain's "peace in our time" Munich pact with Hitler, which gave the German dictator a free hand with Czechoslovakia and encouraged him to launch the attack on Poland that resulted in World War II. Duff and his wife, Diana, subsequently toured the United States to enlist American support for the struggle in Europe. He was made Viscount Norwich and ended his official public career as ambassador to France. His ambassadorship was stormy, at one point marked by a nasty feud with the misanthropic author Evelyn Waugh. On one evening, after Waugh had chanced to make some typically vicious remarks about Lord Louis Mountbatten, Duff ordered the writer from his house, saying: "How dare a common little man like you who happens to have written one or two moderately amusing novels, criticize that great patriot and gentleman? Leave my house at once!"

A number of Waugh's books featured characters based on Lady Diana.

Duff died in Diana's arms of internal hemmorhaging aggravated by his alcoholism on the cruise ship *Columbie* in 1950. It was crossing the Atlantic bound for Jamaica. He was sixty years old.

As a widow, Lady Diana Cooper returned to England to resume an approximation of the glamorous life she had lived since childhood, finding herself in late age as abused by mashers as she had been in youth. On one occasion a drunken Charlie Chaplin pinched her knee black and blue and demanded kisses, which she refused. She remained close friends with Noel Coward and other well-known celebrities into old age, when most of them had died and she had resigned herself largely to a life lived in bed.

A centerpiece of works by Waugh, Coward, and other famous writers of the 1920s, 1930s, 1940s, and 1950s, she lived to see herself lampooned in a 1986 novel by one-time acquaintance Brooke Astor entitled *The Last Blossom on the Plum Tree*. She died that year at the age of ninety-three.

Lady Emerald Cunard suffered financial reverses and was ultimately compelled to abandon her grand house and take up residence in a suite in a fashionable London hotel, though she continued to entertain and maintain something of a salon. She was never able to achieve a reconciliation with her daughter, Nancy, though on one occasion during World War II, when Nancy was living in England, Lady Emerald's car inadvertently nearly ran Nancy down in a London street.

In March 1948 Chips Channon noted in his diary: "Dined with Emerald Cunard who, as she was suffering acutely from bronchitis, looked about 100." Lady Emerald was subsequently diagnosed as suffering from throat cancer. Nancy, then residing in France again, was urged by Lady Diana Cooper to visit her mother before she died and noted her mother had made it known she desperately wanted such a meeting. "Her Ladyship?" Nancy replied. "You must be mad—oh no, quite out of the question."

Lady Emerald died that July. She left what remained of her fortune divided in three equal parts to Nancy, Lady Diana Cooper, and a longtime friend, Sir Robert Adby.

Nancy refused even to attend the bizarre funeral ceremony in which Lady Emerald's ashes were scattered in Grosvenor Square.

Later, Diana Cooper informed Chips Channon that nearly all of the jewels in Emerald's possession at the time of her death were false and that she had died relatively poor.

Though Jamieson Spencer spent much time in London during the war years, he and Channon never met again. Spencer followed his former friend's career in the newspapers.

Channon was given a minor government post in the foreign ministry and undertook a wartime mission to Yugoslavia to visit his longtime friend, Prince Paul, to try to persuade him to keep his country on the side of the allies, but the German occupation rendered that effort moot. Channon was able to avoid what his diaries indicate he feared greatly—military service.

He often told friends "I want to be a peer," but he ended his public career with nothing more than a knighthood.

Unrelenting in his passion for rich food and drink throughout his life, Channon fell into ill health and died at the age of sixty-one in 1958.

Lady Diana wrote of him, "Never was there a surer or more enlivening friend . . . He installed the mighty in his gilded chairs and exalted the humble. He made the old and tired, the young and strong, shine beneath his thousand lighted candles. Without stint he gave of his riches and of his compassion."

Channon wrote of himself: "I adored my fat, beautiful grand-mother, who was such a liar, and so charming and vain and silly and amorous—like me."

Chips's son, Paul, assumed the family Southend parliamentary seat and ultimately became a very popular and successful Secretary of State for Trade.

Channon's granddaughter, Olivia, died at age twenty-two from an apparent drug overdose and vodka binge during graduation partying at Oxford University in 1986.

Major Edward "Fruity" Metcalfe became probably Edward's closest friend in the days and years after abdication, often the duke's only companion. But he was ill treated. Agreeing to be the duke's unpaid aide-de-camp when Edward attempted to perform some contributory role in the defense of France in 1940, Metcalfe awoke one morning in May to find himself abandoned without notice by Edward as the duke fled for the south and the Germans swiftly approached. Metcalfe was also left with the duke's hotel bill.

Living out his life as a typical British gentleman and clubman, Metcalfe maintained his friendship long after the two had ceased to be companions. An American relative of Metcalfe's wife remarked in 1986 on how shabbily the major had been treated by the duke in later years, and on how Metcalfe still refused to speak ill of him.

Peregrine Cust, sixth Lord Brownlow, continued to support Edward after the latter became king, at one point interceding on Edward's behalf with the Archbishop of Canterbury, but without success. Lord Brownlow's highly popular wife, Kitty, an intimate of the future King George VI and his wife, was among the first in British society to warn of Edward's likely abdication.

Brownlow remained closely associated with the British court until his death in 1978 at the age of seventy-nine.

Captain Hendrik van der Heyden was admitted to New York's Co-lumbia Presbyterian Hospital for treatment of a serious infection in both of his hands from burns and shortly afterward announced his retirement from the Lage Lander Line. He, his wife, her brother, and his wife later made a driving tour of the United States. Finding themselves quite taken with the American Southwest, they returned to New Mexico after he settled his affairs in Holland and settled near Santa Fe, where he wrote a book about seafaring in the East Indies. He died at the age of eighty-seven in 1959.

Ludwig van Groot, the *Wilhelmina*'s first officer, was deprived of his master's certificate by a Dutch maritime court after an inquiry into the sinking of the liner as it was being towed to repair docks in Brooklyn. He subsequently became a dockmaster in Nieuw Amsterdam. He was killed at the age of fifty-one while visiting his brother in Rotterdam during the famous surprise German bombing raid on the city in 1940.

Kees Witte moved to Ostend after the Lage Lander Line went bankrupt in 1936, first taking work as an officer on an Ostend-to-England ferry and ultimately becoming first officer of the Belgian liner *Libre* in 1939. With the outbreak of war, he joined the Dutch navy, serving with Dutch elements of the British Royal Navy after Holland's fall and eventually attaining the rank of commander. Driven to alcoholism by his war experiences, which included having two ships sunk beneath him, his maritime career never prospered and he died in the sinking of a tramp steamer in the Java Sea in 1961 at the age of fifty.

The Soviet Union refused to accept Olga Maretzka's remains once her body was recovered from the Hudson River and she was buried in a pauper's grave on Staten Island, within view of the Statue of Liberty. In the notorious purges ordered by Stalin in 1938, eleven of those in her section of the OGPU were sent to labor camps and five were shot.

Though she was never fully accepted by the American Negro community—and was viewed by some American black leaders as a reckless dilettante whose support would hurt their cause—Nancy Cunard covered the Spanish Civil War with great distinction for a large number of Negro newspapers and had many of her dispatches picked up by white newspapers with a leftist or liberal political bent.

After the Spanish conflict and the outbreak of full-scale war in Europe, she returned to England and became an active communist and advocate of alliance with Soviet Russia. Later she returned to France.

In 1948 the right-wing Paris journal *Le Bataille* published an article beneath the headline "Too Revolutionary to be a Communist, the

Rich Heiress has Refused Millions and Nancy Cunard Lives by her Pen in a French Village."

In March, 1965, Nancy Cunard, raving and swearing, was taken by long-suffering friends to a Paris hospital when it appeared she was so ill she could scarcely stand. Demanding red wine, which she was not given, she died in an oxygen tent in a public ward in March 1965 at the age of seventy. She had also asked for and was given writing materials. She started writing a last poem, but never finished.

Henry Crowder, who had briefly been among the more glamorous jazz figures in Paris, returned for good to the United States and by the early 1950s had taken a job with the government as a mail clerk.

"I am a clerk," he wrote Nancy Cunard in 1954. "I handle all outgoing mail of the Coast Guard headquarters. The job is pleasant and the hours of work agreeable . . . And as for music I believe I am now a better pianist than I have ever been in my life. I devote a great deal of time to the piano, and singing. I am not happy, and I am not sad."

By the next year he was dead.

Author and aviator Beryl Markham had said of Alice Silverthorne de Janzé de Trafford: "Loneliness fixed Alice; everyone is frightened of her."

In 1938 Alice was divorced by her last husband. In 1941 her last great love, Josslyn Hay, Earl of Erroll, was murdered in his car on a dirt road outside Nairobi. She herself underwent surgery for cancer of the womb. While recovering, she wrote letters to friends. "I simply can't write again, and there is nothing more to say," she wrote to one. She thanked another for her "sweet" note, but then said, "Life is no longer living when you no longer care whether you are wanted or not."

One day in 1941 she put clean linen on her bed, set fresh flowers about the room, then took a fatal dose of sleeping pills and lay down.

One of the many notes she left said "By the time you read this, I'll have done it again. This time, I hope successfully." In another, she asked that her friends hold a cocktail party in her honor. She was forty-one.

She left no note for C. Jamieson Spencer.

Charles A. Lindbergh continued to pass on German military secrets and other information to the United States military, but his many public speeches urging America to stay out of Europe's conflicts enraged President Franklin Roosevelt. When Lindbergh sought a return to active duty after the surprise attack on Pearl Harbor, Roosevelt refused him. Lindbergh's role was limited to that of a civilian "tech rep" advising American pilots on the use and performance of combat aircraft. While "testing" P-38 Lightning fighters in forward areas of the Pacific, however, Lindbergh was confirmed to have shot down at least two Japanese planes. President Eisenhower promoted him to brigadier general in 1953.

Having pioneered in the 1930s many of the international air routes used by jetliners today, Lindbergh continued to work as an aviation advisor after the war. But he also devoted himself to conservation causes and was credited with developing many advances in engineering and science, including rocketry. He turned to writing, as well, winning the Pulitzer Prize for biography in 1954 for his book *The Spirit of St. Louis.* His wife, Anne Morrow Lindbergh, also became an acclaimed author and poet.

Lindbergh died in his beloved Hawaii in 1974 at the age of seventy-two. He is buried there in a gravesite he designed himself.

Chasey Chatham Parker married three more times, twice to American socialites and once to an Austrian prince who was said to have gone through much of her fortune by the time she divorced him in 1954. She corresponded with Jamieson Spencer during the war. In the early 1950s, when he was living in New York, she had a brief affair with him. He was by then married himself, and the affair ended when his wife threatened divorce.

Anorexic and addicted to alcohol and barbiturates, Mrs. Parker died in Philadelphia in 1973 at the age of sixty-two. Her obituary described her as one of the pillars of Philadelphia society noted for her contributions to charity and the arts.

Nora Gwynne made fourteen more motion pictures, but her career faded during the war years and by the 1950s she was living in relative obscurity in Carmel, California, as the wife of a San Francisco shipping magnate and film company owner. She made a brief comeback in the early days of television hosting an interview show in San Francisco, but it was canceled after two seasons.

After her husband died in 1970, she moved back to Southern California and appeared in cameo roles in several television productions, including one on the series "Love Boat."

\*     \*     \*

C. Jamieson Spencer became a successful broadcast journalist, serving as a counterpart to Edward R. Murrow and Eric Sevareid in England during the early years of World War II. He accompanied the second wave of American forces landing on Utah Beach in the Normandy invasion in June 1944 and travelled with the advancing American troops across France. He reported the ultimate German capitulation in 1945 and covered the postwar Nuremburg war crimes trials.

Switching to ABC after the war, Spencer moved to New York and served in management positions with the network until its merger with Paramount Theaters in 1953, when he and many other original network executives were fired. He then worked in advertising and public relations, residing in New York's Westchester County, but financial reverses and recurrent unemployment forced him to move in 1960.

He married the former Ann Lambreth of Newport, Rhode Island, in 1950 and was divorced by her in 1963.

Spencer attempted to write a book about his wartime experiences but it was never finished. The *New Yorker* magazine published a poem of his about Whitney Ransom de Mornay in 1957.

Whitney de Mornay continued her affair with Jamieson Spencer until December 1941, when he was compelled to leave Paris for England after Germany declared war on the United States. They were never to meet again.

In the late 1930s Madame de Mornay achieved a significant success in the Paris fashion world, but her career was cut short by the war. Her husband Charles, who was Jewish, was interned by the Nazi authorities occupying France in 1940 and ultimately sent to the Buchenwald concentration camp, where he died in 1944, at about the same time Jamieson Spencer entered Paris with Free French forces in advance of the main American armies.

Madame de Mornay was spared Nazi persecution, however, by coming under the protection of a Luftwaffe general assigned to the Paris area, the Count Martin von Bourke und Kresse. He'd been introduced to Whitney by Jamieson Spencer in July 1940. One of the gowns designed by Madame de Mornay in 1939 hangs in the museum of the French Institute of Design.

Count von Kresse underwent corrective surgery on his back and leg in 1937, which, though only partially successful, allowed him to return to active duty as a Luftwaffe officer in command of a Heinkel bomber wing and later as an aide to Reichsmarshal Hermann Goering. Military historians credit von Kresse with helping to persuade Goering to switch from bombing Royal Air Force fighter bases and radar facilities to military targets in England's major cities, a move that enabled the English to win the famed Battle of Britain and buy time to rebuild their air force, eventually establishing air superiority over their own territory and ultimately western Europe.

After falling out with Goering in 1941, von Kresse transferred to his old East Prussian regiment and accepted a demotion to colonel in time to participate in the invasion of the Soviet Union. He fought there and in North Africa, where he was wounded and received several additional decorations.

Promoted again to general, he was reassigned to Paris in 1943 as a staff officer. It was at that time that Whitney Ransom de Mornay became his lover.

He was implicated in the 1944 generals' plot to kill Hitler and found guilty by a Nazi tribunal *in absentia*, but by that time he and Whitney de Mornay had disappeared. Neither the German nor the allied authorities were ever able to learn of their whereabouts, or their fate.

# AUTHOR'S NOTE AND
# SELECTED BIBLIOGRAPHY

This is a work of fiction. There never was a Dutch Lage Lander shipping line with a vessel named the *Wilhelmina*, and in 1935, Edward, Prince of Wales, never made an Atlantic crossing on such a vessel in the company of Mrs. Wallis Warfield Simpson or anyone else in his entourage. The ocean liner and its dire circumstances, like many of the passengers aboard, were created for the purposes of the plot and the story.

But, that accepted, it should be noted that this work of fiction is intended as a historical novel in the fullest sense of that term. Its characters and their circumstances have been drawn as true to life and to their times as years of research can make possible. The goal has been to bring the period preceding and presaging World War II into sharp focus and to provide the reader with a realistic look at some of the people and the events that ultimately propelled the world into the greatest tragedy of modern human history.

Eight of the major characters in this book are fictional. Excepting ship's company and some of the newsmen depicted in scenes set in Paris, New York, and Madrid, all the others were real people who possessed qualities that have herein been attributed to them.

There were terrible riots in Paris at this time and a woman was killed on the balcony of the Hotel Crillon. Prince Edward and his entourage were touring the continent in the fall of 1935 and the outbreak of the Abyssinian crisis and other unrest in Europe did cause some concern for His Royal Highness's safety. Though Edward did not make an Atlantic crossing in 1935, he completed one in similar circumstances a decade before with the Mountbattens and others who appear on the Wilhelmina with him in this story. In the company of Mrs. Simpson and others in this cast of characters, Edward did gain considerable notoriety for taking self-indulgent cruises on the *Nahlin* and other leased or borrowed yachts.

Edward was a hero to his people and demonstrated a deep concern for those victimized by the Great Depression. But he was equally a weak, spoiled, immature, and superficial person whose principal interest was in his own pleasure, whether that meant playing the bagpipes or silly games with wine bottles and matchsticks. His anti-Semitism and attraction to Nazi Germany are well documented. He actually uttered words about freeing Europe from "the tentacles of the Jews" at a dinner party in France in the 1950's—ten years after Nuremberg!

Mrs. Simpson did have shabby origins. Her mother did run a boarding house in Baltimore and Wallis did support herself in China by playing cards and sponging off friends. There is ample evidence that she did not truly love Prince Edward but became ensnared in a monstrous trap created by her own relentless social ambitions and his selfish folly.

Edwina Mountbatten's infidelities and Nancy Cunard's rebelliousness and madness have been well-recorded. The same is true of Duff Cooper's drinking and philandering. His wife, Lady Diana Cooper, was one of the most written about women of the twentieth century. The character of Chips Channon was drawn largely from his own widely read published diaries. His remarks about Jews in this novel, for example, were taken from his own actual statements.

Charles Lindbergh was away from his home and family at the time this story takes place and did relocate to England and Germany two months later. Though the greatness of his achievements cannot be diminished, he was well known for an immature streak and a penchant for practical jokes.

Hermann Goering was every bit the Nazi monster he's remembered as, but historians have speculated on his lack of support for a two-front war, and his withdrawal from active military leadership in the major decisions of the conflict after his failure in the Battle of Britain has been well documented.

There *was* an Alice de Janzé from Chicago. She did shoot her lover and herself in a Paris railroad station and did finally manage to commit suicide in Kenya a decade and a half later.

A substantial amount of the research for this book involved personal interviews and perusals of personal papers and diaries, but other books and published sources were relied upon greatly as well. What follows is a selective bibliography of works that might prove useful to those interested in the period, people, and subjects examined in this novel:

*The Abdication of King Edward VIII,* by Lord Beaverbrook (Atheneum, 1968).

*Ace of the Iron Cross,* by Ernst Udet, (Ace Books, 1970).

*The Airman and the Carpenter,* by Ludovic Kennedy (Viking, 1985).

*American Facts and Dates,* edited by Gorton Carruth and Associates (Thomas Y. Crowell Company, 1970).

*The American Heritage History of World War I* (Bonanza Books, 1982).

*Atlas of the First World War,* by Martin Gilbert (Dorset Press, 1970).

*Berlin Diary,* by William L. Shirer (Bonanza Books, 1984).

*Charles A. Lindbergh: An American Life,* edited by Tom D. Crouch (Smithsonian Institution Press, 1977).

*Chips: The Diaries of Sir Henry Channon* (Penguin, 1970).

*Diana Cooper,* by Philip Ziegler (Alfred A. Knopf, 1982).

*Duchess: The Story of Wallis Warfield Windsor,* by Stephen Birmingham (Little, Brown and Company, 1981).

*Edwina: Countess Mountbatten of Burma,* by Richard Hough (William Morrow, 1984).

*Edward VIII: The Road to Abdication,* by Frances Donaldson (J. B. Lippincott, 1974).

*Ernest Hemingway: Selected Letters,* edited by Carlos Baker (Charles Scribner's Sons, 1981).

*Eight Chicago Women and Their Fashions: 1860–1929* (Chicago Historical Society, 1978).

*The First War Planes,* edited by Andrew Kershaw (Phoebus, 1971).

*Fighter,* by Bryan Cooper and John Batchelor (Ballantine Books, 1973).

*The French Foreign Legion,* by John Robert Young (Thames and Hudson, 1984).

*The German Army: 1933–1945,* by Albert Seaton (St. Martin's Press, 1982).

*Germans,* by George Bailey (Avon Books, 1972).

*The German Wars,* by D. J. Goodspeed (Bonanza Books, 1985).

*The Hemingway Women,* by Bernice Kert, (W. W. Norton, 1983).

*Hitler's Generals and Their Battles,* edited by Christopher Chant (Chartwell Books, 1984).

*In War's Dark Shadow,* by W. Bruce Lincoln (Dial Press, 1983).

*The Letters of Evelyn Waugh,* edited by Mark Amory (Penguin, 1980).

*Matriarch,* by Anne Edwards (William Morrow, 1984).

*Mein Kampf,* by Adolf Hitler (Houghton Mifflin, 1971).

*Mountbatten: A Biography,* by Philip Ziegler (Alfred A. Knopf, 1985).

*A Moveable Feast,* by Ernest Hemingway (Charles Scribner's Sons, 1964).

*Nancy Cunard,* by Anne Chisholm (Penguin Books, 1981).

*Nancy Mitford: A Biography,* by Selina Hastings (E. P. Dutton, 1985).

*Nazi Europe* (Marshall Cavendish Books, 1984).

*The Nightmare Years: 1930–1940,* by William Shirer (Little, Brown and Company, 1984).

*On the Continent: 1936* (Fodor's Travel Guides, 1985).

*Once Upon a Time,* by Gloria Vanderbilt, Alfred A. Knopf, 1985.

*The Only Way to Cross,* by John Maxtone-Graham (Collier Books, 1972).

*Paris: The Glamour Years,* by Tony Allan (Gallery Books, 1977).

*The Penguin Dictionary of Modern History,* by Alan Palmer (Penguin Books, 1983).

*The Prussian Orden Pour le Merite: History of the Blue Max,* by David Edkins (Ajay Enterprises, 1981).

*Queen Elizabeth: A Portrait of the Queen Mother,* by Penelope Mortimer (St. Martin's Press, 1986).

*Queen Mary: The Cunard White Star Quadruple-Screw Liner* (Bonanza Books, 1979).

*Return to Albion: Americans in England, 1760–1940,* by Richard Kenin (National Portrait Gallery, 1979).

*The Red Baron,* by Manfred von Richthofen (Ace Books, 1969).

*Strange and Fascinating Facts About the Royal Family,* by Graham and Heather Fisher (Bell, 1985).

*Wind, Sand, and Stars,* by Antoine de Saint-Exupéry (Harcourt, Brace, 1967).

*Winged Warfare,* by Lt. Col. William A. Bishop (Ace Books, 1967).

*The Wisdom of the Sands,* by Antoine de Saint-Exupéry (The University of Chicago Press, 1979).

*World War I,* by S. L. A. Marshall (American Heritage Press, 1985).

*World War II Almanac: 1931–1945,* by Robert Goralski (Bonanza Books, 1981).

*Wallis and Edward: Letters 1931–1937,* edited by Michael Bloch (Summit Books, 1986).

*War Within and Without,* by Anne Morrow Lindbergh (A Helen and Kurt Wolff Book, 1980).

*White Mischief: The Murder of Lord Erroll,* by James Fox (Random House, 1982).

*Who's Who in Nazi Germany,* by Robert Wistrich (Bonanza Books, 1984).

*Who's Who in the Royal House of Windsor,* by Kenneth Rose (Crescent Books, 1985).

# ABOUT THE AUTHOR

Michael Kilian is a prize-winning columnist for the *Chicago Tribune* whose subjects range from inside Washington politics to East Coast and international high society. His twice-a-week columns are distributed to more than two hundred other newspapers throughout the United States and Canada. Kilian has also been a radio and television commentator and a noted writer on military and aviation affairs. He is the author of eight other books, including four novels.

The son of television pioneer D. Frederick Kilian and stage and radio actress Laura Leslie, Kilian was born in 1939 and grew up in the Midwest and New York's Westchester County. He and his family have homes in McLean, Virginia, and Hedgesville, West Virginia.